Don't Get Too Close to The Darkness Inside...

My name is Lia Hebert, and I know something that might shock most people: Angels are not always the good guys. I learned that after one of them killed my parents.

Since then, my life has been a rollercoaster. In a matter of days since the angel attacked I was taken to Hell, commissioned by the fallen angel Lucifer, and given my own demon guardians. I know what you're thinking: *that's so, rock and roll.* But the reason the angels are after me, and the reason Lucifer wants me is because I can do something terrible—I can make angels fall.

BOOKS BY L. M. PERALTA

THE ARCADIAN STEEL SERIES
The Wings of Heaven and Hell
The Seven Archangels of Heaven
The Seven Princes of Hell

THE ELEMENTALS TRILOGY
The Elementals
The Council
The Creator

United Trace

the wings of heaven and hell

The Arcadian Steel Sequence

Book One

L. M. Peralta

Summary: After the Archangel Raphael murders her parents, Lia discovers she can make angels fall from grace by touching them. With nowhere to turn, Lia is asked by the fallen angel, Lucifer, to make Raphael and his followers fall in exchange for her soul.

ISBN 978-0-9888448-8-9

To Gloria and Louis Latour

part one

collision

one

HE arch of his wings rose above his head. The tips stretched out to the corners of the sky. His soft, blond hair contrasted against the hardened features of his face. He cast his golden eyes down to his staff, deep in the belly of a beast with many eyes and teeth like the pointed studs on a black, leather jacket. Flames erupted around the two figures still in the canvas and yet alive.

The acrid, bitter taste of turpentine and the smell of linseed oil permeated the room. Heat came off the standing work light which forced the shadows into the corners. Deflated paint tubes littered the floor. Stacks of unused canvases leaned against each other on the wall. *For Whom the Bell Tolls* played over the old stereo covered in paint.

A ladder was propped up alongside the finished painting. The top of the ladder reached the tips of the angel's wings. The angel's eyes unnerved me. They seemed to twitch and vibrate like fire in the breeze. The image seemed so…real.

"You like it?" Dad swished a paintbrush in the water of a gallon jug with the top cut off.

His shoulder length, ruddy brown hair was tied back in a ponytail, but a few strands escaped, matted to the sheen of sweat on his brow. He wore a golden cross, wrapped in silver thorns, around his neck.

I nodded. "Who's it going to?"

"A little gallery on Bienville."

I raised an eyebrow. "A *little* gallery?"

"Diavolo." He smirked.

"Marcus Diavolo! Dad, why didn't you say something?"

"I gave his secretary my portfolio last week. I wanted to know for sure first before I said anything to you and your mom. Didn't want to disappoint you."

"You wouldn't have disappointed me. I don't care what the world thinks."

He smiled at me while he dried the paintbrush with a worn rag.

"You need to tell Mom," I said. "She's going to *die* when she finds out."

"No, no, no," he said. "We have something much more important to celebrate tonight. It's your sweet sixteen. You won't get away that easily."

I groaned. "I'm a little too old for birthday parties." I *was* sixteen. At least, that's how old I supposed I was.

No one knew my birthday. I know weird, right? I didn't have a birth certificate. So, my parents made November 11th my honorary birthday. The 11th of November, ten years ago, was the day they adopted me, the day my whole life changed for the better.

Micah and Alexandria Hebert were the only parents I'd ever known. I was found alone in an abandoned house when I was too small for kindergarten. The house was on the market for ages, and the owners lived in Tennessee. They had no idea who I was.

"Li, you know how your mom feels about this. You're the only little girl she'll ever have." He put his arm around my shoulder. "You can celebrate teenage-style with your friends this weekend."

My friends. Yeah, if I had any. I used to have a lot of friends before high school. Felicia Drake and I were friends since first grade. That was until she made it her personal mission to make my life hell. I didn't ask for Mike Breyers to look at me. I wasn't interested in him. He was on the football team, and Felicia had a known crush on him which made him off limits to anyone else. When he asked me to the Spring Dance, she all but lost it.

All throughout freshman year, I would find gum stuck to my locker and get tripped in the hallway by Felicia or one of her new friends. Felicia spread rumors about me and made passive aggressive comments every chance she got. By my sophomore year, the whole school thought I was adopted because my bio-mom went to jail for prostitution, and my birth father was her pimp. So, no, I didn't have any friends. Unless I could count my dad.

"Come on, what do you say?" He squeezed my shoulder.

I laughed. "Dad, you'll get paint on me." I shrugged away from him. "Alright, we can celebrate, but I'll secretly be celebrating this." I motioned to the painting. "Diavolo. Wow."

"Thanks, sweetie." He looked at the backs of his hands and at his palms, covered in paint. Several more splotches stained his white t-shirt. "Can you get the radio? I'm going to jump in the shower." He worked all night. Dad said the muses came for him in the dark. "After school, when your mom gets home, we'll have cake, presents, and we'll drive into the city for dinner."

"Okay." I lifted my backpack from the concrete floor. "I don't want to go anyplace fancy."

Dad winked. "I would never do that to you."

I rolled my eyes and smirked.

"I gotta go." I shouldered my backpack.

"Don't let school ruin your education," he said. He echoed the words of Mark Twain. Although, I'm not sure Dad knew Twain said that first.

I laughed. "I would never do that to you." If not for the history exam in fourth period, I would have skipped school. I bet Dad wouldn't mind if I stayed in my room all day on my guitar. But I didn't do so well in history. I crinkled my nose.

I left the music of Dad's studio behind. I arrived at the corner right as the bus pulled up. The doors screeched open, cutting through the silence of the morning. I took a seat in the back and put my headphones on. *Fear of the Dark* blared in my ears as the bus took off.

The houses blurred through the windows until the bus entered the city and stopped at a light. A man stood at the corner. He wore baggy clothes and a faded baseball cap. Something twitched at the base of his jacket. I turned my attention to the upholstery of the seat in front of me. I didn't want to look back and see its eyes. The eyes were always what got me.

The bus stopped outside St. Andrews, and I walked to class. In third period, I stared at my history test like it was written in Latin. My pen was in my mouth more than it scribbled along the page. The lunch bell rang before I could answer the last question.

At lunch, I sat alone. Friendships were difficult to maintain with a malicious sixteen-year-old spreading lies about me.

"Nice t-shirt," said Felicia. She stood at my table with her gaggle of giggling girls who dressed like her and acted like her. They wore monochromatic colors and heels that I might die in. Felicia's hand reached the side of her lunch tray. Before I could react, her hand with long, polished onyx black nails gripped the plastic fork and catapulted a forkful of coleslaw at me. The coleslaw plummeted onto my t-shirt and covered my left shoulder in mayo, cabbage, and vinegar hell.

"Oops." She covered her mouth with her hand.

Heat rose at my temples. Felicia was the only one in school who knew today was my birthday. I didn't get into fights, and I wouldn't let Felicia Drake ruin my birthday with a trip to the principal's office.

Felicia's heels clicked along the laminate cafeteria room floor. She laughed with the other girls. Her heels were at least three inches high, not that she needed the extra height.

Fall, fall, fall.

She didn't.

I grabbed a handful of napkins and scooped up the mess from my shoulder. The vinegar stung my nose. I tossed the napkins in my tray and threw the rest of my lunch in the garbage. The food didn't taste that good anyway. Soon, I would get ice cream and cake courtesy of my mom.

I went to the bathroom to get the rest of the coleslaw off my shirt, hoping to get the smell out. Armed with a handful of paper towels from the dispenser, I wet them in the sink and leaned in to peer into the mirror and see where the stain was. A sizable white smear was on my black t-shirt and bits of cabbage hung from my shoulder. I wiped at the stain with the towels. I made progress, but the smell lingered.

One fluorescent light blinked on and off. Coldness crept onto my skin. My sweater's arms were tied securely around my waist. I should have put the sweater on before the cold turned my fingernails purplish-blue.

A dark form blurred at the edge of my vision. I tried not to look. I didn't see them more than two or three times a week, and when I did, I tried to ignore them. But this time I couldn't ignore the dark shape reflected in the mirror. The thing crouched in the corner of the bathroom. The creature was thin with skin the color of charcoal and a bald, bulbous head. It faced away from me toward the wall. It shook and whimpered.

Before my parents adopted me, family services took me to a string of psychologists. I saw them. Horrible monsters. They said my hallucinations were a result of what I went through, being abandoned by my bio-mom. That they weren't there.

"Not there. Not there. Not there," I chanted and closed my eyes.

Thud! Tap. Tap. My fingertips squeezed the ceramic surface of the sink. *Did it move?* But I didn't dare open my eyes. I continued to chant.

"What are you doing?" Felicia's voice bounced off the walls. My eyes shot open.

"*Not there. Not there,*" she mocked. "No matter how many times you wish that wasn't the face staring back at you, your reflection will always be the same. So, you can give up."

I glared at her. "You got coleslaw all over my shirt. I smell like vinegar and mayonnaise. Today's my birthday. I know you know that. Did you have to come in here and—"

I broke off. Crimson eyes, wide and round like headlights stained red after a hit-and-run, stared at me through the glass.

My breath trapped in my lungs. I turned away from the mirror.

"You can cry if you want to," said Felicia.

I pushed past her and into the hallway.

The rest of the day, I wore my sweater in class to smother the smell of vinegar. I couldn't get the stain out, and even the thick cotton of my sweater didn't work hard enough to mask the smell. I hoped only I could smell the harsh aroma since the fumes were on me.

I should have taken off my shirt in the bathroom and just worn my sweater, but I wasn't going into another school bathroom, not for a long time. My skin prickled. Was the creature still huddled in the corner? What did it want?

The bell rang. I folded my pen into my notebook and pinned the notebook to my chest. The teacher fought to finish her sentence over the flutter of paper, chatter, and the shuffle of feet. I picked up my backpack and slung one strap onto my shoulder as I headed out the classroom. With my head down, I marched down the hallway. The sun hit my face as I made for the entrance of the school and I ducked my head lower. My hair veiled the sides of my face. I collided into someone. Michael Breyers.

His gray-blue eyes anchored me. "Lia."

I turned to look over my shoulder. Felicia and her troop passed through the doors of the school. She would hate it if she saw me talking to Mike. So, that's what I did. She was over him, but a little light conversation would remind her of my betrayal.

"Hi, Mike," I said. I didn't flirt. I talked about the history mid-term, but I knew that was enough.

Felicia glared at me as she passed.

Mike was on the football team so he turned the conversation to the big game. I ignored him as he droned on.

A man stood across the street from the school. His eyes were on me. His hair was black, but his skin was pale as if never touched by sunlight. I knew that was wrong though. He had been touched by something brighter than the sun. He wore a white t-shirt with a leather jacket and jeans. On his hands were black gloves. Something white arched above his shoulders on either side.

"Lia, did you hear me?"

My eyes were again tethered to Mike's. "Yeah. I have to go." I ripped my gaze away.

I walked home. In a little less than an hour, I was inside. I dropped my backpack at the door. Mom would be home from work any minute.

The bracelets on my wrists knocked against each other as I gripped the bannister and jogged up the stairs.

I opened the door to my bedroom. Posters made the walls invisible. AC/DC, Led Zeppelin, Black Sabbath, and R.E.M. held up the ceiling. The floor was a bed of unwashed clothes.

My Firebird leaned against the wall next to the amp. One of the strings popped the last time I played. Beside my desk was a waste basket full of the crumpled remains of several failed drafts of an essay I worked on for class.

The essay was on Colonialism in early America. The essay wasn't my greatest venture. Studying history was as dull as listening to music through earmuffs. The paper was due next Friday. I sighed.

Sim wandered into my room. She stretched her long feline body and sauntered over to me. I reached down to stroke her fur. "There you are, girl," I said. She meowed.

Sim disappeared in the house. She went missing for hours. Dad thought the house harbored a crawlspace we didn't know about and that Sim wandered into the hole from time to time. The house was old. Dad inherited the home from his mother. I never met her. Both my parents' parents died before they adopted me.

I took off my Kiss shirt. It still held the faint scent of vinegar. I picked up a black t-shirt from the floor and pressed my nose into the fabric. I shrugged, pulled the shirt on over my tank top, and took a quick glance in the standing mirror in the corner of my room. My fingers combed through my long hair, light brown and dyed reddish-pink at the ends. My blood red nail polish looked like tiny misshaped hearts in the center of each fingernail. My nose ring looped over the edge of one nostril.

I flashed a smile and headed out the bedroom door. The front door squealed open as I took the stairs two at a time.

Mom walked in, juggling her purse and a white cake box. She wore flats because heels made her *too* tall. Slim with hair the color of charcoal that flowed down her back like ink, she wore a patterned dress and a dark blazer.

People who didn't know I was adopted said I looked like my dad. Maybe that was because I was so different from my mom. She was a tall, raven beauty, while I was short, right under five two with light brown hair and almond shaped eyes. Mom's skin was light as cream, and mine was tannish and darkened easily in the sun.

"Hey, Mom, can I help you with that?" I grabbed the box from her.

"Thanks, honey. Can you put that on the counter for me?" she asked.

"Sure thing."

She walked down the hall and turned. "Oh, and Happy Birthday!"

"You told me twice this morning, Ma."

She smiled. "I know, baby, and I'll probably say it twice more before the day is out."

I smiled back, shook my head, and rolled my eyes. I set the cake on the counter. A knock sounded at the front door.

Uncle Jonah stood on the porch. His eyes were bloodshot. "Happy Birthday, Li!" He grinned and kissed me on the forehead.

"Hey," I said. "Cake's on the table. Just waiting on Mom and Dad."

Jonah wrung his hands as he walked in. His eyes darted as if afraid someone might jump him.

"You okay?" I asked.

"Sure, sure. I gotta use the bathroom." He wandered down the hall and into the guest bathroom.

Meanwhile, Dad came down the stairs. He wore jeans and a t-shirt. His hair was loose and stringy around his face.

"Did you get a chance to tell Mom the good news?" I asked.

He put his arm around my shoulders and led me into the kitchen. "Shh," he said. "I'll tell her tomorrow. Today's about you, kid."

I wished for a button I could press to set my eyes on roll.

Mom walked into the kitchen. "Okay," she said, "let's cut the cake." Her words came out in a rush of air as if she had been holding her breath.

"Wait," I said. "Uncle Jonah's here. He's in the bathroom."

A look of concern crossed Mom's face. Dad narrowed his eyes as Jonah made his way into the kitchen. He stumbled as he approached the counter. Jonah put his arms around Dad. At first, Dad's arms hung limp, but slowly he brought one up to pat Jonah on the back.

Mom smiled, tight-lipped, and opened the box. She removed the cake which she placed on the table. She took out a box of matches from a drawer in the kitchen and lit the three candles. On the cake, written in curly frosting cursive, were the words: *Happy Birthday, Lia!* They came at me like a neon sign as if I hadn't heard those words enough. I waited through the cringe-y Happy Birthday song and blew out the candles.

Mom beamed, and tears squeezed from the corners of her eyes. I wrapped my arms around her waist and gave her a quick hug. "Thanks, Mom."

She cut the cake, and we all sat on the sofa in the living room while we ate. The sofa faced a brick fireplace. The television was mounted above the mantel. Dad's paintings hung on the walls. A girl stood in a white gown with a raven perched on her head. A dark snake floated through the mazelike cluster of leafless trees rising from the mist. A man sat bent over a heavy book, his face blurred out like a drop of blood in the water.

The airiness of the cake settled on my tongue. Crumbs found their way into my lap. The sharp sweetness of frosting awakened my taste buds as I licked my lips.

Dad finished first and set his plate on the coffee table. He got up and moved behind the sofa. When he came back, he held a box wrapped in silver paper. The box was roughly four feet long and half as wide.

"What's this?" I asked as he placed the box in front of me on the coffee table. Sim weaved between my ankles.

"Open it," he said.

I knelt by the table and ripped off the wrapping paper. I took the top off the box. A black guitar case nestled inside. I flipped open the latch. In the case, a guitar lay in a bed of velvet, but not just any guitar. The instrument was a Fender Stratocaster with a lacquer black finish and maple neck, the same guitar played by Pink Floyd guitarist David Gilmour. I cradled the guitar in my hands.

My eyes widened. I looked up at Dad. "This must have cost you a fortune."

"We've been saving up for it since you were nine years old."

I placed the guitar against my chest and strummed a few notes. The notes carried through the air like whispers. The guitar needed an amp. A Frontman sat in my room for my old Firebird. I couldn't wait to hook up the Strat and play it.

"Hey, I got you something too." Uncle Jonah shoved a small box into my line of vision.

I knit my brows and stowed the guitar back in its case. I opened the box Uncle Jonah handed me. A small heart-shaped locket slid inside the box. It looked antique, not my style, but I was so excited about my new guitar I didn't care. "Thanks," I said.

"Why don't you try it on?" he encouraged.

I smiled thin-lipped. "Okay." I clasped the chain around my neck. The heart-shaped locket dangled upon my black Metallica t-shirt.

"Looks good on you," said Jonah.

"Yeah, I guess," I said. I wanted to get back to my Strat.

Uncle Jonah grumbled something about needing to use the bathroom. He stood and ambled out of the room.

Dad sat down next to me, and I hugged him and Mom. "Thank you so much. A Strat. I can't wait to play it on my Frontman."

"Where do you want to go eat, kiddo?" Dad asked.

"I don't know." I shrugged. "Wherever you guys want to go. I'm good with anything." My eyes swept over the guitar. "I'll be good with anything for a long time."

"How about Urban Ambience?" Dad asked.

"That's all the way in the city," Mom said.

"Yeah, but how often do we get to go out there. It's still early. Plus, you can get that drink you like."

"Well," she said, "we better leave now." She got up from the sofa. I'll go grab my purse. Micah, you might want to check on Jonah. He's been in there an awful long time."

Mom disappeared into the hallway, and Dad walked over to the guest bathroom. He banged on the door. "Jonah, everything okay in there?"

I approached the hallway and listened from the other side of the wall.

"Just a minute," Jonah yelled. The door creaked open, and a thud shook the wall.

"You're high, aren't you?" Dad's voice was tense.

"No," Jonah stammered.

"How dare you, Jonah? You came to my little girl's birthday party high, and you're doing drugs in my bathroom?"

"I wasn't..."

"Oh, yeah. Then, what's that?"

Jonah murmured something I couldn't hear.

"Get it out of here," Dad said.

Feet marched down the hallway, and the front door slammed. I walked into the hall. Dad's arm leaned against the doorframe. His head was down.

"You made him leave?" I asked.

Dad rubbed his eyes.

I shook my head. "He can't help it, Dad. You said to treat people the way you want to be treated, but you've never treated Uncle Jonah that way. You always kick him out."

Mom reached the bottom of the stairs. She put her hands on my shoulders. "Uncle Jonah has a problem," she said.

"But he can't help it."

"It's the kind of problem that's not safe for him or us."

"Uncle Jonah would never do anything to hurt us."

"Not on purpose," Mom said. "We can talk about it when we get home. I don't want you to miss dinner. It's still a school night. How about a rain check? Deal?"

I was quiet for a moment. Uncle Jonah was sick. Dad knew it. I wished he didn't kick him to the curb like that. You don't do that to family. But the hopeful and concerned look in Mom's eyes told me this was not the time to discuss Uncle Jonah's problem. I didn't want to ruin this day for her.

I nodded. "Deal."

STREET lamps spotlighted the interstate. Darkness shrouded the lake. The headlights of passing cars cast odd shadows inside Dad's sedan. I nodded to *Eulogy* as the song blared over the radio, and the rain battered against the windows.

Mom leaned over and put a hand on Dad's arm. She smiled at him. The smile said *I'm happy* and *I love you* without the words. Mom was always good at saying what she meant with an expression or a touch. Dad smiled back.

I wanted to tell Mom that Dad got into the Diavolo gallery. She'd be ecstatic, but I couldn't do that to him. He wanted to wait to tell her. Maybe he'd tell her tonight after dinner. I imagined the look on her face: a smile erupted, and her eyes crinkled to the point of tearing up.

Dad's work belonged in the Diavolo gallery. His paintings were as dark and passionate as rock and roll. I shivered. The angel's eyes punctured my consciousness. He was canvas, nothing more. Art should give you goose bumps sometimes, right?

The rain melted down the window as the railing of the bridge raced. I wanted to bang out a few songs on the guitar. I couldn't play all night. Mom needed to go to work in the morning.

After two or three songs, I'd head down to the living room to watch TV and eat ice cream till two in the morning. I would be groggy when the bus came the next morning, but I'd settle for tiredness if it meant staying up watching bad movies and playing my Strat.

Lightning ripped the sky and jolted my focus to the front windshield.

Mom screamed.

Something slammed onto the front of the car. The back tires left the ground, and the hood crushed under the pressure.

Wings spread against the sky. White feathers loosed in the wind. A staff impaled into the body of the car. The angel's eyes fixed on me. The eyes moved like they reflected flames.

The angel kicked off the car, and I felt weightless.

We tumbled. Metal skid against the road. The sedan headed for the concrete guardrail. I screamed as the radio continued to blare on.

Glass around me shattered, but didn't touch me. The car groaned as pressure caused the front of the vehicle to flatten like a soda can. The seat beside me was caved in, but I was safe. My side hurt from the impact, and I was shaken but otherwise unharmed. The car was turned upside down. The rain stopped.

I unbuckled my seatbelt and fell to the roof of the car. Blood dripped, and my vision blurred.

"Mom, Dad?"

Their bodies dangled from their seats. I reached for Mom's seatbelt.

"Don't, honey," she said. "My legs. They're stuck."

The dashboard crushed her legs, and blood slid over her jeans. The car's windshield was cracked all over.

"I can get you out." I tried to sound hopeful for me and for her.

Dad's hand was on mine. His head lulled back and forth. Heat fought against the misty cold.

Dad let go of my hand. A mixture of pain and sadness lit upon his face. "Go, go. Run!" The words sounded difficult for him to get out as if his lungs were collapsed.

"I can't leave you." My eyes reflected the flames.

His jaw clenched. His face rang with urgency, fear, and something else: regret. The regret wasn't because he was dying, although he didn't want to, regret because he wanted to say goodbye the right way. He cared about stuff like that. But he couldn't say goodbye the right way because he would feel guilty if he didn't use his last words to save me. That was all he cared about, but I cared too, and I wouldn't let them die.

"Mom?"

She looked at me. Blood trailed down her forehead. Her hand stroked the side of my face, and she smiled that smile that said *I love you*.

The wind ripped through me as an invisible force threw me from the car. I rolled along the road until I stopped belly down palms against the ground. I rose on my knees. My feet were unsteady. I tried to run back to the car. "No!" I screamed, my hand outstretched.

The car went up in an explosion of flames and knocked me to the ground. My body melted into the asphalt. Tears ran down my face. My whole world changed.

Sobs racked me so hard I felt like someone punched me in the chest. I held my hands against the ache. A shadow, faint in the dim, veiled me in deeper darkness.

A man stood over me, a man with wings like the creature who landed on our car. I shuddered. But something put me at ease unlike the terror as I gazed into the eyes of the one like him. His eyes were melted gold, and they shone like metal.

The mist curled around us.

"Who are you?" My voice cracked.

"You *can* see me." He squinted like I was something impossible when he was the one with wings.

"Of course," I said. "But why are you dressed like that?"

He wore a long-sleeved shirt with gloves to cover his hands. The material was metallic like silver. Several cuts marred the fabric. *And was that a sword at his side?*

Like a knight out of the Middle Ages, he had a sword with a silver hilt that hung in a sheath at his side. *Had this man, if I could call him that, fought that monster who attacked us?*

Flames still flared from the sedan. I clung to him. "My parents, you have to help my parents." The chances were slim, but I saw other impossible things that night. "Please," I begged.

The golden-eyed stranger shook his head. "They're gone, and you have to come with me."

I rubbed my temples. I must have hit my head when I was thrown from the car. Maybe I was hallucinating. I might have gotten a concussion when I hit the ground. *No, you were seeing things before you were thrown from the car.* I wasn't hallucinating, I just wished I was. This winged stranger asked me to go with him. "I can't. I don't even know you."

"I'm Adriel. I can protect you. But coming with me isn't really up to you."

I gaped at him. "You want to kidnap me?" I reached into my back pocket for my phone. He didn't try to stop me. Dizzy, I backed away and pressed the speed dial for Jonah.

"Uncle Jonah?"

"Lia? How's everything going, hon?" His words were slow.

"We were attacked," I said.

"Attacked? Where are you?" Jonah's voice was clarity mixed with panic.

"We got into an accident on the bridge." My thoughts were clearer. I didn't want to look at the winged man who stood a couple feet from me. I didn't want to admit what I was seeing. *Not now. No time for crazy now.* "Please, come. I think Mom and Dad are dead." I sobbed out the last words. I didn't know if he heard.

"Oh, my God, Li. Stay right where you are. I'm calling the police."

The call ended, and the screen faded to black.

"We don't have time to wait for the police," said Adriel, "and they won't be able to keep you safe."

Keep me safe? My parents were gone. No one would keep me safe anymore. *The world is a lyre, and its music is sorrow.*

My head swam. I fell, but Adriel caught me before I hit the ground, right before everything went dark.

two

IS eyes were cobalt blue, not the eyes of evil, but I grinned in relish while he burned. His staff lie useless on the ground as my fingers curled around his neck. And all around us angels fell. They plunged from the sky, fiery like shooting stars.

My eyelids were difficult to open like honey crusted over them. I blinked. The bed was soft beneath me. Above me was an off-white ceiling and a dusty fan. Dull orange light poured in.

I hauled myself onto my elbows. Every muscle in my body ached, and my skin felt bruised all over. A television sat in the hollowed-out wardrobe.

A presence lingered near me. I glanced to my left. A pair of wings consumed my vision. He stood by the window with his back to me. I yelped and scrambled to the other side of the bed.

"You're awake." Adriel turned, and I breathed a sigh. I didn't understand why his presence brought me such relief, but it did.

A headache was coming on. I rubbed my temples. "Where am I?"

"You're at a motel," said Adriel. "I fought him off. But I was afraid he might return."

"Who?"

"The one who attacked you."

Adriel wore a dark jacket over a white t-shirt and black jeans. A dozen horizontal cuts patterned the jeans, like he got into a knife fight. No, the rips were the style of the jeans unless the knife fight was with a dwarf or someone who crouched a lot.

I hoped that the stranger who pulled me from the scene of a car crash and watched me from my school wasn't the type of guy who got into knife fights.

Although the silvery armor he wore the night before also bore a pattern of cuts. That night, he had a sword. *Where was that weapon now? Had I imagined it? Was I imagining him?*

His wings glimmered in and out of focus like my mind was trying to reject their existence.

I approached him.

"Stand back," he said. "And don't touch me."

I narrowed my eyes. If anyone should be scared, that person was me. Whoever this man was, he had wings like the monster who killed my parents. But despite that, this odd sense of comfort lingered around him, more than comfort. I felt as if he could protect me from anything.

"What the hell is going on?" I asked.

The room smelled musty. The comforter lay at the foot of the bed. I must have kicked the blanket off me last night. Did he watch me sleep?

My danger meter should have been off the charts, but for some odd reason this perfect stranger made me feel safe. He was so familiar.

He stared out the door's peephole. He moved to the window and pulled back the curtain enough for him to peer outside.

I was transfixed by the white wings on his back. A glow came off them, like the moon against the dark sky.

"*Hello?*"

"You'll be safe here at least till morning." He didn't look at me, but continued to peer out the window.

"Safe? What are you talking about? Why would I *not* be safe?"

"Do I have to remind you what happened out there?" He turned around and faced me.

He was tall, more than a head taller than me anyway. His eyes were bright like a light shined behind them. He pushed all the darkness away.

I forced my eyes shut and shook my head. No, he didn't have to remind me that my parents were dead, that a beautiful monster hurdled onto their car and pierced me with those horrible eyes.

Adriel turned away to look out the window one last time before he closed the curtains to the morning light.

"What are you doing?" I asked. "I won't stay here with a stranger in a Halloween costume." I grabbed the door handle. Before I could turn the knob, his gloved hand was around my wrist.

"If you go, he will find you." His voice was a whisper but held more power than any words I'd ever heard spoken.

My heart dropped. Could he mean the man who murdered Mom and Dad? But that was in my head.

"*He* who?" I asked.

"Raphael."

"The painter?"

"The Archangel."

Did he say *Archangel?*

"Um." I didn't know what to say. They couldn't be real. A licensed therapist told me that much. I was in a seedy motel room with a crazy person. Sure, the costume was convincing, but whoever this guy was, he was one of the men who followed me. Maybe he thought I figured out that he belonged to a su-per-secret gang, and they needed to kill me. But that didn't make any sense either.

I was hospitalized because I told my caseworker that I saw winged people and dark monsters. No one else ever saw them. I was the crazy one. The stress was too much. I was hallucinating again. But I never *talked* to one before. Maybe I should have let them lock me up in a psych ward.

"Look," I said. "I know what I'm seeing isn't real. I mean you have wings, and you're telling me that an Archangel is after me. Oh, my god, what am I saying? This isn't real. I'm talking to a hallucination." I turned my back to him.

My fingers twitched, and I pinched my arm, but I still stood in the motel room, and my parents were still dead.

"You can see us, Lia. No one else can, not if we don't want them to."

How did he know my name?

"This is crazy." I shook my head. *What will I say when the police question me about what happened to my parents?* Maybe they'd give me a psych evaluation and put me on meds. Maybe that's what I needed.

"I guess you forgot Sydriel then," Adriel said.

Sydriel? Why did that name sound so familiar?

"How she disappeared when you were four years old?"

"I don't remember anything." I couldn't remember why I was in foster care in the first place. From what I understand, what I've been told, I was found in an empty house when I was four. My mother and father were gone.

"Sydriel tried to keep you safe, but she disappeared. I thought Raphael got to her. He's looked for you ever since, and he'll keep looking for you."

Could this be real? What should I do? Play along, a voice whispered to me.

"What does Raphael want with me?" I asked. "What could *I* do to an Archangel?"

"You can make them fall." Adriel looked at the floor. His voice was like a ripple in a vast sea, afraid that it might lose itself in greater waters.

"Fall?"

"From grace."

My eyes darted back and forth. I wasn't religious. I went to church a handful of times with Felicia and her parents. I never read the Bible, but I knew enough to convince someone I didn't grow up under a rock.

"I thought only angels that broke away from God could fall," I said.

"That used to be the case until you came along," said Adriel. "Raphael wants to track you down, and I'm going to stop him."

I didn't understand. If an Archangel wanted me dead because I could make angels fall, why was this angel *helping* me? Angels were the good guys, right? I knew enough about religion to know that.

Alien life might exist, but who is to say that aliens will be anything like what we think. What if that is the same for angels? *Were* they the good guys?

Adriel's eyes fastened me in place. I didn't see anything in his eyes that might indicate that he had lied to me, but something else made me want to coil myself into a tight, safe ball. The liquid gold turned hard.

To protect someone that you hated would be challenging. Still, if he hated me, he wouldn't have protected me in the first place.

"But, what are you going to do?" I asked.

Adriel shook his head. "I don't know. But that's not what's important right now. I have to make sure that Raphael doesn't find you, or we all will suffer the consequences."

"Well, that's a bit horrifying."

"I've kept you safe here for a few days, but tomorrow, we have to leave."

"Wait. How long have I been here?" I asked.

"Two days."

Horror flashed through me as if cold water was poured down my shirt. "Two days! I need to call my uncle." I searched my pockets for my phone.

"That's not a good idea," he said.

"Where's my phone?"

Adriel shook his head. "Raphael will find you."

I glanced at him. I tasted salt as I tried to blink the tears away. "The last time I spoke to my uncle, I told him I'd been attacked, and my parents were dead. He's the only family I have left. Now, give me my damn phone."

Adriel withdrew my cellphone from his pocket and tossed it onto the bed. I snatched the phone and called Uncle Jonah.

He picked up before the second ring. "Li?"

"Yeah, it's me."

"Oh, thank God." His voice was warm liquid rubbed into cracked and callous fingers. "Where are you? Are you alright?"

"I'm fine," I said.

"They said you were in an accident, that the car hydroplaned and got crushed against the guardrail," said Jonah. "They found your parents. I'm so sorry, Li."

My breath caught. I hoped this was a nightmare. That my parents were fine and that they waited at home for me.

"At first, the police thought you died when the car went up. I told them I talked to you, but they didn't know if that was before or after the car combusted. I made the arrangements for all three of you. But the coroner called yesterday. Said you weren't in the car with them. The police said you might have walked away. That you might have been confused because of a concussion. They're looking for you."

"Arrangements?" I asked.

"The funeral is today," he said. "There wasn't much left." He sobbed over the phone. I waited and listened to his sobs. He sniffled. "I'm sorry I planned the funeral without you. Until yesterday, I thought you were gone too."

I gripped the phone. "What time?" I asked.

"What?"

"What time are they burying my parents?"

"At ten."

"Okay." I ended the call. The phone slipped from my hand and onto the bed. I felt my heart compress into a hard pebble. My cheeks were sticky with tears.

Adriel sat in the worn chair by the window. His wings swept out on either side of the chair. He leaned forward and watched me.

"You have to let me go." I wanted to be strong, but my voice reminded me of a guitar string breaking. "My parents' funeral is today."

"I can't do that," said Adriel. "Not with Raphael on your trail."

"I'll call the police," I said. "I'll say you kidnapped me."

"That won't work."

"They're my parents," I said. "They can't bury them without me."

Adriel's eyes softened like gold in a furnace. "I'll bring you there, but you have to promise to leave with me."

"I don't even know you," I said.

"All you need to know is that I can protect you."

AFTER I washed my face in the motel sink, I gazed in the dingy mirror. My hair was matted to the sides of my face. My fingertips pressed a pink mark, shaped like a toothless smile, along my jaw. The tenderness prepared me for a bruise.

I met Adriel outside the motel. He leaned against a motorcycle in the parking lot. He handed me a helmet.

"A motorcycle? Can't you just fly?"

"I'm not flying you around the city, Lia." He swung his leg over to the other side of the motorcycle. Before I settled in behind him, Adriel's head jerked around.

"Here." He tossed me a pair of black gloves. "Hold onto the grab rail. Don't lean against my wings."

"Isn't that dangerous?" I asked. "Shouldn't I have my hands around your waist?"

"I won't let you fall." He dropped his arm.

The front of the motorcycle was long with handlebars that curved backwards.

I sat behind him and strapped on the helmet. I gripped the metal grab rail that curved from the sides to the back of the motorcycle as Adriel started the engine.

"Hey, what about your helmet?" I asked.

"Believe me," said Adriel. "If I fall, I would be more worried about the ground than my head."

Within minutes, we were outside a café in a squat building with windows lining the front and a few chairs and tables outside.

Adriel got off the motorcycle, and I followed. He reached into his pocket and pulled out a wad of bills, holding it out towards me.

"What's this?"

"Money."

"I know, but it's yours."

"You have money to pay for breakfast?"

"No." The word dragged from my lips.

"Then, take it." He shoved the money into my hand.

"Okay, but I don't need two hundred dollars to buy a cup of coffee and a scone." I took a twenty and handed him back the rest of the bills.

We walked through the glass door. Nestled at the back of the café was a counter where two baristas chatted. A smattering of tables and chairs dotted the room. The odorous smell of coffee brewing assaulted my nostrils.

I never appreciated the pure taste of coffee without any flavoring. For my Mom, the smell was lazy walks through the French Quarter and cold winters in a warm house. For me, the scent of coffee was cramming for a mid-term and a reminder of mornings, which I hated. I didn't drink coffee for the taste, but the ice helped.

The café was empty except for a man with combed hair who sat next to a beautiful woman with long, tussled, blonde locks.

"Do you want anything?" I asked Adriel.

"No," he said.

I approached the counter and ordered an iced coffee and a blueberry scone. The barista with the tight up-do reached into the glass display case with tissue paper and handed me the scone while I waited for my coffee.

I settled down in the chair across from Adriel at a table in the corner of the room. I was stiff and hollow.

I raised the scone to my mouth. "You sure you don't want anything?" I asked guiltily.

"Yes," said Adriel. "I don't eat."

"You don't eat?" I raised an eyebrow.

"I don't need to."

"Okay," I said, "but do you *want* to?"

Adriel was silent. He glanced out the window as if he expected something bad to happen at any moment.

"They can't see you?" I glanced over at the baristas. They gossiped at the counter.

"No," said Adriel. "Only you."

"Lucky me." Blueberry oozed out of the scone and onto my napkin. I wouldn't have been surprised if the jelly found its way to the corner of my lip.

"If only I can see you, how were you able to get that money and the motel room?"

"Others can see me only when I want them to, and *how* I want them to."

Well, that was a great way for a hallucination to explain itself.

"So," I said. "Where are you taking me after…you know?" I wasn't hungry anymore. I flaked off the crust of the scone with my fingernail.

Adriel didn't look at me. He still watched the windows. "Away from here," he said.

"But won't he find me again?" I asked.

"Then we'll move again."

"You want me to go on the run? You do know I'm only sixteen, right? I haven't even finished high school."

"There will be time for that later."

"You mean, when Raphael *stops* hunting me?"

Adriel's eyes fixed on mine. "He won't stop hunting you."

"That was my point," I whispered.

The woman at the other table glanced over at me, a puzzled look on her face.

"Stop talking to me," said Adriel. "People will think you're crazy."

Am I though? I wondered.

THE clouds hung low in the sky. Morning dew dampened the grass. Headstones rose from the ground with names of people who weren't here anymore. I knew only two. I looked at my hands, clasped, as the priest read a passage from the Bible.

Mom's parents died when she was eight, and she aged out of the system. She had no family except Dad, me, and Uncle Jonah. That was part of the reason she was the way she was with me. She wanted me to have what she never did: parents who loved her.

Dad's parents died when he was in his twenties. Mom and Dad had friends, but Uncle Jonah didn't tell them about the ceremony, or else they would have come.

The priest turned to me. "Would you like to say anything?"

I shook my head. My nose stung as the tears started. I took a deep breath. "Why do you believe in God?"

The priest clenched his Bible to his chest. "Because God has provided me a life and a soul and a place to go when I die. He has given you the same opportunity."

Opportunity. I never thought of death as an opportunity. Death was an ending.

The priest placed a hand on my shoulder. He smiled, not showing any teeth. His brows turned down above his eyes.

Jonah stumbled into the ceremony as they lowered the caskets into the ground. He wore a crumpled black suit. His eyes fell to Dad's tombstone which read *Beloved Father, Brother, and Husband. Rocking with the Big Man Upstairs.* His finger and thumb pressed against his eyes as if he could hold the tears in.

Adriel watched me from the tree line. I gulped. I wasn't going with him. He was a stranger. He wanted me to run, but I couldn't do that.

I approached Uncle Jonah. He wiped his tears on the sleeve of his jacket. His hands twitched.

"What's going to happen now?" I asked.

He looked down at his feet. "I have to take you to the caseworker who called me yesterday."

My hands curled into fists, and the muscles in my face tensed.

He reached out to hug me, but I backed away.

"Why?" I asked. "Why can't you take me?"

Uncle Jonah choked back a sob. "I want to, Li, but I can't. The State won't let me. I can't get clean."

My heart felt like it was being squeezed between two brick walls. I raised my fists and hit him in the chest.

He grabbed my arms. "It's okay."

"No, it's not okay," I shouted. "It'll never be okay."

I lost my parents, and I saw something impossible, something that killed them while it stared daggers at me, something that wanted me dead too.

Three

ONAH let go of my wrists, and I slumped against his chest. He hugged me while I cried.

"You have to take me back home." I put space between us and wiped the tears from my eyes.

"I told you. I can't do that," he said.

"Yes, you can. Just for a little while. I want to pick up a few things without some caseworker breathing down my neck."

"Okay." Jonah nodded. "I'll take you, but you have to promise me that you'll go with them. I'll do everything in my power to get you back. I swear to you."

I didn't believe him. Jonah could never give up the drugs. That was what frustrated my parents.

I met Adriel's eyes. They were metal.

"Come on." Uncle Jonah put an arm around my shoulders and led me to the car.

I got into the passenger's seat of his old Pontiac, and he closed the door behind me. White lines ran through the leather upholstery, and the floor of the car was dotted with dry leaves, candy wrappers, and the odd bottle cap. Powdery, white stains mixed with brown and black ones. Particles of dirt settled in the corners and in the cup holders.

Jonah settled into the driver's seat, let out a deep sigh, and grasped the wheel in both hands.

"Uncle Jonah," I said, "have you ever seen something no one else did?"

Jonah turned his head. "You mean like on mushrooms. You should stay away from that stuff, Li. I know I'm not the best example but—"

"I don't do drugs. If you're an example of anything, it's what not to do." I snapped.

Jonah scrubbed his hand down his face.

"I'm sorry. I didn't mean that."

"It's okay." He didn't look at me. He turned the key in the ignition. The car sputtered before the engine was resuscitated back to life.

In fifteen minutes, I was home. The house seemed so vacant from the outside. When I walked inside, I hoped to hear Dad's rock music blaring from his studio downstairs. I wished I'd see Mom's purse and keys on the credenza. But the house didn't vibrate with life the way it used to.

I went upstairs to my parents' bedroom. Sometimes Sim liked to sleep on their bed. Poor thing, I was gone for two days, and she didn't have any food or water.

I stopped at the door. The bed was unmade. Dad's boots were on the floor, paint spattered on the worn leather. Mom's closet was open, stuffed with clothes. The silence and stillness chilled my bones. No sign of Sim. I eased the door closed as a sob rose in my chest.

I checked my room. My guitar was on the bed. Clothes were strewn all over the floor.

Downstairs, I stopped in the hallway. On the wall were photographs of me when I was little. A five-by-seven photograph of me, Mom, and Dad on our vacation to Nashville hung above the credenza. We stood in front of the Grand Ole Opry House next to the guitar big enough for the Jolly Green Giant to bang out a song. Dad wore his black Judas Priest t-shirt and charcoal jeans, a leather arm bangle around one wrist.

His arm was across my shoulders. My hair was shorter, and I wore a t-shirt with cut-off sleeves. Behind me, stood Mom, her long, dark hair tied back. She wore a navy-blue dress. Mom showed her teeth when she smiled. Dad grinned in awe. I smirked. I grabbed the photograph from the wall.

Jonah's voice came from the kitchen. He was on the phone. He faced away from me. "Yeah, she's here now."

"Who are you talking to?" I asked.

Jonah turned around. Lids hid half his eyes as he looked down. A frown wrinkled the skin around the corners of his lips. He ended the call. "That was your caseworker."

"You called them?"

"Li, I'm sorry. You have to go with her."

"So they can put me in some stranger's house?"

"Li—"

I turned away from him and raced back up the stairs to my bedroom. I unzipped my backpack and turned it upside down. The books thudded onto the hardwood. I piled clothes from the floor and my closet into my backpack. Tears dripped onto the fabric as I packed. I placed the framed photograph on top of the pile of clothes in the backpack, but I thought better of it. I wanted the photo close to me.

My fingertips pulled back the tabs encasing the photo in the frame. The frame slipped out of my hands. Glass shattered.

The house shook, and bright light blinded me. I staggered back, tripped, and fell. Posters ripped from the walls. An angel knelt in the center of the room. His white wings were tucked behind him. He wore a hood of chainmail with a silver chest plate. The chainmail covered his arms and legs. Black gauntlets encased his hands. On his feet were boots tipped in steel. He lifted his head, and his eyes fastened on me.

I scrambled to my feet and raced into the hallway. The angel marched after me. *Zing!* He pulled a sword, silver with the image of wings fanned above the hilt. A round orb glowed with light on the pommel of the sword.

I still clenched the photo in my hand. I crinkled the picture as I grasped onto the photograph like a lifeline.

My back collided with the wall at the end of the hallway. The angel stalked towards me. He wanted to exterminate me like a cockroach.

You can make angels fall by touching them. Adriel's words echoed in my head. I hurled myself at the angel, hands raised. With a scream, I clawed at his face. I wanted to tear his eyes out. The angel screamed too.

He sidestepped me. I grabbed a handful of soft and downy feathers and fisted them in my hands as I fell to the floor.

I felt heat, hotter than the fire before Dad's car exploded. I backed away. The angel's wings burst into flames. His eyes grew dark like ink spilled into them. His face paled to sheet white, and embers floated around him.

I looked down at my hands. *The photo!* I searched the ground. Flames licked the edges of the photo. *No!* I stomped my foot down on the flames. I picked up the photo. The fire reduced the picture to half the original size. The faces of Mom and Dad were untouched, but the fire burned me out of the shot. I folded what was left of the picture and put it in my pocket.

The angel's shrieks stopped. The flames subsided, but they disintegrated the white feathers of his wings and left nothing but blackened bones like strokes of charcoal on paper. His black eyes stabbed me.

I darted around him and rushed back to my bedroom. Posters covered a window against the back wall. I slammed the door shut and locked it. I tore the posters from the window.

The door groaned. The wood splintered. I ducked behind my bed and got low to the floor.

The angel walked into the room. Soon, he would find me. What was the point of making angels fall if they could still come after me?

Light pierced my eyes. I stared across the room. A circle wavered in the center of the room. The circle was translucent like water. Another slant of light glowed from the edges of the wavering circle. Inside was a gray world like a circular painting except with more depth.

A woman appeared from the tear. Her golden blonde hair was in tight spiraled curls, and her forest green eyes enchanted me. She was dressed in a tight outfit as if she were going to yoga class. But from the look on the creature's face, she wasn't going to perform downward dog or the child's pose.

The creature froze. "You."

A smile curled upon her lips. With a powerful kick, she struck him in the chest. He staggered back. His sword clamored to the floor. A dagger flashed in her hand. She lunged at him. The creature was so focused on her dagger, he missed when her foot curled around his ankle. She pulled back hard. He collided with the floor.

The portal glowed behind her. Two men exited. One, light-skinned with charcoal black hair and the other dark-skinned with a curved sword at his hip. The two men approached the creature. Each grabbed an arm and hauled him to his feet.

The girl unhooked a set of manacles from her belt.

"I hope you won't make this difficult," said the dark-haired man. His eyes were as black as coals. He wore a zippered midnight blue shirt and fingerless black gloves. A thick, leather belt fastened around his waist. A sword encased in a sheath strung along the belt. Black pants ended in obsidian boots.

"Traitor," the creature hissed through his teeth.

The dark-skinned man wore black pants and a long-sleeve black shirt with padded leather shoulders. He withdrew his blade and tucked its sharp edge under the creature's chin. "I know you're in a lot of pain."

"What do you know about it?" The creature ground out.

"Nothing you're not finding out right now," said the black-eyed man.

The girl folded her arms. The manacles dangled from her hand. "You have a choice," she said. "You can walk on your own into this portal so we don't have to drag you, or I can let Kiran slice your throat open and send you to the Pit."

The cramp in my leg worsened. I stretched my leg. A dull thud echoed behind me. I cursed under my breath. My foot hit my dresser.

The girl looked around the room. "What was—"

The creature let out a howl and lunged back out of Kiran and the dark-eyed man's grasp. He staggered against the wall and flung himself onto the dark-eyed man.

"Nash!" the girl cried.

Nash and the angel rolled onto the ground. The angel was on top of him, his hands around Nash's neck. A dagger gleamed in Nash's hand. He drove the dagger into the angel's side. Thick, black liquid bubbled from the angel's mouth and his hands loosened from around Nash's neck.

Nash rolled from under him and was behind him in one swift, graceful motion. Nash slashed the creature's throat. His chest heaved, and his blade dripped with the dark substance.

My hand flew to my mouth. Tears fell. My eyes ached.

Nash sighed and wiped the dark blood from his blade onto his black jacket. After a considerable amount of brackish blood spilled onto the floor, the angel became more and more translucent. I blinked. He disappeared.

Kiran knelt down and reached into his pocket. He pulled out a pinch of burned leaves, kissed them, and placed them where the angel's body had been.

"They're always so damn strong right after they fall," the girl said. "Tom should have warned us."

"He said it was a Cherub," said Kiran.

Nash shook his head. "He's a Dominion."

"You knew him?" asked the girl.

"No," said Nash. He lifted the angel's sword. "He mounted the orb of light to his sword."

"A traditionalist," said Kiran.

"Hardly," said Nash. "If he hadn't damned himself, I think we might have found him in the Pride Sector of the Angel District. Doesn't look like we'll need those." Nash motioned to the manacles clenched in the girl's hands.

Chirping echoed around the room as if birds sang from the rafters. The three looked at their wrists at what looked like watches with large, flat square faces.

"It's Tom. There's another one. Demon this time," said Nash, "near us. It's in a high school bathroom."

The girl disappeared into the portal followed by Kiran. Nash glanced around the room. His eyes fell on me. My breath caught. I saw something I wasn't supposed to see, would he—?

But he didn't approach me, didn't slash my throat like he did my attacker, he stepped through the portal and didn't look back.

four

"I!" Jonah's voice echoed down the hallway.

My legs wavered like plucked guitar strings as I rose from the side of the bed. I couldn't tell Jonah what I saw. He couldn't do anything about it. He would only worry about me.

Jonah's tall body stood in the frame of my door. "What were you doing down there?"

"Nothing." I slung my guitar strap across my shoulders and zipped my backpack. My hands still shook.

"I stepped outside," said Jonah. "I thought I heard a crash."

"I dropped a frame." I nodded toward the broken glass near the end of my bed. With my backpack in one hand and my guitar on my back, I approached the door.

Jonah moved out into the hallway, and I joined him, but I couldn't stay. I made my way to the stairs.

"Where are you going?" he asked.

"I won't stay in a foster home." I remembered what that was like. To be tossed from one foster family to the next because they couldn't handle the night terrors or the constant proclamations that I saw things other people didn't. The endless line of shrinks who told me the hallucinations were my way of dealing with trauma, what trauma, I couldn't remember. They

wanted to put me on medication. They did put me on medication. "Take care of Sim for me."

Jonah grabbed my arm. "I can't let you leave. You're staying
in this house."

I yanked my arm away. "You're not my dad."

Jonah's eyes widened as if I bit him. He frowned.

Hot tears erupted from my eyes as I tore down the steps.
Three blocks away from the house, the sound of a motorcycle
roared behind me.

Adriel pulled alongside me. "You went back home?" His
voice burned me like a scraped knee.

"I needed to get my guitar."

"Is a guitar worth your life? You could have been attacked
by one of Raphael's followers."

"I *was* attacked." My voice shook.

The gold melted again.

"An angel," I said. "I know what you meant. I watched him
burn."

The angel, the blue eyes, and those beautiful, white wings.
I touched those wings. They felt smooth, soft, and very *real*.
And when I touched them, they erupted into flames and
turned to ash.

"He had a sword. I think he wanted to kill me." My voice
sounded as if I tried to talk through wool.

"But he didn't." Adriel patted the back of the motorcycle.
"We have to go."

"People came to get him," I continued. "They killed him,
and he disappeared."

"Don't worry about that right now," said Adriel. "Raphael
knows where you are. It won't be long before he gathers a
group of his followers to come after you, and they'll be prepared." He handed me the helmet.

I gulped. He was right. Three streets from where I stood, an angel attacked me. I put the helmet on and got on the motorcycle. My guitar rested against my hip. I hugged my backpack between my chest and Adriel's back. I put the straps over my shoulders and gripped the grab rail. My eyes met Adriel's as he glanced over his shoulder. My body no longer shook.

In thirty minutes, we were back at the motel. I hadn't realized how close the sanctuary was to my house. My skin prickled. *What if Adriel was wrong? What if I wasn't safe here?*

I pushed the thought aside as we approached the motel room. I could taste the saltiness of my tears on my lips.

Adriel's hand touched the doorknob, and the handle glowed. The door popped open. He pulled me into the motel room and closed the door. He released me from his gloved hands.

NOT pulling the covers back, I sat on the motel room bed. The mattress felt odd as if filled with nothing but springs and air.

I flipped through the channels on the television. I settled on an infomercial that might put me to sleep. A dark-haired man with a grizzled beard spilled various liquids on a multitude of different surfaces and used one super absorbent rag to soak up the spills. The liquid was gone and, like magic, left no stain.

I wished my messes were as easy to clean up. I had no place else to go for the night. Jonah was determined to call family services on me. I had no money and no friends.

Jonah probably called the police and reported me as a runaway. They would look for me, and once they found me, I would be chucked into a foster home.

Adriel was outside. He said he would stand guard. I assumed he meant to keep others out, but maybe he meant to keep me in.

Adriel had wings and said he was an angel. He was real and so were the people who came to kill the angel I made fall. I had to believe it or admit I was crazy.

My sane mind told me the stress made the hallucinations seem more real. But Adriel could touch me, albeit with gloved hands, and he could restrain me. That was weird. He couldn't do that if he was a figment of my imagination, but maybe *he* wasn't. Sure, the wings and the talk of Archangels could be all in my head, but maybe he did bring me to this motel. He was a real person, without wings of course. But how could I explain the people dressed in black?

Adriel told me an Archangel was after me. Raphael. And I saw him crash onto my parents' car. He was the reason they were dead.

The whole thing was ludicrous to me, but on top of the free room, Adriel graced me with fast food, and I was hungry. I skipped lunch and spent the rest of the day with my eyes locked on the television screen. I couldn't recall what was on mere seconds after having watched it.

How did he get the fast food and the motel room? Angels weren't supposed to steal food or break into motels. He had money, a lot of it, but how did he get it? I couldn't imagine Adriel working a cash register at a grocery store or taking calls at a cubicle desk. Did he steal that money from someone? Angels were the good guys. They weren't supposed to murder either.

I scoffed down the entire meal in minutes and was glad Adriel wasn't in the room to see me chow down. Why did I feel the need to be polite to him? He kidnapped me. I couldn't believe everything he said. There had to be an explanation for all of this.

For argument's sake, let's say I wasn't crazy, and an Archangel was hell-bent on tracking me down. Still, Adriel was an angel too. Why would he have more of an alliance to me than to his own kind? If he was trying to save me, he could change his mind at any time. A layer of hate smoldered in his eyes. The hate was for me, for what I was. What *was* I?

Was it possible to be evil without knowing it? Was I like Damien from *The Omen*? I shook my head. Here I was considering whether I was the anti-Christ. I needed sleep.

I set the bedside alarm for 3 A.M. That's when I would sneak out the bathroom window and decide my next move. Whenever he was around, I had this odd trust in Adriel, but when he was away I could think without that distraction.

I was sixteen. I could get a job and maybe a fake I.D. But where would I sleep until my first paycheck?

My mind darted so much I couldn't sleep. I sat up and turned off the TV. I leaned my head against the headboard and closed my eyes.

Bright light danced behind my eyelids like I fell asleep sunbathing. The bed glided as if on wheels.

"Female, roughly fifteen, found at the scene of a crash. Right lateral bruising, could be internal bleeding. Possible concussion."

My eyes blinked open. People dressed in scrubs wheeled me on a bed down a bright, white hallway. I tried to turn my head. My neck was restrained. A woman's voice spoke, "You're with us, sweetheart. Hang in there. We'll get you fixed up real soon."

I squeezed my eyes shut, but the light still stung. Metal zinged. Were they going to cut me? My eyelids shot open.

Darkness receded. A bright light hovered above me. Out of that light came Raphael. His bright blue eyes stabbed me in the heart as his staff came down.

I jolted up from bed and stifled the scream with my hands. Darkness veiled me in its protection, and the only light came from the television that droned an infomercial about knives. My chest rose and fell in rapid breaths. I grabbed the remote from the bedside table and flicked off the TV. The room was bathed in silence. I put my head in my hands.

Meow! I glanced around the room. A muffled *tap, tap* brought me to my feet. I followed the sound. *Was I hearing things now?* Could I trust anything I saw or heard?

My bare feet swept across the nylon carpet to the bathroom where the sound was louder. My head darted in the direction of the sound. Above the toilet was a small window, the window I planned to sneak out of when I made my escape.

A cat tapped the window with her paw.

I slid the window open, and the cat jumped into my arms. I stroked her fur.

"Sim?"

I looked for any familiar features in the moonlight. She had dark gray fur and unique black markings.

"How did you get here?"

I hugged her to my chest and glanced out the window. On the pavement was a line of white. The line was broken and granules, like salt or sugar, streaked across the ground.

I furrowed my brow and tried to see where the curved line ended. The line coiled around the side of the building.

I brought Sim to the bed, settled down next to her, and pet down the length of her back.

"You shouldn't have come here," I said. "It'll be hard enough to take care of myself."

I found Sim outside our house when she was a kitten. After I fed her for weeks, Mom allowed me to let her inside.

I scratched behind her ear, and she purred.

"We'll have to leave soon," I said. "It's just you and me now."

THE alarm went off. I made sure to keep the volume low so Adriel couldn't hear the noise from the outside.

I turned off the alarm, sat up in bed, and rubbed my eyes.

I stretched my arms over my head but stopped mid-stretch when my eyes caught an outline in the darkness.

Someone sat, in the corner of the room, in the worn, motel armchair. I blinked and looked again. The whites of his eyes glowed in the dark. A slant of angled light streamed in front of him from the bathroom window. The dim glow graced the black fabric of his pants. He wore a black shirt and a black suit. His tie was a trail of crimson. The shadows veiled his face.

"Quite a night we're having," he said with the shadow of contempt in his voice.

I folded my legs up to my chest. "Who are you? What are you doing here?"

"You can call me Bob." His body folded into the chair like a tarantula in a matchbox.

I peered through the darkness. No semblance of wings.

"Are you an angel too?" I said with an edge to my voice.

"I'm no angel, sweetheart." He leaned forward in his chair. His face entered the stream of light. His skin was orange like he had a bad experience with sunless tanning. His eyes were black. The pupils seemed too big. His thin lips were low on his face. His dark hair was slicked back. He looked forty, maybe forty-five.

His hands were clasped in front of him like he was conducting a business meeting. "The difference between me and the angels is that I don't want to kill you."

I narrowed my eyes. He said he didn't want to kill me, but his tone made me feel like that's *exactly* what he wanted to do.

I raised my eyebrow. "Adriel brought me here to help me." I wasn't sure if that was true, but this man might know something, and I wanted to know what he knew.

"Adriel? The young Seraph standing in the parking lot? You think he could stop Raphael?" He stared at me. "I judge by your lack of surprise that you know about Raphael. Even if that little angel could stand a chance against one of the oldest

Archangels in existence, why would he? You know one angel is after you, maybe Adriel pulled you away from the rescue party. Maybe he plans to deliver you to Raphael himself and receive a reward. You don't know anything about him."

"I don't know anything about you either."

"You can see I don't have wings, can't you?" He glanced behind both his shoulders in turn.

"That doesn't mean that you're on my side." I crossed my arms.

"No, I guess not. You'll have to decide." He snapped his fingers, and a large circle glowed alongside him like a tear in the space. A ripple fizzled like lightning and surrounded the circle. Inside was a gray scene, a road and buildings in the distance.

"My boss sent me to rescue you," said Bob. "Don't make me go home empty handed. It could mean the Pit for me."

I stared into the hole as if the opening was a mouth that could swallow me. The tear looked like the one that the people in black climbed through. They saved me from that angel, unintentionally, but one of them let me live despite what I saw.

Sim padded across the bed. Her black and gray form glided in front of me. I reached out for her, but before I could grasp her, her long, sleek body jumped into the tear. She looked out to me from across the gray street.

Bob pressed the fingers of one hand to his thumb in rapid secession as if he played a flute. "Last chance, sweetheart."

five

I climbed through the bright portal. My stomach lurched, and my head swam. A force pulled at me like the momentum that jerks you when riding bumper cars.

My guitar slung across my back, I clenched my backpack. A rush of air, scented like the breeze before the rain, hit me. I looked at the sky. The clouds were layers of gray. I couldn't find the sun. Light came from the ground in the distance. The glow peered between the buildings and gave the whole street a dreamlike quality.

The grimy motel was replaced by a five-star hotel, and all the buildings looked like modern art. One jutted out from the ground like a skyscraper. The building was a mix of grays, whites, and blacks. Another looked like a series of clean, smooth, white and gray boxes stacked on top of each other with floor to ceiling windows along one entire side of the building.

No trash littered the street. No graffiti ran alongside the buildings. Everything looked clean, crisp, and slate gray.

Sim rubbed against my legs, and I stooped to pick her up.

The roar of an engine reared up behind me. I turned around, and Bob sat in a black convertible with the top down. He winked at me.

"Get in," he said. "Unless you want to walk."

The portal disappeared like the zipper on a jacket. The space was unblemished by the rip. The smooth space looked as if the wound could never be reopened.

"Am I...trapped here?" I asked.

"We're all trapped here, sweetheart," Bob said.

That didn't make much sense. After all, how could Bob be trapped if he could make portals appear and disappear at will?

Bob's suit was darker. The suit turned from charcoal black to obsidian. His tie was a bloodier shade of red.

He flashed straight, white teeth. A shiny gold watch wrapped around his wrist.

He looked like a well-groomed businessman, but something felt...*sinister* about him. At least he didn't have wings.

He was either part of my least crazy subconscious, or this was real. This *felt* real.

I pulled open the passenger side door and got in with Sim. What choice did I have? The street was familiar, settled right under the bypass, but the buildings were foreign to me. I wouldn't know where I was going.

The car picked up speed and careened around the corner. Bob jabbed the pedal, and the car jolted forward.

I dug my nails into the seat. Where did this guy learn to drive?

We rounded a corner.

"Where are you taking me?" I yelled as the car sped down the street.

"Someplace much better than that ratty, old motel. Nash won't mind."

Nash, I heard that name before. He was one of the men who crawled through a portal into my bedroom. He inadvertently saved my life, and he killed someone else to do that.

"Who's Nash?"

"He's the guy who owns *this* place." The wheels screeched as we came to a halt in front of a mansion. A literal mansion. The place was lined with gray stone and plaster. It rose at least thirty feet in the air with plenty of large windows along the front face. The brick patio led to a set of stone steps. Lights glowed inside the building.

Bob stepped out of the car, and I followed. He was very tall, at least six foot five maybe taller. He towered over me and the car.

Bob opened the door to the mansion. Who keeps a place like this unlocked?

I walked in after Bob. The walls were alabaster. Mirrors hung on the walls, and the illusion made the place seem larger. A marble staircase rose from the front entrance.

Bob walked up the stairs and gestured for me to follow.

"Why are we going upstairs?" I asked.

"So, I can show you to your room."

"*My* room?"

"You woke up pretty early," said Bob. "It's going to be a few more hours till morning."

"Wait, but what time is it?" I asked.

"3:18," he said, but he didn't look down at his watch or cellphone.

"But it's light outside. Well, sort of."

"Overcast." Bob said. "It's always like that here."

He had to be exaggerating. The weather had to change sometimes.

"Where's here?" I asked.

"Sheol," said Bob.

I narrowed my eyes. "Where is that from New Orleans?"

"South." Bob grinned. "Sheol is always south."

I shook my head and waited for a white rabbit with a pocket watch to scurry around a corner.

"Is Nash home?" I asked.

"Why? Do you want to meet him?"

Do I want to meet the guy whose house I was staying the night in? "Yes," I said. "I don't want to wake him, but, I mean, I am in his house. Are you going to tell him?"

Bob laughed. "He knows who you are."

How was that possible? I just met Bob. Nash did see me before he entered that portal, but it's not like I stepped up and introduced myself.

Bob stopped at a large frosted glass door and slid it open. The room was hospital white. The bed in the center rested on a glass platform that made the mattress look like it hovered.

"You should get comfortable," said Bob. "It won't be long before Nash finds out you're here." He said that like I was a mouse, and Nash was a cat. Like he wanted to hunt me down once he knew I was in his house.

Bob closed the door behind him as he walked back out into the hallway. His footsteps became distant.

I slumped onto the bed with Sim still in my arms. I sighed.

I tried to think of something, anything that could explain all of this. I couldn't be crazy. Crazy people don't know they're crazy.

I shook my head. I pinched myself a thousand times since I met Adriel, and I didn't wake up.

I needed to go through with this, find out why a psycho angel was after me and go home, back to reality. But the death of my parents shattered my reality. What I returned to wouldn't be the home I knew.

Sim bounced to the floor. I laid on the bed. The mattress was firm, and the sheets were cool to the touch.

My thoughts pulled sleep from me until exhaustion extinguished them.

WHEN I woke, the light in the room glowed with the same intensity as the night before despite the large window. I sat up and looked outside. Bob wasn't joking. The sky's color did not change nor was the street wet with rain.

I got goose bumps as I left the warmth of the bed.

Two smaller doors of frosted glass stood in the room besides the door that led out to the hallway. I padded across the cold floor to the door across from the bed.

Behind the door was a closet filled with clothes that hung on either side and a large mirror on the back wall. Recessed lights brightened every inch of the room. A large white chest of drawers was set in the center.

I pulled a garnet red dress from the closet rod. The fabric touched the floor. I frowned and hung the dress back up.

As I browsed through the clothing, I felt like more of an intruder.

Whose room was this?

I left the closet and walked to the door across from the other side of the bed.

Holy shit!

A walk-in shower was built into one corner of the room. Curved glass surrounded the shower. Alongside the shower was a large marble platform with a small step leading up to it. Set into the center of the marble platform was a bathtub and hollowed out into the wall across from the tub was a built-in fireplace. Across from all this was a marble countertop and sink, above which was a wall of mirrors that stretched from one end of the bathroom to the other.

I didn't belong here.

I turned the silver handle on the sink and wet my face in the basin. The water ran cool and clear and felt soothing.

I washed my face with a bar of hard soap that didn't have a scent, dried my face on a white towel, and peered at my reflection. My hair was in tangles. The dyed ends were wet from falling into the sink. My clothes were wrinkled. A bruise purpled along my jawline, and my bottom lip was split.

I pulled open the drawer, and inside was a brush and comb. I ran the brush through my hair until the knots were out.

I reached into my pocket and pulled out the burnt picture of my parents. My face tensed into a frown and lips quivered. The golden locket Jonah had given me hung around my neck. I searched the drawers and found a pair of cuticle scissors. I cut a heart around my Mom and Dad's faces. I had to trim them a few times before they fit inside the locket. Their photographs were side by side nestled within two hearts.

I wore the same clothes from three days ago. They smelled of sweat and blood. I unzipped my backpack and pulled out a t-shirt and cutoffs. They were wrinkled because I tossed them, unfolded, into the bag. I took off my old clothes and put on the new ones.

I thought I should take a shower, but felt weird about it. I'd never been in a house this nice and pristine. I was sure whatever I did would leave a mark. I felt carsick.

I smoothed out my shirt as best as I could. As I ran my hands over my stomach, it rumbled. I'd have to find food for me and Sim. The prospects of that were better than if I had snuck through the motel window.

I didn't like roaming around the house of a guy I never met, but I was eager to find the kitchen. Sooner or later, he would know I was in his house. I hoped he didn't think I was an intruder. Didn't Bob say that Nash knew me? Did he mean my name or what I looked like too? Did he know I was the girl he saw after he murdered that angel?

I made a terrible detective. I couldn't get the right answers if I didn't ask the right questions. I should have told Bob what I knew about Nash. He might have given me more information, like why Nash jumped through portals and killed angels.

I opened the door and tiptoed out of the room. The hallway was empty. Recessed lights bathed the hall in a sun-like glow, and the air smelled clean and sterile like a clinic. Sim followed me.

"No, Sim, you stay." I lifted her from the ground and placed her back in the room before I slid the door shut.

My steps echoed like footfalls in a museum. I bit my lip and squeezed my eyes shut. *Should I take off my shoes?*

I crept down the marble stairs to the foyer. To my right was the living room. To my left was a hallway. I wandered down the hall and stopped.

An entrance opened to the kitchen. White cupboards ran along the walls near the ceiling. Ivory counters settled above black cabinets along the wall and on the island. A stainless-steel refrigerator stood level with the upper cabinets. A coffee pot sat on the counter next to the sink. Light glowed from an oval, white light fixture hanging from the ceiling and from beneath the island.

I pulled open the fridge and peered inside. On the shelves were vegetables, jars of jam, a pitcher of water, plum colored juice, and a bowl of peaches.

I looked through the cabinets until I found an array of glasses and pulled one down from the shelf. I poured a glass of the purplish juice and drank it in a few gulps. The juice was sweet and sour.

I took the cup from my lips when someone appeared through the bottom of the glass.

Nash stood by the coffee pot. He pulled a jar down from the top shelf. He looked no older than twenty. He was tall with charcoal black hair, alarming against his pale skin. His eyes were so dark I couldn't distinguish the pupils from the irises. He wore a thin, sleeveless t-shirt and boxer-shorts.

My eyes hit the floor. "Sorry. Bob said…"

"Good morning." He scooped coffee beans out of the jar. He didn't seem to recognize me although he only glanced at me.

"You must be Nash," I said.

"That's right." He didn't turn to look at me. He lifted the top of the coffee machine and filled the chamber with the coffee beans.

I must have embarrassed him. Did he expect me to leave?

The muscles of his back moved beneath the barely-there t-shirt.

"You hungry?" He still didn't look at me.

"Yeah, I guess."

"Tofu scramble okay?"

"Um, you don't have to cook for me."

"Okay. I thought you might be hungry."

"I am," I said.

"Then how about the scramble?" He turned around and gave me a tight smile.

"Sure." Truth was I never had tofu. Mom used to make me scrambled eggs. She made the best scrambled eggs.

"You can wait in the dining room. It shouldn't take long."

"Where's the dining room?"

Nash pointed to the frosted door on the opposite wall.

I took my glass and ducked out, happy to leave the tension behind me. A marble table was in the center of the dining room. Ten gray, cushioned chairs surrounded the table. Two paintings hung side by side on the wall. One painting was gray with white lines scratched into the canvas. The other was cream-colored with charcoal lines in a mess of spirals.

Dad's paintings showed dark imagery, but they had meaning. I wondered what those paintings meant.

I pulled my cellphone out of my pocket. I should call Jonah. I couldn't tell him where I was. I wasn't sure where I was. But I wanted to let him know I was okay.

The screen lit up. No service. I walked around the room. Still, no service. Weird. Thirty percent battery charge. I turned the phone off and stowed it in my pocket.

NASH walked into the dining room with my breakfast. He had changed into a white collared shirt and dark pants. He left the shirt untucked.

He set my plate down in front of me. The tofu scramble looked like scrambled eggs without the yolks.

Nash stood against the opposite wall and sipped his coffee. His eyes were pointed at the opposite wall where the paintings hung. Did he know the meaning behind those dark squiggles and those sharp, white lines?

The texture of the tofu was spongy. The flavor was earthy, nutty, and spicy. The mushrooms and peppers gave it pops of color. As I chewed, I tried not to scoff the food down. My fork hit the plate with a loud clang. I cringed.

I glanced up, but Nash's eyes still focused on the opposite wall.

I hated to ask, but I needed to get Sim something to eat too. "Um…do you have any tuna fish…it's for my cat."

"Sorry. No." Nash sipped his coffee.

"Do you have any other meat or fish or anything?"

"I don't have any of that here."

That's a little odd. Maybe he was vegetarian.

"Okay," I said. "Is there a store nearby?"

"I'll get you some this afternoon." He took another sip of his coffee. "First, I'll have to bring you into town. The boss wants to see you."

NASH climbed into the driver seat of a sleek red car. A tiny silver horse galloped on the grill. I settled down into the passenger's seat. By Nash's attitude back at the house, I guessed this ride would be painfully silent.

Nash said we were going to see his boss, but he made no effort to tuck his white button-down shirt into his pants. Bob dressed in a fitted black suit and red tie. Did they work for the same guy? And why was this guy interested in keeping me safe from an Archangel?

At least, no one I'd met since Adriel had wings. That was a plus on my reality meter.

The sky was still the same dull gray. The air still smelled like it does right before a rainstorm, and I expected a downpour.

Nash pulled the car out of the driveway and floored it down the street. I braced myself on the dashboard as he continued to zip down the road like he drove for NASCAR. Did everyone in this place drive like a freaking maniac?

The images outside began to blur, and I got dizzy. I thought I might throw up. I grabbed my stomach as the car lurched to a stop.

Nash got out of the car. I stayed in my seat and covered my mouth as I clenched my stomach. Nash's face appeared in the window. He frowned. Was that concern?

He opened the door for me, and I stepped out of the car. My legs shook like cymbals hit with a drumstick. Nash held my elbow to steady me. His touch was warm. The heat seeped beneath the sleeve of my shirt.

We stopped outside a skyscraper that was several stories high like a corporate building. Clouds hid the top of the structure. The glass door slid open. A secretary sat behind a white desk that wrapped around in a semi-circle. Her round, clear face held a tight smile that spread from ear to ear and showed all her teeth. The wide smile made her cheekbones rise, and her eyes crinkle to slits.

"Good morning," she said. "You must be here for your 10:00 A.M. appointment, you can wait in room 1006."

Nash nodded to her as we headed for the elevator. Nash jabbed a button and waited with his hands in his pockets.

I glanced at the button that still glowed: 1000. *One thousand floors? That must be a joke.*

My body jolted as the elevator rose. The sickening feeling festered in my stomach as the elevator lurched upwards. I could feel my breakfast rising in my throat.

The doors opened to a wall of floor to ceiling windows. I walked to the windows and glanced down. I couldn't see the cars below. Clouds obscured my vision. The sky was dark like it was 10:00 P.M. instead of 10:00 A.M. The dark clouds swallowed the building.

I was dizzy. I wasn't afraid of heights, but this was different. When Felicia and I were friends, her parents brought us to Six Flags. Felicia wanted to ride the highest rollercoaster but not unless I rode with her. I never rode a rollercoaster in my life, and I screamed every time the cars dropped, but that didn't make me as sick as when I stood above the clouds.

A warm hand touched my shoulder. I jumped.

"Are you afraid?" Nash asked.

I felt my head nod involuntarily while I said, "No."

He smiled. "This way."

I followed him and scratched the back of my hand as I read the numbers on each door: 1014, 1012, 1010, 1008....

Nash pushed open the door to room 1006. In the room was a white leather sofa across from two black armchairs and a plush rug against the hard marble floor. On a glass coffee table, between the sofa and chairs, rested a wilted lily in a ceramic pot.

"Have a seat," said Nash.

I turned to sit and was startled by a lady in the corner. She wore a white skirt suit and had the same creepy smile as the secretary downstairs.

She glided forward and stopped in front of us. "Can I get you anything?"

"Coffee," said Nash.

Second coffee today. Long night, buddy?

She turned her head and smiled at me.

"Nothing for me, thanks." I needed water. My mouth was drier than a raisin. But I didn't want that strange woman to get it for me.

The woman turned on her heel and left the room. She walked so straight-backed and with such perfect spacing between each step, she couldn't be real. She was like a creepy mannequin brought to life.

After she left, I realized I was hovering above the sofa. I sat down. Nash sat on the other end of the sofa with one arm stretched across the back while the other lay on the armrest.

His hand was inches from my face as his arm closed the distance between us.

My hands were clasped in my lap. My eyes looked down at them. I crossed and uncrossed my legs. Neither pose was comfortable for long. I thought I would break the silence, when the door opened. The secretary walked in with Nash's coffee.

He accepted the cup from her and took one long sip.

The woman retired to the same corner of the room and turned away from us. I squinted at her, but I was glad I couldn't see her face. Her smile might give me nightmares.

The door opened again. Bob strode in, dressed in the same black suit and red tie. He glanced at me and smiled. He held the door open for someone.

Her face was pale and thin with burgundy red lipstick. She wore a fitted, black pantsuit with red cuffs and tall red heels, not that she needed them as her head was an inch from the doorframe.

But what made my eyes go wide and my hands start to sweat, wasn't her height or the rail thinness of her body, but what followed.

As her full form strolled through the doorway, from her back was a set of blackened bones that came up in two angled arches above each shoulder and sank down to thin points near the middle of her calves. They were like wings that lost all their feathers. They were like the wings of the angel I touched.

Bob sat in one of the black chairs across from the sofa while the tall woman stood behind the chair's twin. Her long fingers curled upon the soft leather of the chair's back. Each nail was long and black like a talon.

Run! But I could feel those claws ripping through my body if I made any move toward the door. I glanced over at Nash, but he sipped his coffee and lifted the mug with steady hands.

Bob crossed his legs and folded his hands in his lap. He smiled at me like I was the entertainment.

My eyes darted back to the long nails and up to the woman's face. Her thin lips curled into a smile.

"Have my boys been treating you well?" she asked.

I nodded without thinking. I wanted to ask a hundred questions, but I couldn't will myself to speak.

"I have a few things I need to explain to you first, darling. Then, you can talk, okay?"

I nodded again without meaning to.

"You're being hunted by an Archangel, honey. Well, you probably knew that part. His name is Raphael, and he has an agenda, you see. He doesn't want to kill you. He wants to *use* you. He wants to use you to close the gates of Heaven forever. And I can't have that. Alright, we've got that out of the way."

My voice came back.

My eyes swept from her pale face, and the arched bones rose above her shoulders. She was the boss in this place, this place that was separate from the world. Why hadn't I seen it sooner?

One question burned me, one I wasn't sure I wanted the answer to.

"Are you the Devil?"

"Name's Lucifer, honey. And no, you can't call me Lucy."

I gulped. "Am I…in Hell?"

"I hate that word," said Lucifer. "We call it Sheol. Still Hell, but it doesn't have the same bite."

Either way, I was in Hell. *The* Hell. I don't care what the Devil calls it. Did I die? Was Bob the Grim Reaper?

"Am I dead?"

"No," said Lucifer. "Unfortunately, killing you might not solve my problem. You could still be of use to Raphael."

"Why is Raphael after me? I don't understand. How could he use *me*?"

"Because you can kill angels, my dear. Well, not literally. No one can *kill* an angel. But you can make them fall from grace."

Adriel told me the same. But I assumed Raphael wanted me dead because of what I could do, not that he wanted to use me.

"But why would Raphael want to close the gates of Heaven?" I asked.

"Because he's jealous. He doesn't want you or your kind in Heaven. All those souls to look after, to take care of. You would be his weapon against the angels who resist. Not all the angels agree with Raphael. They still think they are upholding God's will although most of them have never seen Him."

I closed my eyes. I pinched my arm once, twice, but I was still met with Lucifer's black eyes. "Why do you care? If the gates of Heaven are closed, there's only one other place for souls to go."

"Precisely," said Lucifer. "We're overcrowded as it is. I'll have to throw more souls into the Pit."

Bob cringed.

"Besides," she said. "I'm very…particular about the souls I take. Some of course, have to come here, but I like to be selective."

"So, I can't leave."

THE WINGS OF HEAVEN AND HELL   59

"Not unless you want to be Raphael's tool. But I do have a proposition for you." Lucifer drummed her fingers against the front of the chair. "I want you to make Raphael and all his followers fall."

My mind raced. This was not the side I wanted to be on. I wasn't religious, but everyone knows that the Devil is the bad guy...or *girl*. "Why should I do that for you?"

"You're damned. Your soul is on my list. If you want it back, you'll play along."

On her list? I was destined for Hell. How was that possible? "I don't understand."

"Bob, show her the paperwork."

Bob opened the folder in his lap and passed a sheet of paper over to me. The document was in a language I couldn't understand, and the bottom was stained in blood.

"I can't read this."

"Oh, sorry, sweetheart." Bob waved his hand over the paper, and the letters morphed into English.

I skimmed over the contents.

I remembered all those times I clicked agree before reading the terms and conditions. Did I agree to sell my soul every time I downloaded a new app to my phone?

"That smear on the bottom, that's the signature," Lucifer said. "We do them in blood now. Far less tricky."

"I don't remember signing anything," I said. "Not in writing or in blood."

"You didn't," said Lucifer. "Your mother did the honors before you were born."

I narrowed my eyes. *My mother sold my soul to the Devil?*

six

I threw up as soon as the car stopped outside Nash's house. I pushed the door open and leaned my head out so that my breakfast landed on the pavement.

Nash took my arm and led me into the house. He sat me down on a chair in the kitchen.

"Here." He set a cup of hot coffee in front of me.

I don't like coffee, but it seemed like a silly thing to complain about after I found out my mother who abandoned me also sold my soul to Satan.

I used the mug to warm my hands as my arms shook. Steam curled above the cup.

Nash sat across from me and sipped his coffee. "Sorry I couldn't prepare you for that. She told me not to."

"Does this make you a demon?" I asked.

He laughed. "Not everyone in Hell is a demon,"

"I still don't understand," I said. "Why am I like this? Why did that angel explode into flames when I touched him?"

None of this made any sense. I didn't remember my birth mom, and recent information didn't paint a very positive picture.

"Someone must have performed a ritual," said Nash. "Since your soul was already damned that part didn't matter, but you still had to be willing."

"What ritual? I don't remember agreeing to anything. How could this happen?"

Nash put his hand on mine. His touch warmed me more than the mug of hot coffee.

"I'm having a few friends over for dinner," he said. "If you want to join us, there's a dress laid out on your bed."

His hand left mine, and the coldness crept back.

THE dress was blood red with off-the-shoulder sleeves and a skirt that dragged to the floor. The satin fabric was cool to the touch. I had never worn anything like it in my life.

The digital clock on the bedside table glowed 7 o'clock in bright red digits. I changed into jeans and kept on the t-shirt I put on that morning. I was going to dinner, not a ball.

I walked into the bathroom. A bag the size of a purse rested on the counter. I opened the bag. Inside was an array of blushes, lipstick, and eye shadow. I never wore makeup, and I wasn't going to start tonight. I'd make myself look like a clown. But if Nash put the makeup here, did he think I might want it or that I needed it?

I passed the brush through my hair once more and headed downstairs to the dining room. The table hid beneath a white linen tablecloth. A fruit salad sat in the middle surrounded by a plate of rounded slices of bread, a large bowl of pasta with bright green sauce, a platter of roasted asparagus, a rich three-tiered cake with chocolate frosting, and set in front of each seat was a bowl of tomato soup.

Whoa. *Was Nash celebrating something?*

A woman with wavy blonde hair and dark, green eyes framed by thick lashes sat at the table. I recognized her. She was the woman with Nash when he killed the angel. She wore a long, teal dress with capped sleeves. Her lips curled up, more than a smile, an invitation.

Another woman sat across from her. She wore a long, black dress. Her black hair was twisted in a bun and bangs framed her thin eyebrows. Her eyes were dark, narrow, and very close to her nose. Ruby red lipstick flashed against her olive complexion.

I felt like I walked in naked.

The man seated to my far left was the only other person who wasn't dressed like he was going to a wedding. He wore a dingy, gray t-shirt, but still sported a black suit jacket. His hair, medium brown, stuck out on one side. His eyes, set below sharp black brows, were the color of rust.

The dark-skinned man next to him sat straight-backed in his chair. I remembered his name: Kiran. His black hair was shaved close to his head, and a trimmed beard and mustache framed his full lips. High cheekbones accented his angular face. He wore a maroon suit jacket with a white scoop-necked shirt beneath.

Nash stood at the head of the table with his hands on the back of the chair. He wore a fitted black suit and buttoned-down shirt. His posture reminded me of Lucifer's, and a maggot of fear burrowed into my brain.

When his gaze fell on me, he frowned, and the maggot tunneled deeper. He gestured for me to sit down in the chair next to the man with disheveled hair.

My skin tingled. Were these people really demons? They didn't look like demons. Could they be hiding it under a mask like the creatures I saw when no one else did? Or maybe they were like Nash. Not demons, but something else.

If one of them lunged over the table at me and sprouted a tail or fangs, would I be prepared to run?

Right now, I was too hungry to care.

I dipped my spoon in the soup as soon as my butt hit my chair. The soup was cold, which surprised me. But the fusion of flavors played in harmony on my tongue: fresh tomatoes, something crisp maybe cucumbers and a rich oniony flavor. I hadn't tasted anything so good in my life. "Holy hell," I said.

Did I say that out loud?

I felt anything but invisible as the eyes of the other five diners glanced my way.

"Is everything okay?" Nash asked.

I looked up. "Yeah. It tastes amazing."

Nash grinned.

The blonde-haired woman looked over at me. She couldn't be much older than I was, maybe eighteen. "Just wait till you try the rest," she said. "Nash is an excellent cook. I'm Adrianna by the way." She motioned to the guy in the gray shirt. "And this is Tom—"

"*She's* the one?" said the woman in black. "The girl you told us about? What is she twelve?"

"Chandra!" Adrianna snapped.

"I'm sixteen." I leaned across the table and grabbed a slice of bread.

"Bit short for sixteen." Chandra slurped the soup from her spoon.

I dunked the bread into the bowl and waited for the soup to saturate the airy slice. "Haven't hit my growth spurt yet, but when I do, I'll let you know. Wouldn't want to break the illusion that anyone under five four can't possibly have a driver's permit."

Tom sprayed soup from his mouth into his napkin. "Sorry." He snickered.

Chandra jabbed him with her eyes.

Tom continued to smirk behind the back of his hand.

It probably wasn't smart for me to mouth off at a demon, but I was important here. Important enough to earn an audience with the Devil *herself*. So, I could afford a few snide remarks, right?

I cleaned my bowl with the crust. Crumbles fell on the ta-blecloth. I reached for the pasta tongs and served myself a mountain. I slurped the noodles and painted the plate with green sauce.

What was going to happen next? I was basically a prisoner here. *A very well fed prisoner.* Nash had been nice to me, but it wasn't like he was offering me a way out. I couldn't work for the Devil, but I didn't want my soul to be trapped in Hell either. Something told me Hell wasn't all art museums and fine dining. But how was I going to get out of this?

"Lia?" Nash's voice pierced my thoughts.

"Yes?" I looked up from my plate.

"You have a little…" he pointed to the corner of his mouth.

After several seconds, I registered his meaning. "Oh, thank you." I picked up my napkin and wiped the corner of my mouth. I dabbed both corners just in case. My face flushed. "I'm sorry I didn't hear you."

I wiped the crumbs under my napkin. Green splotches dot-ted the area around my dish like a Jackson Pollock painting. Mom used to say, "Slow down, Lia. No one's going to snatch the food off your plate."

"I was talking about our meeting with Lucifer," said Nash. "This will be your team."

"My *team*?" Were we going to play rugby or something?

"Yes, but I'm the captain of course."

"We're going to help you find Raphael and the others." Adrianna's blonde curls bobbed.

"Oh. Thank you…" The thought that the Devil owned my soul consumed me. But she gave me a way to get it back. She was using my soul as leverage to get me to do what she wanted.

"Are we going to kill them?" I asked.

"No," said Adrianna. "Why would you think that?"

"I saw you," I said.

Adrianna squinted at me.

"I saw you kill that fallen angel."

"When did you see that?" Kiran spoke for the first time.

"At my house. Yesterday. I was hiding behind the bed."

"How *can* you see us?" asked Tom.

"I don't know. I just can," I said.

"Well, technically, we didn't *kill* him," said Adrianna. "We sent him to the Pit. He could have come with us willingly. He decided to attack."

"It's a shame." Nash set his fork down.

"So, that's what you do?" I asked. "Bring fallen angels to Hell."

"Them and the demons that lurk on Earth without permission," said Nash. "Usually they overstay their contracts."

"Their contracts?" I asked.

"How *do* you see me?" asked Tom.

"I—What?" *With my eyes of course.*

"Demons can roam the earth for a number of years," Chandra drawled. "They have a certain quota to meet: possessions, signing away souls to Hell. When they don't make their quotas, they hide…on the Earth. We find them and take them back."

"So, you're like demon parole officers?"

"Yeah," said Adrianna. "But we don't do drug tests." Her eyes went from green to solid black. The pupils filled her eyes, leaving no white.

I leapt from the table.

"What?" asked Adrianna.

"Your eyes." The words pulled from my lips in a whisper. But her eyes were normal again.

The others looked at me wide-eyed as I settled back down into my chair. Even in Hell, among a group of professed demons, I was the crazy one.

Tom grabbed my arm. "Did they look something like this?" His eyes were solid black too.

I tried to jump away, but his fingertips dug into my arm.

Tom blinked, and his eyes were normal again. "Sorry." He smirked. "But what did you see?"

"Your eyes are black like hers." My voice shook.

Tom let go of my arm and clapped his hands together. "She's piercing our Veils."

"I don't know why that would be something to get so excited about," said Chandra.

"I've never seen a human do it, have you?" asked Tom. "She's not getting through completely though. Or else she'd be running from the room screaming."

Pierce their Veils? So, they are *demons, and I can see what they truly are* sometimes. The chill recoiled…slowly.

"So, angels and demons and the Devil. They all exist. Anything else I should know about?" I asked.

"Well," said Tom. "There are Cambions."

"Cambions?"

"The offspring of incubi and humans," said Adrianna. "It doesn't happen often. Think of it as a genetic mutation. Cambions are dark magic users. Oh, and they eat people."

"So, they're witches?" I asked. *Wait, witches don't eat people, do they?*

"No," said Adrianna. "They're something different: Half-demons. But there are witches."

"Not that Lucifer wants them running around," said Tom.

Witches, demons, Archangels. I felt like they were pushing against the inside of my skull trying to split my head open.

And tracking down Archangels—it wasn't like there was a class on that or anything. "I don't know where to start," I said.

"Of course not," said Chandra, not looking at me. "You're just a tool. It's our responsibility to get you there." She was dressed like she was going to a ball, but I got the sense that Chandra was a hardened warrior. I imagined her swinging a sword and laughing in the faces of her enemies while tigers in spiked collars roared behind her.

I shook my head. We weren't going to fight anybody, were we? I guess we were. Raphael wouldn't back off just because I asked him to. But this was crazy, they were angels for goodness sake. Besides, didn't angels live in Heaven? Demons couldn't go there, right?

Chandra, Adrianna, Tom, and Kiran were demons. Well, at least Adrianna and Tom were. They had showed me their true colors, their real eyes. According to Nash, Hell housed more than demons, and he implied that he wasn't one. "How are we going to find the angels?"

"With their weapons," said Tom. "Each angel has a weapon made of an extremely powerful metal found only in Arcadia."

"Where's Arcadia?" I asked.

"People call Arcadia the Garden of Eden or Utopia," Tom explained. "Arcadia is a place in Heaven designated for humans."

"Okay. But how will we use the weapons to find the angels?"

"The angel weapons were placed on Earth as a precaution against future rebellion in Heaven," said Kiran.

"Each weapon is tied to the angel it belongs to," said Tom. "Angels are bound to protect their weapons. That is, as long as they aren't fallen."

"If we find them and take them," said Kiran, "they will come."

"Then what?" I asked.

"Then, you use your super special power," said Chandra, "the one that makes you so important." Her words were laced with venom.

"But I'd have to touch them to do that," I said. I'd have to make them scream, make them suffer.

"Angels aren't the only ones who have access to Arcadian Steel," said Nash. "We'll fight them, and you'll make them fall."

seven

Y hand smacked me in the forehead. *What time was it?* I looked over at the clock. 11 A.M. I tossed and turned all night. Each attempt at sleep brought a new nightmare, which wasn't strange when I considered the circumstances.

I was on the run from an Archangel, and my birth mom sold my soul to Satan, who commissioned me to kill said Archangel with my fancy superpower. All I needed was a hardcore rock ballad playing behind me, and people would think I was badass.

I stretched in the bed. I wanted to stay nestled in the warmth of the covers. The chill air kissed my face.

Sim climbed onto my stomach, and I stroked her fur. I filled a bowl with water and left the water by the door for her, but I needed to get her food.

I climbed out of bed, and goose bumps speckled my arms as soon as the warm blanket left my skin. I wore a t-shirt and pajama shorts. I wished I packed something warmer, but I live in southern Louisiana. I didn't have clothes warm enough for the coldness of Nash's house.

I've heard people call Louisiana "hot as Hell." Well, I've got some news for them. Hell wasn't hot. It was as cold as an art museum. It held haunting and beautiful wonders, but bring a sweater.

I picked up my guitar case and laid it out on the bed. The snaps on the side of the case unlatched easily. I felt the smooth body of the Strat. The guitar was perfect. It was the last gift my parents had ever given me, and I couldn't even play it. I couldn't lug a twelve-pound amp around with me.

I scratched Sim behind the ears and made my way to the kitchen. A note was stuck to the fridge.

Went out for a while, but will be back for training. Look in the refrigerator.

Training?

I opened the refrigerator and found another note folded in half and propped up. *For the cat.* Behind the note were several packets of tuna.

I wasn't sure when Nash left the note. If he left earlier this morning, he could be back soon. I poured a glass of juice and gulped it down. Breakfast could wait. I opened a package of tuna and squeezed it into a bowl.

My hand touched the cold, metal banister on my way back upstairs. I pulled my hand away. *So damn cold in this house.* I placed the bowl of tuna next to Sim's water and slid the door shut.

I had a few games loaded on my cellphone, but when I tried to access them, my battery died. I forgot to grab my charger. My guitar still lay on the bed. Wouldn't make much sense to play it. Without an amp, the notes would be soundless.

I could explore the house until Nash comes back. Several rooms were still mysteries to me. Nash must have a television somewhere. Hell might have its own stations. I wondered if shows were weird in Hell. You know, like a game show where the Devil spears the loser in the ass with a pitchfork.

As I passed the foyer, the front door opened. Tom stood and stared at me like I was a bear at a movie theater. He wore a t-shirt with small holes at the hem and a pair of faded black jeans.

"Hi," I said. "You know where Nash went?"

He pressed his lips together. "Nope."

"Do you and Nash live together?" I asked.

"No," said Tom. "I come here for the library, not Nash's abs."

"I didn't mean it that way," I said.

"And I didn't take offense to it."

"Um, where's the library?" I asked.

"Nash hasn't given you a tour? I guess he must not like you. But I do." He winked. "It's a real treat. Let me show you. Seeing is believing."

Nash's house couldn't get any bigger, but it did. The mansion was like Mary Poppins's suitcase. Rooms kept coming out of nowhere.

"Why does Nash need such a big house?" I asked.

"You should see *my* house," said Tom. "Big houses are a thing in the Outer Region. We like to show off. Although Nash has the best library in Sheol. Thinking about the number of books he has fills me with so much envy you'd think I've been hanging out with Leviathan."

"Leviathan."

"One of the seven princes of Hell. Lucifer is one of them."

"But I thought Lucifer was the King—I mean *Queen* of Hell."

"It's more complicated than that," said Tom. "It's a good thing I'm showing you the library. You've got a lot of reading to do."

"Does Nash have a family?" I asked. "I mean, does he really live in this big house all by himself?"

"No one in Hell has a family," said Tom. "Well, that is except for Chandra. She was lucky. Both she and her younger brother went to Sheol, and both accepted contracts."

"She can't be the only one with family down here," I said.

"Hell's a big place," said Tom. "If you did have family down here, it would be very hard to find them. They could be in the Circles or still on Earth fulfilling their contracts. Once they completed their obligations on Earth, they could be anywhere in the Outer Region."

I didn't have family in Hell. The only family I'd ever known were Micah and Alexandria Hebert. They were good people. So, they were in Heaven.

"Can I visit Heaven?" I asked.

Tom laughed. "Are you joking?"

"No."

"Do you think if demons had access to Heaven, they would hang around down here all the time?" Tom asked.

"But the portals. That's how Bob brought me to Sheol. One opened in my bedroom."

"Not all demons have access to portals," said Tom. "They are a gift from Lucifer, and they only grant us access to Earth, not Heaven. And she only grants them to demons who do her dirty work, like us. Without the portals, we'd have to trek all over—" He stopped. "Here we are."

We stopped in front of a set of tall, frosted glass double doors. Sim rested in a fur crescent in front of them. She looked up at me and meowed.

"Sim." I picked up the cat. "How did you get out here?"

"Your cat, I presume," said Tom.

I stroked Sim's fur and felt the soft rattle of her purring. "I don't know how she got out here. I closed my door."

Tom frowned. "Maybe you didn't." He opened the doors. They slid into the wall. I clenched Sim, and I followed Tom inside.

Shelves of books towered from the floor and up to the ceiling. Nash's house was three-stories, and the library ceiling took advantage of each one of them. Ladders on caster wheels ran along the shelves so the books at the top could be reached.

The books had leather covers with creases along the spines. Pages stuck out of the older volumes as if the pages had become loose or were, in some cases, cut unevenly.

The floor was polished white marble. A desk sat in the center of the room. A loveseat and set of cushioned chairs were nestled in front of the frosted glass window.

"This is Nash's *personal* library?" I was in awe of the sheer size. The library must have housed thousands of books.

"Yeah, Nash is a bit of a collector."

"A bit."

"You can uncover a lot of information in these books," said Tom. "Information we can use to locate the angel weapons."

"That would take forever."

"Not really. I've been through most of them. I know what I'm looking for."

"How could you possibly have been through *most* of them?"

"I'm older than I look." Tom winked.

Tom looked no older than the guys I went to school with.

A laugh echoed through the room. A space on the third floor where the shelves stopped housed a loft that led into the third-floor hallway.

Chandra looked down from the loft. She grinned. She reached over the railing and grabbed a hold of one of the ladders. She leapt over and slid down the side rails of the ladder to the marble floor below.

She no longer wore the long, elegant dress she sported at dinner. She wore tight black clothes. Her body, long and lean, reminded me of a cat's. Her long, thin eyebrows were swept over dark almond-shaped eyes that threatened to collide with the bridge of her nose. Her sleek, black hair reached down to her tailbone.

Without a breath, she said, "Do you really think we'll be able to take any angel weapons? A full angel is stronger than ten demons. Have you ever fought an angel? Because I haven't."

Tom raised an eyebrow. "We have someone who can make angels fall with a touch."

"Look at her," said Chandra. "Barely five feet and ninety pounds soaking wet. You think an angel is going to let her get near him? She'll never make an angel fall." She glared at me with such hostility you'd think I killed her dog.

"I already did," I shot back. "That fallen angel Nash, Adrianna, and Kiran killed two days ago, I was the one who made him fall. He burst into flames when I touched him with my bare hands. You might never have fought an angel before, but I have."

Chandra's mouth tightened. "If what you're saying is true, you got lucky." She passed me and walked through the sliding door.

Tom shrugged. He grabbed a book and left me alone in the library with Sim. I put Sim down. She wandered around and stopped every now and then to sniff at something.

I pulled one of the books off the shelf and curled up in the armchair to read. *Winged Warriors: The Seven Archangels.*

The first chapter was about the Archangel Michael. A picture depicted Michael, wings spread and sword raised. His foot pressed down on the head of what I assumed to be the Devil, only the Devil was male. I wondered how many people knew Lucifer was a woman?

Next was Gabriel, he wore blue and white and held a silver horn. His wings were grayish, instead of the pure white of Adriel's wings.

I flipped through the book.

There he was: Raphael, the Archangel who wanted to use me to close the gates of Heaven. He didn't look anything like the Archangel who attacked us on the freeway. I only saw him for a split second, but his eyes didn't hold the same hatred and intensity.

He looked so...kind. He wore a brown shift and held a staff. His white wings were striking against the shadows. The caption read that he was the patron of the blind, of lovers, of shepherds, of the sick, and of guardian angels.

How could someone like that want to shut down Heaven for everyone? Could he have changed so much?

I awoke to a knock at the door. I lounged in the armchair. The book rested open on my chest. Sim curled up at my feet. Nash stood in the doorway. I sat up.

The book dropped onto the floor, and Sim scurried away.

"Sorry." I scrambled to pick the book up.

"We're outside," he said.

"Yeah, I got your note. What do you mean train? Train for what?"

"To hunt angels."

I cringed. He said that so nonchalantly like we were going to hunt rabbits or something. Of course, I might have cringed at the prospect of killing poor innocent bunnies too.

"How are we going to do that?" I asked.

"With weapons. You'll need to know how to use them."

Weapons. Arcadian weapons, the same weapons the angels themselves used. I hoped Nash didn't expect much from me. I could barely run a lap around the football field in gym class.

"Okay, I'll get dressed."

He looked me up and down, and my face got hot. "What you're wearing is finc," he said.

I wore a t-shirt, black leggings, and a pair of laced boots that stopped right above the ankle. In gym class, I wore shorts and a sleeveless shirt. I wasn't sure if I packed anything like that.

I followed him to the back patio. The backyard was open and went all the way to a fence in the distance. Kiran, Adrianna, Tom and Chandra stood on the field, talking. They all wore dark, tight clothes.

"What exactly does training consist of?" I asked before we were in earshot of the others. Surely, we weren't going to come at each other with sharpened swords made of the strongest steel in Heaven.

"Fighting," he said.

I learned that Nash didn't deal in specifics. Either that, or he must have thought I was dense and wouldn't understand anyway.

We faced the others.

"You ready?" asked Adrianna.

"I'm not sure," I said.

"We'll start with hand to hand. Chandra," said Nash. "Why don't you show Lia a thing or two?"

Chandra sighed. "You insult me, Nash."

Chandra stood opposite me. She lowered her head and glared at me. In the dress the night before, Chandra looked delicate, but now, her physique showed. Her body was thin, but toned compared to my skinny frame. She was right. I didn't stand a chance against her.

"You want me to just jump into it?" I asked.

"What better way to train how to fight than to fight?" said Kiran.

"She'll go easy on you," said Nash.

"I'll have to." Chandra smirked. "Or I'll break you."

I glared at her. I might be skinny, but I took on an angel. I could have clawed his eyes out. And anyone could throw a punch, right?

I pulled back my arm and tried to land a punch on Chandra.

She rolled her eyes and dodged my fist. She kicked, and I didn't have time to register my next move before the blow hit me in the stomach, and I landed flat on my back.

Her speed was inhuman. Of course, I wasn't dealing with humans, and even if I was, I still would have landed on my back.

Nash's lips were set as he watched. He probably thought I was hopeless.

I scrambled to my feet, worried I didn't look very graceful. I tried to move my feet a little more, maybe I could confuse her. I attempted to swing another punch, but she was so fast, I saw two of her.

Her fist landed against the side of my face. I felt my teeth click together as a sharp pain rode through my jaw.

I put my arms up to shield my face as another blow landed into the side of my stomach. I bent over.

Don't give up. I didn't want to look like a complete reject, but at the same time I wanted to live through this.

Chandra hit me again, and violent pain went up my arm. I was playing fisticuffs with a demon ten times faster and stronger than me. She had proper training. I didn't.

I tried to dodge the blow, but it landed against my jawline, pushing my head to the side. She was going to kill me.

Dread rose within me until it burst out of me like a firework. The air rippled in front of me like water. Chandra flew backwards and landed hard on her back several feet away.

She looked around, eyes wide, and scrambled to her feet with her hands curled into fists in front of her.

Adrianna, Kiran, and Tom stood with their mouths open. In the sudden silence, my heart pounded in my chest.

"Did you see that?" Adrianna said. "Nash, you didn't tell us she was a witch!"

"I didn't know." Nash sounded uninterested.

"I'm not a witch," I said.

"Yeah, you are. That could come in handy," said Adrianna. "What other incantations do you know?"

A chill shot up my spine, and my skin went pale. *Did I throw myself from the car when I could have saved my parents?*

"Stop it," said Nash. "She has enough on her plate."

"But I'm right, aren't I?" said Adrianna. "You drank demon blood."

"I don't know what you're talking about," I said.

"Maybe your mother or father fed you demon blood when you were little," Adrianna suggested.

"I never drank demon blood," I said. "My birth parents abandoned me in an old house. I don't know anything about them."

Nash's eyes focused on the ground.

Great, I embarrassed him with my pity story.

"That would explain it," said Adrianna. "Lucifer hates witches. She probably sent a demon after your mom and dad. So, they ran."

"She isn't a witch," said Kiran. "Witches know what they are."

"Well, I've never seen anyone do that who wasn't a witch," said Adrianna.

"I don't care what she is," said Chandra. "Do that again, and I'll have your head."

I awoke in pain like someone broke a guitar over my back. I went to the bathroom and looked in the mirror. A bruise purpled below my eye. Several spotted my arms and legs. I lifted my shirt to uncover one the size of a grapefruit on my side.

I had a lot to learn, but there had to be better ways than trying to beat it into me. I wondered how long it had been since Nash trained anyone new.

My body was so sore. I ambled to the kitchen. Nash stood at the stove. The air smelled like French toast, sweet and syrupy.

"How do you feel?" He didn't look up from his cooking.

"Like hell," I said. "No pun intended."

Nash smirked. "You're not going to feel any better tomorrow. I'm giving you a weapons demonstration this afternoon. I don't expect you to spar with anyone, but I do expect you to at least try to wield a sword."

"You've got to be kidding me." I groaned. "A sword?" My shoulders ached. I could barely lift my shirt over my head.

I sat at the table, and Nash put a plate of French toast in front of me. I grabbed my fork as he sat down across from me with his toast and coffee.

"Adrianna likes you," he said.

"She's the only one," I said. "Chandra treats me like I killed her dog."

Nash laughed. "Chandra's like that. She'll come around."

"I thought you were going to let her kill me yesterday."

"Believe me," he said. "She went easy on you."

I rolled my eyes. "She was going about as easy as a boxer goes on a dummy."

"You need this. Once they know what you are, Archangels won't hesitate to kill you, and that fight won't be a ten-minute boxing match."

I cringed at the matter-of-fact way he said that.

"After breakfast, I have something that I want to show you," he said.

I finished breakfast and followed Nash to a door at the far end of the hall. I saw that door when I searched for the kitchen on my first day. Inside was a set of stairs that led down to a well-lit room.

I didn't realize the house had a basement.

At the bottom of the stairs was a floor to ceiling vault. The vault was made of a metal that I never saw before. The metallic surface shimmered in the light like flecks of glitter were embedded in the steel.

Nash pulled on the large handle and opened the door. Upon the metal walls hung swords, daggers, maces, shields, spears, and bows of various shades of silver. Arm bracers, leg guards, and gloves covered in silver at the knuckles dangled from the opposite wall. Silver tipped arrows crowded narrow cylindrical containers on the floor. Like the metal of the vault, these weapons had the same shimmer.

In the center of the armory was a long table.

"What is all this?" I asked.

"These are the weapons we will use to fight the angels."

Nash took a dagger from the wall. "Arcadian Steel," he said. "The brighter the blade, the less alloy it contains, the purer the steel."

"Will we need this many?"

"We might need more."

"But why do you keep the door unlocked?" I asked.

When he brought me to Sheol, Bob walked right into Nash's home without a key.

"People don't steal in the Outer Region," said Nash. "No reason to. They have everything they want even if it's all superficial."

"What's the Outer Region?"

"Where we are now," said Nash. "Sheol is like a giant radiating disk. On the outskirts is the Outer Region. That's where I and a few more privileged souls live, if you can call anyone in Hell privileged, but beyond the Outer Region are the nine Circles. People are tortured in the Circles."

"Tortured. That's horrible."

"That's Hell."

Silence hung between us. What had Nash done to deserve to be in Hell? He seemed nice enough, a bit controlling and dismissive at times, but not a bad guy.

I couldn't trust anything I thought I knew. An angel, one of the good guys, killed the only family I ever had, and demons, the supposed bad guys, were helping me. Nothing made any sense.

"But if we finish this, you won't have to worry about that." Nash placed the dagger back on the wall.

"Will I be able to use one of these?" I asked.

"You will, when you're ready."

I sighed. I didn't think I'd ever be.

"I need to talk to Tom," said Nash. "You can come along."

"What do you need to talk about?" I asked.

"Demon probation officer business." Nash smirked. Nice to see he had a little bit of a sense of humor. It wasn't healthy to be brooding all the time. "Just because Lucifer wants us to hunt angels doesn't mean she wants us to stop tracking demons."

Nash led the way upstairs.

"But wouldn't doing both wear you out?" I asked.

"I don't think the Devil cares about my comfort or anybody's for that matter." The hall led to the foyer. Nash continued up the main staircase to the second floor.

"There's still one thing I don't understand," I said.

"What's that?" asked Nash.

"I'm the way I am because of a spell, right? If Raphael wanted to use someone like me to close the gates, why doesn't he just have a witch perform the spell on someone more...*agreeable* to his goal? The world's full of crazy people who blow up buildings and shoot up schools. I'm sure he could find someone crazy enough to want to keep Heaven *pure*."

Nash and I reached the top of the stairs, and he took the next flight to the third floor. "The spell is very risky," he said. "It's complicated to perform, and if done incorrectly, it could result in death. Unfortunately, the ritual can only be done on mortals."

"So, when my mother did the spell on me, she could have killed me?"

"Possibly."

We walked the rest of the way in silence. My birth mom not only sold my soul to the Devil but also attempted a spell that could have killed me. I had never known her, but the thought hurt me. How could a mother do that to her child?

A loft on the third floor opened to the library. From behind a thin metal railing, I gazed down at the books lining the shelves. As we continued down the hallway, the library was hidden behind the walls.

Nash stopped outside one of the rooms and opened the door. The room was windowless but recessed light brightened the area. Like every other room in Nash's house, the walls were white, and the floor was alabaster marble. Against one wall was a desk with a computer and a low-backed chair. In the chair sat Tom. He crunched down on a handful of potato chips and rubbed his hand on his jeans.

On the computer screen was a blue map of Earth. The map showed orange pulses in several different locations. Some pulses moved more rapidly than others.

"Do we know which one we'll hit next?" asked Nash.

Tom whirled around in his chair. He didn't seem surprised when Nash snuck up on him. I guess he did that often.

"There's one here." Tom pointed to a tiny pulse around what I guessed to be France. "I'm scoping it out tonight. If it's not a Gorgon or a Succubus, you can go after it as early as tomorrow evening. I think it's a Jikininki."

"A what?" I asked.

"A demon who eats corpses." Tom swiveled side to side in his chair. "They like to hang out around graveyards by exten- sion. I think I remember there being a graveyard somewhere in that area and a café that serves the best croissants. Good late-night demon-watching food."

"Let me know what it is," said Nash. He walked out of the room.

Tom looked at the screen.

"A computer?" I asked. "You wouldn't mind if I checked my email."

"No. It's called a Beamer. It detects demonic activity."

"How?"

"Do you know what a Seismometer is?"

"Sure. It measures seismic waves to find earthquakes."

"By measuring the motion of the ground. This works in a similar way," said Tom. "It's connected to Phoners that measure demonic presence. You see, fallen angels and demons give off subtle, but unique vibrations that can't be picked up by human instruments. We get a read, and I go to investigate the source, P.I. style. I stay awhile to determine what type of demon we're dealing with. That way, Nash and the others can be ready."

Tom turned and squinted at me. "How *can* you see us?"

"With my eyes," I said slowly.

Tom frowned. "If every human could see us when we don't want them to, a lot more people would believe in angels and demons."

"I know," I said. "Truth is, I'm not sure why I can see them. I've been seeing them for as long as I can remember. I realized other people can't, so I just hide it. Chills run down my back every time I think of the demons I ignored lurking in the corners. But it's not the demons I should've been fearing, it was the angels."

"You should fear the demons too." Tom turned back to his screen.

THAT afternoon, as I walked down the stairs to grab something to eat before training started, the front door opened.

Adrianna's blonde waves were tied back in a sleek ponytail.
She was dressed in dark tights and a tank top. "I'm so glad you
lived through it."

At first, I thought she might be making fun of me, but her
relief seemed genuine. "Chandra's tough," I said, "but, I'll live.
I have some bruises that's all."

"I'm sorry." Adrianna set her teeth. "I'm not used to being
around humans anymore. I always think they're so delicate."

"That's okay," I said. "If you don't mind me asking, what
are you now?"

"A Succubus." Her eyelashes fluttered. "I used to seduce
men into contracts with the Devil."

Everything about Adrianna looked human, so hearing her
say this made me feel like this whole thing was some big setup,
and Felicia would pop out at any moment and say *gotcha*, but
this would be far too sophisticated for her to come up with.

"Adrianna," I said, "I wanted to talk to you about something you said yesterday when I shoved Chandra."

"You mean when you mentally force-pushed Chandra."

"Yeah, that. You called me a witch."

"Oh, I didn't mean to offend you. I know humans used to
have a major problem with witches, but I thought since you
are one, you wouldn't find it offensive."

"I don't actually. You see, that happened when my parents…"

"I have a few weapons laid out." Nash's voice boomed from
the stairs.

Nash headed down the stairs with Tom as the front door
opened. Kiran and Chandra stood in the front entrance. Kiran
held a long sword strapped to his waist.

We walked out onto the field, and Nash picked up a sword from the long table outside. "I want to give Lia a demonstration."

"I'll spar with you," said Kiran. "That should give her a proper demonstration."

"No, thanks," said Nash. "I doubt a proper demonstration amounts to you knocking me on my ass in three minutes."

"Two," said Kiran with a smile on his face.

"Tom." Nash tossed Tom the sword.

He caught the hilt in mid-air and walked out to the center of the yard.

They held out their swords in front of them.

"One, two, three," Nash counted. He swung his sword, and Tom's blade met his. Tom lunged at Nash, but Nash stepped aside. Nash defended himself against a rain of blows. He let Tom tire himself out.

Nash's blade sped along Tom's, knocking it from his hands and launching the blade to the ground. Nash removed a dagger from his side and pointed it at Tom's neck.

"I didn't know we could carry a secondary," said Tom. "You don't fight fair, Nash."

"I live in Hell." Nash smirked.

"Alright," said Tom. "Best two out of three, but drop the dagger."

Nash tossed the dagger to the ground.

Tom picked up his sword. He challenged Nash with a storm of blows, but Nash defended against every one of them. Tom battered Nash's knuckles with the flat of his sword. Nash dropped his sword, and Tom, with the point of his blade, flipped Nash's sword into the air.

The sword flew several feet away.

"Oh, is that how we're going to play it," said Nash.

Before Tom could land his blow, Nash dodged it, grabbed Tom's wrist, and twisted. Tom dropped his sword, and Nash plucked it from the ground and tossed the blade to join his.

Tom shrugged, dropped his shoulders and put up his fists. He jabbed, and Nash dodged, returning the punch as Tom ducked.

They continued to jab and punch, dodging each other's blows with expert fluidity until Nash backed up and said, "Run for your sword."

He took off down the field, but as Nash reached for his blade, his own dagger was across his neck.

"When did you scoop that up?" Nash asked.

"Right before you ran down the field." Tom released him.

"I'd better take that." Kiran stepped forward and offered his hand.

Tom gave Kiran the dagger.

"Alright then, last one." Nash handed Tom his sword and picked up his own.

Sparks of light came off the blades as they met.

The swords danced. Nash and Tom's movements were fluid and natural as if the weapons were mere extensions of themselves.

After several minutes, I didn't think the dance would ever end, but Nash's blade swept along Tom's, and Nash made a circular motion. Tom's blade was caught as if in a funnel. The sword flew from Tom's hand and into the air. Nash caught the hilt and pointed both swords at Tom's chest.

That was rock n' roll. No way I'd ever learn to fight like that.

After they fought, I tried wielding a sword with Nash's instruction. He let me swing into the air a few times and tried to teach me form. Chandra snickered the whole time. I really wished I could have practiced on my own first.

Nash gave Tom, Adrianna, Kiran, and Chandra time to practice together. He sat beside me while the others fought. A thin sheen of sweat painted his brow.

"No offense," I said. "But why use swords? Guns exist, you know."

"Yeah." Nash wiped his forehead with a clean, white towel. "But guns run out of bullets."

I narrowed my eyes. Couldn't Lucifer *give* us all the bullets we needed?

"You see," he said, "Arcadian Steel is a very special metal: No metal found on Earth or in Sheol could pierce an angel's body. Arcadian Steel is a heavenly metal, and it's difficult to forge. We have a very limited supply down here. Waylon would hate if we carelessly embedded bullets into angels, only to have them fly away with the precious metal. We do have guns, but we try to limit their use to emergency situations."

"Who's Waylon?" I asked.

"He's the blacksmith. Only one around who knows how to forge Arcadian Steel."

"But how do you have Arcadian Steel down here if it only comes from Heaven. I mean, they didn't let you walk right in and take it, right?"

"The Steel we have was taken in the Fall. When the rebel angels fought, when Sheol was created."

"Oh," I said. "You mean when the angels rebelled against God?"

Nash pressed his lips together. His eyes were hard.

"But I thought nothing could kill an angel," I said.

"Well, that's mostly true, but Arcadian Steel can slow them down a lot. Angels can still feel pain. They can lose limbs. Of course, they regenerate within a few months."

"What if you cut off their heads?" That seemed to work with zombies and vampires.

"You won't be cutting off angels' heads," said Nash. "I've never known of anyone who has, and I'm not sure that would work anyway. But that doesn't matter, once they fall, they'll be down here."

"That'll be awkward."

"Lucifer has a special place for them."

The sweat on my skin cooled, and goose bumps speckled my arms.

VER the next few weeks, I practiced sword fighting with Nash and Tom, hand to hand combat with Chandra, and grappling with Adrianna. Kiran gave me advice when it came to sword fighting, and I was grateful that I never had to practice with him. I got enough bumps and bruises from the others.

At the end of each week, Nash treated us to a nice fancy dinner. Everyone dressed up except me and Tom, but he at least tried to look presentable in his rumpled suit jacket.

One afternoon, Nash drove me into town. He drove slower than he had the first time and glanced over at me a few times.

My face warmed whenever I felt his eyes on me.

I didn't know where we were going, but I didn't care. I was happy I didn't have to train today.

Nash turned onto a wide, dirt road. It was strange seeing it among the perfect angular buildings and clean streets. But as the road continued, I couldn't see the town beyond the leafless trees.

Nash stopped the car.

"Where are we?" I asked.

He got out of the car. I followed him, wondering why he was so solemn. The road opened to a barren plain. Nothing but dirt and sky stretched for miles. The scent of smoke stung my nose. The clouds hung low like birds too fat for their wings.

Nash held out his hand and stopped me in my tracks. I gasped as I looked down. I almost stepped into a gorge larger than Nash's training field. The hole was so deep, I couldn't see the bottom. Staring into the dark abyss was horrifying.

Nash kicked a rock off the edge, and it tunneled down.

I waited for the rock to hit the bottom and echo its final descent, but it never did.

"What is this?" I asked.

"The Pit," he said.

I gulped and stared into the fathomless depths. I heard of a sinkhole that buried a house in Florida. On the news, witnesses claimed that the hole was deep, but I couldn't imagine that hole was as endless as the one before me.

"It's where we go if we fail in our duties. It's where we will go if we die on Earth."

"Demons can die?" I regretted my words. Some who lived in Sheol were demons, although Nash explained to me that he wasn't one, but I still didn't like the word. Adrianna, Tom, and Kiran were demons, and they were among some of the nicest *people* I'd met.

"I use the word *die*," said Nash, "because it's the simplest way I can explain it. But it's not literal death…or it's not what humans call death. But when we're down there, we can never come back. Our eternity is an endless fall."

"That sounds awful." I backed further away from the Pit.

"I wanted you to know what the stakes are," said Nash. "I also wanted you to know that I'm not just doing this because Lucifer demanded me to. I don't want you down here. It's not where you belong."

I didn't know what to say. I gave him a thin-lipped smile. I wasn't anybody to him. Why would he be doing anything for me?

I tried to fight against my defensiveness. When my parents died, all that was good in the world died with them. Hell seemed like an odd place to find something good.

"We should go back to the house. I don't like being here," said Nash.

I could sense his discomfort and was glad it was because of the bottomless pit of doom and not my less than ceremonious response to his sacrifice.

When Mom and Dad were alive, I was more trusting. No one ever hurt me before.

The car zoomed through the dark, misty streets of Sheol. I held onto the sides of my seat. Nash's brow furrowed. Being near the Pit bothered him yet he brought me there anyway. He wanted me to know something he wasn't saying.

"Do you think this will work?" I asked.

"I wouldn't put you through it if I didn't." The evenness of Nash's tone set me at ease. He didn't take his eyes off the street. "Raphael needs to fall."

"I'm talking about the other angels," I said. "His followers. Do we know how many there are?"

"We know enough," he said. "Tom has been researching."

"But we *don't* know how many."

His hands were tight on the wheel. "No."

This wasn't something that was going to end in a few months.

Outside, the street lights glowed in the dim, not quite darkness, in the cold world of Sheol.

As Nash turned the corner, I glanced at something outside the car window. A creature ambled across the street. The thing was a cross between a man and a deer. It was skinny and gray. Antlers protruded from its forehead.

"What is that?" I asked.

Nash looked in the direction I pointed. "That's a Jinn." His lip turned up, and his nose crinkled like he smelled vomit.

"Oh, like a genie? Like the kind that grants wishes and stuff?"

"Where in the world did you hear that?"

"Haven't you ever heard of Aladdin?"

"No," said Nash. "A Jinn is one of the three sapient creatures created by God. You know those people who think they've seen demons? How they describe them as dark, gruesome creatures? Well, more likely than not, what they saw was a Jinn. Jinn can go between worlds at will. They don't need any portals. They're shape shifters and can take on any form that pleases them."

"You don't like them?"

"I don't trust creatures that don't seem bound by any rules."

Nash pulled up to a two-story house. The house was smaller than his mansion but had the same clean lines and smooth modern finishes.

"Where are we?" I asked.

"Kiran and Adrianna's house. Kiran is coming with us. I'm bringing you to see Waylon."

"The blacksmith guy?" I asked.

Nash mentioned him before. He said he was the only one who could forge weapons of Arcadian Steel. But Nash had a bunch of weapons in the vault. Did he think we needed more?

"ARE we going to talk about our strategy to defeat Andromeda?" Kiran asked.

"Is that the angel we're going to hit?" I walked alongside Nash.

He nodded.

"What about a gun?" I asked as we walked. Nash was very dismissive of the use of guns. "I know what you said before, but a gun has got to be the most effective way to fight angels. I mean, they fly, right?"

"Guns are out of the question," said Nash.

Our voices echoed down the tunnel. Sheol had the cleanest sewers I could imagine, not that I journeyed down many sewers, but rats and the smell were both assumable problems. Problems that the Sheol sewers didn't have.

"You want to shoot Andromeda with a gun?" asked Kiran.

"Well, yeah," I said. "I'm not all too confident in my sword-wielding abilities."

"But you are confident in your gun-wielding abilities?"

He had a point. Though Kiran challenged me, I found it hard to resent him. He was so soft-spoken with an accent of which I wasn't familiar. His voice was so soothing I sometimes forgot that he carried a sharp sword at his side.

"Why does Waylon stay down here?" I asked.

"He wants to be left alone," said Nash. "And Lucifer wants to keep an eye on him. This way, she knows where he is at all times, and yet he feels secluded."

I shivered. So, Lucifer had her thumb on this place too. As soon as I entered the sewers, I felt safe within its metal walls, but that was a false sense of security. Lucifer had her eyes everywhere. She was the perfect puppet master.

We continued onward, our footsteps echoed through the cold metal tunnels. Nash quickened his pace. We walked for another half hour.

"Here we are." Nash stopped at a wide corridor.

Heat came from deep within. Waylon's blacksmith forge settled at the end of the wide corridor. Swords, daggers, shields, and bracers hung on the walls like something out of medieval times. Although I don't know if they had sewers in the Middle Ages.

Waylon hit the flat of a sword with a hammer as fire rose around the blade. He stopped hammering when Nash approached him.

"We need a weapon," said Nash.

Waylon looked up at Nash. He wasn't wearing a shirt, and a thin sheen of sweat wet his naked torso. He wore jeans and boots. He hadn't trimmed his beard in a long time, and his dark hair was unkempt.

"I'll assume," said Waylon. "That the she-devil knows you're here."

"She does," said Nash.

Did she? Nash hadn't left the house in the last two weeks, and cellphones didn't seem to be a thing in Sheol.

"We need something lightweight and sharp for Lia," said Kiran. "Something made of Arcadian Steel."

I was about to get my very own sword. I never considered that I might one day own a sword, but the idea did intrigue me.

"Show us what you have," said Nash.

"You think I have a sword like that ready?" said Waylon. "I normally make Arcadian Steel weapons with girth to them. I don't make them for humans." He looked at me, and his eyes narrowed.

"You have something," said Nash. "I know you, Waylon. You'd want to challenge yourself. You just don't want to sell it to us."

"What I don't want is to give it away to you for free," Waylon ground out.

"You won't have to." Nash reached into his pocket and withdrew several gold coins. "Good for dozens of drinks at the bar."

"I don't go to bars." Waylon snatched the gold from his hands. He moved away from the forge and turned the corner down a tight corridor alongside the wider one.

When he returned, he carried a small sword. The blade couldn't have been any wider than a drumstick.

Kiran took the weapon from him and balanced the blade in his hand. He whipped the sword through the air. "It's light. Good balance. Not much power, but she can handle it."

He handed the sword to Nash. The blade glanced off the string of lights that lit the tunnels. He offered the grip of the blade to me. I took the hilt gingerly. I practiced with dulled blades, but I never held a sharpened sword and not one of Arcadian Steel.

The sword was light, lighter than the sword with which I trained. I had no doubt speed would be the likely advantage with this weapon, but I hoped I wouldn't have to get close enough to find out. I frowned. *Of course, I would.* I needed to get close enough to touch Andromeda.

NASH parked the car, and I got out. When I glanced over, his arms were folded on the roof. "I thought we might do a little training today," he said.

I sighed. I thought I was getting the day off and didn't want to see Chandra jeer at me from the sidelines.

"Just you and me," he said. "There are a few things I wanted to show you after seeing you fight Adrianna. Plus, you need to practice with your new sword."

I learned to wear tighter clothes when training. Loose clothes slowed you down, and I needed every second if I wanted to stand a chance against any one of Nash's friends.

I got stronger, but I was nowhere near capable of pinning one of them.

"The main thing you're doing wrong," said Nash, "is that you're not watching your opponent."

"What do you mean?" I asked. "Of course, I'm watching them."

"You're looking too much here." He pointed to his face.

That wasn't true. More than a few times my eyes drifted. I liked looking at Nash. I liked looking at him almost as much as I liked listening to him talk, which he was doing now. I realized I should be listening to the words and not only to the sound.

"Sometimes you might guess what an opponent might do by looking at his facial expressions, but more telling is the subtle movements of his body. I'm going to attack, and I want you to watch my body. Just the body for now, don't worry about getting hit."

"Because you won't hit me?"

"I didn't say that." With that, he punched me in the arm. The punch was light. His fist was barely formed, but I failed to dodge the blow.

"Don't look here." He made a circle around his face with his hand. "Look down."

I saw the motion of his arm, the way his shoulder dipped downed, the way his foot pivoted into the punch. The punch still landed, but I saw it all.

"Good," he said. "But you need to stand straighter."

He placed his hand on my back, encouraging me to straighten it. The warmth of his hand suffused through my back, and I found myself leaning into his touch rather than taking direction.

"What are you doing?" he asked.

"Oh, sorry." I arched my back away from his hand.

Bob walked onto the training field. He was dressed as usual in his fitted black suit and red tie.

Nash paused when he saw him approach. I put my arms down and turned to Bob. Nash closed the space between them, and I walked up to join them.

"I know what you're here for Bob, but she's not ready," said Nash.

"I think she's more than capable of reaching out and touching someone." Bob chewed on a toothpick.

"You know it's not that simple."

"She wants me to go now?" I asked.

"She wanted you to go yesterday," said Bob, "and by yesterday, I mean five weeks ago."

I couldn't do this. I still fell on my ass at every training session, and she wanted me to go and fight a winged warrior of God?

Bob plucked the toothpick from his mouth and held it up to his eyes with a frown before flicking it to the ground. "Kiran tells me you're going after Andromeda first. A wise choice," said Bob. "I've heard Andromeda is getting pretty rusty."

"Andromeda may only be a Dominion, but she is a supremely powerful one."

A Dominion? That didn't sound like the title of an angel of low rank.

"It's only a matter of time before Raphael finds out that she is in Sheol," said Bob. "That angel who was with her is probably spinning his wheels to find her, and who knows what side he's on."

Adriel. I hadn't thought about him in a long time. I imagined his long, white feathers against the stormy sky of Sheol. Could he really be looking for me?

"Maybe he's right," I said. "I'll never be ready, but I need to get this done so I can go back to living my life." I couldn't believe I used the words "get this done" like it was a math test.

Nash looked at me and sighed. "She isn't ready. Lucifer didn't call me in to get her killed. She trusts my judgment."

"I can't go to her with that, Nash," said Bob.

"I'll go to her myself," said Nash.

"Good luck." Bob turned on his heels, and his long legs carried him off the field.

Nash took a long look at me.

I raised an eyebrow. "You're staring at me."

"Staring through you." He was distant but came back into focus as Tom's voice cut through the stillness.

"I was right." Tom approached us. "It's a Jikininki. Disgusting bastards, but it shouldn't give you too much trouble. Getting some training in?"

"I was helping Lia with her form," said Nash.

"Yeah, her form sucks," said Tom.

I folded my arms and glared at Tom.

"Chandra, Adrianna, and Kiran are on their way," said Tom.

STEPPING through the portal was like climbing through an icebox straight into the humid warm air of southern France. The edges of the portal were freezing like Nash had cut a hole into a thin sheet of ice.

My sword was in a sheath at my side as a precaution only. Nash didn't want me using it. Besides, Adrianna explained that the demon was going to get a stern talking to first and if it decided to come back with us through the portal, it wouldn't have to be killed. Comforting thought. I hoped the demon was reasonable.

Large mossy crypts rose from the ground. Names and dates were carved into the cold stones. The thick air smelled like wet grass.

"Come on." Nash's sword gleamed in the moonlight.

Adrianna and Kiran drew their weapons. Chandra had on her brass knuckles.

"Stay behind me," said Nash.

"I won't be able to see anything if I'm behind you." *Maybe that was a good thing.*

We moved in as a group. I was close behind Nash. Quiet sounds cut through the graveyard, the sounds of gnashing teeth. The further we walked, the louder the sounds became.

Dirt flew into the air from a hole in the ground, not hole, holes. Nash stopped walking, and I ran into him. "Oh, sorry," I said. His back was tense.

"Shut up," he said through clenched teeth. He put his hand out, and the others backed away. I wondered what was wrong. Why weren't they marching in there and doing the demon negotiation thing?

The digging and gnashing sounds stopped. Nothing is more uneasy than the sound of silence. My heart no longer had a rhythm to match and thumped erratically in my chest as if played by a tone-deaf drummer.

"Go," said Nash.

We turned on our heels and ran. I made the mistake of looking back. Dark forms crawled towards us. Their thin bodies were like spiders.

"Tom said there was only one of them," said Kiran.

"Tom has been making a lot of mistakes lately." Nash ran alongside me. He kept pace with me. His long legs surely could take lengthier strides than mine.

He stopped and held out his hand. The portal started to form.

"Nash, you can't focus!" Chandra backpedaled towards him.

"I can open the portal." Nash spread his fingers, and the glowing tear appeared in front of him.

Chandra climbed through the portal followed by Adrianna and Kiran. Right before I touched the icy walls of the wormhole from Earth to Sheol, Nash grunted.

My head whirled around.

A demon pinned Nash to the wall of the crypt. Its long claws grazed the stone.

I froze.

"Go!" Nash yelled. His jaw was tense. His hand rigidly held out to the portal.

The demon's body was thin, anorexic-looking. Caked, black filth covered its skin. Its hair was twisted into a single, stiff tangle that ended in a long point at the back of its head.

It did not look like the type of creature that was able, much less willing, to talk this one out.

"Get off him!"

The demon turned its head towards me. Its eyes were round and large. Its mouth protruded, and each tooth was filed to a point. The steel tip of a sword launched through its body and cut it down the middle. Nash withdrew his sword, painted in black.

A low growl sounded behind me. I spun around and another monster so like its dead companion stretched its mouth open, exposing all its teeth.

Nash grabbed my arm and yanked me away from the thing. We ran through the graveyard. Nash gripped my arm so tightly, I knew he'd leave a bruise, but I didn't care. I'd rather have a bruised arm than be a demon's dinner. In front of us was a church among the gravestones.

Nash and I burst through the doors. We sprinted around the altar to the back of the room where a long hallway stretched off to our left. Turning around the corner on all fours was another demon.

We raced down the hallway and into a vacant room. Nash swung the door shut. The doorknob rattled.

"I thought they only liked to eat *dead* bodies." I backed away from the door. I was glad my ribs caged my heart, or it might have beat right out of my chest.

The door started to convulse.

"Go to the window," Nash said.

"I'm not leaving you."

"This is a demon," said Nash. "You can't make it burst into flames with a touch."

The door shuttered off its hinges. The creature burst through the door. Nash pushed me out of the way and shouted something, but I couldn't hear over the ear-splitting cry of the demon. Its long claws swept across Nash's chest, turning his shirt to tatters.

Nash's wrist communicator buzzed. Tom was trying to get in touch with us, but the demon slammed Nash's arm to the ground, shattering the communicator to pieces.

Nash laughed grimly. He withdrew his dagger and sank the blade into the creature's side. The demon lunged at Nash. Nash managed to sidestep him, but not without tripping on a rotted piece of wood that used to be a ceiling beam.

I drew my sword, thin and wavering. Nash was on his feet, his blade gleaming at his side. The creature lurched at him, and Nash's blade came down across its neck. Blood sprayed onto Nash's face.

He paled. "I told you to run." He knelt to the floor and stabbed the demon in the neck. The thing faded, but its blood remained like tar on the wooden floor.

"I thought it was going to kill you." The hand that held my sword still shook.

"And it might have. I was distracted. I'm the leader of this team. You need to listen to me. We have to go. More are coming."

He held his hand out, and a portal appeared. "I'm not sure where this will send us. The location was supposed to be at the front of the graveyard not far from where we came in. But I need you to go first. The danger here is a guarantee."

I climbed through the portal. I was dizzy as I passed through. Climbing through portals upset my stomach like riding a rollercoaster.

nine

THE walls were black around me and stretched as far as I could see. I was in a tunnel with tree roots growing down the sides. Etched upon the walls between the roots were images of angels. The carvings were quite intricate. The angels looked like they were diving or maybe falling.

Nash climbed through the portal behind me. Blood dripped over the arm held to his chest. He wandered over to the wall and surveyed the carvings.

"You're hurt," I said.

"It stings," he said absentmindedly. His fingers ran along the carvings. "Where was your concern when your failure to follow orders almost got me killed?"

"I *was* concerned. That's why I didn't follow orders."

"You could have gotten me sent to the Pit." His words stung, more than I wanted them to. "This carving, it's a depiction of the Fall."

"Like when the leaves turn orange, red, and yellow?"

He eyed me darkly. "Like when the angels rebelled."

"Why are you concerned about a few drawings on a cave wall when you're bleeding all over the floor?"

"Because," Nash moved away from the wall, "demons wouldn't draw angels."

"I don't see why not," I said. "Maybe there are a few demons who are happy to see angels fall. I could see why that might prompt some fallen angel graffiti."

Rattling echoed off the tunnel walls. A man, hunched over a shopping cart, wheeled the cart through the tunnel. His skin was pale. He was bald, and blackened bones protruded from his back.

Nash gave me a narrow smile as if to say *I told you so.*

The shopping cart was full of junk: various articles of dirty clothing and trinkets. He wheeled the cart over to us. Lifting his head, he grinned like he was trying to show all his teeth. "You like my work?"

"How did you get down here?" Nash asked.

"The same way you did," the man said it like it was the most obvious thing in the world. I smiled a little at that. That's when I recognized what hung from the handlebar of the angel's cart. A necklace. Dangling from the necklace was a golden cross entwined with silver thorns.

"That's Dad's," I whispered.

"What?" Nash asked.

The necklace swayed like a pocket watch swung by a hypnotist. "That's my dad's necklace." I pulled the necklace off the cart, snapping the clasp.

The angel reached for the necklace, but I held it to my chest and backed away.

"Where did you get this?" I asked desperately.

"I found it," said the angel. "It's mine."

He tried to reach for the necklace again, but Nash spoke up. "Are there other fallen angels down here?"

"Fallen?" The angel wore a baffled look on his face. "No fallen angels down here. Fallen angels are damned like demons. I am not forsaken." He looked at Nash. "You are the one who is damned." He turned to me. "And you," he squinted, "you are dead. Someone *killed* you." His look of shock deepened.

He took one last look at us and turned his cart around. He retreated the way he came.

I looked down at the necklace. "Does this mean my dad's in Hell?" I didn't understand. What could he have done?

"It doesn't mean that," said Nash. "Whether they go to Sheol or Heaven, personal belongings are dumped here. The landfill must be at the other end of this tunnel. That's where he found that necklace."

"What's wrong with him?"

"The demons broke his mind." Nash's voice was full of pity. "They showed him greed and forced him to take part in it. Now, it's all he knows."

Nash walked down the tunnel where the angel fled. "Come on. I think he might have been coming from the landfill. That's why his cart was full."

"But how do you know that way will lead us out?"

"I don't. But the landfill will be a dead end. It's surrounded by dead space. Besides, that fallen angel had to have gotten here somehow."

I followed Nash down the tunnel.

"Those demons we ran into," I said, "something was wrong with them too, wasn't it?"

Nash nodded. "It's what happens to souls that spend too much time in the Circles. They go mad. They become primitive, worse than that angel. All they know to do is attack. Lucifer doesn't offer them contracts."

"Then who let them out?" I asked.

"I don't know, and that's what bothers me."

Screams echoed ahead of us down the dark, narrow passage. My skin prickled. My legs felt like they would tremble to ash.

"Take out your sword." Nash withdrew his weapon. "If you see anyone, don't ask questions."

My sword shook in my hands. I didn't know what was ahead of us, and my thoughts still quivered with the memory of those flesh-eating monsters in the graveyard.

A small alcove was hollowed out to our left. Ahead of us the tunnel continued to narrow.

Chained to the wall in the alcove was a woman. Her skin was dirty, and she wore a rumpled and filthy white dress. Bruises colored her face and body. She lifted her head.

I gasped.

Her eyes were gone, leaving only bloody, dark sockets.

Despite my fear and the trembling of my hands, I marched forward into the alcove. Nash grabbed my arm. "What do you think you're doing?"

"We can't leave her like that," I said.

"You can't help—" Nash broke off.

Two fallen angels entered the small space, both with blackened bones ornamenting their backs. One was tall and thin with ashy, white hair. The other was broader with inky, black eyes and short, dark hair.

A narrow fissure ripped through the wall, large enough for two people. Nash pulled me with him into the fissure and clamped his hand over my mouth. I clawed at his hand with my fingernails, and he removed it.

I stood so close to Nash, I could feel his heart beat.

The two fallen angels spoke. Nervously, my eyes darted to Nash's. His body was rigid, but his face appeared calm.

"Consider your options, demon," said a high-pitched voice with a sing-song quality to it.

"Don't touch me." The voice was gravelly. "You wouldn't hurt a lady."

"You're not a lady. We know what you are."

A thud, and a grunt echoed through the chamber.

"I feel nothing," the woman said.

"You must feel something. You must know something."

"I know what you're looking for. You want a way out of this place." The demon laughed. "But that's not what the Redeemer offers. You're stupid if you believe that."

"Where is he, demon?" one of the fallen angels asked.

"You're about to have a lot more friends down here," hissed the woman.

"What do you mean by that?"

"Lucifer has obtained a weapon to make angels fall," she said.

"You're lying. No such weapon exists."

"It's a girl. She can bring down any angel with a mere touch."

My hand flew to my mouth. *How did she know about me? How could she?*

"We're not interested in your fairy tales, demon. Where is the Redeemer?"

"I don't know where he is. *My* involvement ended a long time ago. The Redeemer is a cruel man, but I respect him. His callousness is what will end all this torment. I want to stay out of his way. He destroys everything he touches."

"You know more than you're telling us. We could force it out of you."

"You could try." The demon's voice was like ice.

"I think you need time to think."

Footsteps faded in the distance.

I was frozen. That demon knew about me. Who else knew I was here?

Nash pulled me from the fissure and led me around the corner.

"We're not going to help her?" I asked.

"It's too risky," said Nash. "They might see us."

"The fallen angels?"

"They are the Missing. Lucifer has been looking for them."

"So, we're going to fight them?"

"That's not our job,' said Nash.

"I thought you were supposed to keep fallen angels and demons in line?"

"On Earth, not in Sheol."

I pressed my lips together. "I'm not leaving her here."

"You can't do that." Nash attempted to grab me, but I sidestepped him and marched back into the alcove.

I crossed the empty space to the wall and knelt by the eyeless woman. I tried not to look at her gory sockets as I fiddled with the chains attached to the manacles around her wrists. The rhythm of my heart was up-tempo.

"Who's there?" The woman's voice was barely a whisper.

Nash stood between us and the place where the two fallen angels retreated. He raised his sword and gave me a look that said *hurry up.*

"We're trying to get you out of here," I said.

"Dislocate my thumbs," she said.

"What?"

"Just do it." She struggled, and the chains jangled together. "They took my eyes. They took my goddamn eyes."

"Your sword, use it," said Nash.

"To what? Cut off her hands?" My own voice scared me.

Nash chuckled. "You're dark."

"Stop laughing at me, and tell me what to do."

"Cut the chains," he said. "Your sword is almost pure Arcadian Steel."

I scrambled to my feet and held my sword out. "What if I hit her?"

"Aim." Nash was unforgiving. "And come down hard."

I aimed my sword at the chains and pulled back. With all my strength, I swung forward. Sparks made me squeeze my eyes shut. The chains clattered to the ground as the woman's arms fell to the floor.

Nash raced towards us and lifted her to her feet. He motioned with his head towards the narrow tunnel that led away
from the alcove. We raced down the tunnel. The tunnel became narrower as we walked, and soon I was the only one
walking upright. Nash ducked his head, and the woman was
slouched over, clinging to Nash's arm.

The tunnel darkened. I could only see Nash and the
woman's forms like shadows in front of me. I ducked my head
as we journeyed deeper. A panicked thought came to my mind:
*What if this wasn't the way out? What if we kept going until the
tunnel became impossibly narrow, and we became caught inside?* I
was never claustrophobic, but I was getting a lot of new pho-
bias lately.

I was on my hands and knees. Nash and the woman crawled
in front of me. Darkness surrounded me, and the walls of the
tunnel tightened. "Nash?" My voice was small.

"It's alright." Nash's voice was a soothing wave washing
over me bringing me back to the shore. "Just keep going."

My knees hurt as I crawled upon the rough, rocky ground.
My hands felt raw as if the skin was being rubbed off as I padded across jagged terrain. The minutes crawled by before I
could make out the shapes moving in front of me. At first, I
didn't know whether my eyes adjusted to the darkness, or if
light invaded the tunnel. But as the world became clear and
brighter, I knew light was coming in. I took a deep breath.

We exited the tunnel, and the dull atmosphere of Sheol felt
like the brightest place in the world. I could have kissed the
soft, smooth ground I crawled out upon. I turned over and
rubbed my knees. My pants protected them from getting
skinned. The air stung my hands. My palms were red, and my
right hand was bloodied. I wiped the blood on my hip.

Nash helped the woman to her feet. She turned her head
back and forth, but she didn't have eyes to see. Maybe her

sense of smell had sharpened, and she smelled that the air around her was no longer the musty odor of the tunnels.

Behind us was a sewage pipe low to the ground, not of metal but of rock.

Mist rolled through the trees and rocky ledges rose from the land. The ruins of a stone building were strewn in front of us. The building was different from the modern architecture of the Outer Region. Arches and columns spread to the gray sky.

A raven cawed. He sat on a leafless tree with bark white like bone.

The woman stumbled to the ground. Nash lifted her into his arms and held her against his wounded chest.

A set of stone steps led up to a rocky cliff. Nash took the steps with ease despite the extra weight he carried.

At the top of the stairs were rows of black trees without leaves. Their twiggy branches reached up to the sky as if begging to be taken away from this place.

We trekked for an hour before we left the forest behind and were back in the world of modern architecture and expansive streets.

Nash approached a bus stop bench and sat the woman down. "I'm sorry," he said.

The woman was reluctant to let go of his arms, but he moved her hands to her sides. He turned away from her and met me at the curb.

"You're leaving her there?"

The woman felt along the bench. Her jaw tensed as her fingers explored.

"She'll be fine," said Nash. "Someone will come and take her where she belongs. Once her wounds have healed, she'll regain her strength. You saved her from the worst of it."

"I guess," I said.

"If we hurry, we'll be back before morning." Nash marched down the street with long purposeful strides, and I followed.

The world is a harp, and its music is blind. The woman touched along the sides of the bench and turned her gory sockets to the sky.

Ten

OONLIGHT streamed through the sheer curtained window of the dirty room. I was small, so small, a child. I couldn't reach the windowsill in the cold, dark room. My life was full of dimness and darkness.

A long time passed since anyone spoke to me. I forgot the sounds of human voices and other voices, voices I had long ago stopped listening for.

A memory came to me of a woman who held me to her breast and whispered quiet assurances to me while I cried. I forgot the details of her face when I woke, but I did remember that her cheeks were sunken, her lips cracked, and her eyes sad. I reached up a small hand to comfort her as she did me.

She placed me in a small bed. Panic tensed her jaw shut. She left me in the night but not by foot or car. She disappeared, no body to find.

But I held the memory of her embrace, not like you would remember a quote or math problem but the way you remembered how to ride a bike or use a fork. A muscle memory, one that I used when I was alone and frightened.

And I was alone and frightened.

I ran my hands along the dark walls. The house felt different, and I knew someone opened a door. The world was drawn in like a breath, and light flooded my small room.

I saw their faces. Men who carried flashlights charged into the room. Their eyes were wide when they saw me. Someone grabbed me around the waist and pulled me from the room.

Their arms weren't the warm, comforting arms of the woman who left. Instead, these arms frightened me. I cried. I wailed. I saw what was in the room with me.

A cage, large enough for a lion. White feathers littered the floor.

"Lia, wake up!"

THE voice jolted me from my sleep. A familiar voice, but one I couldn't place. I thought the sound came from inside the room, but when I looked around all I could see was a large, dark figure which loomed above me, a figure with featherless wings.

I grabbed the sword at my bedside. The light, sharp blade was the one Nash bought for me. I raised the sword against the approaching figure while my free hand messed with the curtain that cascaded down the windows behind the bed.

With the curtain pushed aside, the room was bathed in the dull light of Sheol.

The figure who advanced towards me was an angel. *Was* an angel. What color were his eyes before they turned dull gray? He reminded me of the angel who attacked me in my bedroom. The first angel I made fall.

Steel glinted in the light. He held a long dagger. He wanted to cut my throat in my sleep.

He ran his blade along my sword to the hilt and knocked the weapon out of my shaking hand. The sword clattered to the floor and glided across the smooth surface.

I raced to reclaim my blade.

The fallen angel was upon me. His shadow darkened the space where my sword lay, where my body lay on the ground.

I hit the floor on my back and kicked him in the stomach as I ground my teeth. He staggered back.

Sim watched me from the bed with her amber eyes. No panic controlled her gaze, more of a serene watchfulness like nothing of interest was happening at all.

I grabbed my sword and leapt to my feet. I wouldn't wait and let him regain his composure. I would strike. I would be wild and dangerous. Maybe I might scare him. Maybe he didn't care if I hurt him.

I couldn't kill him, although that thought hadn't crossed my mind in that moment. At the time, anyone could be killed, that included me, and I wouldn't let myself die.

My sword ripped into his stomach and cut a long, shallow tear from hip to hip. Blood seeped out the color of tar.

I swept my blade up into the air and brought it down upon him again, but this time, he was ready. He gripped the sharp edge in his fist. His thick blood dripped down the blade like black paint.

The door opened.

Nash's face was full of surprise and unease. I didn't know if all that worry was for me or for himself when Lucifer found out that he let me die in my bedroom.

I dropped to the ground and pulled the sword down with the weight of my body. The fallen angel screamed as the blade slid across the palm of his hand.

He raised his dagger. Nash grabbed his wrist and twisted until a loud crack resounded.

"Ahh!" His grip loosened on the dagger, and Nash caught the handle. In seconds, the blade was against the angel's neck and pressed into his skin.

"Shh," Nash said. "That's enough. If you don't leave this house, I'll saw at your neck with this dagger until your head hangs from your torso by a thread. I'll do so much worse than the demons who'll find you and put you back where you be-long."

"I don't belong anywhere anymore," said the fallen angel. He glared at me with a hate that couldn't be trumped by any-thing. His eyes looked predatory like those of the angel that killed my parents. But he was not that beautiful monster.

Nash removed the dagger from the angel's neck. The crea-ture darted away from us. He leapt through the window. The glass shattered around his body. I rushed to the window. He hit the ground, landing on his feet like a cat from a fence.

"You let him go?" I eyed Nash. What the hell was he think-ing? That angel was after me. Now he had the opportunity to strike again.

Nash looked at me unapologetically. "You look like you could use some coffee."

"I don't drink coffee unless it's mixed with one of twenty different flavors and has ice in it."

"Tea, then," he insisted and motioned to the door.

NASH poured the tea into the cup in front of me at the coffee table. He sat in a chair alongside the sofa, and watched me until I picked up my cup and sipped.

The tea scalded the roof of my mouth. Nash sipped his like the heat didn't bother him at all.

"What was all that about?" I asked. "What if he comes back?"

"He won't," said Nash.

"How do you know that?"

"They'll find him before he has the chance. He must have escaped, but they'll put him back."

"Escaped from where?" I blew on my tea to have something to do. My hands trembled. I placed the cup back on the coffee table before the liquid spilled over the edges.

"It's better that you don't know. It'll be easier to do what Lucifer asked." Nash sipped his coffee.

"What do you mean?"

"When you make them fall."

"But if he escaped," I said, "what's to stop him from coming after me again?"

"Oh, they'll make sure he won't escape again."

"Shouldn't we tell Lucifer?"

Nash's eyes darted to mine. "Not unless you want him to be tossed into the Pit. I can make that happen. But I don't think it's necessary. You handled him quite well."

He might have killed me if Nash hadn't shown up, but the way Nash smiled told me to take the compliment. It was the first he had given me.

"He was an angel of low rank and fallen, but that was impressive how you were able to hold him off alone." His smile held charm and a look of danger to it like the smile of a comic book villain.

Nash was very critical of my training. He wasn't afraid to discuss my weaknesses. But now he beamed like a boy who finally taught his dog to play fetch.

"You're ready," he said.

"Are you saying that because you don't want to talk to Lucifer?" I asked. He told Bob a week ago that I wasn't ready with such finality that I thought I'd never be.

"I did talk to her," said Nash. "She trusts my judgment. We have a special relationship."

I wondered what special relationship Nash shared with the Devil. It must be *really* special if she trusts him with one of her most powerful weapons against the angels: me.

"So, does that mean, we're fighting Andromeda?" I asked.

Nash nodded. "Which means you need rest."

I looked down into my cup. "I don't think I can go back to sleep."

"You can sleep on the couch. I'll stay and watch over you. You'll feel tired once you lie down."

"It's been hard to sleep in general. I'm used to sleeping with the television on."

"I can tell you a story."

"Like a bedtime story?" My eyebrow quirked up.

"If you want to call it that."

I set my mug on the table and laid down on the couch. I closed my eyes as Nash's voice filled the room.

"Once there was an angel. She was the most beautiful angel in the heavens, and she was named after a star."

"A Bible story?" I pursed my lips.

"No, this isn't in the Bible."

I turned my face back to the ceiling.

"The beautiful angel had a beautiful heart, but she also had a weakness for a fellow angel who convinced her that everything she knew was a lie. So, she used her charm to rally other angels to fight to reveal the truth.

"The battle went on for hundreds of years, but the angels didn't feel the passage of time. But they did feel their wounds, cut with Arcadian Steel weapons. Friend stood against friend. Brother against brother.

"And then the revolutionaries lost. Their wings burst into flames, and they plummeted to Sheol. No god looked down on them with mercy."

"The most beautiful angel, that was Lucifer, right?" I yawned.

"Yes."

"But I thought the angels rebelled because Lucifer didn't want to be ruled by God?"

"Is that the story they told you?" Nash's voice was low and soothing.

I slipped into sleep. Fear and exhaustion caused me to melt away. As I drifted, I recalled the way Nash looked at the walls of the tunnel where the images of the angels falling from Heaven were etched. Sadness glazed his eyes. I wanted to ask him about that sadness, but I couldn't stop myself from sinking.

THE ice pack fell from my shoulder for the seventh time, and I left it on the pillow as I strummed the silent notes on my guitar.

"Are you in a band?" Adrianna perched on the end of my bed. Her blonde hair was pinned back and wound in an elegant bun. Her long, green dress pooled to the floor. Her lips were painted ruby red.

"No," I said. "I'm not really friends with a lot of people my age."

She frowned.

"Is there something I can help you with?" I eyed her.

"I thought I'd help you pick out something to wear for tonight," she said. "That way you don't have to wear a ratty old t-shirt and jeans."

"Thanks." I glared at her.

"Sorry. Kiran says I don't possess an awful lot of tact. But I wanted to help. Nash enjoys his dinners. We try to make them special."

"I'm not getting dressed up just to have dinner," I said.

Adrianna's lips formed a hard line. "Nash wasn't too pleased when you showed up dressed like you were going to a rock concert."

"Is Nash always so controlling?" I asked.

"He's the leader of our team." She got up from the bed and opened the closet door. "And because of him, we've ferried thousands of demons and fallen angels back to Sheol."

"Except when you kill them."

"That doesn't happen very often." Adrianna pulled a long red dress from the closet. "Nash has done this for a *long* time.

Sure, he might be a little bit of a control freak, but he's an expert at what he does. That's what makes him so enticing and, well, his looks don't hurt."

"I thought you were with Kiran." I looked at her, puzzled.

"I don't want to be *with* Nash. Doesn't mean I don't have eyes. This one should do." She pulled a dress out from the closet.

The red dress was the one Nash laid out on my bed my second night in Sheol. "Fine." I grabbed the dress from Adrianna and closed the bathroom door behind me. Ten minutes passed before I figured out how to get the dress on without stepping on the skirt from the inside. I managed to zip the gown up myself to my great relief.

"It's very billowy," I said as I exited the bathroom.

"It's supposed to be that way," said Adrianna. "Trust me, you look great. But your hair."

"Yeah, my hair is always a problem." I ran a hand through my brown hair to the dyed red tips.

"I can fix that." Adrianna brushed through my long hair and used bobby pins to pin it back and away from my face.

"Now makeup." Adrianna clenched a zippered bag. A grin split her face.

"No makeup," I said.

Adrianna frowned. "It'll make you look more even."

Dark circles began to grace my eyes a few weeks ago.

"At least let me do your eyeliner," she said.

I shook my head.

"At least take out that nose ring." Her hands were on her hips.

"The nose ring stays," I said.

Adrianna pouted. "Suit yourself, but next time, you'll let me give you a fresh face. You look like you haven't slept in days."

I moved with the care of a tightrope walker, not wanting to trip over the long dress. I managed to get to the landing of the stairs without tripping, which was more of a feat for me than swinging a sword.

The dining table was set and platters of food were in the center. Kiran, Tom and Chandra were already seated. Nash walked in from the kitchen. His eyes washed over me, and I thought I saw his lips twitch at the corners.

He approached me, and I stood with baited breath. He touched the small of my back, and a flush swept over me. When he pulled my chair out, I sat in a hurry. A tiny ball of air gathered in the center of my chest and didn't dissipate until Nash took his seat at the opposite end of the table.

I sipped my soup in silence. Nash stole the occasional glance at me. I knew that because I was eyeing him too. Was it that much of an improvement?

I hated Adrianna for making Nash's good looks so glaringly obvious to me. I noticed before, but her closeted conversation made it a fact I could no longer avoid. Added to that were her knowing smiles from across the table. I blushed and cursed myself for it.

"So, where are we going to fight this angel?" Chandra took a bite of her food.

Tom held up a finger as if to say *wait a minute*. He wiped his lips with a napkin and left the room.

"Won't Raphael know if Andromeda's weapon is taken?" I asked.

"Not unless she tells him." Adrianna put her fork down. "But that's unlikely. She has no reason to suspect us. She'll probably think it's archeologists."

"Do archeologists often find angel weapons?" I asked.

"If they do," said Chandra, "they're not alive long enough to tell about it."

At least one demon found out I'm in Sheol. Was it such a stretch to think Raphael might find out too?

"You're quiet, Nash." Chandra turned her eyes to him.

He looked at me from across the table. "I'm worried about the demons we discovered in the graveyard. Someone freed them from the Circles and tried to hide them on Earth."

He didn't mention the demon we found chained up and questioned by fallen angels. Didn't he think that was worth discussion too? He didn't want to tell Lucifer about them either. Why was he protecting those angels?

Tom returned with a large book. He opened the tome on the table, pushing aside the platters and dishes. Across both pages was a map. He pointed to a place on the map somewhere in South America. I didn't recognize the place. I had never been anywhere but Louisiana...and Hell, of course. I skirted by in geography, remembering locations and names for tests and quizzes and forgetting them in the weeks to follow.

Dad was always critical of education, specifically the institutes of education. "Schools ruin curiosity," he'd say. He never had to explain to me what he meant by that. He didn't want school to destroy my sense of wonder.

When you're forced to memorize boring facts that don't matter much to anyone anymore, you tend to lose your interest. When it came to topics outside of school, I wanted to absorb information with voracity. I bet if Rock was taught in school, I wouldn't have grown up listening to *Black Sabbath and Machine Head.*

But Mom always said I needed to do well in school. I could understand that too. I did want to go to college one day.

"Where exactly are you pointing?" I asked.

"The Galapagos Islands," said Tom. "Andromeda's Chains. That's where we should find them."

"Do we have a more exact location?" asked Nash.

"Cerro Azul, located at the base of the volcano. We might have to explore the surrounding area too."

I hoped Cerro Azul wasn't an active volcano. A militant angel was after me. I didn't need to be worried about lava too.

"We'll have to fly there." Tom closed the book.

"Fly?" I remembered Adriel and his wings.

"On a plane." Tom raised an eyebrow.

"Can't Nash open a portal?" I moved the food around on my plate.

"He would have to open a portal in the Circles to get to Cerro Azul right now. Sheol spins like a disk over Earth. That's why we have to be careful about our calculations when returning. Like Earth rotates around the Sun, Sheol doesn't remain in one place, and it moves very quickly. I don't want to go backpacking in the Circles." Tom took the book off the table. "I'd rather take a plane."

So, Sheol moved. That explained why Nash didn't know we'd end up in those caves when we returned. On Earth, we barely moved a mile from where Nash opened the initial portal, but in Sheol we moved more than an hour's walk to Nash's house.

"How long are we staying?" I asked.

"Hopefully, only a couple days," said Nash.

"But that sounds like a lot of ground to cover in a couple days," I said.

"Not with this." Adrianna reached into her bag and withdrew a glass orb that looked like a fortune teller's crystal ball.

"What is it?" I asked.

"The Orb of Metatron."

"Who?"

Chandra sighed. "She doesn't know anything, does she?"

"Metatron the Archangel," said Kiran. "He never had a weapon of his own. He grew distrustful of his fellow angels so he designed this orb to detect angel weapons. That way he would know if they were near and meant him any harm."

How were they able to get such a powerful defensive weapon from an Archangel? I dismissed the question. Of course, they fought Archangels in the past. That's why Lucifer qualified this team to help me in my task. Maybe Metatron was a fallen angel?

"The orb will glow when we get near Andromeda's Chains," said Adrianna. "That's how we'll know for sure we're in the right place."

eleven

I packed my bag the next morning and pulled on a pair of black jeans from the closet and a loose, white shirt. The jeans looked like they came out of a fashion magazine. I put on a pair of laced up boots that covered the hem of the jeans. The outfit didn't seem like the right attire in which to fight Archangels, but what was?

Bob promised to take care of Sim for me. I pet Sim before I left and told her that I would be back. I hoped I would be back.

After we jumped through a portal back to Earth, we needed to take a plane to Ecuador. I guess there are no planes in Hell, which is odd since there were cars. But, there were no cellphones either, and Nash didn't have a computer or television.

You couldn't say Sheol was technologically behind because of the modern-day selection of cars and sleek look of the architecture. Sheol was technologically selective. I'd have to ask about that.

I was afraid to step through the portal again. I felt a nauseating pull when I stepped through my first portal and headaches and queasiness when I jumped through the portals with Nash. The pull was undeniable like the Earth wanted me, but the tug weakened the more portals I entered. Would my body gravitate to Sheol now?

I tried not to think about it as I stepped through. Instead of the pull, what met me was more of an unsettling push like someone shoved me in the hallway at school. I stumbled as I came out on the other side. I felt dizzy.

I opened my eyes. The world was bright and colorful, not like the dull, cloudy gray atmosphere of Sheol. My head felt like someone crashed cymbals right next to my ears.

I rubbed my eyes as the sun blurred my vision. I breathed in and noticed that the air, although chilly, was less cold and dry than in Hell.

My back was to a wooden fence at the end of an alley. A large, rusty dumper blocked the view of the street.

"Come on," said Nash. "We have to get to the hanger."

The hanger was a couple of blocks down the road. Tom wanted to send us straight to the hanger, but Nash said it wouldn't be smart to let demons see us enter a portal right behind the distillery. One demon knew about me, Nash wanted to keep it at one. Tom grumbled as he wheeled two bags of luggage.

"It wouldn't be so hard if you didn't have to bring all those books," said Adrianna.

"These books are the reason we're not searching for Andromeda's Chains on the moon," Tom said.

The moon *would* be a good hiding place for angel weapons.

"But we already know where we're going, right? I can't see why you brought them along," she said.

"I don't know why *you're* complaining," said Chandra. "I have to carry the weapons." Chandra held a large black suitcase in one hand and a duffle bag on her opposite shoulder.

A private airplane sat in the loading bay. It was a good thing, too. Airport security wouldn't let us get by with a bottle of water much less a suitcase full of weapons.

"Hello, Mr. Nash." A man waited at the steps of the plane. He looked to be in his early fifties with a gray beard and bright, clear blue eyes. He wore white slacks and a black suit jacket with gold bands at the cuffs. He bore a pin of golden wings above his breast pocket.

"Good morning, Frank," said Nash. "You have the itinerary?"

"Yes, sir."

Nash placed his bag on the cart beside the steps, and everyone tossed their bags in as well.

The wind blasted through the open space with no trees or buildings to stop the onslaught.

Inside the plane was a beige sofa along one wall, and across from the sofa were two large, brown leather chairs that looked comfortable enough to sleep in. Between the two chairs was a square table, and on the wall, was a television. I longed for the static drone of the TV while I slept. Maybe that was why my nights were sleepless.

I plopped down on the sofa followed by Adrianna, Kiran, and Chandra, who sat on the opposite end as far away from me as she could get. Tom took his books out of his bags, which he lugged up the steps himself. Nash sat in the chair across from me.

A flight attendant entered the plane. I was relieved to see that she wasn't one of the robotic women from Lucifer's skyscraper.

She was a pleasant faced woman with a natural smile and warm, pink cheeks. She looked like she smelled of peaches. She wore a clean, white buttoned down shirt tucked into a simple, black skirt.

"Can I get you anything?" she asked.

"Coffee," said Nash.

"How do you take it?"

"Black."

"Root Beer?" I asked.

"I'll take an iced tea," said Adrianna.

Tom's nose was in his book as he waved the flight attendant away.

At the cost of signaling to everyone that I had never been on a plane before, I pushed up the blinds and watched the ground shrink below us. My ears popped as we ascended.

"What is the weapon we're looking for again?" I asked.

"Andromeda's Chains," said Tom.

"Chains?" That doesn't sound like much of a weapon.

"Yes, Chains," said Chandra as if she was annoyed. "They are heavy and bathed in fire. You wouldn't want to get hit with them, especially a mortal like you. They would crush your skull." She smiled in relish at that comment.

If I had to guess how many demons were aboard this plane, I'd say, *At least one.*

As night fell, Nash showed me to the back of the plane where two rows of sleeping bunks nestled across from each other. I curled up on the top bunk and peered out of the window behind the blackout blinds to see the stars.

Adrianna and Kiran slept in the bottom bunk opposite me. Kiran put his arm around Adrianna's waist.

I awoke. The others had left their bunks. I noticed the sheets of the top bunk across from me had been disturbed. Someone had crawled in while I was asleep. I wondered if it had been Nash.

I imagined his gaze upon my sleeping form before he closed his eyes. My heart thumped that up-tempo drum beat I started to hate.

But my heart wasn't the only thing acting funny. I sensed a difference in Nash's mood toward me after I fought with the fallen angel. He had more respect for me than he had before. He watched me more and stole glances at me as I moved around the house.

THE WINGS OF HEAVEN AND HELL 127

I rolled over and pulled open the blinds. The light assaulted my eyes. I blinked until I became comfortable with the brightness.

The islands were in the distance, a forest canopy of green surrounded by clear, blue water.

The plane landed at the airport, and Nash called a car to take us to the hotel. Large white columns stood at the front entrance. Once I got to my room, I tossed my suitcase onto the king-sized bed.

This hotel was above and beyond the seedy motel that Adriel brought me to. The room was double the size. The bed was dressed in clean, white linens and a comforter. An abstract painting, taller than me, hung on the wall across from the bed. The painting reflected the bright, colorful atmosphere of the island. Off to the side was a private balcony with two lounge chairs and a clear, glass railing so that it wouldn't obscure the view of green trees and the beach in the distance.

Nash and the others went to brunch at a café down the street from the hotel. Nash said he ate at the café before and recommended it, but I was still too anxious to eat.

Tomorrow we were supposed to travel to the base of a volcano to steal an angel weapon. From the time our hands touched that weapon, we would be on that angel's radar or more like her hit list. She would attack us, and I had to stop her.

If I didn't, my friends would die, and if they died on Earth, they were destined to the Pit where they would fall forever.

But, no pressure.

I unpacked my bag and put on shorts and a t-shirt. I sat out on the balcony all afternoon and enjoyed the sun on my skin. I hopped into the shower, towel dried my hair, and got dressed.

A knock sounded at my door. Nash stood in the hall.

"Are you hungry?" he asked. "There's a little place in town."

"Let me guess, it's highly recommended," I said.

"Very highly." He smiled.

I didn't come down for breakfast because my nerves were on edge. I didn't eat on the plane either. My stomach rumbled, and I clenched it as my face grew hot. "Actually," I said. "Something to eat would be great."

"Okay, get dressed. I'll be back in an hour."

I looked down at my outfit. Great. If I knew Nash, this *little* place he was talking about was probably pretty fancy. I hadn't packed any dresses. Why would I? I came to Ecuador to fight, not to prance around town in my finest.

"I didn't bring anything dressy," I said.

"Don't worry about it," said Nash. "I'll have something brought up to you."

I was about to tell him not to bother, that I would order room service, but he was halfway down the hall as I clenched my stomach and tried to quiet another rumble.

Half an hour later, I answered another knock. A man in a white suit stood outside with a black garment bag and shoe-box. He offered them to me. When I took the items, he still stood at the door.

"Thanks." I gently shut the door.

I tossed the bag on the bed and unzipped it. Inside was a black skirt and silk, black tank top with lace along the neckline. I frowned, but at least, I wouldn't have to walk around in a floor length ball gown. I donned the outfit and tucked the shirt in. Inside the shoebox was a pair of red flats. I slipped those on and looked in the mirror.

My hair was in tangles since the plane ride. I tried to comb out the tangles, but the warm, humid air of Ecuador made my hair frizz as if touched by static electricity.

Satisfied that I did my best, I flipped through the channels of the hotel television until I heard another knock at the door.

Nash wore a fitted gray suit and button down white shirt. The top two buttons were undone, letting the collar casually sit back along his collar bones. His dark hair was swept back.

I walked with Nash to the elevator and into the hotel lobby.

A black car was parked outside the hotel. Nash walked up to the vehicle and opened the door for me. I climbed inside, and Nash sat beside me.

I looked around. "Aren't the others coming with us?"

"Chandra wanted to spend her night at a resort. She tried to get us all to go, but I declined."

The first question that came to mind was *Why?* But how could I ask such a dumb question. The answer was obvious. Chandra didn't want me to come, and Nash took pity on me and decided to take me out to dinner.

The driver pulled away from the curb and drove down the winding streets.

"You look nice," I said.

He flashed me a smile. "Thanks." The smile faded. "Are you nervous about tomorrow?"

Nervous, that word didn't seem to fit what I felt, a mixture of fear, nerves, and something surreal. A small part of me that floated on the outside, watching all this unfold and not buying it at all.

"I don't know," I said. "My mom used to say you can never have just one emotion. Emotions always come in layers. Some are stronger than others, sometimes they can overwhelm others, and sometimes they can all be so mixed up you don't know what you're feeling. That's where I am right now."

"Everything will be fine," he said.

The car stopped outside a restaurant with a stucco finish and an iron gate. The building was surrounded by palm trees.

The inside of the restaurant was bathed in an orange glow. Rustic wooden beams accented the ceiling. On the walls was a beige textured finish. A feature wall was painted a reddish-orange with framed pictures of bison, horses, and tropical birds.

Nash pulled my chair out for me before he took his seat. With anyone else, I would have thought better of this, but Nash had a flare for formality.

The table was set with a white linen table cloth, porcelain plates, wine glasses, and cloth napkins that were folded to look like little hats.

Nash placed his napkin in his lap, and I followed suit.

I ordered an iced tea, and he had tonic water. This was the first time he asked for something other than coffee. I thought he was a caffeine addict.

At one table over, two girls talked conspiratorially and stole glances at Nash. They were dark skinned and beautiful. The smiles on their faces told me that they were swooning over him. I felt a little insulted by their apparent gawking. Nash could be my boyfriend for all they knew. *My boyfriend.* What was I thinking?

I was thinking Nash was good-looking. His dark hair contrasted with his smooth white skin. His eyes were like ink, dark and fathomless and...looking right at me.

My face flushed, and I looked away as if I hadn't just been staring. I tried to eat slowly. After days of copying Adrianna, I developed some good table manners. At least, I didn't eat so fast anymore.

Nash ate like it was a dance. He savored each bite and never gestured with his utensils.

He put his fork down. "Do you like it?" he asked.

"Huh?"

"The pasta?"

"Oh, yeah. It's really good." I should have said that his pasta was better. It was after all. No, I didn't want him to think I didn't enjoy the meal.

After one last bite, I set my fork down and wiped the corners of my mouth with the napkin. I took a sip of tea and swished it around in my mouth, hoping I didn't have anything stuck in my teeth.

He looked up at me, and I swallowed.

"If you could live forever," he said," what would be more important to you: to retain the mind or the body that you have now?"

"That seems like a very philosophical question," I said.

"It's just a question."

"Okay then, I guess I'd have to choose my mind. I don't want to start forgetting things or go insane. I think that's my greatest fear, to lose myself."

Nash smirked. "That's quite an answer."

"Are you making fun of me?"

"Not even a little bit."

I smiled. "Okay, now you. Which would you rather keep: your mind or your body?"

"I'll keep my looks," Nash said with a grin that showed off his white teeth.

I laughed. This was a different side of him.

"Okay. I have a question for you, but it's not a philosophical one."

"Shoot."

"What's your favorite rock band?"

Nash smiled and shook his head. "I don't listen to rock n' roll."

I stared at him agape, teasing him a little.

"Is that a sin?"

"Yes," I said.

"Send me to Hell." Nash settled back in his chair. "What's your favorite song?"

"I listen to a lot of Metal, Megadeth, Iron Maiden," I said. "But my favorite song is Mad World by Tears for Fears."

"Never heard it."

"Wow. It's too bad we don't have a radio back at the hotel. Do they have radios in Sheol?"

"Afraid not."

"I guess I could play it for...wait I can't. My guitar's electric so I'd need an amp."

"You left it back home?"

"Well, yeah. An amp is a bit too big and awkward to take with me. But I couldn't leave my guitar...my dad, it was the last thing he bought me. I'm sorry. I didn't mean to..." I blinked my eyes a few times to stop the tears. I smiled and hoped that might help. "Sorry."

"How did he die?"

"Both my mom and dad died in a car crash." I didn't say that Raphael caused that car crash. It was so easy to say *car crash*, I forgot I was talking to someone who wouldn't think I was crazy for saying I saw an angel. "Now that I know Heaven is real, I'm sure they're up there. They were good people. Sorry."

"Why are you apologizing?"

"I just...I don't know." I dabbed my eyes with the napkin. I wanted to change the subject. "So, where did you learn to cook?"

"Self-taught, and I've had a lot of time to practice."

"How long exactly?" I raised an eyebrow.

He watched me through hooded eyes. He opened his mouth to answer when the waitress approached our table. She asked if we wanted anything for dessert, and Nash ordered a coffee.

Maybe he was a caffeine addict.

"A couple hundred years," he said. "But cooking practices change and improve all the time."

Whoa. *A couple hundred years.* I was afraid to ask Nash how old he was. Would it even be a number I could fathom?

I imagined how talented I could be if I practiced the guitar for a couple hundred years. I envisioned myself on a stage in the hazy dimness of Sheol with Nash, in the front of the crowd, cheering me on as I played. A chill ran down my back. I was getting too comfortable in Hell.

WE walked along the base of the volcano. Smooth, sloping curves of land skirted around the rocky mound. The terrain looked dark and dangerous in contrast to the bright blue skies above.

My sword was at my side, and a dagger nestled in a smaller sheath on my belt.

Tom looked at a map. Adrianna walked far ahead of us with the Orb of Metatron. She was unarmed. The Orb glowed in the presence of Arcadian Steel. If she had any on her, it would continue to glow, and we wouldn't know if we were close.

My foot slipped, and I might have fallen to the ground if a warm hand hadn't taken me by the elbow to steady me. Nash was by my side. He smiled, let go of me, and walked on.

Chandra glared at me. "Keep up," she said as she passed.

I took a quick drink of water from my canteen and followed the others. We walked around the base of the volcano for half an hour.

"It's glowing," Adrianna called to us.

The orb was brighter than a spotlight. Streams of light glowed between Adrianna's fingers. A break scarred the ground at her feet, a foot and a half wide and three feet long. The chasm's depth was unfathomable.

"Rope," said Adrianna.

Chandra took the rope from her side and threw one end down into the chasm. She clasped the other end in a firm grip.

Adrianna handed the orb to Kiran and climbed down into the hole. "Throw it down to me," Adrianna yelled. She echoed up to us.

Kiran dropped the orb, and Adrianna caught it.

Nash's voice was by my ear. "You'd better come with us. Just in case." He climbed down after Adrianna.

Chandra held the rope by herself.

I took hold of the rope and climbed down. I climbed a rope in gym class once. I couldn't get a fourth of the way up. But after weeks of hard training, my arms were stronger. I climbed down, and as I got three feet from the ground, I felt the rope slacken. My feet hit the ground sooner than I expected, and I fell backward on the hard, rocky surface.

Chandra smiled down at me. "Sorry, my arms got tired. You must be too heavy."

I stabbed her with my eyes. Too bad she wasn't looking.

I got up before Nash or Adrianna could come and help me. I didn't want to seem weak.

The chasm was a lot deeper than I expected. A tunnel led in the direction of the volcano.

I walked with Nash and Adrianna as I braced myself against the rocky wall. The fall hurt my leg, and I was sure to have a nasty bruise on my thigh the next morning.

The orb glowed brighter as we journeyed on. The tunnel ended in a solid rocky wall. I looked around. I didn't see a weapon.

"It's a dead end," I said.

"No." Adrianna touched the wall and brought the orb up to it.

I shielded my eyes as the orb blazed with light.

"Kiran!" Adrianna yelled. "Come meet us down here, and bring your sword."

Kiran jogged up to where we all stood. He looked at the wall.

"Here." Adrianna patted the wall.

Kiran stepped forward. He held his sword above his head, and in one swift motion, he plunged the sword into the rocky wall. The blade sliced through the rock like a pocket knife through a cardboard box.

He drew a wide circle with his blade.

"Stand back," Nash shouted.

Kiran's blade came full circle around to his initial cut, and the wall cascaded down like thunder.

I managed to clamp my hands over my ears in time.

When the dust settled, I peered at the place where the wall used to be. A small hollowed out space was hidden behind the wall. Inside was an ornamented, gold box. Adrianna knelt and opened the box.

I walked up and stepped around the remnants of the wall. Inside the box was a coil of silver chains. The links were longer than my thumb and five times as big around.

Adrianna lifted the chains from the golden box. "They sure are heavy," she said. She held one end of the chain and wrapped it around to her elbow until she formed a manageable circle. She put both hands through the center and held the chains on her forearms as we walked back to the chasm.

"More rope," Adrianna shouted.

Chandra threw down another length of rope.

Adrianna tied the rope around her waist and secured the chains. She climbed. Kiran's hand supported her back until she climbed out of his reach.

He and Nash ascended, one at a time.

I was nervous to climb back up, afraid Chandra would wait till I got to the top and drop me, although I knew she wouldn't. I assumed I needed to be alive for my angel death touch to work.

I clasped Nash's outstretched hand as I reached the top.

A bright white light, brighter than Metatron's Orb blinded me. A violent shutter of wings sounded above us, and when I opened my eyes an angel hovered before me.

She was beautiful. Her pale skin glowed in the light, and her white hair matched the ivory of her wings. On her elegant face was a look of utter disgust. *Andromeda.*

"Adrianna, get the weapon away from her," Nash yelled.

Chandra threw Adrianna her sword, and Adrianna darted away as Andromeda plummeted towards us head first.

I hadn't realized she would know so soon. I thought maybe we'd have a week before she arrived or at least a day.

I tried to back away, but stumbled to the ground.

Nash pulled me up. "Your sword," he screamed.

I looked at the others. They all had their weapons drawn.

I pulled the sword from the sheath at my side. The blade felt heavier in my hands than usual.

Andromeda landed on the ground before us. "Worms," she said. "Why did you come?"

Nash stepped in front of us.

My heart fell.

Andromeda swung her leg. Her foot hit Nash in the jaw, and he twisted in the air. His outstretched hands stopped his face from meeting the ground.

Chandra yelled and threw her sword against Andromeda as Nash stood. Andromeda raised her shielded forearm to block the blow. The Arcadian Steel sparked against her arm bracer.

Angels have Arcadian armor, I realized, and we didn't.

Kiran swung his sword at Andromeda. She deflected the blow with her armored forearm. They dodged and jabbed, moving like eels in a fish tank. Their movements were swift, controlled, and confined.

Nash interrupted the dance.

He let out a whirlwind of slices, faster than I had ever seen him wield a weapon before. But Andromeda blocked each one. Until one landed and sliced through her arm. A trickle of silver blood seeped from the wound.

Andromeda's teeth were set in a grimace. She glared at Nash and looked to where Adrianna ran. Andromeda's large, white wings swept into the sky and sailed toward Adrianna. Adrianna was a fast runner but despite this Andromeda was above her in seconds.

"Let's go!" Nash shouted. "We can't let her get her hands on those chains.

Andromeda was upon Adrianna. We could see them in the distance as we ran towards them. Kiran was in front of us.

Adrianna drew her sword and slashed at Andromeda. Andromeda grabbed the sword in her bare hands.

She screamed as the blade cut into her flesh. Silver blood, as slick as oil, covered the blade's surface. Andromeda wrenched the blade from Adrianna's hands and tossed it. The blade flew several yards away. I didn't see it land.

Andromeda smacked Adrianna across the face and sent her spinning to the ground. Adrianna rose and wiped the blood from her lip and faced Andromeda once more. Adrianna ducked and dived for Andromeda, wrapping her hands around the angel's waist. She tackled Andromeda to the ground and tried to trap Andromeda's legs in hers.

Andromeda beat against Adrianna's back with a flurry of blows, but Adrianna held strong. Andromeda reached for the chains and pulled them from Adrianna's waist.

The chains were surrounded in flames as soon as they touched Andromeda's hand.

Adrianna must have felt the weight of them leave her or maybe the heat of the fire. She let go of Andromeda's waist to pin her arm to the ground. But Andromeda was too fast. She saw her opportunity and rolled on top of Adrianna, whipping the chain behind her and bringing them down near Adrianna's face.

Adrianna wrapped one leg around the side of Andromeda's waist and pinned the other against her thigh. She tilted her body and flipped the angel onto her back. Andromeda's wings were flared out against the ground as she held her head up. Adrianna walked her foot up to Andromeda's shoulder and wrenched Andromeda's hand from around her.

Andromeda pulled back her arm as far as she could, and the chain hit Adrianna on the back, ripping her shirt and the skin beneath.

Adrianna screamed in an agony that I never heard before.

Andromeda landed another blow to her back before the first scream ended. Andromeda tossed her against the rocky ground and stood as we arrived.

Kiran raced to the ground beside Adrianna. Her eyes blinked open and closed as if she had trouble keeping them open.

Andromeda swept her chain at us, but Nash's blade collided against it. The chain wrapped around his sword and pulled the blade from Nash's hand. Nash withdrew a second sword from his side.

Kiran rose to his feet and roared. In his mouth and nostrils embers burned as if he was on fire from the inside. He rushed at Andromeda, and his blade sent sparks against her arm bracer as she blocked him.

Andromeda raised her chains above her head.

I knew what I needed to do. I pushed pass Chandra and Tom.

Andromeda didn't look at me. She didn't know what I was.

Right before her blow landed, I reached out and threw myself against her. I made contact, but I landed hard on the rocky ground. I used my hand to break my fall, and an audible crack sounded as the flat of my hand hit the rough terrain.

Andromeda's wings burst into flames. Her chains hung at her side. She screamed. I thought I couldn't imagine a scream more agonizing than Adrianna's, but Andromeda's was.

Andromeda flew into the air and sailed away as the fire died to embers and left her feathers black and ashy. Those feathers would soon die and fly away from the bones like blackened confetti. Andromeda would only have one place to go—Hell.

MY shoulders slumped. I had either been very brave or very stupid. Adrianna was on the ground gasping for breath but alive. Nash stared at me. His eyes were wide with a look of quiet gratitude. As hardened as he was, he didn't want anyone to die.

Kiran dropped his sword and ran back to Adrianna's side. She had marks all over her body and a long cut on the side of her face. Blood cascaded from the cut down to her ear and jaw. She bled like any human, but the blood was black like that of a fallen angel. Blood pooled around her on the ground and leaked out of a fatal wound around her stomach. Andromeda's Chains cut away the fabric of her shirt and left deep gouges in her flesh.

Warm tears wet my cheeks. She wouldn't survive this. Chunks of flesh were missing from her body and spurting blood like soda from a shaken can.

"We have to go back!" Kiran yelled.

"We can't," said Tom. "If we open the portal right here, right now we'll be in the Ninth Circle."

"We can't let her die," said Kiran. "She'll go to the Pit."

Nash's jaw was set. He didn't say anything. He opened the portal.

"What are you doing?" Tom asked.

On the other side was a barren plain of ice. The chill bit my skin. The cold air fought against the humidity of the Islands.

"He's right," said Nash. "We don't have a choice."

Tom's eyes were wide. "Nash, we could spend an eternity there. If anything is second to the Pit, it's the Ninth Circle."

"I'm not going to let her die," said Chandra. "Pass her to me on the other side." She stepped through the portal and disappeared through its center.

Kiran lifted Adrianna from the ground. Her body slumped in his arms. Her head lulled against his chest. She was too weak to grimace from the pain. I'd heard the body will protect itself from pain after a while so the mind wouldn't fall to pieces. He put her through. His arms disappeared on the other side.

I walked forward as I clasped my hand gingerly around my wrist. I think it was broken. Nash put his hand on my shoulder. "No," he said. "Tom, take her back with you."

"What?" I said. He wasn't going to leave us, was he? We were a team. "I'm going with you."

Nash narrowed his eyes. Was he angry with me? "I can't let you come with us. The punishments in the Circles are designed for immortal souls, not for you. If you died, that could mean the Pit for me."

If the Ninth Circle was second only to the Pit, I couldn't comprehend the tortures they might face there.

But they had to do this for Adrianna. I hoped she would be okay. The whole thing was crazy to me. She could die on Earth, but not in Hell. Would she be able to regenerate or something? But if she did, what would happen to her and the others once they were in the Circles? Would the demons let them leave?

My breath caught. What if Nash became *stuck* there? Would I ever see him again? Would Lucifer make me join a new team and fight with strangers?

Nash climbed through, and the portal disappeared.

TOM and I boarded the plane. In Sheol, although many places on its outskirts were like Earth, the Circles were another matter, and the area that contained them was much greater than its outer edges.

The thought that Nash might not come back from the Ninth Circle entered my mind again. Was he lost forever?

I thought back to the battle. We nearly lost. That angel could have killed us all. Adrianna. Was she going to die? I couldn't imagine she would survive those wounds on her back and stomach. A human would have died in an instant. I still couldn't wrap my mind around the idea that she wouldn't die if she died in Sheol.

And Andromeda was a *lesser* angel. The only angel I spoke to was Adriel, and I didn't know what rank he was. But if Andromeda was powerful enough to take on five trained fighters, how much stronger was Raphael?

I gulped.

Not to mention, if Raphael found out what we were doing, he could come after me. What if, Andromeda warned him. She flew away. Nash and the others hadn't been able to do their fallen angel bounty hunter thing. Would she go to the gates of Heaven and warn them, tell them where I was?

Raphael's army would find me. All my friends would die and become destined for the Pit. If they died, I would never be free. My soul will be lost forever in Lucifer's chains. We better find the other weapons fast and pick the angels off one by one before we go up against an army of angels bent on destroying us.

Tom cracked open a book and poured over its pages. How could he read at a time like this?

"Tom?" I asked.

"What?" He didn't take his eyes off the book.

"Will you look at me?"

Tom picked up his head. "What is it?"

"*What is it?*" I stared at him. "Our friends are lost somewhere in the Circles, and we're not going to talk about it?"

"What is there to talk about?" He held the book open in his lap. I knew he wanted to look back down at it. He wanted to escape my eyes and my judgment. Or maybe he didn't care. I hoped it was the former.

"Tell me about the Circles."

"You want a lesson on the Circles right now?"

"Yes."

"It won't clear your mind."

"Just tell me."

Tom closed his book and placed it on the small table beside him. He grabbed the pen and pad of paper at the end of the table. "Imagine that Hell is a circle." I moved to the chair opposite him as he drew a circle on the piece of paper.

"This region here—hey, what's wrong with your wrist?" He watched me as I cradled my wrist in my lap.

"I think I broke it."

"You need to go to the hospital."

"That's going to be difficult while I'm thirty thousand feet in the air," I said. "Can't someone in Sheol set it for me."

"Sure," said Tom. "But that would require me to tell them that you're human."

"Would that be a problem?"

"We'll stop at a hospital in the city. Soon as the plane lands. I wish you would have said something before we boarded."

"I was more worried about Adrianna," I said. "I'm still worried about her, about all of them. Please, distract me."

Tom eyed me curiously, but he didn't ask. "This region here." He pointed to the edge of the circle. "Is the Outer Region where Lucifer and a few honorary demons, such as myself, live." He drew another smaller circle inside the larger one. "Here." He pointed to the edge of the second circle, "is Limbo, and this…"

"Wait," I stopped him. "What's Limbo?"

He shook his head. "This is going to be a starting-from-scratch type lesson, isn't it?"

"I don't know a lot about religion," I said.

"This isn't religion. This is Hell."

"Well, I don't know a lot about Hell either."

He sighed. "Limbo is located right outside the Outer Region. It's the First Circle of Hell. Religion will tell you Limbo is a place for non-Christians and unbaptized babies, but that isn't true. It's an intake office."

"A what?"

"Where people first go before they're assigned to a Circle or obtain a contract. Lots of paperwork. If you obtain a contract, you have to follow the tenants of said contract which will perhaps earn you a place in the Outer Region instead of an eternity of torture."

"Why doesn't everyone take the contract?"

"Morality is a funny thing," said Tom. "There are some things people aren't willing to do in the face of the unknown. No one knows how bad the tortures of the Circles are until they experience it themselves. Also, some people just don't get offered contracts."

"What about the unbaptized babies? If they don't go to Limbo, where do they go?"

"Babies go to Heaven." Tom smirked. "Baptisms don't mean much. Well, they don't mean anything at all. The mechanisms for getting to Hell are much more complex than that. But I thought we were talking about the Circles."

"Okay, so what comes after Limbo?"

"Thought you'd never ask." He drew yet another circle within the smaller one.

"I think I can do without the diagram," I said.

"Fine." He crumpled up the paper. "Right outside Limbo pass the river is the Second Circle. It storms there, gets awful windy. The winds are so rough they can rip the skin from your bones." He said it like he was telling a ghost story.

My mouth formed a hard line.

"If you don't believe me fine," said Tom, "but I'm going to tell it the way I want to tell it."

"Who's in the Second Circle?"

"Adulterers mostly, mixed with a few others who use sex appeal for immoral gains. There are a few marketing executives down there and not because they cheated on their wives."

"Seems like a silly reason to go to Hell."

"There are lots of silly ways people have gotten to Hell. Cerberus, the three-headed dog, presides over the Third Circle, reserved for the gluttons who are forced to doggy paddle through his shit."

I crinkled my nose as the image hit me, hard to avoid although I tried.

"The Fourth Circle houses the hoarders and the money grubbers. Hades runs a tight ship. His demons place heavy weights on the chests of the tortured. There are a lot of priests down there."

"I thought Hades is from Greek mythology."

"Mythology is just a word for a religion that's no longer practiced. Hades bears more than a passing mention in ancient Greek religion, but he's existed before the world was made."

"Hoarders don't deserve to be in Hell. I mean, the people on the show are slobs, but they're sick. They're not evil."

"If only evil people went to Hell," said Tom, "Lucifer would only have a few thousand psychopaths down there."

"How many Circles are there?"

"Nine, and they get worse with each level."

Nash and the others went to the Ninth Circle, the worse one. No wonder Tom acted so hopeless. "Tell me about the Ninth Circle."

"But I haven't gotten through the others yet."

"I don't care. Just tell me if they can make it."

Tom shook his head. "Not likely."

"But..."

"What they did for Adrianna was a Hail Mary," said Tom. "If she died on Earth, she would be banished to the Pit. Torture is better than that, even Ninth Circle level torture."

"So, what happens now?" I asked, my voice a whisper.

"All we can do is wait."

Before Tom and I went back to Sheol, we stopped at a hospital in the city where a doctor set my wrist and put it in a cast. She said I had a fracture. My wrist and a large portion of my forearm would be in the cast for at least three weeks. When Tom and I arrived back at Nash's house, a black sports car was in the driveway. Bob kept his promise to take care of Sim.

Bob rolled down the sleeves of his shirt when I opened the door. He grabbed his coat off the rack.

"You're back," he said. "And in one piece." He smiled devilishly.

"No," I said. "We have a problem."

Bob's smile dropped faster than a bowling ball from a Ferris Wheel.

"Nash and the others are in the Ninth Circle," I said.

Bob tilted his head to the side. "What are they doing there?"

"Adrianna was injured," said Tom without emotion or urgency.

What was wrong with him? Hopelessness was one thing, but I thought he cared about his friends.

"And they entered the Ninth Circle so she wouldn't die on Earth," Bob concluded. "That's a shame."

"You have to get them out," I said. "They're there because of Lucifer." *They're there because of me.*

"Sweetheart, I can't get them out of the Ninth Circle. I couldn't save them from the First."

"Tell Lucifer," I said desperately.

"Oh, I will," he said. "But that won't free them either."

"I don't understand."

Bob sighed. "The Circles were created for the damned. It's not like you're asking me to break them out of prison. That would be quite easy. But the Circles are a different matter. It's impossible."

I was angry, but tears were in my eyes. The Circles weren't difficult to get out of as Tom implied. They were impossible to escape.

I looked at Tom. He didn't seem at all surprised by this. Because he knew. That's why he sounded so hopeless and shallow. He knew, and he didn't tell me.

But he did tell me. I just didn't want to listen.

Bob walked passed me, and I kept my back to him as he spoke, "I'll tell Lucifer, but it won't bring them back."

I heard the door open and shut behind me, and he was gone. Tom bent his head and walked away.

The world is a guitar that needs tuning, and its music is broken.

The tears dripped down to my chin. I wiped them with the back of my hand. They were out there because of me. Nash said he would fight angels for me, and now he was gone.

call it a loan

LYDIA walked with Robert arm in arm. She leaned her head against his shoulder as they strolled through the park under the fading light. It was night now.

For two years, they dated. They met at Faulkner House Books in the French Quarter. She opened a copy of Macbeth when he walked in. The little silver bell chimed, and she looked up.

His hair was dark brown, and his eyes were the space between the stars. He wore a red scarf around his neck and held a coffee. The night was chilly, much like this one.

Lydia pulled her shawl around her as her teeth chattered against the wind. The dark trees were backlit by the warm glow of the streetlamps as they walked the narrow track and passed ponds of brown water where delicate, green lily pads floated. She wasn't sure why Robert was so silent, but he was only quiet when he was nervous.

She squeezed his arm tighter as he stopped. "What is it?" she asked.

"Lydia," he started, "I have something to tell you. Well, actually something to ask you."

Her dark hair tickled her as the light breeze drew the tresses against her face. She couldn't remember a time when he sounded so serious.

"Okay," she said.

That's when he fell to one knee.

Her breath caught. She thought she was prepared for a moment like this. It wasn't entirely a surprise. They were together for years and talked about marriage before. Still, silence hung in the air, and she couldn't breathe.

Robert reached into his pocket and revealed a tiny, black box. He opened the box, and the diamond glittered in the moonlight.

"Lydia," he said. "Thank you for giving me the best two years of my life."

Lydia grinned and did a dramatic curtsy.

Robert chuckled and continued. "I've gotten to see your finest qualities, mixed with a few little quirks."

Lydia's short laugh came out between wide spread lips set into a smile that she wasn't sure she would be able to wipe from her face.

"You're perfect, except for one thing" he said. "The only thing I would change…" He looked at the sky for a moment as if he was thinking about it. Then he looked back down at her. "…is your last name…"

Her eyes glistened.

"Will you marry me?" he asked.

Lydia's response was caught in her throat. She couldn't take her eyes off Robert. She didn't notice the men until they stood in front of them and behind. Her eyes widened, and her smile evaporated like water in the sun.

The men were dressed in dark clothing. The men to her left and right were very tall, taller than Robert. One had his hair tied back in a ponytail, while the other's scraggly, curly hair hung on either side of his head, bordering a fully-grown beard. Directly in front of her was a shorter man with a long nose and hair shaved close to his head. She could sense two larger men behind them.

Robert stood up and pocketed the ring box. He wrapped his arm around Lydia's trembling shoulders.

The men tightened their circle around the young couple.

"Oh, don't let us stop you," said the shorter man. His voice was higher pitched than she expected, but confidence dripped from his words and told her this was not a man to be messed with. "What were you going to say, pretty lady?" His hands were in the pockets of his dark jeans.

The man with the ponytail smiled. He was missing one of his front teeth. He gripped a knife. She guessed the other men were armed as well. She could feel the heat which radiated off their bodies as they stood behind her.

Lydia glanced down the street. They were in the light of a single street lamp, but no one else was in the park. Robert must have chosen to come here so they could be alone. He knew a big show at the restaurant would have been too embarrassing for her.

The way the short man moved his hand to the pocket of his leather jacket made her think one heart-stopping thought. *He has a gun.*

"Why don't you tell us what you were going to say?" The short man didn't give up.

Robert spoke first. "This isn't necessary. We'll give you whatever you want. Just let…"

"What I want," interrupted the short man, "is to hear her answer."

This might be her last chance to tell Robert how she felt. Her heart dropped at the thought. "Yes," she whispered, her voice hoarse.

He leaned in closer and smirked. "You're gonna have to speak up, dear. I didn't quite catch that. I've always had trouble hearing, or so I've been told."

"Yes," she said slow and clear. She looked up at Robert. "My answer is yes." She tried to smile, but that was impossible.

"Wonderful!" he shouted and still smirked, "Put it on."

Lydia stared at him like she was trying to fit together the first pieces of a jigsaw puzzle.

"The ring. You said, yes, didn't you?"

Robert fished the black box out of his pocket and opened it. He took the ring out of the box and placed it on Lydia's finger. His hands shook, and he dropped the box to the ground.

Lydia could tell Robert tried to maintain his composure. His nostrils flared, and he shook not only from fear, but from anger.

The short man sneered. "I'm going to make this very easy. I wouldn't want a young couple to miss their wedding day."

Lydia shuttered at the threat.

The two men alongside him glared at them. Their hands were also in their pockets. Heavy brows shadowed their eyes.

"All you have to do is give us everything in your pockets. Anything you have."

Lydia's hand trembled as she handed her purse over to the tall man as Robert reached into his pocket for his wallet and cellphone.

"Take it," he said. "We don't want any trouble. We're meeting friends here later. They should be coming around soon."

A lie. No one was coming to meet them. Robert was trying to make the men leave sooner so this whole ordeal would end.

The short man smiled, and went through Robert's wallet. He pulled out a picture of Robert and Lydia, the one they took last Christmas, a month ago. They both wore ugly holiday sweaters and stood in front of the Christmas tree.

"This one you can keep." He flicked the picture into the cold night air. The photograph drifted to the ground. "But, we're not done. Aren't you forgetting something?" He glanced down at Lydia's hand. The ring encircled her finger.

She hadn't got the chance to admire the full beauty of the diamond or feel her heart thrill as she fanned out her hand to look at it.

She had no family. Her parents died in a car accident when she was eighteen, six years ago. But she kept several good friends. Christine, her friend since high school, would have giggled with glee at the thought of her best friend getting married. She would have grabbed Lydia's hand and held it captive until she got a better look at the ring.

That was a fantasy now. Robert probably put all his savings into the ring, so he could surprise her with something beautiful.

Lydia was about to take the ring off when Robert said, "No."

"No?" The short man lifted his eyebrow.

"You have our money, our phones," said Robert. "Leave us alone." The edge in his voice scared Lydia, a mixture of pride, fear, and anger.

The short man laughed. "You think that's how this works?"

"Robert, let's give them the ring," said Lydia.

"You better listen to her, Robert," the short man said. "This goes one way."

Robert's whole body trembled, and he clenched his fists. "You have what you came for."

"Oh, for shit's sakes." The short man pulled the gun from his pocket and pointed it at them.

Lydia's eyes widened. She held out her hand. She started to whisper. An incantation nestled in the back of her mind as she stilled the trembling of her outstretched hand. The words wouldn't work. They never had, not as they did for her mother and her grandmother. She was powerless. But before she could finish the words, the short man was pushed backward, as if he were shot from a cannon. His feet left the ground as he flew against the trunk of the tree behind him.

A gunshot rang through the air.

Lydia wasn't sure if the shot resonated from the short man's firearm as his back hit the trunk or from one of the other men who surrounded them.

"Holy shit!" one of the men shouted.

The other men hastened into the darkness.

The short man scrambled to his feet and stared at Lydia. His hands trembled as he placed one against the trunk to steady himself. As soon as he got his footing, he darted down the path and into the gloom.

Lydia could still feel Robert at her side. He tried to say something but choked on the words.

Blood dripped on the pavement in front of her, a startling red under the light of the park lamp.

Lydia turned to Robert. A lump caught in her throat as her eyes trailed down. Blood covered the front of his shirt.

She grabbed his arm as he stumbled to the ground. "No, no, no," she chanted. She knelt at his side. Their cellphones were in the hands of those men. Robert was a head taller than her, and his muscled body was too heavy for her to carry.

"Help!" she screamed, but her scream was dampened by sobs. Tears blurred Robert's face like rain down a car window.

"You need to get up." She tugged on his arm in vain. "We need to get you to a hospital."

Robert coughed, and a spatter of blood sprinkled onto her light blue dress. His eyes panicked and pleaded. His hand was slippery with blood as Lydia tried to clench it, but it slipped as if oil coated his fingers.

"You have to get up!"

But Robert closed his eyes.

"What a shame," a voice said above her. The voice was layered, like two people spoke at the same time, using the exact same words. One voice sounded like a man's, but a deeper voice came like a growl as he spoke and echoed his words.

Lydia jerked her head up, afraid that yet another mugger came to take advantage of her desperate situation.

The man stood. He wore a dark suit with a bright, red tie. His face was clean-shaven, and his dark hair was slicked back. He looked like a lawyer or an accountant. What was he doing in the park at night?

"He's not dead yet, you know," said the stranger. "You could run out into the street, call for help, but I can tell you that won't do anything." The man looked at his watch. "He has ninety-eight seconds left. If you had put pressure on the wound, he might have gained, I don't know, ten seconds or so."

Lydia pressed both hands against Robert's chest where the blood issued forth. The rusty smell of blood stung her nose as she leaned over him.

The man glanced at his watch again. "Look at that, he just gained thirteen more seconds. My, my, my!"

What was this man talking about? She thought he might be a lunatic, that his mind was so far gone, he would be of no help at all. He might be dangerous. But she didn't have time to choose her friends. Robert was dying. He needed to go to the hospital as soon as possible.

"Do you have a cellphone?" she asked. "Please, call an ambulance."

The man shook his head and knelt across from her. Robert's form rested between them. "Unless, an ambulance arrives in forty-five seconds. It won't matter." He winked.

"What are you talking about?"

"He doesn't have time for me to explain what you already know, Lydia. How long have you pretended to be a normal college girl?"

"Tell me what you want." Lydia narrowed her eyes.

"To make you an offer. But there's not much time for ne-gotiation." The man snapped his fingers, and a scroll of paper appeared in his hands.

Lydia's vision blurred from the tears. Maybe she hadn't seen him take the scroll from his pocket.

"I don't have anything to give." Lydia hoped that wasn't the end of the conversation. Whatever this man wanted, she would gladly give it to help Robert.

The man cocked his head to the side. "You don't have an-ything to give, yet. But as you know, I must make my quota. People are so much less desperate now-a-days. They care so little. But you care a lot, don't you, Lydia?"

She knew what he was. He wasn't a man although he ap-peared as one, but when she searched for his shadow under the light of the lamp, she couldn't find one.

"What do you want?"

"A simple trade. His life will be spared if you offer me the soul of your firstborn child."

Lydia laughed a dry laugh. The story of Rumpelstiltskin entered her mind. If the love of her life wasn't dying on the floor before her, she might have asked something cheeky like, *Will I have to guess your name?* But instead, she said, "I have no children."

"Call it a loan," he said. "And the best kind because it ac-crues no interest."

The thought of selling an unborn child's soul to the devil left a bad taste in Lydia's mouth. She and Robert discussed the idea of having children after the conversation about marriage. They both wanted to make sure that they were on the same page for all the important things before they decided to get hitched.

Robert's breaths came out slow and shallow. Lydia couldn't imagine her life without him. She would miss the way he in-serted her name into popular love songs that he sang in the shower, the way he flared his nostrils whenever he got angry, and all the other little things that he did every day that she didn't feel grateful enough for.

For their second anniversary last year, they went to Augusta, Georgia. By the end of the week, they visited Meadow Garden and the Institute of Art. They wandered the streets of downtown, listened to outdoor jazz shows, and went to a production by the Symphony Orchestra. The city was so beautiful that at the end of the week, Lydia said that she loved being able to spend the entire week with him in such an amazing place, but that the time they spent together seemed too short. All Robert said was, "Don't worry. We have forever."

The demon's offer didn't matter. In less than a minute, Robert would be gone. They talked about children and agreed that one day, that would be a possibility. But as Lydia gave the demon the answer he wanted, she changed her mind about that possibility. Lydia wasn't having any children.

part two

invictus

Twelve

FOUR weeks passed since Nash, Adrianna, Kiran, and Chandra entered the Ninth Circle. I filled those weeks with books about the Circles, the Archangels, and Sheol. Nash had quite a library and no television. I found it hard to distinguish fact from fiction, however. After everything I'd seen, I was willing to believe a much larger range of things than I had before.

Many days, I was bored, and nothing brought me comfort except petting Sim. She followed me wherever I went throughout the house. I missed my music. I couldn't play my guitar, and I left my MP3 player at my house.

I wondered if MP3 players were a thing in Sheol.

I cut off my cast myself with a dagger from Nash's armory. I made sure the steel was darkened: a duller blade than the sharpness of pure Arcadian Steel, but still sharper than blades of other metals.

I lounged in the living room with a book in my lap when a knock echoed down the hall. I answered the door. Bob stood outside.

"You shouldn't be shut up in this house all day, sweetheart," he said.

"I told you, I'm not fighting angels for Lucifer until Nash comes back," I said.

He smiled. "You know, not many people defy the Lady of Darkness. She won't wait much longer."

I folded my arms. Lucifer needed me. I could make angels fall, and it would be much harder to do that if I wasn't a willing participant. "What do you want?"

"I would like to invite you to one of our trial proceedings," he said. "I thought you might enjoy the show."

I raised my eyebrows.

"A demon has failed to meet his one-hundred-year quota," Bob said.

"Why would I want to go to something like that?" I asked. I had been to court a number of times since the police found me in an abandoned house. I was glad when my parents adopted me, and the court visits ended. I couldn't think of anything fun about sitting in a cold courtroom and listening to people talk.

"Because, my dear, you need a bit of fresh air. You look depressed. I wouldn't want you to go killing yourself."

I uncrossed my arms. "Alright. Just let me get dressed." I closed the door.

I came back wearing a black knee-length dress and a pair of black flats.

I tried to hold my breakfast down as Bob sped down the street. He parked outside a marble building with a wraparound staircase.

I waited to see officers at the door who would look in your purse and make you go through a metal detector, but no such security existed.

"Bob, does Sheol have MP3 players?"

"You want an MP3 player?"

"Sure," I shrugged. "If you got one lying around."

Our feet tapped on the marble as Bob and I walked across the floor to the courtroom. I wished I had worn two sweaters.

This courtroom was colder than the one in New Orleans if I remembered correctly.

I hadn't entered a courtroom in ten years. It smelled like aged carpet and old books.

Bob opened the doors of the courtroom and gestured for me to walk inside. The room was packed tighter than a rattlesnake in an ant farm.

Demons talked and laughed. Some looked like people although many had black eyes. Others looked like the creature I saw in my high school bathroom with charred skin and blood red eyes.

"This is the most exciting entertainment in Sheol," Bob said.

Exciting entertainment. I'd been to quite a few court hearings as a foster kid. Once I was placed with a foster family, I went to court every five or six months until I was adopted. Exciting wasn't the word I would use to describe a court proceeding.

"Trust me," said Bob. "You'll have fun." He gestured to an empty seat near the front of the courtroom.

"Where are you going?" I asked.

"Well, you see, I have a special seat." He pointed at a chair off to the side of the judge's bench. He left me on my own in a sea of demons.

The woman next to me glanced over. She had large teeth and a rail thin body. She looked human, but her face was too symmetrical, too perfect. "Oh," she said, "you know Bub."

"Bub?" *She must have a strange accent.*

"Oh, I call him Bub because it's closer to his real name." She winked.

I thought Bob's full name was Robert. I'd never considered that it could be anything else.

Bob took his seat.

A railing separated the audience from the judge's bench and the two tables up front. Two men in suits sat at either table. They were the prosecution and defense attorneys.

The man at the left table wore a pin-striped suit, and his hair was slicked back with gel that made the hair look plastic. The man on the right wore a brown suit and glasses. Another man sat with him at the table, the defendant. Although he slumped in his chair, his torso was longer than his attorney's. His skin was as pale as a corpse.

A door opened behind the judge's bench, and Lucifer took a seat. Instead of a black judge's robe, she wore a long, blood red robe of the same style, length, and texture. Her dark hair was pin straight. Her burgundy red lipstick matched her red heels, which I caught a glimpse of when she walked in. She was a flame, commanding my attention.

I expected the courtroom to quiet down once Lucifer entered, but the conversation and laughter continued.

I knew to rise when the judge entered so I stood, but no one else did. When I was about to sit back down, a man stood up from behind the short railing. The bailiff? He shouted, "Get up everybody! Get up!"

A few people listened. The rest only laughed.

"Okay," said Lucifer. "Sheol versus Malzal."

No one told us to sit back down, but the people who did stand, including me, slowly went back to their seats.

"Good morning, Your Honor," said the man in the pin-striped suit, "Virgil Geoffrey Netherson for Sheol."

"Morning, Your Honor." The man in the brown suit stood and wiped his sweaty forehead on a napkin. "Ambrose B. Letchfield for the defense."

"Good morning, gentlemen," said Lucifer. "Mr. Netherson."

"Your Honor, the deciding factor on whether Mr. Malzal is guilty is the answer to this question: Did he meet his quota?" said Netherson. "The answer to that question is no."

The audience howled with laughter.

Netherson continued. "As the record shows, the defendant was commissioned to collect one thousand souls, yet he has only submitted contracts for nine hundred and ninety-two souls."

"Your Honor," Letchfield interrupted, "if I may, Mr. Malzal doesn't deny that he failed to meet his quota, but he would like to mitigate his punishment with a defense."

"I will hear any testimony related to mitigation of the punishment at the sentencing hearing," said Lucifer. "Does your client wish to plead guilty and move onto sentencing?"

"No, Your Honor," said Letchfield. "We would like to proceed with trial."

"Alright." Lucifer sighed and rested her chin in her hand as she leaned her elbow against the judge's bench. "Prosecution, bring forth your witnesses."

"The Prosecution rests, Your Honor. I believe the record speaks for itself," said Mr. Netherson.

"Objection," said Letchfield. "Despite what Mr. Netherson says, nothing has been introduced into the record."

"Fine." Netherson slumped his shoulders and rose from his seat. "I call Xander O'Reilly to the stand."

"Ooo," several members of the audience cooed.

A short, balding man rose from the sea of demons and approached the front of the courtroom. Demons jeered at him as he passed while others cheered. I wondered if bets had been placed.

I raised my eyebrow as the bailiff helped him climb over the railing. Xander O'Reilly took a seat in the chair alongside the judge's bench.

Netherson got up from his seat and approached the witness stand. "Mr. O'Reilly, state for the Court what you do for a *living*."

The crowd laughed at Netherson's emphasis on the word *living* as if that was the greatest pun imaginable.

"I'm the records keeper for Sheol's demon contracts. I work in Limbo."

"Do you know Mr. Malzal?"

"No, not personally, but I know his quota."

"And what is his quota?"

"Objection, Your Honor, hearsay." Letchfield's hair was plastered to his forehead by a thick layer of sweat.

"Your Honor, I'm referring to an official, notarized document," said Netherson.

"No such document has been introduced," Letchfield countered.

"Objection sustained," said Lucifer.

"I'll rephrase," said Netherson. "How do you know his quota?"

"I have to collect and file his contracts."

"Ah ha," said Netherson. A ripple of excitement ran through his voice. He reached for a folder on his desk and withdrew a sheet of paper. "And what is this?" he asked the witness.

"Why, that's Malzal's contract."

"Ah…" the audience trailed off.

"And what does it say?"

"It says that Malzal had one hundred years to collect a thousand souls in exchange for one hundred years in the Outer Region."

"And how many sales contracts for souls did he produce after that one-hundred-year period?"

"Nine hundred ninety-two."

"I have no further questions for this witness." Netherson went back to his seat.

Lucifer looked to the defense attorney. "Mr. Letchfield."

Letchfield remained seated. "No questions, Your Honor."

Xander O'Reilly left the stand, and as he attempted to climb back over the railing, he fell onto the other side. Giggles erupted from the audience. When O'Reilly stood back up, they threw apples at him as he walked down the aisle. The apples were bruised, and their mealy guts spread across the floor.

"Mr. Netherson?" Lucifer's voice rang through over the noise of the crowd.

"The prosecution rests."

"I have one witness," said Letchfield. "I call my client, Mr. Malzal."

Malzal glanced at his attorney with a look of pale horror. Letchfield whispered to him, and Malzal nodded. He walked up to the witness stand and took a seat.

"Mr. Malzal, were you able to make your quota this century?" asked Letchfield.

"No." Malzal whispered.

"Speak up," said Lucifer.

"No." Malzal increased his volume.

"Why weren't you able to?"

"I was stuck in a possession." Two bulbous nubs appeared at the temples of Malzal's large forehead.

"Will you please explain?"

"Sure, a young girl...woman. I had to have her."

I cringed at his choice of words.

"So, you possessed her?" asked Letchfield.

"I did, and it set me back. I had to wait until I was exercised, but as you know priests aren't the go-to-guys nowadays. Instead, her parents brought her to a hospital where the doctors put her on all kinds of psychotic drugs. The drugs affected me, and I got...trapped."

"The involuntary drugs you were given prevented you from letting go of the possession?"

"Objection, Your Honor." Netherson didn't bother to get up from his seat. "Leading."

"Sustained," Lucifer said.

"What stopped you from letting go of the girl?"

"They pumped her with drugs. I took over her body so the drugs affected me too. I couldn't think straight enough to get out." Ridged points poked out from Malzal's skin where the nubs had been.

"How were you able to escape?"

"I threw a fit. Had her speak a little Latin. Threw stuff around the house. Floated up to the ceiling. The whole bit. So, her parents called for a priest. They were scared out of their wits. At first the priest refused, but I blabbered in several different languages and floated above the bed."

Malzal's teeth were as sharp and needle-like as a cobra's. *Why hadn't I noticed that before?* The Veil was lifting. "After that, he decided to perform the exorcism. The exorcism was unofficial and all, but still worked. I crawled from the Second Circle of Sheol back to the Outer Region, explaining all along the way that I had contracts that needed to be delivered."

My thoughts burned. Malzal escaped the Second Circle. That meant that Nash and the others had a chance.

"And how long were you possessed before you were able to escape?"

"Three years. The last three years of my contract."

"Thank you, Mr. Malzal. I'm so sorry you had to go through that ordeal. No further questions, Your Honor."

"Anything for this witness, Mr. Netherson."

"Yes, Your Honor."

Netherson remained seated with his pen in the corner of his mouth. He pointed the pen at Mr. Malzal when he spoke. "So, you possessed a girl, and you got *stuck*?"

"That's right."

"Did you have to possess her? Was that part of your contract?"

"No, but..."

"You just wanted to, is that right?"

"Well, sure I wanted to but..." The horns curled above his head, twisting from their fleshy nubs.

"In fact, you had three more years left before you decided to take that little vacation."

"Is there a question?" asked Letchfield.

"Nothing further, Your Honor."

Malzal quietly left the witness seat and shuffled back to his attorney. His forehead wrinkled, forcing his eyebrows low above his eyes as the weight of the horns pressed the skin down.

"Do you have any other witnesses?" Lucifer tapped her long, dark fingernails against the bench.

"No, Your Honor."

"I'll hear closing now."

Netherson stood up and straightened his jacket. "Your Honor, what we have here is a simple breach of contract. Malzal was asked to deliver a thousand souls to Sheol. He was given an adequate period of one hundred years, and yet he chose to wait until the last three years of his contract to take a *siesta* inside some girl. Your Honor, I ask that you find this man guilty."

The crowd hooted, and demons clapped.

"Your Honor." Letchfield raised his voice. "Mr. Malzal toiled for one hundred years to deliver Sheol one thousand souls. He was a mere eight souls short of his quota due to the fact that he was wrongfully imprisoned. I ask that you consider that in your decision, Your Honor, and find Mr. Malzal innocent of these charges."

Letchfield wiped his forehead and patted his client's shoulder.

"I have considered the testimony and the evidence." Lucifer twined her fingers together. "I find that Mr. Malzal has indeed violated his contract, and despite his excuses, I find him guilty."

"Move for sentencing," said Netherson.

"Of course," said Lucifer.

"Please Your Honor, give us time to prepare."

"No, you've had your captive audience, Mr. Letchfield. I'll proceed with the sentencing now. Alright. Before the Court imposes a sentence, I will call upon each attorney. Is there anything else you two would like to gab about?"

"No, Your Honor," said Netherson.

"My client would like to say something, Your Honor."

"If he must."

Malzal stood. "Your Honor, Morning Star."

A few snickers emanated from the audience.

The horns, brown and twisted, rose three feet above Malzal's head. "Your Honor, I humbly ask that you allow me to fulfill the remainder of my contract plus one thousand more souls. I can get those souls for you in less than fifty years."

"You couldn't get those souls for me in a hundred."

"Please, Your Honor. I ask that you not condemn me to the Circles. I'm deeply sorry for this whole ordeal. Please let me continue to gather souls for you."

Lucifer snickered. "You committed adultery in your former life and were to spend eternity in the Second Circle, isn't that right, Mr. Malzal?"

Malzal nodded. "That's right, Your Honor."

"And the only reason that you're not in the Second Circle, is because *I* allowed you to gather souls for me."

Malzal remained silent.

"It is by my grace, that you aren't swept up in a whirlwind of filth and lust, having your flesh ripped off for an eternity by its powerful blasts. You know what that makes you, Mr. Malzal? A traitor. And if there's one sin more deplorable than all the others, it's treachery. Especially when it's against me. I hereby sentence you..."

Silence hung over the room for the first time in the entire proceeding.

"...to the Pit."

Laughter, cheers, and boos echoed through the room as Lucifer smiled from her bench.

Malzal's face went paler as two burly officers took him by each arm. His attorney whispered to him, but the pained expression on Malzal's face didn't fade as he was carried away.

"Please, Your Honor," Malzal shouted, "send me to the Ninth Circle. I beg you, please!"

Lucifer rose from her seat. "Court is adjourned." She slammed the gavel.

BOB drove me back to Nash's house. As the car idled outside the garage, I asked, "Why did you show me that?"

"I wanted you to see what it's really like down here," he said. "You got to see what very few people do before they have to choose. You got a chance to see Hell the way Lucifer runs it. What Nash has, he had to screw someone over to get it, maybe even a lot of people. You shouldn't be so worried about him."

"I'm not fighting angels until he comes back." My voice was firm and didn't waver. Did Bob think he could get me to stop caring about Nash?

Bob shrugged. "I tried." He flashed me a mouth of white teeth. "In Sheol, you have to look out for number one. Sometimes that means destroying parts of yourself. The part of you that has loyalty to Nash is going to get you in a lot of trouble.

I suggest you burn it away before your whole being is in the fire."

I reached for the handle.

"Just remember," he said. "In Hell, a man chooses himself over everybody else."

I opened the car door and slammed it behind me.

Later that afternoon, I went to Nash's library. I scanned the books for any titles that might help me to find out more about the Circles. I found one titled, *Seven Princes, Nine Circles.*

I opened the book. I wanted to know everything I could about the Ninth Circle. Maybe I could help Nash and the others out.

I found a brief description near the beginning of the book. The Ninth Circle was reserved for those who committed treachery. It is divided into four rounds each beneath a frozen, icy lake. The worse the sin, the deeper the tortured are buried.

I leafed through the book to find a more detailed description. My fingers flew from page to page as I searched for words that might be relevant to my search. I stopped when I turned the page to a picture of a large fly with bulbous red eyes. The caption read that this creature was Beelzebub, one of the seven princes of Hell, right-hand man to Lucifer herself. He is the demon of gluttony.

The words of the woman in court came back to me. "Bub…it's closer to his real name."

Beelzebub. Bob?

Thirteen

I T was midnight, and still I could find nothing to help me formulate a rescue plan to save Nash, Adrianna, Kiran, and Chandra.

I read books upon books about the Circles, and all I found out so far was that they're terrible. Each Circle was a different level of torture from being torn apart by hellhounds to being trapped inside a fiery tomb.

I slammed the big book onto the coffee table.

Tom lounged on the couch as he looked through one of his great tomes. He jumped when the book hit the table.

"How can you just sit there?" I said. "We have to find a way to get Nash and the others out of the Circles."

Tom swung his feet to the floor and grabbed an apple out of the bowl on the table. "We're not going to do that." He bit into the apple.

"We have to do something."

"You don't understand," he said. "You don't just walk out of the Ninth Circle. What Nash did was very stupid. Some demon down there is probably making him his bitch right now."

I folded my arms and sunk down on the opposite end of the couch. "So, what, we give up?"

"We give up on Nash, yes," said Tom. "But Bob found us a new team. We'll have to work with them. If we don't, it's the Pit."

"I thought they were your friends."

"You can't keep friends in Hell."

You can't keep friends anywhere.

"How did you get here anyway?" I asked.

He grimaced.

"I'm sorry was that a rude question?" I turned my head to the side.

Tom sighed. "Actually, it is, but I know you're trying to be mean right now because you think I don't care about Nash as much as you do. I'm not giving you my life story, but suffice to say, I chose to be in Sheol."

"Why would anyone *choose* Hell?"

"Some people are suited for it." Tom smirked.

I folded my arms. "What about the Circles?"

"Not everyone is tortured. Lucifer offers deals: collect a hundred souls, possess so-and-so, or wander the Earth wrecking the lives of humans."

"That seems like a lot of work for someone who *decided* against paradise."

"There are lots of theories." Tom returned to his book.

"Then, why don't you talk about them?"

Tom looked at me. "Because you're far from able to discuss them. Contrary to popular belief I don't like to hear myself talk."

"Try me," I said. "I'm able to hold my own with the best of them."

Tom sighed. "Some souls are destined for Sheol. They don't make a conscious decision, but the guilt eats them up inside. They don't believe they belong anywhere else. But for those who choose it, the payoff is a life much like the one they lived on Earth, except they're at the top. They live in nice houses, get the best booze, and don't pay for any of it."

He sneered. "The best part: they get to skip Purgatory. Everybody sins. They got it so locked up in Heaven, they don't let anybody in until they've purged. You think doing bad things to other people is shitty? Just imagine getting shitty stuff done to you every day for hundreds of thousands of years. Starving. Running through walls of flames. Most humans aren't in Heaven, they're in Purgatory. It's not as bad as the Circles, but Lucifer gives everyone who wants it a way out. A lot of people take it. There aren't very many humans who even know what Heaven is like."

"Why does Raphael want to shut the gates to humans if there aren't that many there?" I asked.

"Well, just because *most* humans are in Purgatory, doesn't mean there aren't still a lot in Heaven too. There are more people in Heaven than there are on Earth, but three times that many in Purgatory. If Raphael's anything like the original Fallen, then it's the thought of humans living in Heaven at all that bothers him. Imagine being an angel and feeling like somebody's butler. Humans are whiny, little bitches, no offense."

I darted my head towards the front hallway. Voices echoed into the living room.

Tom and I got up from the couch and headed for the door. Bob and three others stood in the foyer. Three men, all dressed like they were ready for training.

"Here they are now," said Bob. "Lia, Tom, this is Malcolm, Alex, and Chip."

"Hi." Tom shook the shorter man's hand. "You must be Chip."

"No." Bob patted the tall, blond man's shoulder, "this is Chip. That's Malcolm."

My skin prickled. Malcolm was only a little taller than me, but his skin was blood red, and his eyes were black, snake-like slits.

"Malcolm likes to go au naturel," said Bob. He didn't mean unclothed. Malcolm wore the same black clothing as the rest of the party, but it didn't hide the forked tail that whipped from behind his back.

Bob looked at me. "Alex is Chandra's brother, so it's kind of the same, right? He can't fight too well, but he looks a bit like Nash, doesn't he? Well, except for the eyes."

I folded my arms over my chest. "Bob, you're not replacing Nash."

Bob put his hand on my shoulder and led me away from the group. I squirmed beneath his touch. "Listen," he said. "I did what I could for you, Lia. I did, but the boss isn't having it anymore. You've got to collect more than one fallen angel or the deal's off. I'm afraid, she'll have you thrown into the Pit and that'll be the end of it."

I uncrossed my arms and looked at him wide-eyed.

He pursed his lips and shrugged his shoulders. "Look, why don't you work with us, okay? Once Raphael is gone, Lucifer doesn't have to worry about him finding another way to lock down Heaven, and you don't have to worry about your soul. These guys," he nodded his head over to the group, "they're good. Maybe better than Nash and the others. And, if you like Nash that much, you could always go back to him if he ever makes it out of the Ninth Circle. What do you say?"

I glared at him with narrowed eyes. "One training session," I said, "but I want you out of this house, *Beelzebub*."

He smiled when I said his true name.

"Alright." He put his hands up in surrender. "I'm out. You do your thing. Oh, and I got you something." He reached into his pocket and withdrew an MP3 player. "Peace offering."

WE practiced all afternoon. It felt weird to use Nash's weapons and his training field. I landed on my back more times than I liked.

"They're good," said Tom.

I took a swig of water from the bottle I carried. "Yeah, that's what Bob said."

Tom sighed. "Look, I've been hanging with them for what you would consider an eternity. So, yeah, it really sucks that they're gone. I wanted to finish this fight with Nash, but if we don't do this, I'm destined for nothing but the Pit. I don't know what Bob said to you, but knowing him it was probably a threat. If Nash gets out of the Ninth Circle, it will be because of him, Kiran, Chandra, and Adrianna. There's nothing we can do out here, but continue to fight."

"I'm sorry," I said. "But I'm not going to stop trying. I'll train. I'll fight angels. But I'm not going to stop looking for answers."

Alex, sweaty after fighting Malcolm, settled down next to us while Malcolm and Chip sparred together.

"Aren't you worried about your sister in the Circles?" I asked.

"Chandra can handle herself. She started fighting when she was twelve. I see her more now than I ever did in life." He swallowed a long draw of water.

I looked at Tom, critically. At least Alex had hope.

"Anyway, I hope you don't mind if I use the shower." Alex stood up.

Tom winked at him. A subtle smile lit his face.

TOM swiveled in the chair. "I've checked it out," he said. "It's an Archdemon, but he's alone."

"He's in New Orleans?"

An orange dot on the screen radiated circles from its center.

Tom nodded. "Demons like the city. It has a great night-life." He smirked.

A demon in *my* city. I wondered if I'd seen him before, if he was one of the ones who frightened me over the years. Perhaps he was. I couldn't let him lurk around.

"Do you think the others would be up for it? It would be their first time," I said.

Tom shook his head. "No, it wouldn't."

I put my hands on my hips. "What do you mean?"

"I sent them after Andromeda last week."

"You found her?"

"Yeah." Tom ran a hand through his hair. "She didn't get far from where we left her."

"Why didn't you tell me? I could have gone with them."

"That's why I didn't tell you. I'm not sure I should even be telling you about this one."

"Just because Nash isn't here, it doesn't mean I'm no longer part of this team," I said. "Making angels fall isn't the only thing I'm good for."

"But it's a pretty big thing to be good for," said Tom. "Every time I send you out there, I'm sending you to possible slaughter."

I folded my arms. "I can't let everything Nash taught me fade away. I can't get soft."

"You haven't gotten *out* of soft."

I groaned.

"Did Andromeda tell anyone?" I asked.

"About you?" Tom shook his head. "It's not likely she met with any other angels where she was, and not being able to fly, she couldn't have made it back to Heaven. Besides, no angel will listen to an angel without light."

I wasn't so sure about that.

I met Malcolm, Alex, and Chip outside on the field. "No training today." I stopped in front of them. "We have a demon to track down."

"A demon?" Malcom squinted at me. "We didn't sign up to hunt our own kind."

I hated the way he looked at me with those thin, black eyes. He was always scowling. Maybe that was because demon faces were less expressive. He couldn't be angry *all* the time.

"Well, someone has to do it." My hands were on my hips. "Lucifer won't be happy if we ignore a demon who's been loafing around on Earth."

I thought of Nash. He wouldn't pass up on a demon hunt. This was what he did. He ferried thousands of demons back to Sheol, and he was good at it.

"I'm the leader of this team. We're going to fight." That always worked for Nash.

Malcolm pursed his lips. "Fine." He, Alex and Chip shuffled out of the room.

"That's our new team," I said to Tom. "They won't even hunt demons."

"They don't want to turn on their own," said Tom. "We're not looked upon very highly by our demon brethren."

That night, Alex opened the portal, and we stepped through into a dingy bathroom with tiled walls and wooden stalls.

Too bad Lucifer wouldn't give me the ability to open portals. Going through portals was nauseating, but it would be nice to go where I wanted, when I wanted. I'd still have to consult with Tom though. Portals could go anywhere since Sheol was like a disk, rapidly bisecting sections of Earth. Knowing me, I'd probably portal myself into a volcano.

I led the way out of the bathroom and into a dark hallway that led to a room with a bar and pool table. Loud music played and people talked, danced, and drank. The door was open to a

crowded street of people walking back and forth down the covered walkways and in the middle of the road. Lights glowed
from signs beneath balconies with black iron railings.

We walked out onto Bourbon Street, and although we were
all dressed in black and wore swords at our hips, we didn't gar-
ner a second glance.

"How are we going to find the demon here?" Alex peered
up and down the crowded street.

The stench of beer stung my nostrils. "Come on." My feet
stuck to the brick street as I walked. People stumbled and
laughed, but one man weaved through the crowd on deft feet.
He wasn't drunk, and he wasn't with anyone.

"There." I pointed out the man.

"Him?" asked Malcolm.

"He didn't come here for the party," I said. "And he doesn't
seem to be making a beeline towards the strip clubs."

We followed the man. He was tall, maybe the same height
as Bob with long, black hair pulled into a ponytail and dark
skin. He wore a fitted jacket and dark jeans. His hands were
in his pockets as he walked.

He walked down Canal street. Cars drove by and parked
behind a gate under the overpass. Carts and tents were set up
by the homeless. One woman huddled among the trash in a
dirty tank top. A man in tattered clothes was petting his dog.

Tarps covered the ground, and graffiti was etched into the
stone walls like a gallery without gatekeepers. Broken and dirty
lawn chairs leaned over next to an empty, blue shopping cart
and a flat, gray mattress.

Low hanging clouds covered the stars and saturated the sky
with thick, black tar. The tar melted from the sky and sent
deep shadows to the edges of the city and between dark alley-
ways.

The passing cars hummed. The smell of exhaust tingled my nostrils. I held the back of my hand to my nose, stifling a sneeze.

Chip crept ahead of us. Something whished beneath his coat. Chip had a tail! The tail was long and thin like a lizard's. I'd lifted the Veil again. It would be nice to know how to control that.

The further we walked, the quieter the streets became. I rubbed my arms. The silence unnerved me. The quiet always did that to me. That's why I found it hard to sleep without the TV on.

The demon stopped at a house several blocks away. We watched him from a few houses down. He walked inside. I signaled for Malcolm, Alex, and Chip to follow me. We approached the house. Malcolm swung the door open. The creak cracked the silence.

Chip wore a worried look on his face. I passed him, moving into the dark and musty house. Worn wood floor trailed down the hallway. The plaster walls were gray in the night.

On my right was a living room with a sofa on wooden feet and a small television with bunny ear receptors. To my left was a dining room. The long table had a dozen cushioned chairs around it. A dusty chandelier was above the table.

Stairs were in front of us, and upon the stairs were black footprints. With a wave, I signaled the group to move forward. I drew my sword. The metal zinged as I released the blade from its sheath and took the stairs.

The footsteps led to a room. I opened the door and looked around. A small bed was catty-cornered in the room.

On the bed was an old woman. Her skin was leathery. Her body was thin and wrapped in a loose nightgown. She sat upright in the bed. Her eyes were a milky blue.

The others stepped behind me as I spotted something in the opposite corner. The form was tall and black with red eyes.

A circle glowed around us.

"He tricked us," said Malcolm.

The demon unhinged itself from the wall and walked to the edge of the circle. "Mari tricked you," he said. "She was always a most capable witch even without her sight."

"Belial." Malcolm wore a look of recognition.

"You know him?" I asked.

Malcolm gulped. "We shouldn't have come."

"That's right you shouldn't have come," said Belial. "No demon can leave this circle."

"Well, I'm not a demon, and I'm not afraid of you." I stepped out the circle and faced the demon, my sword in front of me.

Belial squinted. "Lydia." He breathed the name and stepped closer to me despite the sword raised against him.

"I thought you were dead."

"I'm not Lydia," I said. "I don't know who you're talking about." I backed away as he tried to touch my face.

"No, you're not Lydia," he said. "But you are someone close to her. You look just like her."

Lydia. I had never heard that name before. She was a woman I looked just like, but who I didn't know. "My mother?"

fourteen

Y mother.

"What do you know about my mother?" My sword was still pointed at him.

Belial put his hands up, but his voice was uneven and mocking. "Hey, we're all friends here. I wouldn't hurt the daughter of one of my own."

"What do you mean one of your own?"

"Lia, don't talk to him," hissed Malcolm. "Just break the ring and let us out."

"Do that," said Belial, "and you'll learn nothing from me."

I looked back at Malcolm, Alex, and Chip caged by an invisible force. Their eyes were desperate and afraid. But I saw hundreds of demons like Belial. It wasn't until later that I realized it wasn't Belial's appearance that frightened them, but his power.

"How do you know my birth mother?" I asked.

Belial's lips spread to either side of his face and long, pointed teeth were visible beneath short, reddened gums. "She is one of my own. A witch. She was one of the best."

The small, old woman whimpered in the corner.

Belial looked upon her with compassion. "So, are you, my dear, Mari." That seemed to appease the woman. Her lips stopped quivering in a frown, and she returned to her blank gaze. She concentrated on keeping Alex, Malcolm, and Chip entrapped within the glowing circle.

Belial continued, "When I saw Lydia for the first time, she cradled you in her arms in a tight blanket. She was afraid I came for her child. Lydia was so desperate, so fragile. She had done something terrible. She made a deal she couldn't turn back on so I helped her."

"You helped her perform a spell?" I asked.

Belial frowned. The moonlight touched the side of his face. His skin was black and scaly like a lizard's. "I'm flattered you think *I* can do magic, but that's not the case and unfortunately, I haven't taken the time to study many spells especially the arcane ones like the one your mother wished to perform. She didn't understand why she didn't know magic like her mother and her mother's mother. She knew a few incantations but had no power."

I narrowed my eyes. "So, how did you help her?"

"I allowed her to drink my blood."

My hand tightened on my sword. "I don't understand."

"My blood gave her power. It is what made her a witch."

I shook my head. "And you just happened to come to her at the right time?"

"No." Belial shook his head. "I didn't know your dear mother from Adam. Someone told me about her. He called himself: The Redeemer."

The Redeemer. That was the second time I'd heard that name: first from the mouth of a fallen angel and now from this demon.

"He told me to tell Lydia about the spell that could help her daughter."

I squinted at him.

"I didn't care one way or the other," said Belial. "I've spent thousands of years looking for desperate souls to become my creations. I would have told her anything. But I knew the spell wouldn't work. Even an experienced witch who could lure an angel couldn't perform such a spell without someone dying in the process and utterly ruining the whole thing. But I don't tell my children what they can and cannot do with their magic. Lydia wouldn't have listened to me if I warned her against it, and I doubted she would have become what I wanted her to become for any less. But you are here so I guess she didn't kill you. Maybe she decided not to do the spell after all."

"She did do the spell," I whispered. "And it worked."

Belial looked at me in surprise. "You little liar."

"I've touched angels, and I've seen their wings burst into flames and their eyes grow dark. My mother turned me into a monster."

Belial's face twisted into a grimace of anger. "Your mother earned herself a one-way ticket to Hell to save your life, girl. Her mistake was made before you were born, and she sacrificed everything to fix it. You're mortal. I can smell it on you and running around with demons. You're undoing everything your mother gave her soul for. She should hate you." His words were laced with venom, and he lurched forward.

I tried to avoid him but fell to my back. As his dark shadow covered me, I reached up and dusted the salt particles, breaking the circle.

Belial's lips curled into a smile. On all fours, he crawled to the open window and leapt out.

I scrambled to my feet and rushed to the window, thinking I might find him in a mess of broken bones, but nothing but tall grass and overgrown bushes rested below.

The woman on the bed screamed a shrill, long scream. She chanted in words I couldn't understand. The bed rattled, the legs thudding on the floor in an off-beat rhythm. My feet lifted from the ground. I tried to grip the windowsill, but that didn't stop my body from hitting the ceiling.

I looked around the room, panicked. Alex, Malcolm, and Chip floated near the ceiling beside me. We were dropped. My body hit the floor with a loud thud. My elbow hit the wooden baseboards, and pain screamed up my arm. My sword clattered beside me.

"Open the goddamn portal," Malcolm screamed.

Alex scrambled to his feet. His fingers were spread, hand out to the empty space. But before he could open the portal, an unseen force slammed him against the wall.

The old woman continued to chant. Malcolm unsheathed his dagger and aimed for the woman.

"No," I screamed.

The dagger flew towards her. But right before the blade sank into her chest, the dagger stopped in mid-air, turned, the tip pointing away from her, and shot towards Malcolm.

The blade sank deep into Malcolm's red chest. Blood oozed from around the dagger and onto the floor.

The old woman stopped chanting. She sniffed the air. She was on her hands and knees on the bed like a cat. She crawled from the bed to the floor where Malcolm's blood soaked the floorboards. She started lapping it up with her tongue, scooping it up into her hands and sipping it.

I dry-heaved as the blood ran down her face and over her white, loose nightgown. She searched the ground for more.

While the woman was distracted, Alex opened the portal. Malcolm held a hand to his chest. We rushed through and returned to Sheol without Belial.

WE climbed out to the street in front of Nash's house. Distances in Sheol didn't match the distances on Earth, but I hadn't quite figured out the ratio.

"We don't hunt demons," Malcolm grunted. He pulled the dagger out of his chest, and more of his blood spilled onto the street. I was a little sick as I thought about the woman kneeling in the gore and feeding it into her mouth.

"Look, I'm sorry," I said. "But if we can't work as a team to hunt demons, then we'll die if we go against an angel. Nash—"

"Nash isn't here," said Malcolm. "You can't run things as if you're saving his place. Lucifer wants us to hunt angels, not demons. Demons and angels are completely different. They don't have the same fighting styles, the same weaknesses. Who would think killing demons is good practice for hunting angels?"

"Nash did," I said. "And he's coming back. You're just warming his seat and not doing a very good job of it." I found it easy to be mean to Malcolm. He didn't look human.

I walked back to the house and climbed the stairs to my room.

Sim sat at the edge of the bed, and stared at the corner of the wall near the ceiling.

"What are you doing, silly cat?" I scratched her behind the ears and dove into bed. Everything hurt, and I'm sure I earned a few bruises from falling from the ceiling. I was lucky I didn't have any broken bones.

Sim yawned, jumped onto the bed, and strode over to me. She laid down on my chest, and I stroked her fur. "You miss Mom and Dad, don't you?"

Sim meowed and purred as I scratched under her chin. Sim liked to follow Mom around the house and curl up at her feet wherever she stopped. I think Mom loved Sim the most. I was glad she found her way to me. Mom wouldn't have trusted Jonah to take care of her.

Neither Mom nor Dad trusted Jonah to do anything, and now I understood why. When I was younger, I stayed after school to try out for the school play. Jonah was supposed to pick me up. Mom worked late, and Dad had the flu. He could barely get up to use the bathroom. Night fell when Dad's car pulled up. Jonah wasn't answering his calls, and I hadn't gotten home, so Dad dragged himself out of bed and came to get me.

His face lit up with relief when he saw me. He cursed Jonah, the first time he'd done that in front of me. He tried to shelter me from all that was bad in the world. I think that was the day things changed between him and my uncle.

Now, I hated him too.

I opened my locket and gazed at the pictures of Mom and Dad. They both looked so happy.

I turned over onto my side, and Sim leapt off the bed to wander around the room. I stared at the blank, white wall. I had been in Sheol for two and a half months, I missed Christmas and New Year's. If I stayed much longer, I'd miss Mardi Gras and Easter too. But I didn't have anyone to spend them with anyway, and I had nowhere to go once I left.

I didn't like the twisted way Belial interpreted what my birth mom did to me. She *saved* me? She turned me into a horrid tool.

Goose bumps peppered my skin. I blinked as I tried not to cry.

fifteen

I strummed my guitar. I didn't have anything to amplify the sound, but I didn't want to lose my calluses. While I played, I listened to music on the MP3 player Bob gave me.

I hadn't spoken to Malcolm, Alex, Chip, or Tom since we found Belial. I didn't come down for training or dinner but snuck downstairs late at night to eat leftovers cold from the fridge. Tom didn't look for me. He was probably happy to have the library all to himself.

Bob's car was in the driveway a few times. I dared him to come upstairs and tell me what Lucifer expected of me. I'd tell him where to shove it.

A knock came to my door. I had the same feeling I get when I'm presenting something to the class for a school project, an edgy nervousness that I hadn't expected in a situation so familiar. I answered the door.

Tom stood in the hall. Dark circles colored the areas under his eyes. "I'm going to be gone for a couple of days. I know you probably wouldn't have even known I was gone, but I thought I'd be nice and tell you anyway. Just in case you come looking for me."

"Where are you going?"

"To track a demon." He yawned the words.

"You don't look like you're up for that?"

"I'm fine. I just didn't get any sleep last night."

"It won't matter anyway," I said. "You'll never convince Malcolm to hunt it."

"No, but it's still my job."

I raised an eyebrow. "I could go with you."

"That's alright. Someone should stay in case Nash comes back."

I squinted. "But you don't think Nash is coming back."

"Look, Alex is going with me. I'll be fine."

"Okay," I said slowly. Part of me was a little relieved he didn't want me to go.

That evening, I went to the library and pulled any books that might be useful and piled them near the armchair. I read or skimmed most of them. I drank a cup of coffee as I read and tried to stay awake. I blared the rock music on my MP3 player to full blast. Midnight neared when I picked up the last book. I reread the same sentence three times.

I slammed the book closed. I wasn't getting anywhere with these books. I hadn't come across any loopholes or shortcuts. I put my head in my hands and closed my eyes.

Maybe Tom was right. What choice did I have anymore? Wait!

I was the only one who could stop Raphael. I refused to go up against anymore angels without my friends, but Lucifer forced my hand on that. Tom and I couldn't do much to help them if we went alone, but if *I* went, Lucifer would come after me. She'd send all her generals too. Maybe a few fallen angels.

Bob's threat was empty, and I knew that. The war for Heaven would go on with or without me. If Lucifer thought throwing me into the Pit could stop Raphael, she would have done that already. I was her prized possession, her ticket to making Raphael kneel. All I needed to do was enter the Circles and survive.

I didn't tell Tom what I was up to. He would try to stop me.

I pet Sim and wrote a letter to Tom. He'd be away for two days and wouldn't find it until I was gone. The First Circle was several miles beyond the Pit, and each Circle was a thousand miles wide.

No amount of planning would prepare me for what I was about to do. I might die, and, if I did, no more deals could be made. Lucifer would have only one place for me—the Pit.

I grabbed a small bag from the closet and packed some food. After I secured my dagger and sword to my side, I grabbed the keys to Nash's car.

I never drove before, but it couldn't be too hard.

As I raced down the stairs, the door opened, and my heart stilled. I would be discovered. My plan to save Nash and the others would be dashed.

My hand gripped the bannister as the door crept open, and Nash stood with his back to the dull gray sky of Shoel.

I cleaned the cut above Nash's eye with gauze from the first aid kit. Bruises patterned his face and neck.

Nash's eyes were distant as if he imagined something terrible. What awful things had he experienced in the Circles? Would he ever be the same?

"Adrianna?" I asked.

"She's okay," said Nash. "Her wounds sealed up. Though, like the rest of us, she got a few new ones along the way. Kiran is with her."

I didn't ask about Chandra. I felt guilty for that later.

I was surprised to see cuts and bruises on Nash. He didn't even bruise when he trained with Kiran.

I taped a bandage to the cut. "Okay, all done."

"One more," he said.

He pulled up his shirt and revealed a long, angry slash across his chest. Blood seeped from the wound. The blood was dark because of the amber light of the living room.

"I think you might need stitches for that one," I said.

"In the kit." He gestured with his head as he removed his shirt.

"You want me to stitch you up?"

"Who else is going to?"

"There aren't any hospitals in Hell?"

He laughed. "You can do it. Just pinch the skin together as you thread the needle through. It heals on its own, but it'll take time. I don't want to ruin another shirt while I wait. I also don't want to go through the pain of dried blood sticking to the bandage."

I picked up the needle and thread. Felicia's mom taught me the lost art of hand stitching. She was a little bit of a hippy. Felicia's lack of enthusiasm about sewing seemed to bother her so she was happy to get me involved. My fingers were deft and capable from years of playing the guitar.

Nash cringed as I pinched the skin back together and eased the hooked needle through. I sewed from one end of the cut to the other. The wound closed as I sewed.

Nash gritted his teeth until I finished.

I wrapped the bandages around his torso and taped the loose end. As I wrapped, I noticed large round wounds on Nash's back near his shoulder blades.

"Do you need me to look at your back?" I asked.

"No, just minor cuts, but nothing too terrible. Most of my injuries healed before I got back."

"Yeah," I said. "You were gone for a long time. I thought you might be gone forever."

A couple weeks passed, and I told Bob that I didn't need my new team anymore. He was surprised that Nash made it out of the Ninth Circle and through the other eight on the way out.

As Nash's wounds healed, he sat out on training as did Chandra, Adrianna, and Kiran. I practiced my stances under Nash's instruction.

Adrianna and Kiran showed up for dinner a couple nights later. Adrianna looked like she was never in the fight at all. I was sure the cut along her cheek would scar, but her skin was clear and white as always. She wore a shirt that cut off right above the waist, no gouges, no bleeding. All was healed as if she received the most advanced plastic surgery on the planet.

She knocked the breath out of my lungs when she gathered me into a hug. "You saved my life. I'll spend an eternity repaying you."

I patted her shoulders, but was more comfortable once she released me from the embrace.

"You look...*great*," I said.

"Don't act too surprised," said Adrianna.

"No, it's just, I thought you were going to die out there. But now, it's like I should have never thought that in the first place."

"I could have died," said Adrianna. "I would be in the Pit if not for you. The way you ran at Andromeda like that after seeing what she did to me, that was amazing. You set that bitch on fire to save me."

I smiled, thin-lipped. I couldn't let her die. She fought Andromeda because of me.

A week later, we were back to talks about angel weapons.

I heard so many names back and forth that I stopped listening. All I needed to know was when we were leaving and where we were going.

No angel that we encountered since was as bad as Andromeda. I didn't know if that was because they were weaker, or we were getting stronger.

We managed to trap a few angels in conversation while I crept up behind them. It seemed wrong to trick them like that. But I wanted to get this done and go home.

Nash hadn't been open with me since he returned from the Circles. He retired to his room for days on end and only came out for training.

When I told him about Belial and how he mentioned the Redeemer, Nash seemed concerned, but he didn't say anything to the others. Maybe he thought he could figure it out himself. This Redeemer guy was bad news. He might be the same guy who let those flesh-eating demons out of the Circles.

I cooked for myself, which proved a disaster every time. One day, I thought I would set Nash's house on fire. Sim watched me from the kitchen doorway as smoke rose to the ceiling, and I coughed enough to make my throat hoarse.

Sim's eyes followed me as I turned on the faucet, grabbed the sprayer, and doused the flames. She was like a gazelle watching a lion devour a zebra.

Since I spent more time downstairs in the hopes that Nash would come talk to me, I moved Sim's bowls down to the kitchen. She roamed around the entire house, rubbed against my legs more, and purred every time I petted her.

So far, my efforts to make myself available were in vain. I thought that Nash kept himself so locked up because I started to explore the house. Maybe he regretted our one-on-one dinner in the Galapagos Islands. The Ninth Circle changed him.

Whatever happened, I wondered when Nash would go back to his old self—the guy who had started to show interest in me.

As I read on the couch, Tom appeared in front of me through the portal. His hands were on his knees. His breaths came out in a sharp, rapid rhythm. Seconds later, Alex appeared behind him, equally winded.

"What happened to you?" I asked. "Nash was worried about you. He said you'd never taken so long to scout."

I looked from Tom to Alex. Alex had a wry smile on his face.

Tom looked puzzled. When he summoned enough air to speak, he said, "Did you say Nash?"

"Yes, Nash. They're back."

"Safe?"

"Yes, all of them."

"How long?"

"A couple weeks. Right after you left actually."

Tom looked confused. "We found a colony," he said breathlessly. "A colony of Cambions. I need to talk to Nash. He needs to go now."

"Tom?" Nash walked into the living room.

Tom's mouth hung open like he didn't believe me until then. He approached Nash and pulled him into a hug. I'd never seen them show such affection before. I forgave Tom then. He had wanted Nash to return, he just thought it was impossible.

They released each other, and Nash patted Tom's shoulder. "How did you..."

"They threw me out," said Nash, "when I started instructing Hades on how to torture people."

Tom shook his head. "I wouldn't believe it unless I saw it."

"And not even then," said Nash.

Tom smirked.

"What's going on?" asked Nash.

"Cambions," said Tom. "We found a bunch of them in an abandoned hospital near Mumbai. Cambions move around a lot so it's a goldmine we have to bank on."

"I'll get the others," said Nash.

"I'll get my sword." I started towards the stairs.

"No." Nash turned around to face me. "You can't come."

"Why not?" I asked.

"Cambions are strong, and it's a colony."

"Lots of demons are strong. I've fought them before. They've talked to me. I—"

"We won't be talking to them," said Nash. "Cambions are half-demons. Lucifer wants them exterminated."

I folded my arms.

"Let's go." Nash marched away with Tom and Alex.

I raced to my room to grab my sword. I glanced out the hallway windows. Nash opened the portal, and Chandra was the first to step through. I quickened my steps and took the stairs two at a time.

The portal was still open, but the field was empty. I ran toward the glowing tear and leaped through. Heavy, humid air hit me. The street was deserted. Behind a black, iron gate was a hospital. The sign on the gate was so faded, it was unreadable.

The warm breeze, disturbed the dead leaves beneath a branchy tree. No street lamps lit the way. *Who builds a hospital in the middle of nowhere?* Maybe that's why the place shut down.

I jogged through the gate and into the courtyard. The others stood in front of the hospital.

Nash turned to face me. "What are you doing? I told you to stay behind."

"They're only half-demon," I said as I approached the doors. "So, shouldn't that mean that they're half as strong?"

Adrianna shook her head. "A Cambion has twice the spiritual energy because it is both human and demon."

"Riiight," I said.

Nash pressed his lips together. He reached out his hand to open a portal. "You're going back."

"Stop." I yanked his arm back down. "You know you shouldn't open so many portals. What if you're too drained to open the next one?"

Nash grimaced. "You shouldn't have followed us." He approached the building.

The windows and doors were boarded up. The red bricks had long, dusty black lines running through them. The smell of wet earth scented the air.

"How did they get inside?" I asked.

Adrianna tested the boards. "Cambions who favor their demon halves can make themselves temporarily incorporeal. Long enough to pass through walls. But it requires a lot of energy. They'd have to rest and eat up for several days after that."

The front of the hospital was surrounded by dense vegetation. The lower half of the outer walls was stained green.

"Well, it looks like this is going to be a good-old fashioned break in." I hacked at the walls with my sword. The wood splintered beneath my blade. Once the boards were no longer an obstacle, I kicked the doors open. They opened with a dull creak and dust fell upon my shoulders.

I looked back at Nash. I felt badass, but if Nash was impressed he didn't show it.

"Follow me," he said. He stepped into the abandoned hospital like it wasn't the creepiest place on Earth.

The light pooled in from the full moon and revealed a dirty tiled floor, and the once white hospital walls were a dingy gray. I held my breath and waited for a demon to jump out from the shadows.

Nash withdrew his sword with a zing and marched down the corridor.

The first floor of the hospital was a maze of empty hallways, abandoned metal gurneys, and quiet rooms. Squares of dirt marked the space of every missing tile. The humidity and heat inside was more intense than outside the hospital.

We stopped in the large empty space that led to the stairwell. Four hallways led away from the space. The ceilings went all the way to the upper floors with half walls lined along hallways so you could look down and see the landing.

"Why would Cambions want to live *here*?" I asked.

"They're hiding from Lucifer," said Alex. "That's why they're always moving. But they don't want to be alone. They can't have families, you know."

I looked at him. "What do you mean by that?"

"Cambions can't have children," said Adrianna. "They're infertile like mules."

"Oh," I said. Despite the heat, a chill ran down my back as I glanced up at the darkness above us. Anything could be lurking in the shadows. "Do you think they're…up there?"

A form moved in the shadows above us. Dread wrapped its fingers around my heart and stopped my breath. Figures with pale faces stood at the half walls overlooking the landing. They jumped.

Feet thundered to the floor. Laughter echoed. Someone hissed, "Dinner!" More of them dropped to the floor and surrounded us on all sides. They looked normal, like people, but their fingers ended in long, dirty claws.

They whispered and chanted, "Dinner!"

Adrianna's back was to mine.

"They want to eat us?" I asked. *Why were so many demons interested in eating people?*

"Only you," said Adrianna. "That's why Nash didn't want you to come."

I gulped. "Why are they acting like this? I thought they were part human."

"They haven't fed." Adrianna cut down one of the creatures. The circle tightened. "If they don't eat, they go mad with hunger, forcing them to feed."

"But—" I broke off. *This isn't a colony. Someone locked them in here.* A Cambion with wild hair and dry, cracked skin lunged toward me. I backed away and knocked into Kiran and Nash. I put my sword between the demon and myself.

Blood sprayed around me as swords slashed through the bodies of the creatures, but behind them were others, and still more watched from the rafters and the balconies that overlooked the small landing at the bottom of the stairs. My breath spiked. I wielded my sword mechanically, and cut into at least two of the monsters.

My face was sprayed with blood. My blade was painted with gore that dripped down the hilt and over my hand that fisted the pummel in a tight, urgent grip.

An invisible force tore my sword from my hand, and my bloody palm clenched around nothing. My eyes swept the room. The weapons were torn from the hands of my friends as well, and we stood defenseless before the monsters.

"Welcome, friends." A tall man stepped out from the shadows, but something in his calm demeanor and the glint in his emerald eyes told me this wasn't a man. He *was* good-looking. He had dirty-blond hair and clear skin.

"Quentin," Adrianna's voice was a whisper, but somehow the man heard it.

"Oh, if it isn't the lovely Adrianna."

Adrianna stabbed him with her hard, green eyes. "What are you doing here? Are you responsible for these?"

"Most of them are my children, yes." He moved along the balcony on the second floor.

"Are you crazy?" Adrianna shouted. "Why didn't you return to Sheol?" Her hair gathered together and became slick and scaly like snake's skin. I blinked, and it returned to soft, blonde curls.

"I missed my quota." His fingertips grazed the railing. "With each one of my children, my power increases. I can't get enough of it."

"You can never have enough children to put up a good fight if Lucifer comes for you."

"You think I did this *only* for power. Why would I lock myself up in this place? I was *asked* to do this, and in exchange, I don't have to spend an eternity in the Circles."

"Asked by who?" Nash's voice came from behind me.

The Redeemer, I thought. He has stained fingers from dipping his hands in everything.

Quentin's mouth curled up on one side. "We are sleepers, and for now, we dream. You were wrong to come and tempt us with this human."

He looked down at me, and my blood curdled. His hand rolled into a fist, and the weapons that were pulled away from us hovered in the air and pointed towards us in a circle of swords. He wanted to stick our own weapons through us like needles into a pin cushion.

As the steel wavered, thoughts clouded my mind. I was going back to Sheol to spend an eternity. Nash, Adrianna, Kiran, Chandra, and Alex would die in this place and forever be destined to the Pit. I would never see Mom and Dad again. I clasped my locket in one shaking fist.

But, in a rush of air and confusion, the Cambions around us were thrust back and skewered onto the blades that surrounded us. Two alone shuttered on the end of my blade. The bodies of others hung on the blades of my companions like a gory wreath.

Quentin's face darkened. "What was that?"

Adrianna's eyes met mine with a look of both shock and fear. The swords fell to the floor, and the bodies came with them.

Nash pulled his sword out of the two bodies that were tossed on the ground like puppets. He cut off the head of the shocked creature that stood in front of him.

Quentin and the Cambions that stood with him on the balconies were thrust against the wall and into the shadows.

"Lia," shouted Adrianna. "Whatever you're doing keep doing it."

"But I'm not doing anything," I said.

Adrianna tossed me my sword as a Cambion came at me. His jaws gnashed like a rabid dog's. I ran my sword through his neck.

The air smelled coppery. Mixed with the humidity and moldy smell of the hospital, I thought I would be sick. But I continued to slash my sword at my enemies, liking the thought of their teeth in my flesh even less.

A mess of bodies littered the floor so that I could no longer see the tiles beneath. Adrianna turned to the stairs when Nash's hand gripped her shoulder. "If we don't stop Quentin, he'll make more of them."

"We can't go after him," said Nash. "We don't know how many more he has lurking in the darkness. We need to go." He looked at me.

He wanted to leave because of me. Hasn't he seen that I could handle myself without even trying to? I wanted to tell him that, but my lips quivered like the strings on a violin.

sixteen

I grabbed the spear from the ground and ran. It hadn't worked this time. The angel must have known something was up. He felt me behind him. I needed to get him away from the others. All I needed to do was touch him, and it would all be over.

I tripped and knelt among the stalks of corn. This was it.

The wings flapped above me. I waited as the sound grew louder and louder. *A little closer.* I rolled over onto my back and thrust the spear into the air. The pointed edge invaded the angel's body. Silver blood spilled onto my chest and neck. I continued to push until the spearhead jutted out from his back.

He tried to pull back from the spear, but he screeched in pain as he realized the spearhead had sharp teeth on the back end.

But I didn't need much time. I ducked my head and *slam!*

His gauntleted fists came down upon my back, and I plummeted to the ground. His blow knocked the breath from my lungs.

I sensed him as he struggled above me, attempting to pull the spear from his body. Loud screams battered my ears, and silver blood dotted the ground. I couldn't let him pull the spear out.

I crawled along the ground and reached out in front of me. The sudden loss of oxygen made me dizzy, and my vision blurred.

My hand landed against something cold and smooth. Arcadian Steel. The angel's boots were made of it. But Kiran's sword had cracked his armor in places. One of his leg guards had shattered under the repeated blows of pure Arcadian Steel.

I climbed up his leg until I touched smooth, exposed flesh. The scream brought me utter satisfaction.

The loud guttural shriek of despair was mixed with hopelessness as he suffered the knowledge that he was damned for all eternity.

He stumbled back. His wings burned and set the stalks of corn on fire.

The corners of my vision crept into darkness.

WHEN I awoke, I was in the arms of Adrianna.

"Did I get him?" My memory was fuzzy.

"You got him," said Adrianna. "He's chained up in the cargo hold."

I sat up. We were on the plane.

"You shouldn't have grabbed the spear and ran off on your own." Nash turned his back to me.

I was ashamed, not because of what I had done to the angel, but because since Nash returned, all he did was criticize me. I should have known that he would be upset that I took matters into my own hands.

Nash wasn't too keen on the idea of me sneaking up on the angel anyway, but Chandra said that was the best I could do. For once, I agreed with her.

It was easier for them to distract the angels and for me to get them unaware than it was for Nash and the others to beat them down until they were weak enough for me to approach. Nash's way always led to injuries that took weeks to heal.

I was fine doing it this way. It got the job done sooner, and we could move on to the next angel as my way caused very few, if any, injuries. This time, however, things didn't go as planned.

I sat up and crossed my arms over my chest. "I'm sorry," I said. "But if I wouldn't have done that, he would have gone after you."

"And we would have handled it," said Nash.

I narrowed my eyes. "I know that, and then what, someone gets nearly killed, and you attempt another journey through the Circles all over again?"

Nash leaned forward. His face was inches from mine. "It's not about us. If *you* are mortally wounded, you die. Simple as that. We can't open a portal and save you."

Nash stormed into the sleeping quarters and slid the door closed behind him.

"I think you made him mad." Chandra smiled as she took a seat in the brown plushy chair opposite the white sofa.

"He's worried about you because he cares," said Adrianna.

"You must see something I don't," I said.

"Listen," said Chandra. "This is what Nash does. This is the culling phase."

"Chandra, stop," said Kiran.

"No, she deserves to know," she said.

Tom looked up from his book, but returned to it once he heard Chandra's next few words.

"Nash likes his girls…interesting. Whenever, the next hot, young demon comes down to Sheol, he wants to know her story, how she got to Hell. If the story is interesting, he dates her for some time, and then he slowly purges himself of her."

"That isn't true," said Kiran. "Sheol can get lonely. Nash has been with women in the past. He found out they weren't his type. It's hard to live an eternity with the same person."

"Do you believe that?" asked Adrianna.

"It is for some people," said Kiran.

Adrianna's lips formed a hard line.

Chandra smirked. "Guess this is another gutter ball for good old Nash." Her eyes threatened to collide with the bridge of her nose.

"You're jealous." Tom didn't look up from his book.

"What did you say?" asked Chandra.

"I said you're just being a bitch." Tom's voice was nonchalant. "Nash dated you for three weeks, which is like what? A second in the face of eternity, and he couldn't stand you for that long."

I grinned. So, that was the reason Chandra was so terrible to me all the time. She was another Felicia, jealous that a guy might like me over her. I guess jealous girls are everywhere, even in Hell.

But maybe Chandra was right. Nash decided that I wasn't interesting enough, and he decided that right away. Or maybe I read the entire situation wrong, and he hadn't been interested in the first place. I was the same to him as I was to Lucifer and Raphael, a tool to get what they wanted. In Nash's case, he used me to avoid the Pit.

That didn't matter anyway. I needed to do this. What scared me was that I got used to making angels fall. That angel I destroyed in the cornfield, I might have considered beautiful once, with its clear blue eyes and delicate white wings. But not anymore. So many of them tried to kill me. I thought of them as monsters and nothing more.

Lucifer said she would release my soul if I did this for her, but Tom told me that some people were destined for Hell. What if I wasn't allowed into Heaven anyway?

I have the power to make angels fall. So, I must be one of the bad guys. I guess everyone has the potential for evil, but I used my power to help the Devil. Surely, that would earn me a spot in Hell. But if Lucifer didn't take me and God didn't want me, where would I go?

Still, I wasn't fighting just any angels. I fought the ones who wanted to lock Heaven down to humans. These angels went against God's will, right? I hadn't read the Bible, but I was sure that God made Heaven for human souls. I must be doing the right thing, and the only path that would get me back home.

I had found a small alcove with a plush armchair to hide away in. I looked up from the book I was reading. Soft, sure music echoed down the hall.

I stood, placing the book down on the chair.

The music became louder as I walked down the hall. I peered through the open doorway. A grand piano was nestled in one corner, and Nash stood in the center. His long fingers cradled a violin.

His chin was pressed against the instrument while his other hand clasped the bow. He wore black pants and an untucked, rumpled shirt. His hands were rapid and sure. The sound vibrated down the strings in clear, quick notes.

Nash's slender fingers ran along the strings as he swept the bow across as gracefully as he wielded a sword.

His eyes shot open, and when he saw me, he stopped playing.

"Please, don't stop," I whispered. "I didn't know you played. I didn't even know you liked music."

"Everyone likes music." Nash knelt and placed the violin in a velvet lined case.

"When you said you hadn't listened to Rock…"

"I wasn't lying. There is more music in the world than rock n' roll. When you've had as much time as I have, you become interested in learning lots of things."

"I was starting to think there was no music in Hell."

Nash looked up at me as he closed the violin case. "There is. It just has no emotion."

"That song you played." I stepped closer. "I felt something."

Nash stood. "I thought you were trying to get out of here."

"I am."

"Then why are you being so reckless?"

"Reckless? I'm doing what I was asked to do." I was baffled.

"You're taking risks, improvising, going against my orders."

"Your *orders*."

"I'm the leader of this team. I'm the one who was charged to protect you."

"I'm trying to protect *myself.* My soul is hers. If I don't do this, I'll end up here. I want to get this done. I wish you could understand that." I turned, ready to march out the door when Nash's hand wrapped around my arm.

He spun me around into his embrace, and I felt his breath on my lips. His hands pressed into my back. His warmth spread through me.

My hands clenched against his chest, feeling his heart beat like a drum, and my heart beat with it. The up-tempo melody filled my ears, every other sense, but touch and sound, was dulled. He pulled in closer to me. My lips trembled. My palms sweat. He stopped.

Nash pulled away from me. His eyes were half-lidded as he looked down to mine. "You should go." His voice was uneven. "We're leaving tomorrow."

I pressed my lips together, feeling silly that I thought something was happening between us. "Where?" I asked.

"Italy," he said.

seventeen

I peered through the window of the plane. Below was a cluster of buildings that seemed to float on the blue-green sea. We landed at the airport and walked to the nearest café to eat lunch.

The canal flowed alongside the walkway. I marveled at the water as we walked, and gondolas passed.

Adrianna and Kiran walked arm in arm ahead of us. An image of Nash and I with our hands together, fingers entwined, flashed in my mind. We walked side by side, my head leaned against his arm. We watched the gondolas pass. *Do you want to ride one?* I shook my head until the image broke away like an unmoored ship from the coast.

Adrianna pointed to something and took off with Kiran.

"Where are they going?" I asked.

"Wouldn't worry about them if I were you," said Tom. "This isn't their first time in Venice, even though they look like a bunch of tourists. They'll find the hotel on their own. I'm going there now if you want to join me."

"This *is* my first time," I said. "I think I'd like to enjoy it for a little while."

"Okay, but you should stick close to Adrianna and Kiran."

Chandra followed Tom, but didn't try to catch up with him. After what he said to her a few days ago, she might beat him in a dark alley.

When Chandra left too, I thought Nash might go with her, but he stayed with me. Of course, he stayed with me. The others left so he had to stay. He needed to protect me and make sure that I wouldn't try to escape.

I was a prisoner. Sure, I didn't want my soul to end up in Hell for all eternity, but if I didn't care about that, Lucifer would find another way to make me do what she wanted.

We strolled along the stone pathway. A tall column with a winged lion rose in the air, reaching into the heavens.

I don't remember who first told me that Heaven was above us. I always pictured angels on clouds. When people died, I thought they became angels. I wondered if any of that was right.

Hell wasn't at all what I expected. I didn't know about the Outer Region. I thought Hell was fire, brimstone, and pitchforks. I didn't realize how much choice was involved or at least the illusion of choice. People could feel so strongly that they belonged in Hell that they ended up there.

I always thought good people go to Heaven, and bad people go to Hell. But it was so much more complicated than that. Things weren't that black and white. People aren't good or bad, they are a mix of complex morals and wrongs that paint who they are. I always knew that, and it made this duality of Heaven and Hell seem so silly. Humans don't quite fit in either one. It's like they were never designed for us in the first place.

I stood on the arched bridge that overlooked the canal. A gondola floated below. Nash placed his hand on mine.

I looked up at him, and our eyes met.

"There you are," I said.

"What?" he asked.

My eyes quivered. "For weeks, I thought I did something to make you mad."

"Oh, you made me mad lots of times by putting yourself in danger."

I put my hands on my hips. "You've been a jerk."

"I did go to the center of Hell."

"I don't know how to read you," I said.

He stared at the water. "Things got...complicated down in the Circles. I thought that you would be upset with me when I returned."

He cared enough to worry that I would be angry with him?

"I wasn't upset. I was relieved."

"I want to show you this city," he said.

"Why?" I asked.

"Because you chose Heaven. That's why you're doing all this. But if you go there, you'll never see all the wonders this world holds."

"The *wonders this world holds*? What is that, a ballad?"

Nash grinned, but slowly his expression turned dark. "Human souls don't come back from Heaven."

"Maybe that's because Heaven is so wonderful. Maybe the people there are too happy to come back." I grinned.

"Perhaps," he said. "But I want you to enjoy this life before you go."

He acted as if my time alive was short. I guess it was short to him. Nash had been alive a long time. Maybe alive wasn't the right word. He might have lived in Sheol for hundreds of years on top of whatever time he spent on Earth.

Was that the real reason he was distant? He might never see me again. He said things got complicated in the Circles. Maybe he meant that he had time to reflect on the fact that our time together would be short. If I survived, I would be going back home to Earth and after I died, I would move on to

Heaven, or maybe Purgatory first, and I would never see him again.

I remembered how I felt when Nash was lost in the Circles. The thought that we might never be together again made me feel empty. I didn't realize that Nash was faced with the same thing. I shook my head. I had to let go of this fantasy. Nash didn't care about me like that.

By the time the sun went down, Nash and I visited Doge's Palace, walked through Saint Mark's Basilica, saw a glassblowing demonstration, gazed upon art at an outdoor sculpture museum, and rode in a gondola to a restaurant where we sat outside and admired the Grand Canal.

As the sun fell on the city, we sat on a bench near the water. The lights of the buildings glowed in the darkness and their reflections stretched into the canal. Nash's eyes were vacant. His lips were pale and tense. Mine quivered.

I awoke the next morning, feeling better than I had in months. I joined the others for breakfast at Caffe Florian Venezia. Nash ordered his usual coffee. He smiled at me. I don't think he listened to a word Tom said as he explained where we were going that day.

"The only clues I have on the Twinblade point to symbols of rebirth. At first, I thought it was something to do with Jesus, but he didn't seem to fit. Then, I found this."

He passed a piece of paper to the center of the table. The image depicted a bird, wings spread, surrounded by flames.

"The Phoenix," said Adrianna.

"Precisely. And only one place in Venice has risen from the ashes multiple times. So, the Twinblade must be in…"

"Teatro La Fenice." Nash took another sip of his coffee.

I slumped my shoulders. I should have known I couldn't captivate Nash's attention like that.

"That's right, how did you know?"

"I'm older than *you*, Tom, and that's saying a lot."

"Where?" I asked.

"Teatro La Fenice," said Tom. "It's an opera house in Venice. La Fenice means the Phoenix. That's where our angel hid his weapon."

"How poetic," I said.

LATER that day, Adrianna took me to an Italian boutique. She bought me a dress, long and black, with off-the-shoulder sleeves and long, black gloves that went past my elbows.

"I don't think this is good angel-fighting attire," I said.

"You can't wear leggings and a t-shirt," she said. "We're going to the opera." She faked a posh accent, twirled one hand into the air, and took a bow.

That evening, we entered the foyer of La Fenice. Two red velvet carpeted staircases were built side by side bordered by an intricate, black railing. Marble columns rose in every place imaginable. Bright chandeliers decorated the ceiling in glowing brilliance.

I couldn't help but blush when Nash stole a glance at me. But I worried when he didn't look a second time. Was he running hot and cold again? Was I imagining it?

Around the corner was the entrance to the opera room. Thick, red carpet bordered the doorway.

A clock was set in the ceiling among the golden designs that spread down to the walls. Along the walls, starting at the very top of the opera room were private boxes going down to the red velvet chairs below.

A golden bird with its wings spread adorned the short wall above the stage.

Tom stepped up to me. He must have traced my gaze because he said, "The phoenix. It's an appropriate symbol for this place. There have been three fires here, one in 1774, then again in 1836, and the last in 1996. Yet, it has risen from the ashes every time."

Tom knew enough random trivia to be on a game show. I guess that's what happens to you when you read a lot of books.

At the back of the room, sat a private viewing box, four times the size of the smaller boxes, and trimmed with the golden bust of angels.

A large chandelier hung in the center of the sky-blue ceiling where painted angels flew together in romantic poses.

Thick velvet curtains, trimmed with gold, bordered the stage.

Adrianna peered into her bag. The Orb of Metatron glowed. "It's bright," she said. "The Twinblade must be close."

I studied the room closer. My eyes rested on the large box trimmed in gold. Something strange glowed on the trim above the box. I squinted. The pattern on the left didn't quite match the pattern on the right.

"Maybe it's in another room."

"No, wait," I said. "Up there." I pointed to the box that hung ten feet from the ceiling.

"The royal box."

I nodded. "You see the trim. It's not quite right."

Nash, wide-eyed, gazed at me. "How did you know?"

"Maybe it's my fancy Sight ability," I said. "You know, seeing beyond the Veil and all that."

"We have to get up there," said Adrianna.

Chandra stood.

"No." Kiran grabbed her arm. "We'll attract too much attention."

"He's right," said Nash, "We'll have to wait until the theater clears."

The opera was three hours long, but I lost track of time as I became engrossed in the beauty of the voices and the performances. The opera was in Italian so I didn't understand what they said, but body language and tone helped me along.

A woman was forced to be with a man whom she did not love to save the painter who she did.

I teared up as the woman threw herself over the edge of the cliff. The actors bowed, and the audience clapped. Shouts of "Brava" resonated through the audience as the young woman took the stage.

Time ticked by as the theater cleared.

"We could get the blade if we access the seating above the royal box," said Tom.

We walked up the stairs to the viewing boxes. Chandra leaned over the top of the royal box and reached for the sword. Kiran held her so that she wouldn't fall. She pulled the sword from its place among the golden trim. Kiran pulled her back.

"Here it is." She held the blade across both hands.

"He bathed it in gold." Nash smirked.

Golden tendrils wrapped around the hilt. Feathers frozen in steel made up the cross guard. Two blades like a tuning fork rose from the handle.

"Hiding in plain sight," said Kiran. "I can't wait to meet this angel."

We waited in silence as the minutes dragged on.

"Where is he?" asked Adrianna.

Every other angel came to claim the weapon in mere minutes. As soon as the weapon touched our hands, we heard wings as they swept above us, but this time everything was quiet.

I imagined the angel as he burst through the sky-blue ceiling of the theater, causing the chandelier to crash to the ground and leave sparkly bits of glass among the red velvet seats. But that didn't happen.

Tom shrugged. "Guess he's not coming."

Not coming? That hadn't happened before.

"Keep your eyes open," said Chandra. "He might be a little late to the party."

"I don't like this," said Nash. "If he's not coming, he must know there's no way to save his weapon like this."

"But I thought angels were bound to protect their weapons," I said.

"They are," said Nash. "I'm suggesting this angel might know our plans and will wait for the right moment to strike. Other angels have been bold and went in blind. If this angel knows what we're doing, he might have a better plan."

"Maybe he's fallen," I said.

"He's not," said Nash.

WE spent five days in Venice, and the angel never showed. Nash did as he promised and continued to show me around the city. We went to several more places with rich architecture and beautiful paintings. A few of them reminded me of Dad's paintings. I wiped the corner of my eyes and blinked away the glisten that clouded them.

Nash smiled a lot, but at times I caught a grimace or frown on his face. Was the time he spent in the Circles still bothering him?

Nash held my hand to steady me as I stepped into the gondola. The moon and stars dotted the sky. Warm, Mediterranean breezes washed over me. I sat in the small boat, and Nash sat beside me.

Behind us, a man in a striped shirt steered the gondola with a long paddle. The streetlights glowed on the water. The boat drifted along the canal.

My hands were in my lap. My shoulder brushed against Nash's arm. "When you said you wanted me to see the world, did you mean with you?"

Nash squinted. "You won't need a chaperone forever, Lia."

"You *can't?* Is that it?"

We passed beneath a bridge. On either side of us, buildings rose out of the water. Nash's hand was on mine, but he yanked it away as if my skin burned him. "I've been trying to figure out a way to fix this. Lucifer is a liar. She won't keep her end of the bargain."

"You mean let go of my soul?"

He nodded.

"And you knew all along? Why didn't you say anything to me?"

"What would I say? Lucifer would have tossed me into the Pit if I tried to warn you. I can't do anything if I'm falling into an endless hole."

"What should I do?"

"Trust me. I'll figure something out. We need to keep doing what we're doing. But hunting angels won't set you free."

I looked down at my hands. "Maybe I'm not doing this only for me."

Nash sighed. "Lia, I—"

Thud!

The paddle hit the side of Nash's head, and he slumped over into my lap.

"Nash!" I looked accusingly at the man who operated the gondola. "What the hell are you doing?"

His arms flew in a frenzy as he paddled wildly down the canal. I was cold all over. His eyes went solid black, and a grin crawled across his face.

I lifted Nash's head and tried to shake him, but he was out cold. I searched his waist. Strapped to his hip was a sheath and dagger. I pulled the dagger and pointed the blade at the demon. "I'll cut your throat."

His laugh was deep with an echo behind it. Goose bumps rippled across my skin. I faced him as I knelt in the gondola, afraid if I stood I might fall into the water.

The demon drove the paddle into the water, and the gondola halted. My hands shook. The demon licked his lips. I gripped the dagger tighter as the gondola shifted in the water. I grabbed onto the edge with one hand. Weight made the gondola tilt as if someone jumped in with me.

I spun around. Another demon with white eyes like close-up stars was in the boat with us. He smiled, and his teeth were all pointed like a shark's. His skin was black and flaky like he had been burned.

The gondola jerked, and my blade fell to the bed of the boat. I scrambled to get a hold of it. The white-eyed demon lunged at me. His hands were around my throat. I clawed at his hands with my fingernails, and the blackened skin flaked off. Beneath was blood-red flesh that oozed white pus.

I felt movement behind me. My eyes strained upwards. Nash was awake. His hands flew to the sides of the white-eyed demon's head. His thumbs went into its eyes. The demon screamed. Nash screamed.

The black-eyed demon plunged the dagger deep into his back, right between the shoulder blades. Despite the wound, Nash continued to dig his thumbnails into the eyes of the demon that attacked me.

Meanwhile, the black-eyed demon wielded his paddle. I reached up and yanked the dagger from Nash's back. Nash grunted through his teeth. I stood on shaky legs.

The demon raised his oar above Nash, ready to hit him, but he wasn't watching me. I sank the dagger into his stomach and let my body drop down. The blade was so sharp, it cut down the middle of his body to his groin. All that was left of him was the black blood like tar at the front of the gondola.

Nash no longer wrestled with the white-eyed demon. The demon lay in the bottom of the boat, dark gouges where its eyes used to be. Nash bound its hands with rope.

"What are you doing?" I asked.

"I want to know why this demon attacked us." Nash grabbed the oar that floated on the surface of the water. He set his teeth as he rowed.

"Let me do that," I said.

"I have it."

"Nash, that demon stabbed you. Let me help."

He handed me the oar. I rowed to the edge of the canal. Nash climbed out and lugged the body with him. I stood under the street lamp. The boat idled away. I left the oar inside.

"Come on." Nash pulled the demon up from the ground.

"Nash." I tried to stop him, but he had the body of the demon across his shoulders.

Midnight fell by the time we met up with the others. Nash dragged the demon to the alley behind the hotel. The demon came to. His sockets dripped thick gobs of blood.

Adrianna knelt and yanked a fistful of his hair back. "What color were its eyes?" she asked.

"White," I said.

Adrianna looked up at Nash. "He was possessed by a Jinn? How do you expect us to get any information out of him?"

"He might remember something," said Nash.

"That's doubtful." Tom approached with his hands in his pockets. "The Jinn wouldn't let him see, and it's probably already fled his body."

"But Jinni can form," said Adrianna. "I once saw one morph from a man to a deer."

"Why would a Jinn need a body if they can change into anything they want?" I asked.

Nash shook his head.

"Even the most practiced Jinni find it difficult to hold their shape for long periods of time, especially on Earth. That's why they like to hang out in Sheol. Possessions are sometimes easier if they want to confront someone. Maybe it needed this particular form for some reason."

"It wanted the demon to come at us with all it had," I said quietly. "It didn't think we would catch it. It was going to kill us. So, finding out it was a possession wasn't even in the cards. The Jinn wanted the demon to come after us with no fear of the Pit."

"Or someone asked it to possess that demon," said Chandra. "It's time for us to start naming our enemies."

"You think maybe Raphael..." I stopped.

Nash shook his head. "If Raphael knew where you were, he'd come himself, or he'd send angels."

I took a deep breath. "Who else?"

"I don't know." Nash looked at the others. He kicked the demon in the back. The demon let out a scream. "So, you *are* awake. Tell us everything you know. I won't hesitate to send you to the Pit."

"I was at a bar," he stammered.

"In Sheol?"

"Here! I was having a drink when I felt like something was being forced down my throat. I blacked out, I swear. Why can't I see?" He sobbed. "I can't see."

Nash hauled him to his feet.

Adrianna bit her lip. "If they tracked us here, we should leave."

"What about the angel?" I asked.

"If he hasn't come by now," said Kiran. "He isn't coming."

WHEN we returned to Sheol, Nash and I walked into the living room of his house. The others went home, and we left the demon several blocks away where the portal opened. He still crawled on the ground and asked about his sight. I pitied him.

He reminded me of the demon Nash and I found in the tunnels. We had abandoned her too. His body was taken over by something else. He hadn't meant to attack us.

Nash threw his jacket down on the couch. The leather had a long tear where the dagger went in. His white shirt was stained with black blood that grayed out around the edges of the stain.

"Let me see your back," I said. "It might need stitches."

He pulled off his shirt and sat on the coffee table. I squinted. The two rounds sores, situated at the shoulder blades were on either side of the gash in his back. They looked like big cigarette burns. I assumed he got them in the Circles. I didn't want to bring his mind back there.

The stab wound was shallower than I expected it to be. I saw the dagger go in to the hilt. My fingertips grazed the edges of the wound. The swell of his muscles tempted me, and I thought about running my hands along them as well.

Nash craned his neck to look at me. "If you wanted me to take off my shirt, all you had to do was ask."

I gazed at him quizzically. Was he flirting?

His grin dropped. "I was kidding." He turned away.

"It looks like it closed up some."

"I heal fast," said Nash. "Well, not as fast as I used to."

I thought back to the wounds I tended when Nash came home from the Circles. Either those wounds were recent, or they had been initially worse than when I saw them. But the wound still seeped blood. I leaned in closer. The penny scent of the blood stung my nose. The color was dark, not red but black.

"What are you doing back there?" Nash asked.

"Nothing," I said. "Stitches will stop the bleeding."

"You just want to stitch me up like a voodoo doll. If I didn't know better, I'd say you like threading people up."

"Maybe." I shrugged. I left the room to get the first aid kit.

I still thought about the angel who didn't come to claim the Twinblade. I didn't catch his name, but I guess it didn't matter much. I had nine fallen angels under my belt, names were frivolous at this point. Nash kept their weapons in the armory.

What if he didn't show because Raphael was on to us? What about the other Archangels that were on his side?

We needed to get rid of them before Raphael decided to attack. They were bigger threats than lesser angels, especially if they grouped up and tried to take us down.

I sat down next to Nash and threaded the needle. The needle rested against the gauze on my lap as I cleaned the wound with a moist cloth. The white, textured cloth wasn't a dull pink as I removed it from the wound, it was gray.

"I want to take down an Archangel next," I said. I pinched the edges of his skin and knit them together.

The cold air in the room drifted around us and threatened to steal the warmth from our bodies. Warm blood ran over my finger as I pinched together the next section of skin.

"I don't think that's a good idea." Nash's hands gripped the edges of the table as the needle passed through his skin. "Archangels are much stronger than the angels that we've gone up against."

"I can't stay here forever," I said. "I might never be strong enough. I need to do this, Nash. I know what you said about my soul, but maybe I can stay in Sheol with you. That doesn't mean everyone else shouldn't have a choice."

Nash turned around to face me. He grabbed my hands. His lips twitched. "I know why you want to do it, but it's a bad idea, Lia. Trust me."

"I do, but I think it's time."

Nash laughed. "That's because you are mortal. Not every-thing needs to happen in a flash."

"Don't call me mortal like you're trying to berate me. It might be a flash to you, but for me, it's been almost a year. I've done what you've said—"

"No, you haven't. You challenge me constantly." Nash sighed. "Let's hunt a few more regular angels before we start going after Archangels."

"We might not have much more time," I said. "That angel who didn't show up. He knows what we're about which means Raphael probably knows too. Someone attacked us tonight. You could have died."

"That wasn't Raphael, and if someone wants to kill me, it's going to take a lot more than that."

I wanted to believe him, but although Nash had the best intentions, his methods were faulty. If Raphael found out about me, we'd be in big trouble if he still had all his generals.

I finished stitching Nash's back and walked up the stairs as he sauntered off to the kitchen to make a pot of coffee. I was too tired to stay up a minute later.

I crawled into bed. Sim nestled up to me. That's when I realized I was gone six days and hadn't been around to feed her. I turned on the bedside lamp. Her food bowl was full. Bob must have come by while we were gone and fed her. I re-minded myself to thank him for that. I turned off the lamp and closed my eyes.

THE next afternoon, I finished training with Nash and the others. Tom talked about our next hit. He droned on and on, and I stopped listening, trapped in my own thoughts.

What if Nash was wrong? I had more than myself to worry about. Adrianna wrapped her arm around Kiran's. Nash's face was a mask of concentration as he listened to Tom do his fa-vorite thing in the world besides reading: lecturing.

Chandra, as she stood, glared at me with her arms folded, and mouthed the word "*what?*" as I looked at her. Her skin was changing color from tan to obsidian black. Not only that, but the flesh hardened like the shell of a scorpion.

I broke the hum of Tom's voice. "I think we should hit an Archangel next."

Silence nestled in the air for a moment. Nash's expression was a look of disappointment mingled with frustration.

"That would be something," said Tom.

"No way," said Chandra. "She's going to get us all sent to the Pit."

"You didn't let me finish." Tom raised an eyebrow. "That would be something absolutely crazy. But Lucifer wants us to go after Archangels," said Tom. "We would have to do it eventually."

"Maybe after a few years of training," said Kiran.

Years? I didn't want to make Sheol my home for years. The longer I stayed here, the longer it would be before I started my life. I wanted to go to college and study music. Mom and I talked about it last year. The thought of leaving Nash entered my mind again. I lowered my eyes and frowned.

"Kiran's right," said Adrianna. "We need more training."

Adrianna was against me too?

"We have to do this," I said. "If we wait years before we fight one of Raphael's Archangels, they might gang up on us. He'll find out what we're doing. The sooner, the better. It'll be easier to take on one Archangel than to fight all of them at once."

Kiran nodded.

"I think that sounds like a wonderful idea." Bob approached us from the house.

Nash eyed him darkly.

Bob peered at him with a smile both playful and threatening.

"I thought it would be easier, if the Archangels—" I started.

"You can stop selling it," said Bob. "Just do it." He patted Nash on the shoulder.

I backed Nash into a corner. Bob knew it. He would tell Lucifer if Nash discouraged me from going after an Archangel. Guilt birthed a lump in my throat. Nash complained about me challenging his authority over the team, and I did it again.

"We're going to need more abled bodies," said Nash.

"That can be arranged," said Bob. "I've got all the resources at my fingertips."

eighteen

THE chill left my bones as I walked into the sanctuary of warmth the hotel provided. The lobby of the hotel had a high arched ceiling supported by thick marble columns capped in gold.

A small chandelier hung above a bed covered in white linen. In front of the bed was a small loveseat and table.

A large, marble tub was set in the center of the bathroom and clean, white towels were folded into shelves hollowed into the walls.

I took off my large coat and tossed it on the bed.

In the corner of the room was a brown package with a red bow. Who left that? I felt eyes on my back. I whirled around. Nash leaned inside the doorframe to the adjoining room. How long had he been standing there?

His subtle smile unarmed me.

"I hope you don't mind," he said. "I ordered room service." He walked in without asking.

"No, I guess not." I wanted to soak in the warm tub, but I still felt guilt over forcing this decision on Nash. I figured I had to let him win sometimes.

"I need to talk to you about something," he said.

"Okay." I sat down on the loveseat.

He settled down beside me.

A spasm radiated through me that left me with goose bumps.

"I need you to be careful tomorrow," he said.

"You too."

"No, I mean, you need to protect *yourself*. Let us weaken Uriel first."

"Why can't I sneak up on him like usual?"

"Lia, this is an Archangel we're talking about. There will be no sneaking up on him."

My eyes considered his, and I could see the seriousness in them. But I couldn't stand by if he was in trouble. If it came to that, I would have to intervene. But worrying about me would distract him.

"Alright," I said. "I'll wait for your signal." A lie.

He touched the side of my cheek and that warm bath seemed like the lesser option.

When the food came, Nash set the platter out on the small table he pulled up to the loveseat and lifted the bottle of wine. He poured two glasses and set one down beside my plate.

"I'm underage," I said.

I was sixteen, seventeen in three months, but I thought the legal drinking age in most parts of Europe is eighteen.

He laughed. "You're fighting an Archangel tomorrow, you're old enough."

I looked up at Nash. He gave me a thin-lipped smile. He didn't think we were going to make it. That's why he was allowing me a glass of wine. He thought it was an experience I might not get to have. What else did he want me to experience tonight?

I shook my head and cautioned myself not to overthink this. This wasn't a last supper. Nash appreciated food. He probably appreciated wine too. It was nothing more than that.

"I'm okay." I pushed the glass away, but it tipped over the edge of the small table. My reflexes improved since I came to

Sheol. I dropped my fork and caught the glass, but the wine still tossed over the lip, and a sizable splash landed on Nash's shirt.

"Oh, I'm so sorry," I said.

"That was a pretty good catch," he said. "It's alright. I'll change. It'll only take a second."

He opened the door between our rooms. He removed his shirt as he walked through the doorway to his room. *Adjoining rooms.* He was being cautious.

On his shoulder blades were the two, long oval-shaped wounds. In the center they were white, like bone. The edges were red and black like burnt paper curling back.

I had wondered if he got them in the Circles, but when I bandaged him up, he said that there were only scratches on his back. These wounds were much larger than scratches.

Why didn't he tell me about them? I could have sewn them up, and they might not have left such horrific scars. No, that wouldn't have helped, the scars looked the same as they did when he returned. They were wounds that wouldn't heal.

But maybe he didn't get those scars in the Circles. The scars might have been much older than that. Where *did* they come from?

When he returned, he carried a black guitar case. Nash sat beside me in a fresh, black shirt and passed the guitar case along to me.

The case tipped, but Nash caught it. "Careful," he said.

I undid the latches on the side of the case and opened it. Inside was a black Fender Stratocaster with a mahogany neck. "You brought my guitar."

I looked at the guitar and felt a sense of longing. A question I had been trying to avoid entered my mind. *Were Mom and Dad in Heaven?*

I remembered what Tom said. Not all good people go to Heaven. What if they were in Sheol? I shook my head. It wasn't possible. They were good people, too good to be part of Lucifer's kingdom. No god would let that happen.

"I brought it because I got you this." He gestured to the corner of the room to the large box wrapped in brown paper with a red bow.

"What is it?" I asked.

"Something I thought you might like. Open it."

I moved the Strat from my lap to the bed. I walked over to the wrapped box and started to tear away the brown paper. I looked at him. "Don't tell me…"

"Just open it."

The wrapping fell to the floor and nestled in the corner was a Peavey 6505.

"You said you needed an amp." Nash knelt on the floor next to me.

"Thank you," I said slowly.

"You don't like it."

"No, I like it. With the guitar…It just brings up memories, that's all."

"Bad ones?"

I shook my head. "Thank you." I hugged Nash. His body was tense. "Are you worried? About the Archangel?" I asked.

"Yes, I am," said Nash. "But you're right. If we don't start hitting them, and Raphael finds out what we're doing, we'll be dealing with them all at once."

"There are seven of them, right?" I asked.

Nash nodded. "You've been studying."

"When you were…gone," I said, "I explored your library quite a bit. I wanted to learn everything I could to get you out of the Circles."

"Only I could have gotten myself out of the Circles."

I didn't want to think about Nash in the Circles, not after everything I'd read about them. He had to go through every one of them to get home.

"I didn't really know if I could believe everything I read in those books. So, there really are seven?"

"They don't all side with Raphael," said Nash. "Definitely not Michael."

"How many are on Raphael's side?"

Nash looked down at his glass of wine. He pushed it to the end of the table. The glass was half-full. "We know about Gabriel and Uriel. Possibly Phanuel."

That left Michael, Raguel, and Sariel. There used to also be Ramiel, but Ramiel had fallen from grace after he slept with a human and was replaced by Phanuel.

The one we were going after, Uriel, was the angel who warned Noah of the coming flood and saved mankind from the devastation. I didn't know if that was just a story. If it was true, Uriel's opinion of humans had certainly changed since he sided with Raphael.

Nash stared forward as if he could see through the wall.

"Nash?"

He turned to face me.

"Tell me we're going to get out of this, and that I'll get the opportunity to use that amp you got me."

Nash smiled. "Play it now."

"I'm a little rusty. I haven't played in a while."

"Go ahead. Play."

I removed my guitar from its case and hooked it up to the amp. I took a deep breath. I strummed "This Means War." I felt the sound in my chest as music filled the room. Maybe this would be the last song I ever played.

The world is a drum, and its music is a death march.

THE dull sky hung over the Russian city. The buildings were quiet and brown grass grew between cracks in the street. Several of the structures were crumbling and in need of repair, but no one was around to maintain them.

The city was a relic. Still standing, but forgotten.

I kicked over a pebble with my boot.

"What happened here?" I asked.

"People thought the city was haunted," said Tom. "A group of Jinn took over and scared people away."

Jinn. They were what people confused with demons because they could transform into any terrible thing they wanted.

I imagined one of those creatures with its thin, gray body and horned head as it stalked through the streets of the silent, abandoned ruins. A chill went down my back.

"What did they want with the city?" I asked.

Tom shrugged. "Jinni motivations are beyond me. I've tried to study them, but that only led to more questions."

"Nash!"

We turned around. Thirty or so demons stood behind us dressed in dark clothes with weapons and shields at their sides. Chip, Malcolm, and Chandra's brother, Alex, were among them.

"Bob sent us." Malcolm approached Nash.

"Good," said Nash. "We're going to need you."

Malcolm's red skin was a pop of color in the snowy city. They all wore the same silver bracers and arm guards as the rest of us. The armor was made of Arcadian Steel and a lesser alloy. Even against angel weapons, it would take more than a single strike to break through.

A bright light emitted. Everyone turned towards the brightness. Adrianna pulled out Metatron's Orb.

"Are we close?" I asked.

Adrianna shook her head. "No, this is strange. We haven't moved, yet the orb is getting brighter and brighter."

The atmosphere darkened, and clouds like dark tendrils came down upon the Earth. The sky exploded with light as twenty silver winged angels hovered above us.

Lightning flashed across the sky as the dark clouds swept over the buildings. The wings of the angels glowed against the gloom.

"Nash," I said, "do you see Raphael?"

"No," he said. "But you need to hide. Get behind those ruins."

A few feet behind us were the ruins of a fallen building. I snaked through the crowd of demon warriors and knelt behind the stone debris. I peered over through an opening in the stone and watched as an angel flew down in front of Nash.

My breath caught. The angel was a head taller than Nash. His long, white-blond hair flowed in the wind. His gray eyes glared down at Nash and reflected off the light of his sword that was bathed in cerulean flames.

They knew we were coming. That's why Uriel had his weapon.

Uriel's fiery, blue blade met Nash's. "Hello, Nasriel," he said.

Nasriel?

"How did you know?" Nash asked.

"Did you think Andromeda wouldn't deliver the message to me?" asked Uriel. "You left her broken. Yet still, she tried to save her brethren. While you stand here a traitor."

Of course, Nash wasn't a demon. He was a fallen angel, and he was fighting his brothers.

Nash pushed him back, and Uriel sprung into the air and flew above us. Nash ran along the street and jumped over the debris and ruins of buildings. Uriel darted down to meet him. As Uriel landed in front of him, Nash met his blade. Sparks flew in the distance and steel on steel echoed through the battered streets.

Uriel wrapped his wings around him as he spun. Nash's blade hit upon the wings and sent sparks like a tire rim along pavement.

His wings were armored. They were dipped in Arcadian Steel.

My eyes darted to the others. Adrianna and Chandra fought back to back against an angel with silver hair. Kiran, Tom, and a few other demons battled angels not far from where I hid.

I glanced at the battle between Nash and Uriel.

Uriel flew to the top of one of the buildings. Nash climbed the metal stairway to the roof.

He was trying to wear Nash out, but when Nash reached the top, he didn't even seem winded. The battle continued as their blades met once again.

Nash pointed his sword and impaled the steel into Uriel's shoulder. He walked forward, sinking the blade in deeper, but Uriel grabbed him by his shirt and threw Nash into the air. Nash still held his sword tight, and the blade sailed from Uriel's body as a spray of silver blood flew like splashed paint before it hit canvas.

As Nash was still in the air, Uriel lifted his blue sword. Uriel's blade went through the center of Nash's body. As he lifted Nash with his sword, Nash's feet dangled from the ground.

Time stopped.

"No," I screamed and bolted toward the building, too far away. I'd never make it through the throng of fighting angels. I wasn't thinking straight. All I saw was red. *I'll make every last one of the them fall.*

I stepped over the bodies of the fallen and dodged the blows of the fighters. No one aimed for me, *yet.*

An angel stepped in front of me as he battled with one of the demons. I touched his skin as I passed, not stopping to see his wings burst into flames, but I could hear his screams. They followed as I ran. They'd follow me forever and in my dreams to haunt me.

I raced through the crowd and tripped over the body of one of my allies. He lay in a pool of dark blood. His eyes were frozen, fixed on the sky. *Alex.* Tears painted my face, and I rubbed them away, smearing dirt across my cheeks.

As I scrambled to my feet, an angel landed in front of me and faced me. I withdrew my blade but hadn't managed to swing before his steel-clad foot kicked me in the stomach. All the breath came out of me in a rush of air. My sword clattered to the ground.

The angel raised his blade above me.

This is it. I'm going to die, and my soul will be destined for Hell.

Right as the thought entered my mind, another angel flew down between us. His back was to me. He held a demon blade probably picked up from one of the dead.

His blade sparked against the rebel angel's, and they turned to the side. I could see his face.

Adriel.

A thin, silver fabric covered his body from the neck down, and his wings were bathed in the same silver as Uriel's. He was fallen-proof.

Adriel cleaved the angel in the leg, and the limb rolled out from under him.

"I have to get you out of here." He offered me his gloved hand.

I took his hand, and he lifted me up. He put his arms around me.

"Wait," I said, "Nash is up there with Uriel. He's hurt."

"Nash." Nash's name was natural on his tongue. *Did he know him?* Adriel looked toward the building as I pointed.

His wings unfolded, and he lifted me into the air with him.

I held my breath as I looked at the ground so far below us. A shiver went through my body. Only the warmth of Adriel's arms gave me any comfort.

His feet cracked the concrete of the building as he landed and released me.

Uriel was gone.

Nash lay on the ground, blood escaped from the large wound in his chest. The blood wasn't red or silver, but black.

"Nash." I ran up to him.

Adriel stepped closer to us.

Nash looked at him as the glow of Adriel's wings engulfed us.

"Get away from me." Nash grimaced.

"You need to be healed," said Adriel, "or you'll die."

Despite Nash's protest, Adriel knelt and pulled off his glove. He touched the center of Nash's chest. Light emitted from his touch.

I pulled up Nash's shirt. "There's no wound," I said.

"He'll be sore, but he'll live," said Adriel. "We have to go."

"Get your people out of here," he said to Nash as he pulled me up from the ground and back into his arms.

"Don't you dare take her," Nash shouted. He tried to stand, but he stumbled.

I didn't want to go, but I didn't have a choice. Adriel clasped me. The air whooshed around us as his wings lifted us from the ground. Nash's form got smaller and smaller until he disappeared in the distance.

The redeemer

TODD stamped the paper and handed it back to the small woman. "Move to aisle four and fill out form A3."

"But I've been waiting here for seven hours," the woman said. She had died in her nightgown, poor thing. Her gray hair frizzed around her face. Her pale blue eyes were stern and impatient. If she obtained a contract, that would all change. Todd wouldn't be able to recognize her. She could look anyway she wanted. Most people chose to be young again.

Todd, like many people, thought he would want to look like a celebrity or someone ruggedly handsome. But when he got here, all he wanted was to look twenty again. He was thirty-four when he died: automobile accident. He spilled hot coffee in his lap as he drove to the boring job he hated and swerved into oncoming traffic.

"They said my husband was here. He died eight years ago, but I'd believe it, the old bastard. He used to kick the dog, you know, and boy, did he have a mouth on him. Cursing is against God."

Todd fought not to roll his eyes. His first day on the job, he might have comforted a woman like this, told her that she would be with her husband soon, and that it was such a tragedy that either one of them had to die. But Todd had seen thousands of women just like this one, always looking for their husbands. Most men died before their wives. A lot of wives assumed their husbands went to Hell.

"You'll have to move along, ma'am," Todd said.

The woman narrowed her eyes at him, but thankfully she moved along and left Todd to his boring job.

The intake office was beautiful on the outside like a medieval gothic castle with seven walls surrounding it, but inside it looked like the DMV: cold white walls, laminate tiled floors, and workers that were bored past death.

He idly wondered if Heaven's intake office was like this: endless lines of people waiting to find out how they would spend eternity.

When he was alive, Todd used to do data entry for Flex Global. At the time, he thought that was the most boring job in the world.

He spent his day in an office much like this one while he was at a computer, typing in words and numbers into an excel spreadsheet. After a week, he stopped caring what those words and numbers meant.

What he failed to realize was that that job was temporary. What he was doing now, this was forever.

"Next," he called.

A tall man in a black, hooded cloak stepped up to Todd's desk. Todd looked up at the man. His face was shadowed by the hood. He had an odd presence about him, something lingering and ominous.

Looks like I've got myself a serial killer today, Todd thought. Although the idea of this didn't amuse him. He had seen more old ladies, but many serial killers nonetheless. Enough that the idea of them bored him only slightly less than the old ladies.

"Form, please." Todd held out his hand to receive the man's form and move him along.

When the form wasn't forthcoming, Todd looked up at the man.

"I need information," the man said in a low voice.

"Form," Todd said.

The man put his hand down on the table. Pinched between his two fingers was an insect a little larger than a watermelon seed with orange stripes along its back. "This insect doesn't have a name because it has yet to have been discovered by modern man. The Egyptians used it to torture their enemies and get confessions. If I let it go, it will burrow deep beneath your skin and lay eggs. Those eggs will hatch and even more of the little critters will crawl beneath your skin. It won't kill you, of course. But you'll have to tear the flesh from your muscles to rid yourself of them."

Todd blinked. *Was this guy for real?* "Sir…"

"Do you want to test me?" His hand moved closer to Todd, and Todd flinched.

Being in Hell was one thing. But, being in Hell with a parasite crawling beneath your skin, unable to sleep, was quite another.

Todd cherished the time when he got to sleep. It was his favorite part of the day. He still dreamed that things weren't as mundane as they were. It gave him a bit of momentary hope in the morning which he appreciated, although it quickly faded the moment he walked out the door.

"What do you want?" Todd asked.

"Information. I need to know if Lydia Chen has been processed."

Todd went to his computer and searched. He wasn't going to find anything. The Records Department had been slacking off since 1997, or perhaps even earlier than that. That's just when Todd got there. "I'm not seeing anyone by that name."

"What about her married name: Lydia Palermo?"

Todd typed. "No, not there either. Look, sir, if you're trying to find your family, you're not alone. It's one of the first things people try to do when they get here. Sometimes, they get lied to. This Lydia, she might not be here. She might be in Heaven. I'm sor…"

"If she's dead, she's here," said the man. "What about Robert Palermo?"

"I can't sit here searching through all your relatives. Now if you would please just hand me your form."

The man let the bug go. It raced toward Todd like a magnet. Todd shrieked, and a hand slammed down on the table. The man smashed the bug before it could reach Todd. He left the line.

Todd stared at the bug flattened against his desk. Its guts were splayed in crimson and black.

part three

luminated

nineteen

ADRIEL'S arms protected me, like a winter coat, from the chilly air that whistled around us. We were far from the abandoned city. What had Adriel been doing there? That angel would have killed me. Could it really be that Adriel planned to deliver me to Raphael?

So many bodies littered the city's cold ground. If we couldn't take down an Archangel, what was the point? What if they came to every battle? What's more, they had their weapons. They were on to us.

Adriel hovered in the air and sank to the ground. A cabin nestled in the woods not far from where we stood.

Adriel tucked his wings and walked toward the cabin. "Come on," he said. "I'll make you some tea. You must be freezing."

I followed him into the cabin. It was the size of a dorm room with a sofa and a kitchenette off to the side. I sat down on one of the bar stools at the kitchen peninsula.

Adriel searched inside the cabinets. Most of them were empty. He found the tea. He fumbled around the kitchen until he found a pot which he filled with water and put on the stove. He sighed as if the whole ordeal was more difficult than fighting Archangels.

"I'm sorry, I don't have anything here to eat," he said. "I'll get some food for you tomorrow morning. The sofa unfolds into a bed so you'll be more comfortable."

"I'm not staying here," I said.

"Raphael will find you if you leave."

"What do you think is stopping him from finding me here?"

Adriel turned to me with fierceness in his eyes. My heart leapt but calmed quickly. No threat tainted his golden eyes. "I've been trying to protect you," he said. "You ran away from me and made a pact with Lucifer. Possibly the worse thing you could have done."

"Worse than Raphael finding me?" I challenged.

"The Devil is not a cartoon character with horns and a tail. Lucifer is evil."

"Take me back to Sheol." I folded my arms. "If you don't, Nash and the others will find me. I'll go back anyway, and you won't be with me."

He hesitated at that. The thought of not being with me pained him. I could see it in his eyes. But he barely knew me. Maybe he was promised something in exchange for keeping me alive as Lucifer promised to return my soul if I completed my task.

"I bet you had a lot of trouble sprinkling salt in the snow," I said. "You can't keep them away from me."

"I'm not going to hand deliver you to them either." Adriel looked out the window above the sink.

"Will you look at me?" I shouted.

Adriel pulled himself away from the window. His golden eyes were trained on me. He was so tall, he looked ridiculous hunched over the sink like that.

"I know Lucifer's a liar. I know she might not keep her end of the deal she made with me, but I need to do this. I'm not letting Raphael kick my parents out of Heaven. They deserve better than Sheol. People die every day, good people. I'm not going to let Hell be their only option."

Adriel's eyes softened like smooth, melted gold. He *was* beautiful, but every time I looked at him I couldn't help but be reminded that beautiful creatures can do terrible things.

"Alright," he said. "I'll take you back, but I'm coming with you."

Could he do that?

I didn't know how Lucifer would feel if I brought an angel with me into Sheol. It had to be against the rules, but I was more worried about what Nash might think. For some reason, Nash and Adriel hated each other, and I had a feeling it went beyond simple angel versus demon hate.

After all, Nash wasn't a demon. He was a fallen angel.

But so far, all the fallen angels I had seen had bones protruding from their backs where their wings once were. Did that mean that someone sawed Nash's off? That would certainly explain the wounds. I cringed. I doubted the process was like pulling off a fingernail, probably more like sawing off an arm.

ADRIEL flew over Fengdu, China. The town nestled at the foot of a rolling, green hill. Set into the hill was a white tower with a face carved into the anterior.

"Fengdu is a transitory place," he explained. "Many souls stop there on the way to the afterlife."

"Like ghosts?" I asked.

Adriel's feet touched the stone steps, and he released me into the alley. The shadows receded away from the glow that surrounded Adriel. He glowed brighter in the Arcadian Steel armor than he did in regular clothes.

"Disembodied souls," said Adriel.

"Yeah, ghosts," I said.

Adriel shook his head.

We walked down the paved streets until Adriel stopped outside a small building with a green roof. The four corners of the roof sloped up to the sky, and a sign hung by two lengths of rope. I couldn't read the Chinese characters.

"What does it say?" I asked.

"Miss Jiao's Tea House."

"What are we doing here?"

"We came here to pass over."

My skin prickled. "Pass over means *die*," I said.

Adriel frowned.

"It's a euphemism," I said. "It means *die*."

"Why can't humans say what they mean?" he asked. "We need to pass over into Sheol. Why would anyone say *pass over* when they mean *die*?"

"Because death makes us uncomfortable." *And sad.*

We went inside. The wooden interior made the room feel warm. Flat mats and tables that you could only reach if you sat on the floor were situated throughout. On the long, narrow table in the back was a tea kettle. Steam issued from the kettle, and it smelled as if tea had been freshly brewed.

A woman, shorter than me, walked from behind the red partition that covered the back door. She had smooth, black hair and olive skin. She looked to be in her early twenties.

"What are you doing here, Seraph?" She folded her arms.

My jaw dropped. She could see him. She could see Adriel, an angel, standing next to me.

"Who's she?" the young woman asked.

"Her name's Lia," said Adriel. "She's like you."

I raised an eyebrow at Adriel.

"No one's like me," said the young woman.

"This is Jiao," said Adriel. "She's going help us get to Hell."

Jiao raised an eyebrow. "I'll do nothing of the sort."

Adriel lifted his hand into the air and opened his palm. Between his fingers was a small packet of green moss.

Jiao's eyes went wide. She reached up and tried to grab the packet.

Adriel lowered his hand, and Jiao snatched the packet from his grasp and held it to her face.

"Aramoti Tea," she cooed with reverence.

"I'll let you have that if you help us."

"Oh, alright," she said. "And I won't ask you why you want to go to that dark, evil place."

She turned and walked back behind the partition.

I raised my eyebrows at Adriel. "What did you mean I'm like her?"

Adriel sat on the floor at one of the low tables. "She knows tea magic."

"I don't know tea magic. How can she see you?"

"Just like you she can see beyond the Veil."

"Did her mother sell her soul to the Devil?" I asked.

"No, she sold her own. She's a witch."

Like my mother. I couldn't understand why anyone would drink demon blood. The stuff smelled like bile and was thicker than human blood, not that either sounded appetizing.

"How does an angel know a witch anyway?"

Adriel looked uncomfortable.

Jiao came back with a pot of tea. She poured the tea into each of our cups without spilling a drop. "Drink slowly. If you rush it, you could end up killing yourself." She looked at me. I guess Adriel didn't really need the warning.

I took a sip of the tea. Nothing happened at first, but the more sips I took, the more the world around me became unfocused. Things in the room started to change or disappear.

I blinked. I was in a different room. Jiao was gone, but Adriel was still with me. The room became darker. The legs of chairs were around me. Demons played at a pool table on one side of the room. Only some looked like men.

A horned bartender served drinks to demons in the forms of men and women sitting at the bar. The room smelled like beer and old carpet.

"Hey, what are you doing here?" The bartender pulled a shining, silver switchblade from his pocket.

The demons at the pool table stopped playing and stared at us. A few of them removed weapons from their belts.

Adriel and I got up from the floor. The tips of Adriel's wings reached the ceiling. Adriel lit up like a glow stick in the dark room.

The demons closed in on us. One grabbed my arm. His skin was black and blistered. Pointed teeth grinned from his too-wide mouth. A tail whipped behind him.

Adriel took the demon's wrist and twisted it until he knelt on the ground. Another, this one looked human, jabbed a dagger at Adriel, but he dodged the blade, picking him up and throwing him against the wall.

When the other bar patrons saw this, they backed away.

"Come on." Adriel grabbed my arm in his gloved hand.

We ran from the bar and out onto the street.

"I recognize this road," I said. "Nash's house is a few blocks that way." I pointed, and Adriel followed me down the street.

I hastened down an alley that cut across to Nash's house. I didn't want any demons seeing an angel walking through Hell. What if they alerted Lucifer? The bar patrons might do that.

Adriel kidnapped me twice, but I didn't want him thrown into the Pit. I wasn't sure what his motives were, but he was trying to protect me in the best way that he knew.

I opened the door and walked into Nash's house.

"Nash!" I called.

He rushed up to me. I thought he would hug me, but he pulled back. "What is *he* doing here?" Nash looked toward Adriel.

Adriel stood in the doorway. "I wasn't going to leave her," he said. "And I'm not leaving without the Twinblade."

I turned to him. "The Twinblade?"

"I saw you take it." He glared at Nash. "Return my weapon."

Why didn't Adriel come when we took the sword? He had to know I wouldn't have fought—

I backed away from Adriel. "You *are* with Raphael."

"No, I'm not," said Adriel. "You know that."

Did I? Why would Nash send us after Adriel if he wasn't our enemy?

Nash's eyes seared into Adriel like fire into flesh.

No. Anger drove Nash. Adriel would never deliver me to Raphael. "Did you send us after him because you hate him?" I asked.

Nash's eyes darted to mine.

"Return my weapon," Adriel said again.

"Over my dead body." Nash withdrew his sword.

I stood between them. "No!"

"Lia, make this bastard fall," said Nash, through gritted teeth.

"I'm not doing that, Nash. He saved me. He saved *you*."

Adriel smiled from the doorway. "It seems you've had this place warded."

"Yeah, I did," said Nash. "So, sons-of-bitches like you couldn't get in."

"You're not doing right by her," said Adriel. "She shouldn't be out fighting angels."

"I have to," I said. "My soul belongs to Lucifer."

"What?" Adriel had a pained expression on his face. He hadn't known the details of my deal with the Devil. Now he understood why I was backed into a corner. "No."

I nodded. "I have to do this, or my soul will be damned."

"What's *she* doing here?" Chandra stood on the landing on the second floor. Adrianna's hands were on her arms as they shook from the sobs.

She shrugged Adrianna away and raced down the steps towards me. Chandra plowed into me. I stepped back to steady myself. Nash got between us, and Adrianna held Chandra's arms.

"How dare you come back?" she screamed. Tears leaked from her eyes. "Alex is in the Pit, and it's all your fault. If you hadn't been so hell-bent on going after an Archangel, he'd still be here."

"Chandra, let's go." Kiran approached us from the hall.

Tom was behind him. His head was down. He hugged a large book to his chest.

"No," said Chandra. She pointed at me. "You did this. And if they weren't here to protect you, I'd tear your flesh into a million pieces and eat it." She wrenched herself free of Adrianna's grasp and marched out the front door.

Adriel flinched away from her as she passed. *Had she noticed an angel standing in the doorway?*

"It's okay," said Adrianna, but her voice was weak. She didn't believe her own words. She only used them to comfort me, but I didn't deserve comfort.

"No, it's not," I said, "I need to be alone." I rushed up the stairs and collapsed on my bed.

Sim sneaked out when I opened the door.

Chandra was right. All those poor souls that risked everything to help me were spending an eternity in the Pit. And I was the one who wanted to go after an Archangel.

I put my face in my pillow and screamed.

Uriel knew we were coming. That's why he was ready for us, and if he knew, that meant Raphael knew too. We couldn't win. Our plan to pick off his followers was dashed. We only collected ten angel weapons, including Adriel's Twinblade.

But now that Raphael knew what we were up to, the next time we went after an angel weapon would be our last.

I stood before the Pit. No light could enter it. Darkness was a theme in the music I listened to.

I used to think darkness was the night sky or the reflective surface of a turned-off television screen. It's hard to imagine nothing.

The Pit wasn't darkness. It wasn't a room with the lights turned off. Nothing lie beneath that darkness.

I wished I could reach in and pull Alex out of that hell, but he became part of it. That was my fault.

I stood at the edge of the Pit. In a moment of terror, I thought I might jump. No more battles would be fought because nothing would be left to fight over. My breath caught as my foot inched forward.

I shook my head and drew my foot back. An ironic smile crossed my lips.

"I knew you wouldn't jump."

I whirled around.

An angel stood behind me. His eyes were gray. The long, light brown locks hung limp around his angular face. His skin was unblemished. Soft, white wings were tucked at his back. The light around him didn't set me at ease.

I drew my sword.

His eyes latched onto the flash of steel. "That's not the reaction I usually get from humans." His lips curled into a smile.

"What do you want?" I asked. Why wasn't he lunging at me?

"Just to talk."

An instrument hung at his side. A long, silver horn. No weapon. He didn't come to fight me, but still I didn't sheath my sword.

"Who are you?" I asked.

"My name is Gabriel."

Shit. I was talking to the Archangel, Gabriel. "Are you with Raphael?"

Gabriel smiled. "I am."

I gulped and took a step back before I realized how close I was to the Pit. I cringed as I imagined my descent and thanked the stars it didn't happen. "Then you know who I am."

"I do."

"So, you know if I touch you, your pretty feathers will turn to ash."

His smile didn't fade. "I don't know what the Devil's promised you, but you're on the wrong side."

"I'm on the side that wants my parents' murderer dead."

Gabriel's eyes softened. "Raphael can be reckless with his ambition."

My grip on the hilt of the sword tightened. Gabriel spoke as if Raphael had gotten a speeding ticket. "As soon as I find Raphael, I will make him fall."

Gabriel glanced toward the Pit. "You think they're your friends, don't you? Demons look out for themselves. I would send every one of them to oblivion. That's what I'll do to the ones you call friends. But if you come with me, I'll have no reason to kill the roaches in the basement."

And Nash wouldn't have any reason to keep fighting. He and the others would be safe. But everyone who died would have to go to Sheol. I couldn't make that decision for them. It wasn't right.

"I won't go with you," I said. "And if you stay a second longer, I'll do everything in my power to keep you down here, and we both know how little that would take."

Gabriel stood strong, but his eyes twitched. "That's disappointing." He kicked off the ground and darted into the sky. The light emitted from his body. I shielded my eyes.

THE next day, I strolled around the backyard. My head was down, and my hands were in my pockets. Sim walked along with me, occasionally stopping to try to catch something I couldn't see.

I hadn't told anyone about Gabriel's little visit. It worried me that I didn't. Was I really considering Gabriel's offer? It would mean safety for my friends, but, no, I couldn't do it. I couldn't be the reason all those souls ended up in Sheol, including my parents.

Wings flapped above me.

Adriel landed by my side. "I'm sorry about what happened yesterday."

"Where did you go?" I asked.

"I watched from the sky. That is, when the thick clouds of Hell didn't roll in to block my vision."

"You didn't sleep."

"I didn't need to."

I wondered what it was like to watch the world sleep every night for your entire life, but I had a more burning question.

"Are you one of Raphael's followers?" I asked. "Please, tell me the truth."

A few days ago, Adriel wounded another angel to save me, but I couldn't shake the thought that he might want to deliver me to Raphael himself. Bob said as much back at the motel when I first met him.

Adriel seemed hurt by my question. "No," he said. "I don't follow Raphael or Michael, for that matter. I've been away from angel politics for a long time. I haven't walked through Heaven's gates in many years."

"Then why are you following me? Why are you protecting me?"

"I'm trying to save you from Raphael. I want to stop him."

"Then why not just kill me? Destroy his weapon."

"I won't do that."

I wondered if he could. Could an angel kill a human without falling from God's grace?

"The Twinblade, that's how you found me," I said.

"Yes, once I discovered that you meant it no harm, but that you were using my blade as a trap, I followed you."

"So, you've been following us this entire time?"

"It's not like I had a choice. You had my weapon, but I would have followed you anyway. You shouldn't be doing this, Lia."

"Doing what?"

"Making angels fall. Only God has the right to punish his children."

"Then why did he give me this power?"

"God didn't give you this power."

I stopped in front of him. "If that's all true, why are you protecting me?" I folded my arms.

"Because," he said, "I'm your guardian angel."

"My what?" I raised an eyebrow.

Adriel held my eyes. "When Sydriel went missing, I took her place. Sydriel was the angel you saw when you were four, much too old to still see angels. I didn't want you to see me. It wasn't right, so I watched from afar."

"Sydriel was my guardian angel?"

Adriel nodded. "No one knew she was gone for a long time, a decade. That's when I started watching you."

"If Sydriel was my guardian angel, then why would she leave me?"

"I don't think she did," said Adriel. "Sydriel has been a guardian for centuries. She has never left her charge."

"Maybe she left me because of what I can do, because of what I am."

"No. Something must have happened to her," he said. "As I watched you, I tried to find out what that might be. Did you ever touch her?"

"I don't know," I said. "I can't remember."

Adriel shook his head and sighed.

"Were you and Sydriel friends?"

His eyes darted to the ground. "We were on a different path, but yes, we were friends."

"What do you do?"

"I'm of the Seraphim, defenders of the Throne of God."

Defender of the Throne of God. Was that why he could cleave that angel's leg off without breaking a sweat?

"So that would make you?"

"Of the highest Order."

Whoa. Too bad Adriel wasn't on our side. Well, he *was* on my side. At least he didn't want to offer me to Raphael, but he didn't want me fighting angels either.

I didn't want to fight angels.

I was tired, and I didn't want any harm to come to my friends. I knew the only way they would stop was if I was gone. Maybe I was wrong to come back here.

"If you're my guardian angel, you'll help me find a way out of Sheol, for good this time."

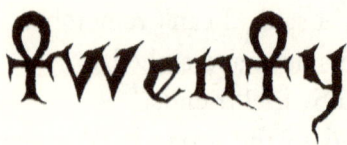

Twenty

I shut the front door to Nash's house. Adriel waited for me on the sidewalk. He wore a white t-shirt and dark jeans. Black gloves covered his hands.

"We don't have to walk far," he said.

"What happened to your armor?" I asked.

"I had to sell it."

"To get me out of here?"

He nodded.

"Couldn't you have just flown me out of here?"

"*I* could have, but not with you. A thick dome surrounds Hell like a layer of rock. I could break that rock without injury to myself, but you would get hurt. I could also be warded from reentry. This way is better. Follow me."

We walked down the street until we came to an alleyway and traveled into the darkness. I held Sim to my chest. Her warmth comforted me.

"Wait here," said Adriel.

Someone stepped out from the shadows. He had a long, snake-like body. This was the man that Adriel sold his armor to. The thought that he had given his beautiful, shining armor to this seedy man made my stomach lurch.

"The portal," said Adriel.

"Of course." The man twisted his finger in the air, and a rip appeared, wide enough for Adriel and me to pass through.

"I'll go first." Adriel stepped into the portal.

After a few seconds, I stepped in after him.

The night was warm and humid, on the edge of autumn. We were on the side of the road in front of a forest and across the street from a small, roadside diner.

"Where are we?" I asked.

"I'm not sure," said Adriel. "You go over to that diner, and grab something to eat."

"But I don't have any money."

"Don't worry about that. I'll be back soon."

"You're leaving?" I asked.

"I'll be back before you're finished eating."

The hum of insects quieted as I walked to the other side of the street. I hid Sim beneath my jacket. She was asleep and wouldn't bother anyone. I opened the glass door of the diner and walked inside. Cushioned wooden booths lined the windows at the front of the diner.

A plump waitress smiled and came from around the counter. "Sit anywhere you like, hon."

I slid into the booth in the back corner though the diner was empty. I placed Sim in my lap beneath the warm coat.

The waitress came over to my table. "Can I start you off with something to drink?"

"Water is fine. Can you tell me where I am?"

She raised her eyebrow.

"I've been on the road all night, and I fell asleep in the car."

"You're in Statesboro, hon."

"Oh."

She studied the parking lot outside the window. "Where's your car?"

"Uh, my boyfriend dropped me off. He went down the road to find a gas station. I was so hungry, I couldn't wait."

Did I just call Adriel my boyfriend?

The waitress eyed me for a moment, but smiled. "I'll get that water for you."

When the waitress returned, I ordered eggs and sausage. "Can I get a second order for my boyfriend?"

"Sure, hon."

I watched the window for any sign of Adriel as I waited for my breakfast. I hoped he would come back soon. I didn't want the waitress to call the police on me because I couldn't pay. They might run my name and find out that I was a runaway from New Orleans.

I was far from New Orleans, though. I think Statesboro is somewhere in Georgia.

The waitress set my food on the table and set out a place across from me for my "boyfriend." As she strolled back to the counter, Adriel walked in. The bell above the door chimed.

The waitress jumped. "Oh, my, I'm sorry, hon. The wind must have blown the door open."

Adriel sat down across from me. He passed me a paper bag. I peered inside. Rolls of bills were at the bottom.

I raised an eyebrow and moved the bag onto the seat next to me.

I made sure the waitress was gone before I asked, "Where did you get all this money?"

"Never mind that. It should be enough to get you food and a bus ticket."

"You're not coming with me?" I asked.

"I am. But I don't have my bike. It's better if I follow you from above."

"I got you breakfast." I gestured to the plate in front of him. "You can take it to go, so the waitress doesn't freak out when she sees food float up in the air and disappear into nothing."

"I don't eat."

I narrowed my eyes for a moment. Oh, that's right. He'd said so back when we first met. Whoa. *Was that almost a year ago?*

I shrugged. "Yeah, you told me. I thought you were joking." I guess that made sense. Angels couldn't die. Why would they need to eat?

"If I could eat," said Adriel, "I wouldn't eat the carcass of another sentient being." He eyed the meat like it was road-kill.

I swallowed the sausage I was chewing, and ate the eggs instead.

"So, where are we going?" I asked.

"You should stay here for a while," he said.

"You're not staying."

"I'll be watching."

"That's creepy," I said. "No one else can see you. You could stay with me."

He shook his head. "That's not possible."

"Well, watching from a distance is weird."

"I'm a guardian, that's what I do."

I pushed my plate away and folded my arms on the table. "Why did they think that I needed a Seraphim to guard me? I mean, you defend the throne of God."

"You mean Seraph."

"Huh?"

"I'm of the Seraphim. I am a Seraph."

"Sorry. Why would I need a *Seraph* to guard me?"

"I volunteered."

"You didn't even know me."

"I wanted to find out what happened to Sydriel."

"What did you find?"

"I found angel blood in the house where you used to live."

"Angel blood?"

"That's right. A lot. Whatever happened to Sydriel, she was badly injured, and whoever hurt her had access to Arcadian Steel."

"An angel."

"Or a demon."

The waitress came back to the table and refilled my orange juice. She glanced at my plate. "Not liking it, hon? I can get ya something else."

"No, thank you," I said. "I'm not feeling too well. You can take it back."

The waitress eyed me, but she took my plate.

"You can take that one too," I said. I looked across the table at Adriel. "He's not coming."

She grabbed that plate too. "You need me to call someone, hon?"

I pulled my phone out of my pocket. I'd been in Sheol for ten months. My phone long since died. I didn't have any service anyway. No one to pay the bill.

"Yeah," I said. "Is there a phone I could borrow?" I asked. "I'll pay. Mine died, and I need to make a call."

"Sure." The waitress reached into her skirt pocket and handed me a smartphone with a cracked screen. She walked away from the table and wiped down the counters. She glanced over at me every few seconds.

I dialed Jonah's number. The phone rang for so long, I thought he wouldn't pick up, but his groggy voice was on the other line. "Hello?"

"Uncle Jonah?"

"Li? Where are you?"

"Are you going to call family services on me?"

"No."

"I'm at a diner."

"Where? I'll come pick you up."

"It's far," I said. "I'll come to you, but only if you promise not to involve the caseworker."

Silence leaked from the other end of the line.

"Uncle Jonah?"

"Alright," he stuttered. "I just want you home, Li. I need to know you're safe. I'm staying in Mid-City. Renting a place on North Rampart."

I bought a bus ticket to New Orleans. My head lulled against the glass, and I slept for most of the way.

A full night's sleep was difficult to come by in Sheol. It was too quiet. At least, I had the hum of the bus to still me to sleep.

I awoke still tired. I had a lot of catching up to do.

When I got off the bus, I walked to North Rampart Street. I wandered down the narrow street of raised houses without front lawns or driveways. Houses were painted bright orange, neon pink, and other colors that would be more suitable at an abstract art museum than on a residential street.

Cars were packed along the sides of the street, making the street narrower. I couldn't imagine driving down it, squeezing my way, just barely scraping double-parked cars along the cracked, shaded street.

I glanced down at the address I had written on the palm of my hand. This was the place. I turned the handle of the barred door and knocked.

Coughing and shuffling came from inside. Jonah opened the door. Dark circles surrounded his blood-shot eyes.

"Come in. These streets aren't safe at night." He wore a ruffled t-shirt and a pair of striped pajama pants.

I stepped inside. A galley kitchen was to my left. To my right was a short hallway with two doors, and behind the kitchen was a small table with two chairs. The living room was bare except for a small television against one wall.

I put Sim on the floor, and she explored the apartment.

Jonah ambled into the kitchen. "Go ahead and drop your stuff anywhere." He poured coffee into a mug. "Do you want anything? Water, tea? I have orange juice."

"I'll take coffee," I said.

Jonah squinted. "But you don't like coffee."

"I didn't know you knew that about me."

"I think it's kind of a crime here to not like it."

"It's starting to grow on me. That bus ride was killer."

Jonah poured a second cup and brought both to the table. I sat across from him and sipped the coffee, lukewarm and bitter, but I didn't care. I was tired and too on edge to sleep.

Uncle Jonah's knee bobbed up and down which caused his whole body to tremble. He gulped his coffee like someone might snatch it away from him. His hand shook as he brought it back down to the table.

"This is a small place," I said.

"Just moved," said Jonah. "Couldn't afford the rent at the old place."

"Why aren't you staying at Mom and Dad's?" I asked.

"They left everything to you, Li. The house, the paintings, your mom's trust account."

"Uncle Jonah, I need that money."

"You can't get it. Not until you're eighteen."

"I won't need it when I'm eighteen. By then, I'll have a job and my own apartment. I need that money now."

Jonah sighed. "You're idealistic. Your dad did that to you. Micah made you believe anything is possible. But the world's not like that. It knocks you on your ass, a lot, and not everybody can be whatever they want to be. You don't always get what you want."

He was right. What I wanted was for my parents to be alive. I wanted to be safe and warm at home.

Instead, I was on the run.

"Why are you shaking like that?" I asked.

"Withdrawals. It's better now," he said. "I joined a group. I think it's really helping this time."

"That's good," I said.

"It will be, once it's over."

I smiled. He was trying. That's what Dad would have wanted.

"Can I stay here?" I asked.

"Where were you staying?"

"Please," I said.

Jonah's eyes swept up to the ceiling. "I could get in a lot of trouble for this. But I don't want you sleeping under some bridge. You can stay as long as you need to."

Twenty one

I pet Sim and poured food into her bowl. I found a job, waitressing at a local café. College students came for coffee and lunch. I would have started my junior year in high school and looking for the right college would have been the most important thing to me.

A month and a half passed since I left Sheol, and no sign of angels wanting to take my head off or put me in chains. I felt normal. I liked normal.

A few colleges existed in the area. Each with its own music department. I had taken the bus to a few of the colleges and looked around.

I'd love to major in music. I didn't know if I could pick electric guitar as my instrument.

An amp sat in one of the music rooms. I got into the habit of bringing my guitar and hooking it up. I played long into the evening and didn't get back to Jonah's apartment until night.

He was never there. Between work and his group meetings, the only time I saw him was around noon if I wasn't working. That was right before he would shuffle into his bedroom to sleep. I was glad he was getting help. Dad would be proud.

Sometimes when I was on the bus or walking to work, I saw Adriel out of the corner of my eye. I thought it was creepy that he was always watching, but it gave me a sense of comfort too. I knew that if anything happened, he would rush in to help.

The music building was pretty much empty for the night. I should probably get back to the apartment before it got too late, but it felt good to get carried away with my guitar.

That night, I played like no one could hear me. I tried more complex songs and wasn't afraid to put my body into it as I slid across the floor and jumped around like I was performing a rock concert.

"You're really good."

I stopped, and the sound of my guitar echoed and faded.

A guy with curly, brown hair smiled at me. He wore a t-shirt and jeans. A backpack hung from one shoulder. He was a good-looking guy, and he didn't look that much older than me.

"Thank you," I said. "I was just messing around."

"Sorry to interrupt," he said. "I left my notes." He plucked a notebook from one of the aluminum folding chairs. He saluted me as a way of goodbye.

"Wait," I said. "You're a music major? What instrument do you play?"

What was I doing? I didn't need the distraction. I knew I would never see Nash again, but I was still thinking about him. I needed to get over him, but tossing a new guy into the mix wasn't the best way to do that.

"The drums," he said. "My dad used to play at Fritzels. Jazz."

"You play Jazz?"

"Yep. Since I was a kid. You practice here a lot?"

"Just about every night. I'm Lia by the way."

"Carson. Well, I'll see you around, Lia." He grinned and turned on his heel.

After he left, I packed up my guitar and walked to the bus stop. An old woman sat on the bench. Her hair was covered by a shawl tied beneath her chin. She coughed a loud hacking cough.

I stood at the opposite end of the bench. The woman continued to cough, and I thought about asking her if she was okay, but I couldn't bring myself to pierce the silence between the coughs. I glanced over at her, and my skin crawled.

She looked up at me, and for a moment the Veil was lifted. Her skin was cracked and bleeding. Her eyes were black, no pupils, no whites, but one solid color.

A demon.

I reached for my sword reflexively, and, in the same moment, realized the blade wasn't at my side. The woman continued to stare at me as I backed away. The air became thin and still. The sky seemed darker than seconds before. My breath spiked. I turned and ran from the bus stop.

I ran for five blocks and reached the next stop. No one else waited for the bus. My body shook, and I couldn't bear to sit. As soon as the bus pulled up to the curb, I was on it.

When I got home, I locked the deadbolt. Jonah was at work, and the apartment was quiet. I spotted Sim on the couch, and relief settled upon me like a warm blanket. Petting Sim always put me at ease.

I placed my guitar case against the wall and plopped down on the couch. Jonah bought the couch a few days ago. He was doing well with his meetings and his new job. He still suffered from withdrawals, but he seemed less jittery in the mornings.

The couch was my new bed. Jonah offered me his room, but I said I didn't mind the couch. I woke up every morning with a stiff back, but it didn't bother me that much. I was searching for something different than Sheol to prove to myself that I hadn't become accustomed to the comforts of the Outer Region.

I stretched out on the couch. My feet barely reached the opposite end. I kicked my shoes off and removed my socks with my toes.

The air from the vent against the wall left a chill on my skin, but when the sound of its humming ceased, dread wrapped its fingers around my throat. The image of the woman at the bus stop burned behind my eyes. I grabbed the remote and turned on the small television, a beacon of light in the cold, dark room.

I wished I hadn't left my sword, not because I wanted to hunt the monsters but in case they attacked me. What if I saw one in Jonah's apartment?

I turned to face the plush back of the couch and closed my eyes. I didn't need the images on the screen. The gentle lull of the voices was enough to let sleep take me.

THE clasps of my guitar case were cool against my fingertips. The case popped open with a satisfying squeal of the hinges. I lifted my guitar out of its velvet casket. It came to life again every time I played it.

"Hey." Carson dropped his backpack to the floor. Two drumsticks bound together in his fist.

"Hey." I parroted back. I wanted to choke the silence. "Trying to get some practice in?"

"Thought it might be fun if we played together." He grinned. He sat on the stool behind the drum set in the corner of the room.

"I don't know Jazz," I said.

"You don't need to," he said. "I can play anything."

I squinted my eyes. "Okay," I said. The words pulled out of my lips.

"You start. I'll follow the melody."

I plugged my guitar into the amp and played the first cords of "Come As You Are." My heart beat with the drums as Carson tapped in harmony. Each third note rang out like breaking water. The clear, sharp noise mesmerized my eardrums.

Together we weren't perfection, but something else: potential.

The last note of my guitar faded into rippling silence. We played three more songs after that and met again the night after to play more.

Soon, we played every night. I even learned some Jazz. For two nights now, Carson walked with me to the bus stop. We talked about music mostly. The occasional mention of the latest movie or internet meme felt surreal to me. Normal stuff. I had to remind myself of that. Especially when I saw them.

Sometimes they walked down the street or lurked in the corners. When I tried not to look, a stray glance froze the blood in my veins. They watched me. They knew I could see them. That's why they showed themselves to me—black eyes, skin touched by embers, clawed hands, and cruel smiles. They got joy from scaring me.

I celebrated my seventeenth birthday with Sim. I ordered a pizza and bought a cupcake from the café where I worked.

I still missed Nash and the others, but knowing that they weren't risking their lives against warrior angels made me feel better.

"Can I take you out sometime?" Carson asked.

"Yeah, that would be great," I said. "Where did you have in mind?"

"There's this Italian place in town. The decor isn't spectacular, but the food is great."

"Okay," I said.

"We can go after this if you want."

I glanced down at what I wore. A black t-shirt and jeans. I was uncomfortable going to dinner without wearing long, beautiful dresses, but I wasn't in Sheol anymore. Regular teenagers went to dinner at places where you could wear jeans.

We took Carson's sedan to the restaurant. The front of the building was glass with white paper blocking the view of the outside, which was a busy street surrounded by other businesses.

I was so used to Nash's cooking and the nice restaurants that he took me to that I felt like the food was less than remarkable. The pasta was more like Chef Boyardee than fine Italian cuisine. Still, it was nice to feel normal for once and to be on a date with a normal, *human* guy.

Carson brought me on a few more dates, and I still met with him to play guitar and drums. He was a nice guy. He wanted to follow in his dad's footsteps and become a professional drummer.

I didn't tell him that I was on the run from the foster care system and a militant army of angels. Instead, I told him that I lived in a small parish outside New Orleans and that I wanted a fresh start so I moved out here.

I smiled as I walked home from work. For the first time in months, I was happy. I had Carson, and a job. I thought about catching up on school, but hadn't figured out a way to do that without putting family services on my trail.

A mother and her daughter walked ahead of me. An old man with a cane stood at the street corner as he waited for a car to pass. His cane wobbled, and the old man knelt to the ground. He was on his hands and knees in the street.

The young mother gestured for her daughter to stay on the sidewalk as she rushed over to the old man and helped him up from the street. The man smiled. He thanked her and continued down the cross walk.

If Raphael got what he wanted, that mother and her child will never have a chance to enter Heaven. The gates will be closed to them.

And Mom and Dad, would they be tossed out? I clenched my locket in my hands.

I couldn't hide forever. Raphael was hell-bent on closing the gates, and I was his weapon. Adriel might do everything in his power to protect me, but Raphael would find me. But, even if he didn't, he might find another way to get what he wanted.

Could I live with the guilt that everyone in the world would be destined for Hell, and I could have done something?

I searched for Adriel everywhere I went. I would tell him that I wanted to go back. That I needed to go back, but he was nowhere to be found. I knew that he was watching, but he kept his distance.

WE stopped outside Carson's apartment complex. Carson's apartment had the same number of rooms as Jonah's, but each room was more spacious.

"I'll order the food," he said. "Why don't you find a movie?"

"What do you feel like watching?" I asked.

"Nothing with flying cars or government conspiracies but barring that I'm game for just about anything."

My laugh was quiet. Air left my nose as I grinned. I plopped down on the couch and browsed the movies on the TV menu. I landed on a movie about killer tomatoes who ate people, and I stuck with that.

The food came a quarter into the movie. Carson laughed with a mouth full of chow mein. I laughed when he laughed. I glanced over from time to time, but I wasn't watching the movie.

His Adam's apple bobbed as he chortled. He lived without worries. When the credits rolled, and all we had were empty paper boxes on the coffee table, Carson placed his hand on mine. "You have great taste in movies."

"Really?"

"Yeah," he said. His voice was breathy. He leaned in close to me, but his motions were so subtle I didn't notice until his face was inches from mine. He looked down at me and searched my eyes as if he examined a new piece of sheet music—both fascinating and unfamiliar.

"Is this okay?" he asked as he moved closer to me.

My head nodded without my thinking to do it. His lips latched onto mine as if my assent broke a dam, and all the water rushed out. His kiss was soft at first as he explored. But as my fingers pressed into his shoulders, he pressed his lips onto mine with a bruising pressure.

"Do you want to…" He trailed off.

My head nodded away again, but this time my voice joined in. "Yes."

His hand was around mine as he pulled me from the sofa and down the hall. My head was so clouded I didn't look around. My back hit the soft mattress.

Carson's lips covered mine again, and I wasn't so cold anymore. He kissed my jawline, my neck. His hands traveled up beneath my shirt and touched my chilled skin, setting it on fire. My hands grabbed fistfuls of his t-shirt.

His mouth breathed into my ear. "Are you sure?"

I was about to say *yes* when a low rattle sounded from somewhere in the room.

My eyes popped open.

A skinny, red-skinned demon crouched in the corner, its elbows on its knees, hands over elbows, and a wide leering grin on its face.

I pressed my body into the mattress. My hands flew up to Carson's chest. I grounded my palms into him.

"What is it?" Carson asked. "Did I hurt you?"

"There's something in here," I said without thinking.

Carson got from on top of me and whirled around. "Where?" His eyes darted around the room, sweeping over the demon, not seeing it.

With two clawed fingers, held up like the peace sign, the demon pointed to its eyes and slowly turned a long, crooked finger to me.

I crawled backward on the bed. "I don't feel comfortable in here."

"Okay," said Carson. A frown was on his face, and his eyes were full of concern. "We can go back to the couch."

I darted into the hallway and stood at the door. Carson took his time. He grabbed something off the nightstand. The demon's eyes followed his movements.

"Hurry up!" I blurted out.

"Alright, jeez," he said. "Are you feeling okay?" He moved from the bed to the hallway. I watched the demon's face through the sliver until Carson closed the door.

We sat back down on the couch, and he kissed my neck. I looked toward the hallway and imagined the door creaking open and the demon crawling towards us on its crooked, red limbs. If *I leave tonight something might happen to Carson when I'm gone.*

"Stop. I have to tell you something," I said.

Carson pulled away from me. "What's up?"

"There's something in your room," I said.

He squinted at me.

"This is going to sound crazy…"

"You saw something I didn't?" he asked, eyebrow raised.

"That's just the thing, I did. I do. There's a…demon in your bedroom."

Carson scratched the back of his head and laughed. "Look, Lia—"

"I'm not joking," I said. "I see them sometimes. There's one in there right now."

"You're serious?" He whistled air and leaned away from me. "That's quite an ability: seeing demons."

"I've been seeing them since I was a kid. They can only be killed by Arcadian Steel. I have a sword, but I left it behind when I came back."

"Came back from where?"

"Hell."

"Okay, maybe I should take you home."

"You can't come back here," I said. "I don't know what it wants from you, but it could hurt you."

"Lia, you can stop now. It's not funny."

"I told you this is not a joke."

Carson stood and put on his jacket. "I'm taking you home."

"No, you have to believe me." I pulled on the sleeve of his jacket.

He shrugged me off. "All I have to do is bring you home, and that's what I'm doing. Get your coat."

I stared at him, but no amount of standing there was going to get him to believe me. I sounded crazy. A year ago, I thought I was.

Carson drove me back to Jonah's apartment. I looked down as the car idled at the curb. I couldn't look at him, but I could feel the tension between us. I grabbed the door handle and pushed the door open. I stepped out of the car and slung my guitar strap across my chest.

Once I was at the front door, the car pulled away and zoomed down the street. I unlocked the door and stepped inside the apartment. Jonah's keys weren't on the counter so he must have been at work or one of his meetings.

Light came from the living room. I tossed my key onto the counter and turned the corner. I froze.

Three angels stood in the room. Light glowed around them. Arcadian Steel swords hung at their sides. Their soft hair looked as graceful as the feathers on their wings. They wore steel plated armor.

As they charged, a flash blinded me, and, like a bolt of lightning, Adriel faced the attacking angels. He carried a dagger. I wasn't sure what match the dagger would be against their swords.

Adriel slashed one of the angels and left a long, thin cut at the base of his neck. All three angels surrounded Adriel. He cut, slashed, and ducked. But the angels left a pattern of cuts along his arms and chest.

Sprays of silver blood speckled the walls and cushions of the couch. The television screen was cracked, and the small, square dinner table lost its legs.

Adriel was on his back, an angel above him, ready to sink his sword into Adriel's chest. I rushed forward, colliding into the angel's back, feeling his soft feathers against my hands, feeling them burn. The embers flaked into the air like burnt newspaper. The blood pounded in my ears.

A rip like torn fabric cut through the chaos. A portal opened, a tear in space, a glowing open wound. Nash came through that wound, followed by Chandra, Adrianna, and Kiran.

Nash stared at me like I was the lock ness monster. "Grab him," he ordered the others, without taking his eyes off me.

Chandra and Adrianna grabbed either arm of the fallen angel. They moved him through the tear and disappeared on the other side.

Nash's eyes stabbed me. "What are you going to do?"

The glowing portal beckoned. Adriel fought one angel. He dispensed the other one who knelt on the floor. Silver blood leaked out of a massive wound in the angel's side where his armor had given way to Adriel's dagger.

Adriel would be fine. He was a Seraph. I couldn't let him stop me from doing what I must do.

The world is a harmonica, and its music must be played.

"I need to go back." I took Nash's hand, and he pulled me through the portal.

Twenty Two

THE air was still. Everything was dull and gray. The sky looked like a painting. The off-white clouds were motionless. Light seemed to peer through as if my eyes were covered by a thick, dark veil.

Sim's warm body settled against me as I clenched her to my chest. The poor cat passed through nearly as many portals as I had.

The fallen angel hung limply in the arms of Chandra and Adrianna. Nash was at my side. I could feel the warmth of him, but dared not look at him. Kiran stepped through behind us. No one spoke.

We stood so close, but a gulf was between us.

Adrianna smiled at me guiltily. "I'm glad Raphael didn't tear you to pieces."

Raphael wanted me alive, but the thought of him ripping me apart limb from limb still gave me the chills.

I followed Nash as he strolled with his hands in his pockets, but I kept my distance.

Bob was parked outside Nash's house. He said something to Nash with a smile, but I couldn't make out the words.

When I approached, Bob said, "Nice to see you again, sweetheart. It wasn't very kind of you to leave us."

"I wanted to keep my friends safe."

Bob walked with me to the door. "You're lucky they weren't tossed into the Pit after your little stunt."

I hadn't thought of that, but I should have. Of course, Lucifer would be angry, and she would toss the first demon she could get her hands on into the Pit. I felt an unsettling feeling like when I catch myself after a bad fall or when I'm not careful when handling sharp objects. I'd made a mistake I narrowly escaped.

Bob smiled and gestured towards the open door. "After you, my dear."

I stepped into the foyer. Tom was on the couch in the living room. He looked up from the large tome he was reading.

His eyes met mine. He smiled and went back to his book. *Was that sadness in his eyes?*

It had been three months since Alex died, and Chandra wasn't the only one who missed her brother. Tom had cared for him. I never apologized to Tom for letting Alex die.

Nash made us coffee. I sat on the couch next to Adrianna. Nash sat in a chair across from me. His eyes were on his cup.

Nash glanced up. When his eyes met mine, they glistened. He shook his head. He pushed himself up from the chair and walked over to me. "You got what you were looking for?" he asked.

"Yeah," I said. "But I realized I couldn't stay."

"I'm glad you didn't." He put his hands in his pockets and walked up the stairs. When he was half way up, he turned his head. "If you want your old room back, it's yours for as long as you want to stay." He disappeared into the hallway.

"He's been like that the whole time you were gone," said Adrianna. "I think it really got to him that you didn't say goodbye."

How could I say goodbye? Nash would have tried to stop me. They didn't know I was trying to save them. They thought I was being selfish.

That night, Nash hosted a dinner. The table was laid out with a variety of rich food, no doubt all cooked by him.

I wore the red dress. I asked Adrianna to do my hair. I wanted to make amends with Nash.

Tom, Adrianna, Kiran, and Chandra chatted and laughed. I drowned out their voices like the white noise of a TV as it lulled me to sleep. Adrianna stole some glances at me to make sure I wasn't sulking, but it wasn't me she should have been worried about.

Nash had barely taken three bites of the food he had obviously worked tirelessly to prepare. He didn't join in on the conversation, and his eyes avoided mine.

He downed his glass of wine. "I'm going to bed." His voice cut through the banter, and the room went silent as he left.

I pushed the food around on my plate some more before I climbed the steps to my bedroom. My guitar rested on the bed. Sim was curled into a crescent of fur on the pillow.

She watched me as I grabbed my guitar and crossed the room to hook it up to the amp. I strummed a few quiet notes before my fingers picked up speed.

The music was hard and fast. It hit my ears like a hand swatting a fly.

My guitar pick slipped from my fingers, but I continued to play. Despite my calluses, pain flared, and blood dripped onto the cold, marble floor.

The music faded in one long, dissonant note. I slumped to the floor. Fat tears fell among the drops of blood.

I couldn't do anything right. All the shame and exhaustion that made me leave the first time came flooding back. What was I doing? I couldn't defeat an Archangel.

"THIS is the next weapon we'll go after." Tom pointed to the picture in a large book he rested on the coffee table in Nash's living room.

The sword was curved. The hilt was decorated with steel angel wings.

Chandra and Nash hadn't come to our meeting. I doubted either of them would ever forgive me.

I sighed.

"What's wrong?" asked Adrianna.

"If we go out there again," I said, "they'll be ready for us, just like last time."

"And we'll be ready for them," said Kiran.

Over the last week, I trained harder than ever to make up for the months I lost. Nash didn't say much to me, but he did give me instruction. Dark circles crept under his eyes.

"Lia, I need to talk to you," he said.

I nodded and followed him out of the house and to his car. He opened the door for me, and I got in. He started the car and zoomed out onto the street. He drove faster than usual, but I knew he was in control. My stomach was getting used to his driving.

He parked at the edge of the Pit. This was fast becoming our spot, though I didn't want it to be.

Nash chose it because no one would bother us here. No one in Sheol wanted to be this close to the Pit.

Nash stared out into the abyss.

"Nash?"

"How was it?" asked Nash. "On the outside."

I removed my seatbelt and sat back against the seat. I didn't want to tell him the truth, but I didn't want to lie to him either. "It was everything I hoped it would be. I still want to go back to it after we defeat Raphael."

Nash looked up. He closed his eyes.

"I'm sorry, Nash."

I didn't know what he expected of me. He didn't think that I'd stay in Sheol with him forever? After all, the only reason I fought Raphael was so Lucifer would free my soul.

"I don't want to die," I said.

He looked at me with determination in his eyes. "I won't let that happen. But I do think you should reconsider your reasons for doing this." He wanted me to stay with him.

"I know." I looked down. "But there's one good reason. It's Hell, Nash."

"You don't belong here," he said.

That surprised me. But he hadn't flirted. He barely touched me. I was reading him wrong. No, I hoped he saw me differently, but that wasn't reality. If not for Lucifer's orders, he'd want me as far from him as possible.

"After you complete her agenda, Lucifer will never let go of such a powerful weapon. She isn't going to let you go back home, and when you die, she'll keep your soul so she can test whether the ability still lives in you."

"But I have to trust her. If she *is* lying, what other choice have I got?" I asked. "I do have another reason for doing this. My mom and dad are in Heaven. I know they are. I'm not going to let Raphael boot them out even if it means I have to stay down here."

"But you don't know that," said Nash.

"I do." I remembered the strange scars on his back. "Have *you* been there?" I asked.

He shook his head.

I wondered if that was the first lie he told me.

FOOD covered the surface of the table: Caesar salad, stuffed eggplant, roasted potatoes, and risotto. Nash put his heart into this meal as he always did.

He joined in again. He laughed with Kiran at the end of the table. But after what he told me at the Pit, I wondered if his joy was manufactured.

We were all dressed in our usual dinner attire. I wore a long, black dress with lace detail in the bodice.

Despite my feelings about Nash, he, Adrianna, Kiran, Tom, and Chandra had become my family.

The only person who was missing was Adriel. He'd done so much for me, but he didn't support me fighting angels, and I needed to fight angels to keep my friends alive.

I wondered if he still watched me from a distance. Perhaps he did.

A flash flooded in from the windows.

We fell silent.

"What was that?" asked Chandra.

Nash bolted from the table, and we all followed. He threw open the front door as the sky flashed bright again.

Lightning zipped across the gray and came down like thin arms, seeking to take all Sheol with them.

And there they were, clad in silver, their wings bathed in Arcadian Steel. More than fifty angels.

"Holy hell," said Tom.

"They're attacking Sheol," said Nash. "Come on, grab the weapons."

We rushed down to the armory and grabbed our weapons. As we made our way out the door, the angels descended.

"Get in the car!" Nash shouted. "There's no time."

We threw the weapons in the trunk and piled into Nash's car. It was a tight fit. Adrianna sat on Kiran's lap.

Nash sped down the street.

"Where are they?" asked Kiran.

"It looks like they touched down near the Pit."

"Near the Pit?" Chandra's voice wavered.

"I'm afraid so," said Nash. "Hold on!" He curved around the corner.

Something hit the car like a brick. Wings flared out as an angel, sword raised, knelt on the hood of the car. Images of my parents hanging from their seats hit me. I couldn't breathe.

"Oh, shit!" said Tom.

Nash jerked the wheel, and the angel jumped off the car and hovered above us. The car skidded to a stop. Nash turned around and looked at us. "Alright, we're getting out. Grab the weapons. We can do this."

I nodded.

We raced out of the car. Kiran opened the trunk, and we removed our weapons.

Angels and demons fought before us. More black blood speckled the streets than silver.

As soon as Nash grabbed his weapon, he ran into the fight and met swords with an angel. Nash's toned arms brought the sword down on the angel. I remembered how it felt to be wrapped in the warmth of those arms, as his lips hovered inches from mine, before they pushed me away. They were capable of so much tenderness and yet so much destruction.

I felt a hand on my shoulder.

"I hate you," said Chandra, "But you're the only one who can kill angels. Stay behind me, and touch as many of those bastards as you can."

Her blade cut into the body of the angel in front of her. She pierced his skin, and silver blood oozed out.

I lurched forward, ducked my head, and grabbed his exposed wrist. His wings burst into flames, and his were the loudest screams in all Sheol. I stayed near Chandra, careful not to breathe in the dust of his ashen feathers.

Kiran and Adrianna fought together. Silver and black blood covered them.

Tom was not far from where Chandra and I stood. The angel he fought wielded a silver axe. His shield clashed with the axe and sent sparks like falling stars down onto the street.

Chandra tore the hem of her dress until the skirt was right above her knees. "Look out," she screamed.

I ducked, not knowing where the threat was.

Chandra's sword forced the blade away from me and pushed the angel who wielded it back. The angel kicked Chandra in the stomach and sent her sailing across the field.

"Chandra!" I shouted. I dodged the blade in time.

I ran. I avoided the fighting angels and demons until I made my way to an alley and sank down against the wall, hidden in the shadows.

I looked across the field for Nash and the others, but I couldn't make out anyone. They were lost in a mass of bodies and flashes of steel.

But I did see one face I recognized: Adriel. He was above the battle, scanning the skies, looking for me. But he didn't have a weapon. He wasn't wearing any armor because I asked him to take me back home, to the home I abandoned once again.

I wasn't doing any good, hiding in the dark. It was my fault Adriel didn't have his armor or a weapon. I looked to my right. There was Nash's car. No one was around it.

I glanced to the left and the right to make sure no one looked my way. I raced for the car and slammed the driver's side door shut. The keys were still in the ignition. Blood spattered on the windshield. I turned the key, and the engine sputtered. I hoped the car could get me to Nash's house and back.

After I turned the car around, I sped off toward the house.

As I walked into the foyer, Sim padded down the stairs. She hissed at me. Her teeth were sharp and snakelike. I looked at her quizzically. She never hissed at me before.

I threw open the doors of the armory and pulled Adriel's sword from the wall. The Twinblade.

The sword was heavier than I anticipated. Edged on both sides, the blade ended in two sharp points. Below that, golden wings made up the cross guard.

Chandra lifted the sword effortlessly from the wall in La Fenice. I could barely lift the sword above the ground. I dragged it up the stairs and out to the car.

I had to get it to Adriel. He was a Seraph. Once he had his sword, he would save my friends.

I turned the key in the ignition. The car made a loud screech, but wouldn't start.

"Come on," I urged.

I turned the key again, and the car sputtered to life. I backed away from the house and followed the road back to where I left Nash and the others.

I slammed on the brakes, but the car wouldn't stop. The wheels assaulted the bodies of the fallen warriors and slammed into the fighters, sending bodies over the car. The car barreled toward the Pit.

The black abyss threatened to swallow me and Nash's car for all eternity. The metal screeched as a javelin tore through the roof and into the ground.

The car stopped half way over the edge.

The breath was caught in my throat.

The long, steel javelin pierced the car and held the vehicle in place.

I climbed to the back and grabbed Adriel's sword. I didn't want to face what was out there, but I desperately wanted to get out of the vehicle that was two wheels in the grave.

I opened the driver's side back door and climbed out of the car, skewered on the javelin. The front of the car tilted from side to side, and the wheels still rolled.

The earth shuttered as an angel landed in front of me. Around his neck was a silver horn. The angel with the silver trumpet, God's messenger.

Gabriel.

I spun around, anger rose like a tidal wave behind my eyes. I used every bit of strength I possessed to point Adriel's sword at Gabriel.

"That isn't yours, is it?" Gabriel asked. "But you're used to taking others' things, aren't you?"

My voice trembled despite my efforts to slow my breathing. "Get out of here," I said, "you don't belong in Sheol."

"And you do?" He shook his head. "I came here to warn you. I do follow Raphael, but I don't condone the reckless way he killed your parents."

I gulped. My arms burned from holding the heavy weapon. "You came without him."

Gabriel nodded. "You're playing a game beyond you, girl. Raphael wanted you to gather the angel weapons. He wanted you to make those angels fall."

"Why would he want me to go after his own followers?"

"*His* followers?" Gabriel shook his head. "The more angels you took down, the less who would stand up against him. He instructed his followers to retrieve their weapons, long before you started your quest."

I squinted. "How did he know what I was doing?" But we *were* taking down Raphael's followers. Gabriel was trying to confuse me and make me think Raphael had the upper hand.

"He watched you all along."

Sim's sleek body patted toward me. Her body morphed and stretched. The fur fell out in heavy clumps. Horns grew from her head.

A Jinn?

Not Sim. This was a demon. One that sided with Raphael and had been watching me the entire time.

"You should come with me, Lia," said Gabriel. "Your soul is damned anyway. The Devil never keeps her promises."

"No," I said. "I'm not doing this for Lucifer. Don't come any closer, or I'll spit in your face. That should be enough to make *you* fall."

"You're a sinner." Gabriel glared at me. "Whatever deal Lucifer made with you, it won't matter. You've made angels fall. You don't belong in Heaven. But it isn't too late. You can join us."

The Jinn circled me. I was painfully near the Pit.

The Jinn stood in front of me. I had barely seen it move. It gripped the Twinblade in its hands and bared its teeth at me. They were still pointed like Sim's, but its mouth was much wider. My heart thumped like a beating drum, and I let go of the sword.

The Jinn crawled over to Gabriel, and the Archangel took the Twinblade from him.

"What do you say? They can't reach us where we're going. You can stop all this fighting."

I thought of Mom and Dad. Maybe I didn't deserve eternal bliss, but they did. "I won't help Raphael close the gates of Heaven."

Gabriel looked at me like I was a puzzle he was trying to figure out.

Adriel landed in front of us. He had a silver blade in his hands. "Give me my sword, Gabriel."

"You lost this weapon when you left your post, Seraph."

"I'll cut you to pieces," said Adriel. "Years will pass before you're whole again."

"You would attack your own? You should have fallen a long time ago." Gabriel thrust the Twinblade against Adriel's sword.

Adriel bent his knees and struggled against his own angel weapon, but he righted himself. The steel clashed and battered. Flakes of gold left the Twinblade, showing the silver beneath.

I set my teeth and waited for my opportunity to grab a fist-ful of Gabriel's feathers and bring him to his knees.

The Twinblade came down on Adriel's sword, and the sword shattered. Gabriel slammed his shoulder into Adriel. But Adriel turned and grabbed Gabriel around the neck. Gabriel dropped the Twinblade and elbowed Adriel in the face. Adriel staggered back. Gabriel reached for the Twinblade, but Adriel tackled him. They both went for the sword. Adriel grabbed the hilt of the blade.

Gabriel held the blade in both hands until silver blood oozed from his palms. One shaky hand released the blade and reached for the horn at his side. He raised the horn to his lips.

Adriel let go of his sword and darted to me. He removed his shirt and tore it in two. He balled the shirt in his fists and pressed the fabric against my ears.

Gabriel brought his lips to the mouth of the horn and blew.

Adriel's shirt did nothing to muffle the sound. My ears rang, and I knelt. I wanted to clamp my own hands against my ears, but instead balled them into fists. I couldn't do that. I would touch Adriel's hands if I did. My nails bit into my palms.

Gabriel stopped blowing his horn. He screamed and hurled the Twinblade into the Pit.

Adriel's hands left my ears. He soared down. Down into the abyss.

No!

I brought his weapon here, it was because of me that Gabriel managed to get a hold of it. I couldn't let him die because of me.

Tom's words came back to me. *Angels are bound to protect their weapons...as long as they aren't fallen.*

I jumped.

Gabriel bellowed, "No!" But his voice was lost in the fathomless depths of the Pit.

The wind rushed around me.

All it would take was one touch.

Too much space separated us. I couldn't reach him. I had to push within. I let all the anger and pain boil inside me, and I pushed backward against the air. The force jolted me down.

I flew with him. I touched his bare chest.

Something awakened. An image flashed before my eyes. A woman knelt in a pool of silver blood, an open book before her, and the headless body of an angel.

Adriel's wings burst into flames. His scream echoed in my ears, a desperate howl. His eyes flashed as he watched me fall beside him.

He took me in his arms, and warmth spread through my body. He flew up with the last of his blackened feathers and left a trail of ash over the Pit.

epilogue

I sat alone on the edge of the Outer Region of Sheol. The sky was the same color it had been when I first arrived, but I could see a greater depth to it. The sky was shades of gray-blue. The angels came to Hell and brightened the atmosphere.

I stared out over the Pit. A week passed since they came.

After I jumped into the Pit to save Adriel, Lucifer released the demons of the Nine Circles into the Outer Region. The angels left after that. Nash and the others had a difficult time getting all the demons back into the Circles, but at least the angels were gone.

The sound of a car roared behind me. Nash got out.

"You walked here?" His hands were in his pockets.

"I wanted the quiet," I said. "Besides, I don't have my driver's license."

I *had* driven Nash's car and would have felt pretty badass doing it if I wasn't fighting for my life. I tried to smile, but couldn't. So, I glanced back over the chasm that swallowed Adriel's weapon and nearly swallowed him too.

"That didn't stop you from driving my car," said Nash.

"Looks like Bob got you a new one," I said. The new car *was* fancy. Not that the old one wasn't, but Bob always went a bit overboard. The silver horse galloped on the grill. The red paint shimmered in the new light of Sheol.

Beelzebub was the Prince of Gluttony after all. He lived everyday like the next would never come. There was something to be said of that, but I wasn't in the mood for poetry.

"I didn't know they would come here," said Nash. "You shouldn't have come back."

"No, I should never have left."

He looked at me.

"I didn't ask to be what I am. But, now it's my responsibility. I can't sit by and let Raphael close the gates of Heaven. I can't let him kill my friends."

Nash's ashy black hair was still, like a painting. That was so odd. No wind drifted through Sheol, making everything a still-life, like one of Dad's gory masterpieces.

"When you jumped," said Nash. "I thought I lost you."

"You saw it."

"I saw everything. Why did you save him?"

"I couldn't bear to see him die. He saved me."

We sat in silence, lost in our own thoughts. I didn't know if Nash forgave me for leaving. My leaving hadn't bothered him most. What bothered him more than anything was that I left without telling him and that I left with Adriel.

In the evening, Adrianna, Kiran, Tom, and Chandra came to Nash's house. They always dressed in their finest, but this night was special. Wounds healed, and we celebrated our victory.

I told them that Raphael had been watching us the entire time, using Sim, or what I thought was Sim to spy on me.

What had happened to the real Sim? I hoped she wasn't on the streets hungry. Perhaps another family took her in.

Adriel wasn't with us, not that Nash invited him. I hadn't seen him since the day after the battle. His feathers were gone, all turned to ash. The bones of his once beautiful wings protruded from his back and made him look more like a demon than an angel. Sadness crowded his eyes, so deep that I could not fathom it. It made me want to cry with him. He was bound to Sheol.

I knew this wasn't the end, but at least we defended our turf.

The angels would come back for me. Raphael would come for me.

As a precaution, Bob instructed demons to ward every inch of Hell with protections against angels. Angels had never entered Sheol before.

I didn't tell them what I saw, as I fell into the Pit. The images were strange, and I still didn't understand what they meant. Something familiar hit me when I touched Adriel.

"So, they know about you," said Tom. "If we leave Sheol, they'll come for you. The wards won't hold forever, and they only last three years. Then, we have to wait another three years before they can be replaced."

"We'll figure something out," said Nash. "For now, let's enjoy this meal." His confidence was so steadfast that some of it had spread to me.

I *was* in danger. An Archangel was after me, but I can make angels fall. I was part of a war over Heaven. But something in me changed. I could feel it. My past goals seemed unfathomably small. So much more was at stake.

But I wasn't alone.

The light flooded through the windows. The sky was brighter since the angels emerged from the clouds.

The world is a clarinet, and its music pierces.

excerpt

If you enjoyed
THE WINGS OF HEAVEN AND HELL,
look out for

THE SEVEN ARCHANGELS OF HEAVEN

Book Two of the Arcadian Steel Sequence

By L. M. Peralta

the seven archangels of heaven
THE ARCADIAN STEEL SEQUENCE
BOOK TWO
L. M. PERALTA

prologue

THE reedy branches reached to the ashen sky. A slash of light hung among the clouds where the angels descended, their wings white and thickly feathered. The shining armor and Arcadian weapons they wielded gleamed in the light above them.

Never again would Adriel feel that eternal warmth or the tickle of feathers against his back. He was in a world of never-ending gloom from which he could never leave.

He trekked across the lands beyond the Angel District. Headstones were embedded in a vast plain of barren soil. In the distance the earth met the gray sky.

Adriel didn't dare think what was beyond that, the Circles perhaps. He thought of the cruel punishments Lucifer enacted on accursed souls, and for once, he felt pity. As an angel, he never held sympathy for the damned. They were damned for a reason, but now that he was damned too, these thoughts came readily to his mind.

Adriel avoided the grave markers that patterned the ground like gory stepping stones. Dust stung Adriel's nose, and sweat stained his brow.

He walked with a heavy stone upon his shoulder. The physical weight of it caused him little struggle, but its symbolism carried much weight.

He was fallen.

His stone would rest among the others. His name etched upon it. The marker was not like a headstone found on Earth, in remembrance of a loved one. It was not to honor what he was. It served as a symbol of his shame, of his fall from grace.

Adriel sank the stone into the ground, packed beside three others. Although he did not struggle, he did notice the weight of it. That had never happened before.

His hands were reddened from gripping the gritty surface of the stone. That had never happened before either.

He sighed as he beheld the sky.

A place of unimaginable bliss and serenity loomed far above him, and its gates were locked to him forever.

He didn't blame Lia, but he wondered if, given the chance, he could have retrieved his weapon and flew out of the Pit. But the Pit would have swallowed him up like a black hole. The farther he descended, the stronger the pull down would have been until he was lost in an endless fall. The pressure would have torn the feathers from his wings and the skin from his body. He would live through all that pain for an eternity.

What was worse, the pain or this hopelessness?

The air around him changed. Soft footfalls padded across the dry, cracked earth.

Adriel turned his head.

Nasriel approached him. He wore a black suit and a black shirt like a mourner at a funeral.

Appropriate, Adriel thought.

Nasriel stood over him as Adriel's fingertips bit into the flat headstone.

"I'm sorry," Nasriel said.

The wind pushed the hair around Adriel's face. A few strands stretched away from him as if they struggled to leave his ill-fated head. His hair was dark gray when the locks used to be black as midnight. It matched Nasriel's more closely now.

"Where's your headstone?" Adriel scanned the vast distance.

"Why? So you could put yours next to mine?" Nasriel asked.

The grittiness of the stone beneath his hands left impressions in his no longer impervious skin.

Nasriel shook his head. "I don't remember."

Adriel closed his eyes. "It feels so . . . lonely. I used to be able to sense the others, our brethren, but now, there's nothing. I just feel this terrible disgust for what I've become."

"That will change with time," Nasriel said.

"Will it?"

"A lot of time."

Adriel stood. Tension crept through his shoulders. Was his back bowed?

Nasriel glanced over Adriel's shoulder. "I can help you saw off the bones if you like."

Adriel had not yet looked in a mirror, and he did not want to. From the corner of his eye, he could see the blackened bones that had once been covered with soft, white feathers. He knew his golden-brown eyes had darkened to black, and his hair had become ashen. That transformation happened to all fallen angels, but he didn't want to see it.

"They can get in the way sometimes," Nasriel said, "and it's not like they're of any use anymore."

Nasriel needed no special shirts to accommodate his wings. They were gone. *How long had it been since he severed his wings from his body?* Knowing Nasriel, he probably chose to do it as soon as he plummeted to Hell. Nasriel never let emotions get in the way his aims. He always followed through.

"No," Adriel said. "I want to keep them to remember what I was."

Nasriel grimaced. "You might as well rid yourself of them. It's not like angels have ever *risen* back into God's good graces."

"They remind me of my shame," Adriel said.

Nasriel raised his eyebrows. "This didn't happen to you because you went against your god. It happened because a girl burned you. That's the problem with you, with the others. Why would you want to follow a god who would slough you off so easily?"

"God didn't do this to me."

"No? The creator of all things can't find a way to bring your Grace back?" Nasriel laughed.

Adriel clenched his jaw, and the muscles in his body tensed. He knew what he felt, but the feeling was never so intense before.

Adriel's hand wrapped around Nasriel's neck. He didn't squeeze, but he held Nasriel in his grasp. He was proud of his control, especially in the face of such burning rage. The pride and wrath were unfamiliar, yet so satisfying.

Nasriel pulled Adriel's fingers from his neck and thrust his arm away. "You guarded his throne for millennia. We both did. Not once did he grace us with his presence or show his damned face. What do you owe him?"

"My life."

"I hope you're thinking about that when you enter the Angel District." Nasriel spit on the ground. He turned and walked away with his hands in his pockets, not bothering to avoid the headstones, but planting his feet down on them like they were pavers.

He became a black dot in the distance, a speck, a bug, a fly like the rest of them. Adriel was no better.

"It's time."

Adriel turned toward the voice.

A man stood a hand taller than Adriel. He wore a black suit and red tie. His hair was slicked back, and his golden wrist-watch gleamed in the light.

"Beelzebub." Adriel's nose crinkled as he said the demon's name.

"You can call me Bob," he said.

"I'll call you by your true name," Adriel said.

"Suit yourself. You won't be seeing much more of me any-way."

"That will be a blessing."

"Trust me. Where you are going there are no blessings." Beelzebub strolled past Adriel and led the way to the lands beyond.

Adriel stared after him.

Beelzebub turned his head. "It's not a short walk." Beelze-bub grinned, and when he did, there was no joy in it. His grin threatened like the smile of a crazed killer.

"You've been demoted to ferryman?" Adriel asked.

"I volunteered, my fallen friend."

"Why?"

"Isn't that interesting," Beelzebub said. "You've come with a newfound curiosity."

Adriel hadn't considered it. He had never asked many ques-tions before. Now, he wanted to know the answers for reasons other than utility. He was, as Beelzebub had said, curious.

"Do you still want to know?"

Adriel was quiet. He was ashamed that he did *want* to know. It was a part of what he had become.

"Of course, you do," Beelzebub said. "I heard you were Ser-aphim. We don't get many of those down here. Since you're done polishing God's throne, you're not a Seraph anymore."

Adriel frowned. He wasn't some monkey at a zoo. "I left my post a long time ago," Adriel said.

Bob walked on, and Adriel followed.

"Against Michael's orders, I assume," Beelzebub said. "I never did understand that. How Michael, an Archangel of lower rank, can order around the highest choir of angels."

Adriel grimaced. He didn't like the familiar way Beelzebub spoke about his brethren.

"I know you won't tell me about it," Beelzebub said. "You're not the first angel who's fallen. They're all loyal to a fault when it comes to matters of Heaven or angels. Well, that is apart from the original Fallen. Most of their souls have been demonized. I've heard the guilt goes then. I could put in a good word for you."

Adriel cringed. He had never seen it, but he had heard of angels turning into demons. If anything was worse than becoming a fallen angel, it was becoming a demon. He couldn't imagine any fallen angel choosing that horror.

A cluster of buildings came into view beyond the horizon. A tall, iron gate surrounded the buildings.

Beelzebub stopped. "There it is," he said. "The Angel District. Welcome home." He approached the gates where two giants stood. They were identical except one had a swollen eyelid. The corner of the eye creased so he looked like he was winking.

They carried broadswords at their sides.

"Morning, Bob," the unblemished giant said. "Looks like you have a new one for us." He glanced over at Adriel.

"That I do," Beelzebub said.

"We'll take good care of 'im." Shut Eyed grabbed Adriel's shoulder.

The giant's hand was cold and moist.

Adriel shrugged him off.

"Testy one," Unblemished said.

Shut Eyed reached for the sword at his side and clubbed Adriel's head with the flat of the blade.

Adriel sank to the ground, putting his hands on the sides of his head. Ringing accosted his ears as he put his head to the ground, trying to make it stop. It wasn't the pain that bothered him, although it was there. If he stood right away, he knew he would stumble. He was on the ground the moment the blade hit him. He didn't want to let those demons see him stagger as well.

After a moment of spinning, Adriel stood up, careful not to show any expression of pain on his face. Pain was more acute now. He wouldn't forget that again. Next time, he wouldn't show it. He would set his feet and bear it.

"That's alright," Beelzebub said. "I wanted to take him in myself. We have ourselves a Seraph, boys."

"*This* is a Seraph?" Unblemished asked.

Shut Eyed laughed. "He don't look any different."

"I'm not Seraphim," Adriel said. "I'm a fallen angel."

"That's what I like about you lot," Unblemished said. "You got humility." He and Shut Eyed pulled either side of the gates and opened them to Beelzebub and Adriel.

"Good luck, ex-Seraph," Unblemished said as he and his twin brother sealed the gates behind them.

Beyond the gate, a gravel path curled into the cluster of buildings. Trees, naked of leaves, surrounded the path. Their branches leaned toward the trail as if they wanted to capture those who treaded it.

The music of the city grew louder. A series of beats sounded without vocals. Adriel's muscles tensed. Despair rose beneath the song. The screams and cries coming from the city echoed the feeling the music gave Adriel.

"What will happen to me in there?" Adriel asked.

"Others will hold a mirror to your shame," Beelzebub said. "And it won't matter because you'll feel it anyway, right?"

"Then, what's the point?"

"Those who feel shame are the weakest here. They hesitate and prefer to live in self-pity," Beelzebub said. "If you were human, your shame would damn you to the Circles. But fallen angels feel pain differently from humans. Their greatest pain is the shame. And no one has more shame than a fallen angel. That is why this place exists. Do you know the best way to make a man feel better about himself? Show him a man who's far worse off."

Beelzebub patted Adriel on the back. "You'll be an example to others. But don't look so glum, my boy. You've hit bottom. You need fear nothing more now. There isn't any further to fall."

Adriel recoiled at Beelzebub's touch and his words, but he was right. Adriel didn't have any further to fall. It didn't matter how he had fallen. He was down here. The Devil had him now.

Beelzebub strolled onto the street, and Adriel followed. Bright neon lights assaulted his eyes, and stabs of loud music came from all sides. Adriel's vision blurred.

"Whoa." Beelzebub gripped Adriel's arm to keep him upright. "I know. The lights are brighter to you now. It will take some getting used to. Your eyes aren't what they were when you used to look into the light of God, but they're still better than a demon's and certainly better than a human's. Come on."

Adriel blinked a few times, and his eyes adjusted to the light. The lights were pink, yellow, green, orange, and blue. Demons crowded the streets. They chatted, drank, and laughed. Their skins were crimson, obsidian, and burnt with eyes of black and red. Horns curled from a few heads, and teeth were like the points of daggers.

"Pick them up," a deep voice roared.

Desperate hands scrambled to grab the glittering coins from the ground. Fallen angels sank to the earth on their hands and knees, not in prayer, but to lift money from the dirt. Their necks were collared, and chains led from the collars to the hands of horned demons, barking at them while the crowd hooted and laughed.

"Eat it!"

A demon shoveled a thick, brown gruel into the mouth of a fallen angel in chains. The angel's stomach bloated like she was pregnant.

"Hit him!"

Demons forced another angel to lash the backs of his brethren with an Arcadian whip. Whelps and lines of black blood were drawn across the backs of angels who knelt on the ground.

Adriel's heart clenched, and a sting erupted behind his eyes. Both were sensations he wasn't accustomed to.

"What is this place?" Adriel grabbed the collar of Beelzebub's shirt.

A grin split Beelzebub's face.

Adriel fisted the fabric of his shirt. "Why are you smiling, you devil?"

"They let these things happen to them," Beelzebub said, "and you will too, because you hate yourself."

The fallen angels were collared, but they didn't fight. The collar seemed a mere symbol to their shame. Adriel, too, wanted to hurt himself. The thought of pain, the feeling of punishment, would for that moment cloud his mind and help him to forget he was doomed.

Adriel lowered his eyes and released Beelzebub. He did hate himself. Regardless of the circumstances, he had failed in his duty. He should have stayed at his post as defender of the Throne, but he left to find a friend and stayed to protect a girl who lost her guardian angel. None of which were his assignments yet he failed in those as well.

Beelzebub smoothed down his shirt. "Now, let's get a collar on you."

He twisted around the corner, and they strode down the street. Adriel's ears numbed to the music, the shouts, and the jeers. He didn't want to look at what happened to his fellow fallen angels.

"Here we are." Beelzebub opened a door in the alley. Graffiti marked the door with the word *dog-catcher*.

Inside, a fat man squatted at a workbench with a soldering tool. Hours of sweat drenched the front of his yellowed shirt. He held an iron collar that had not yet been welded shut. He glanced up at Beelzebub and Adriel as they walked in. He had a glass over one eye to help him see his work.

"It's done," he said. "Now, let's get it around his neck."

The room was dark, a relief to Adriel's eyes. But a bright light glowed above the table where the man worked. The brightness stung as Adriel bent his head, pressed his cheek onto the table, and allowed the man to reach his neck. The light caused him pain, but he *could* look into it. Beelzebub was wrong. Adriel could see the light of Heaven, only not without sacrifice.

One

I sat on the end of my bed. The rumpled blanket was cool to the touch. My feet dangled in the cold. My hands gripped the mattress. I closed my eyes and breathed in through my nose.

I wore a thick sweater and hadn't changed out of my pajama bottoms. What was the point?

Nash hadn't returned. I wasn't sure where he had gone.

But with the trainings, the hunt for angel weapons, and the attacks on over a dozen angels, I didn't have time to process my feelings for him. I had feelings, but they were jumbled puzzle pieces on the floor.

I hated the way he treated Adriel, but there was something about Nash, something undeniable.

Sim's food and water dish rested near the door. The food in it grew mold.

My feet padded across the cold floor. I picked up the dish and brought it to the bathroom. I tossed the food in the small trash can and rinsed the bowls in the sink.

Sim was never here. My skin crawled at the thought of the creature that was here—a Jinn, imitating my cat. The Jinn spied on me and reported to Raphael my whereabouts and what I was up to. That's how the angels knew when to come. That's how they knew to retrieve their angel weapons.

The real Sim, what became of her?

I grabbed a towel and dried the bowl.

It was my fault the angels attacked Sheol. Adriel losing the Twinblade and worse, his Grace, was my fault too. Worst of all, Raphael knew where I was, and he knew what I was after. I had no way to stop him. Dad and Mom were in Heaven, but because of me, they wouldn't be for long.

I dropped the towel and hummed the food tray against the wall. The plastic chipped and fell to the floor.

I screamed and beat the wall until the sting bit my hands. I gripped the edges of the sink.

"Lia?"

I walked to the door and slid it open.

Nash stood in the hallway. "Are you alright?"

"Sure." I struggled to keep the tremor out of my voice. "What's up? Why are you dressed like that?"

Nash wore a black suit like he was going to a funeral. "I was visiting a friend."

A dead friend? But all Nash's friends were dead and not dead at the same time. They were immortal. Everyone was. I will be or am too because when I die, I'll go to Heaven if Lucifer keeps her end of the deal. Big *if.*

"We have to go," Nash said. "Tom found a fallen angel. We need to bring her to Sheol."

Fallen angels and demons were standard Sheol Parole Officer fare. Nash oversaw enforcement. I wasn't complaining.

Hunting fallen angels and demons meant spending some time on Earth where the air wasn't so stale. I couldn't stand the stagnant air of Sheol and the way the weather never changed. I missed listening to rain drum against the windows while I strummed on my guitar.

"Okay. I'll get dressed." I slid the door closed and pulled on a pair of black pants and a shirt. I wrapped my belt around my waist and slid my sword into its sheath.

My hand stopped on the hilt of my sword. My skin prickled. *What if this was a trap?* Raphael might be trying to lure me back to Earth so he could send my friends to the Pit.

I rushed out of my room and met Tom as he came down the stairs from the third floor. "What if Raphael planned this?" I asked. "What if he made that angel fall to trap us? He can't come to Sheol, so he making us come to him."

Tom narrowed his eyes. "You sure don't bury the lead, do you?" Tom sighed. "The fact that you thought of it means Raphael won't do that. He wouldn't try something that even you could figure out. Besides, Raphael can't *make* an angel fall. Angels must go against an order they believe is from God."

I shook my head. "Then, why hasn't Raphael fallen?"

"Clearly, he believes he isn't going against God," Tom said.

I narrowed my eyes. "But he is. God made Heaven for humans, and he is directly opposed to that."

"It gets complicated when the message isn't coming from God Himself."

"Then from who?"

"You have a fallen angel to hunt," Tom said. "We can talk more about Heavenly politics when you return. But an angel can't decide to go against God to become fallen if he believed that very sacrifice to be in the name of God. Therefore, Raphael couldn't get one of his followers to do it unless they believed that what Raphael pursued was an act opposed to God, and, if they believed that, they wouldn't be one of his followers."

Choice and belief matter a lot in both Heaven and Hell. That fascinated me. You could end up in Hell because you believed you belong in eternal damnation, and angels could fall on the mere belief that their actions are against God.

Tom turned away from me and continued down the hall-way.

"You aren't coming with us?" I asked.

"Can't," he said. "I have some scouting to do."

I considered what Tom said. I saw Raphael around every corner. I had to stop doing that or it would paralyze me.

Chandra leaned against a column at the landing of the stairs with her arms folded. Her hair was tied back, and her brass knuckles were secured to her belt. When she saw me, she grimaced, unhinged herself from the column, and walked away.

She didn't like me before, but after what happened to Alex, she'd never forgive me.

Adrianna, Kiran, and Nash chatted on the sofa in the living room. I stopped behind the wall and watched their reflections in the mirror opposite the room.

"It was that damn cat," Kiran said.

"It always tried to bite me." Adrianna looked at her nails. They were painted red and made her emerald green eyes pop. "I should have known something was wrong with it. Animals love me." She smiled.

"What are we going to do now?" Kiran's curved sword rested in its black sheath invisible against his pants except for the silver hilt.

"I haven't figure that out yet." Nash bent forward and rested his forearms on his legs. "But we can't go after the other angels, not yet. We need another strategy."

"I'm ready." I stepped through the archway and into the room.

Kiran and Adrianna gave each other an awkward glance.

"Good." Nash stood. "Let's go. Wait. Where's Chandra?"

"Here." Chandra walked into the living room. *Did she see me eavesdropping on their conversation?*

I looked at her. She didn't look at me. She avoided my existence. I was glad she ignored me. The only alternative relationship we could have had was one a lion has with an antelope.

Nash held out his hand and opened a portal. The edges of the portal glowed like a hole burned through the space and showed what lie beneath.

Chandra climbed through followed by Adrianna and Kiran. They disappeared onto the other side.

I clenched my locket, which protected the photographs of my parents. The only ones I had left. Letting my feelings out never helped me so what was the point of all that effort? Sometimes, I couldn't help it.

Despite what you might believe, bottled emotions aren't the dangers. The fear is that if you bottle up your emotions, they come out in a rush to meet you and not in the best of ways. But perhaps the true danger wasn't the emotions themselves and the consequences of the rush, but the very practice of keeping them quiet. If you keep them silent long enough maybe you become numb.

Numb was the opposite of what I felt with Nash.

"Go ahead," Nash said.

"What?" I asked.

"The portal."

"Right." I approached the glowing circle. I turned to Nash. "I'm sorry."

"For what?"

"For everything that happened. I'll never leave again, not until this is done. And I'm sorry about Sim too. I ruined everything."

"It threw things off course," Nash said, "but you didn't know about the cat. How could you? I'll figure out what needs to be done. In the meantime, stop blaming yourself. Self-pity doesn't look good on you." He nodded to the circle.

He was right. I couldn't let the thousand little thoughts in my head stop me from doing what I needed to do. I can't change the past, so let's start working on the future.

I stepped through the portal, ready to take a breath of clear, moving air. I breathed in a deep lungful. Dust tickled the back of my throat. I bent over, feeling like I might cough up my insides.

The air smelled of mold. The walls were gray blended with vomit green. Cracks ran through the plaster. Dim light struggled to get through the dirty paned glass window above the second landing.

I stood on the stairs. Black iron bars supported the stair rail. Cobwebs showed their wispy patterns between the bars. Light invaded the stairway through a small window on the front door. Someone had nailed boards to the doorframe.

The stairs groaned. I didn't want the distressed wood to give under my weight, so I rushed up to the landing before the next flight of stairs.

Chandra, Adrianna, and Kiran looked down at me from the second floor. Adrianna gestured for me to join them. Their weapons were drawn.

Nash's warmth suffused my back. He stood close behind me. I didn't hear him on the stairs. The portal must have sent him straight to the landing.

Strange. Portals changed location on Earth so quickly, but at least it kept us from running into each other.

We met the others upstairs.

The hallway walls ended in dirty baseboards. Cracked picture frames failed to protect the photographs inside, covered in thick layers of dust. The doors were ajar to two of the three rooms on the second floor.

A roach darted in front of me and scurried into a crack in the baseboard. *Don't worry. We aren't taking you to Hell.*

Chandra pointed to the room at the end of the hall. The door was closed. We crept toward the room with our weapons drawn. Chandra turned the knob and swung the door open.

I held my breath. Fallen angels get a burst of adrenaline right after they fall. The angel who attacked me in my bedroom didn't need his Grace to crush me like a monkey does a coconut.

The room was empty except for a curtain that floated in the breeze, which came in through the broken paned glass window. Holes blemished the torn, gray curtain.

"It's the only room we haven't checked," Chandra said.

"She must be downstairs." Kiran looked to Nash.

He nodded.

If I was a fallen angel, and I heard movement upstairs, impossible not to hear in this creaky, old house, I'd have made a run for it. We would have heard boards being torn from the front door if that was the case.

To my right was a closet with dingy, white folding doors. As I approached the closet, I squinted.

Low breathing came from behind the slats.

"Lia, what are you doing?" Adrianna asked.

"Shh! Listen." I stepped closer.

Dad always said I had excellent hearing despite all the Metal concerts I'd been to.

I imagined black eyes as they peered at me from the closet shutters. Imagining what waited for me wasn't hard to do. So many things jumped out at me from the dark. But I never got used to them. My skin crawled, and goose bumps erupted across my flesh.

I clenched the hilt of my sword.

My hand shook as I reached for the doorknob. Before my hand touched the knob, the door burst open. I jumped back.

The fallen angel emerged from the closet. She wore a dirty, shapeless dress. Her skin was pale and eyes as dark as the Pit.

Her dark gray hair was in stiff tangles. Her bony, featherless wings rose in the air above her head. Black cuts patterned her exposed skin.

She screamed and rushed us. Dark blood dripped from her mouth.

Adrianna grabbed her wrist and pinned her arm back, right between the bones of her wings. "You need to come with us."

The angel screamed like a wild animal and tried to pull away from Adrianna, but Adrianna's hold was firm.

The angel gritted her teeth. She forced herself forward and pulled until the loud crack of a bone breaking filled the room. She slipped from Adrianna's grasp and scooped a piece of broken glass from beneath the window.

The angel held up the piece of glass. The shard cut into her palm, and fresh blood dotted the floor. Her other arm rested limp and mangled at her side.

Kiran whipped his blade, and the sword flashed in front of the angel. The sword cut into the arm that held the glass. The shard and her hand fell.

The bloody stump was still raised to us in a grim salute.

The floor creaked and groaned and splintered. The floorboards gave.

My back hit a flat, hard surface. Plaster and dust fell on top of me. Despite the pain, I rolled over so nothing heavy could hit me in the face. I choked the dust out of my lungs and forced myself up. I sat on top of a dining room table.

Adrianna lay under a pile of floorboards and sheetrock. I moved the stuff off her as she came to.

Debris shifted across the room. Black bones angled out from beneath cracked floorboards and ceiling dust. Like a rabbit caught in a garden, the angel's eyes quivered.

She ran. I climbed over the debris and raced after her. I fell and grabbed her ankle. She struggled and plummeted. I grabbed my dagger from its sheath and plunged it into her calf. She howled.

The dagger pinned her leg to the floor. I climbed up her body, straddled her back, and held the joints of her wings down so she couldn't move the featherless, sharp bones. Indents were gouged into the bones as if she tried to cut them off like Nash's.

Blood speckled my hands. I swallowed the bile that rose in my throat.

Nash and the others met us in the hallway. Sheetrock dust powdered their dark clothes.

"I got her." My lips tightened into a cruel smile.

Adrianna's eyes were wide. Chandra grinned like she had gotten me to eat a poisoned apple.

Nash approached me and offered me his hand. His face was expressionless. I took his hand, and he helped me up.

Kiran pulled my dagger from the angel's leg. He and Nash grabbed her by both arms and lifted her.

She continued to struggle.

Nash jerked her arm. "Who gave you these cuts?"

She looked at him. "I did."

"Why?"

She stopped struggling and craned her head over Nash's shoulder to look at his back. "Don't you hate yourself?" Her eyes met his. "I do, every day, since I turned into this monster."

Nash furrowed his brow. "There's a place in Hell where you will be punished."

She ground her teeth. "I don't want to go to Hell. I want to die."

"You already have," Nash said, "and now, you have to come with us to die again and again."

"Please, I can't go there. Please."

She begged, begged not to go where Lucifer sent angels, where she sent Adriel. After all he had done for us, I couldn't let him suffer in a place angels begged not to go.

Nash turned away from her.

Her head dropped to her chest, and tears marked the floor. She lifted her head and looked for a savior. Her eyes rested on me. She blinked as if her eyes deceived her. "A human? Who are you?"

She recognized me the same way demons did. A light in my eyes signaled my humanity and distinguished me from the poor costumes demons choose to wear.

"Don't worry about her," Kiran said. "Are you opening the portal?" he asked Nash.

"What are you doing with demons? You're the girl Michael talked about."

"Michael? The Archangel?" I asked.

"The one and only," the fallen angel said. "He knows Raphael is looking for you."

Nash's face turned dark. "We have to leave. We shouldn't stay this long. We have her, let's go." He let go of the angel's arm and opened the portal. "Lia, come on." He waved me over.

"What's going on?" I asked.

"Just go through the damned portal. We'll talk later."

I climbed through the portal. I waited for the others. Chandra and Kiran stepped through with the fallen angel. Blood ran down the angel's leg where I drove the dagger in.

I don't know what came over me. Was the dagger necessary?

She struggled on the ground. One arm mangled. The other a stump. She would have had a hard time getting back to her feet. I could have easily climbed on top of her without stabbing her through the leg.

Adrianna and Nash followed. The portal blinked out of existence.

Nash's mouth formed a hard line. "Handle the angel. Lia and I need to speak with Lucifer."

I hadn't seen Lucifer in a long time, but I wasn't itching to meet with her again. The chill from our first meeting never left my bones. But another Archangel was after me, and the thought of that left me colder.

The world is a drum, and its song is thunder.

two

HE skyscraper disappeared into the clouds. Lucifer was at the top, the highest point in Hell. The smell of burned leaves tickled my nose. The air grew misty and cold close to the building, colder than other parts of Sheol, at least, colder than the parts I had seen.

Other darker, deeper parts of Sheol existed that I hadn't visited, like the Circles and the depths of the Pit. I had no intention of seeing either.

But with two Archangels after me, I might not have a choice but to visit the deepest and darkest places of my nightmares. Michael and the other Archangels coming after me made sense. They had to stop Raphael from doing what they believed was against God or their inaction would condemn them.

Nash walked with me through the sliding doors.

"Is he working against Raphael?" I asked.

"I know as much as you do," Nash said.

At the welcome desk sat one of Lucifer's clone secretaries. They weren't mirror images of each other, like identical twins. But they dressed alike, had the same wide smile, and wore their hair in the exact same way. They walked to the same rhythm, like they listened to the same song in their heads too. However, I doubted the clone secretaries ever listened to music.

The secretary's hair was pulled back so painfully, it stretched the corners of her eyes toward her hairline. She gave us a toothy smile as Nash and I walked to the elevator.

I didn't look back at her. I feared she turned her head to follow our movements. I didn't want to see her staring back at me with that creepy smile plastered on her face.

"We should have questioned her," I said. The fallen angel may have known more than she told us, right? What motive would she have for giving us the whole story?

"We couldn't do that at that house," Nash said. "Besides, if I chose to keep this from Lucifer for any longer than the time it takes us to get here, she'd have my head."

Lucifer had her thumb on Nash. But, at the same time, she trusted him. He was the only fallen angel she allowed to roam around the Outer Region. But why? What was it about Nash that none of the others had?

I made a mistake and looked back.

The secretary's grin took up half her face as she leaned over her desk to watch us. Her hands clasped in front of her like she was trying to hold onto a fly she caught.

The urge to run zinged through my body like sharp steel.

"Let's not talk about this here." Nash pressed the button for the elevator.

The elevator dinged as the doors opened. I stepped inside, and my heartbeat quickened. The doors closed on her face, and I shut the image away.

My heart sank in time with the sudden drop. It's funny how elevators create that falling sensation when they're going up. *Must I fall first before I succeed?*

"Are you okay?" Nash asked.

I gripped the railing. My sweaty palms made the steel slippery. "Define *okay*."

Ever wonder how a wild horse feels in a pull trailer? A moment of panic when you don't know what's going on and you're not sure if you're going to be okay, that's what I felt. But I had some degree of control over my own destiny.

"I don't think it's hit me yet," Nash said, "what that fallen angel told us."

"What do you mean?" I asked.

The elevator stopped.

Nash pressed the button for the top floor, but the button wouldn't stay lit. Nash jabbed it a few more times, but it didn't glow at all.

"What's going on?" I tried the button myself.

"I don't know."

"Are we stuck?"

The elevator moved up again.

Nash furrowed his brow. "I guess it was nothing."

The elevator zoomed ahead twenty more floors and jolted to a stop. This time, the doors slid open.

Nash paused. "Strange." He pressed the button to close the doors, but they remained open. "Well, I guess we aren't being given a choice."

"There's always a choice," I said. "I could get on your shoulders and pop the top to the elevator shaft. We could climb up or down."

Nash narrowed his eyes.

We entered a hallway. The walls were cream-white with ornate arches evenly spaced. Candle-lit chandeliers hung from the ceiling and lush, white carpets rested against the dark, hard-wood floors.

"Where are we?" I touched a statue of a cherub that sat on a pedestal. The cherub was a fat baby with curly hair and wings that reached the top of his head.

Cherubs don't look that way. They are full-sized angels with four faces. I guess they needed all those faces to guard Arcadia, the place in Heaven humans went to when they died.

"Bob lives here." Nash strode to the door at the end of the hall.

I followed him. "Bob? I wonder why the elevator stopped here."

"I wonder the same thing." Nash opened the door that stood three or four inches below the tall ceiling.

The door opened to a dining room. Burgundy red paint colored the walls. To my left was a floor to ceiling depiction of a forest painted in dark greens and pale yellows. To the right was an archway that led into another room. On the ceiling hung a chandelier. A red lampshade covered each light.

In the center of the room was a table for ten. The table was of a dark wood, and the chairs were padded with white fabric. On the table were platters of food: a roast turkey, slices of bread, cheese, a rack of lamb, a whole roasted pig, sausages, biscuits, gravy, mashed potatoes, pasta, and fruit. No part of the table was untouched.

At the head of the table sat Bob, or should I call him, *Beelzebub*, the demon of gluttony and right-hand man to Lucifer.

A white napkin was tucked into his collar. He held a fork and knife. He wore his traditional black, fitted suit and red tie. His hair was slicked back as usual with a thick layer of grease. His Rolex watch gleamed in the light.

Was he going to eat all this food by himself?

He smiled at me and Nash. "Good morning."

I narrowed my eyes. You have to be careful when snakes slither on the ground.

"You've made quite a feast for yourself," Nash said.

"Well, you know I didn't make this myself," Bob said. "You should invite me for dinner sometime."

"I'm afraid I don't have enough food in the kitchen to sate your appetite." Disgust laced Nash's words. I wasn't sure if the disgust was over the meat or the excess.

Bob grinned. "You probably don't. I suppose you're looking for Lucifer."

"The elevator malfunctioned," I said. "You should get that fixed unless you're trying to scare people to death."

"You're the only one in Sheol, we could scare to death, my dear." He smiled.

"It wasn't a malfunction." Bob put down his utensils and removed his napkin. He wiped his mouth. "Lucifer has re-routed all initial contact to me."

Was Lucifer getting too many Jehovah's Witnesses at her door?

"So, you'll have to convince me it's something worth her time," Bob said.

"It's Michael," Nash said.

Bob's mouth tensed.

"We have a source who says he's looking for Lia," Nash said.

Bob stood and approached Nash. "Is that so? Michael. He's a feisty one. Follow me." He smoothed down his suit jacket and strolled past Nash through the door.

We followed Bob to the elevator. The doors slid open, and we stepped inside. Bob reached into his pocket and pulled out a key. He tapped the elevator control panel. Below the buttons was a keyhole.

"Newly installed," Bob said. "It's the only way up past my floor."

A whole floor! Each floor of this place could house ten midsize apartments. My house could fit inside one floor of Lucifer's skyscraper three times.

Bob turned the key, and the elevator bucked upward as if resuscitated.

My fingers played across my palm. Couldn't Michael wait until I killed my parents' murderer? I could face him after that, after I did what I needed to do.

The elevator doors opened. A mild, burning odor weaved through the air like someone had blown out a candle in front of me. We followed Bob down the hall and into one of the many rooms that stood in a line down the hallway.

I recognized this room, the same room where Lucifer told me my birth mother sold my soul to her. The white sofa was the same one Nash and I sat on. I remembered Lucifer's long nails as they bit into the back of the chair she stood behind.

A clone secretary nosed the corner of the room. A bun pulled back her dark hair. Her long legs ended in black heels. She turned as we entered the room and approached us with a wide grin. "Can I get you anything?"

"Coffee," Nash said.

"Never mind that." Bob put up his hand. "Tell Lucifer Nash needs to speak with her about the Archangel Michael."

The secretary blinked. "Michael." Her smile remained, but her face tensed. She hesitated, perhaps hopeful Bob would say more, but when he didn't, she moved along and shut the door behind her.

Nash sat on the couch and put his arm across the top, the way he sat when we first went to see Lucifer.

"Nash..." I frowned.

"What?" He looked at me as if I had the results of a cancer screening.

"Can I sit there, where you're sitting?" I asked.

He raised an eyebrow. "You want me to move?"

"How can I sit there if you don't move?"

"You could still sit here." His lips curled into a smile.

My face warmed. Definitely flirting. Should I flirt back?

"Scoot over." I nudged his shoulder. Not flirting.

He moved over to where I sat last time, and I took his seat, but that subtle change didn't put me at ease.

The door opened behind us. My skin crawled like it wanted to run away from my bones.

Lucifer entered. She was dressed in a tight, red skirt with a fitted black, business blazer. The heels she wore had her towering over Bob.

The secretary scurried in behind her and handed Nash his coffee. She clasped her hands together and bowed her head toward Lucifer. "Can I get you anything, Morning Star?"

"Leave." Lucifer waved the secretary away.

With that smile, Lucifer didn't look worried that this conversation involved Michael, but Lucifer could put on a damn good performance when she wanted to. A smile didn't mean a thing.

She sat across from us in one of the padded, leather chairs. She crossed her legs. Her featherless wings fanned out on either side of the chair. "You have something to tell me about Michael."

Bob stood not far from where Lucifer sat. What I couldn't read on Lucifer's face, I could read on his. His brows knit together, and his face slumped into a frown.

Michael was not a good topic for them.

Nash opened his mouth to speak when one of the clone secretaries with the wide smiles came in. Her heels tapped across the marble floor as she approached us.

"Morning Star." She bowed to Lucifer. The smile plastered on her face spoke that she wouldn't be in trouble for interrupting the Devil's meeting, but that was far from the truth. "31,855 souls funneled in an hour ago."

Lucifer narrowed her eyes. "We received our quota this morning."

"I know, your Greatness, but 31,855 more were received after the original quota."

"I'm busy. Offer them the standard contract." Lucifer waved her away.

"We have, but 28,111 have refused it."

Lucifer's eyes darkened, and her lips curled. She stood. "Then, throw them into the Pit!" Her voice bellowed. A voice echoed behind hers like she wasn't the only one who spoke, but another deeper voice repeated her words.

Goose bumps erupted on my skin, and a chill settled so deep in my bones, I would never be able to shake it.

Since I met her, in all the times I thought of Lucifer, knowing she was the Devil, my heart had not shuddered at the thought until that moment.

The secretary still smiled, but the corners of her lips twitched, and her eyes spelled alarm. A bead of sweat trickled down her forehead.

Nash, who was sipping his coffee, gulped down his last swallow.

Lucifer smoothed out her skirt and sat back down. She sighed. "Pick out one third of them and make them the offer again. Call their names one by one in earshot of the others. It'll have more effect. The others will wonder why they haven't been chosen. They'll panic and beg to take the deal. If they don't, chuck them into the Circles."

The secretary nodded and left the room. Her heels hurriedly clicked down the hallway.

Lucifer turned back to me. The way her face became so calm so fast sent a colder chill down my spine. I saw why she had a reputation for being a good liar. I bet she would have made an amazing poker player.

"Peter isn't letting people in like he used to," Lucifer said.

"Peter?" My voice shuddered. That surprised me.

"The gatekeeper to Heaven, my dear," Lucifer said.

"Oh, right," I said.

From what I'd read in Nash's library, Peter was one of the Twelve Apostles of Jesus. Jesus gave him the Keys to Heaven. "I knew that."

Nash took a loud sip of his coffee. He was usually a quiet drinker. Was he signaling for me to shut up?

I didn't plan on saying too much more anyway. I didn't like how my voice wavered. It made me sound weak and afraid, and I didn't want Lucifer to think I was afraid.

"We have a problem." Nash put his coffee down on the table. "We hunted a fallen angel this morning. She told us that Michael has his eye on Lia."

Lucifer smiled, but didn't show teeth. She settled back in her chair, and the bones of her featherless wings crackled. "I thought this might happen. Where's the angel?"

"She's in Sheol," Nash said.

"Good."

"Well, what are you going to do about it?" I asked, not able to catch my words before they tumbled out.

She glanced at me. "You might need to make Michael fall."

I gulped. I didn't need another angel in the way of my getting to Raphael. I felt remorse for the others. I would feel none for him.

"You are strong, stronger than when I met you, but you will need help." She spoke to me, but she looked at Nash. She made it his responsibility to protect me.

"She can't." Nash leaned in. "You and I know that, Lucifer. You can't ask her to do something you know is impossible."

Lucifer laughed. "I can ask, but it's not worth my time. My interest is in Raphael. I can't have her killing herself going after Michael."

She didn't want me to attack Michael, but if he attacked me, I'd be on my own. Killing him was my responsibility, not hers.

Nash settled back against the couch. Relief and worry painted his face. He expected Lucifer to do something, but I wasn't sure what. Fight Michael herself maybe.

Did he think the Devil would stick her neck out?

A dark thought crossed my mind.

"Could Michael and Raphael be working together?" I asked.

Lucifer squinted at me. "I doubt it."

"Then why is he after me?" But I already knew. Raphael wasn't the only one who needed to be stopped.

Lucifer clicked her fingernails together. "Because, my dear, he wants to destroy you before Raphael can use you against him."

Three

ASH drove fast. I wanted to talk to him about what Lucifer said to us. The Archangel Michael had his eye on me because he wanted to kill me. Not a pleasant thought. But Nash took the turns at such high speeds, I couldn't bring myself to start a serious discussion while he drove like that.

At this rate, it wouldn't matter if Michael was after me, I would die in a car crash.

"Slow down!" I screamed.

He slammed on the brake, and my seatbelt cut into me and knocked the breath out of my lungs. It took me a moment to catch my breath again. "Nash, what the f—"

"She's not doing anything about it." He gripped the wheel.

"She asked about the angel," I said. "Maybe she plans to question her."

"That won't do any good if she can't stop Michael. She expects you to do it. We have to get home." Nash pressed down on the accelerator, and the car zoomed ahead.

He slowed down a little, but still sped along. He didn't look at me. His mouth formed a hard, thin line. His eyes focused in front of him. I hoped he was looking at the road and not looking past it, lost in his thoughts.

I wished I could have spoken with Lucifer first. She wasn't the most delicate person. I could have sat down with Nash and explained it to him in his own home where he wouldn't have to drive after the news.

I knew this wouldn't be quick and painless, but I didn't need to add another warrior angel on the list of angels that wanted me dead. I had taken the wings from angels who would be happy to see me in the Seventh Circle of Hell, but never an Archangel.

I remembered the first Archangel we tried to take down: Uriel. That hadn't gone too well. I feared for Nash's life that day.

Today, Nash feared for mine.

Or at least I hoped he did. It could also be that he feared Lucifer. If he failed to protect me, there was no telling what she would do to him.

He pulled up to the house, and I jumped out of the car.

Nash didn't say anything to me. He went straight to the front door and walked inside. I hurried after him into the house.

I was ready to tear him up for driving like that and shutting me out when he should have been talking to me. I was the one who should have been panicking, not him. My life was in danger. He stole my anxiety and made it his own.

"Nash, can we at least talk about this?" I asked. I wanted him to say something to me, anything that might bring me hope. Raphael was an Archangel, and he was after me too. I didn't get what was so much worse about Michael. Well, besides the fact that Raphael wanted to *use* me while Michael wanted to *kill* me.

But either way I was screwed. Raphael wouldn't let me live past his agenda anyway, not if he didn't need to. The thought of me touching him and taking his wings would scare him too much. Even if he needed to keep me alive, I'd be a prisoner for the rest of my life.

Was Michael the angel who told Mary that she would give birth to the son of God? Or was that Gabriel?

Gabriel. He tossed Adriel's sword into the Pit, all because Adriel had helped me. His eyes were so empty when he did that. If Michael was anything like Gabriel, maybe there was reason to worry.

Paranoia hit me like a boulder rolling down a steep hill. I had experienced it before, many times. I never knew when it would hit me, but every time it did, something bad would happen.

I felt it right before my parents died, before the day I nearly drowned in the school pool, and the day I met the Devil.

Warmth suffused my back as if someone stood right behind me, whispering in my ear what was to come. Only I couldn't hear it because the message wasn't in words but in feelings.

It happened more often now. The only trouble was I didn't know what to connect it to. I didn't know what or who it warned me against.

Nash marched down the stairs to the armory. He opened the door and gathered weapons in his arms. He pulled the weapons down from the wall and piled them onto the table by the door.

He went back and forth from the wall to the table. The angel weapons hung against the back wall. I helped harvest those weapons, not for the weapons themselves, but to lure angels to me so I could touch them and take their Grace away. I wondered where the fallen angels were now.

"Nash, can you please stop for a minute and talk to me?" I pleaded. My voice cracked. At first, I wanted to talk to him for the sake of my own curiosity and my need to be comforted. Now, it was more about grounding him.

"What's there to talk about?" he asked. "Michael is after you. We need to train."

"I don't understand. What makes Michael, a single Archangel, any more of a threat than Raphael and his entire army of angels?"

Nash stopped and looked at me like I had grown two heads. His tone grew grave. "Michael defeated Lucifer single-handedly after taking on an army of demons without breaking a sweat. That's why she's too afraid to do anything herself. If he comes for you, we won't be able to stop him. *I* won't be able to stop him."

I remembered once again, as I had many times, that I was in a world where I didn't know all the rules. What was more, I didn't understand the complexity of Nash's feelings for me, but I did know something. He wanted to protect me.

I put my hand on his arm. "It'll be okay, Nash."

"You should be scared. You don't sound scared."

"You want me to be scared?"

Nash turned to me. His dark eyes hardened to black crystals. "I don't want you to have a reason to be, but I want you to be scared when you should be. Being scared might keep you alive. Being scared might make you fight harder. It might make you think clearer. It could mean the difference between life and death. So, yes, I want you to be scared."

"I am," I said. "But we'll beat him."

"Maybe, a slim maybe, if we stay on top of this." He moved the weapons to the table and packed them away in a bag.

He shut me out again, focusing on something physical. Something tangible, something he could control. But I could tell his mind couldn't let go of an image of me. Was he thinking of my death? Was he playing out all the many ways we could fail?

I drew him away from his task, placed my arms around his neck, and hugged him. It took a moment for him to realize I wasn't letting go.

He wrapped his arms around me and pulled me in. His breath warmed my neck, pushing the cold away until it receded in ripples across my skin. Goose bumps erupted in the places he didn't touch, but they made me appreciate the warmth more.

I was glad I was the one comforting him. It had pushed the apprehension to the back of my mind. On the way back to Nash's car, after we left Lucifer's skyscraper, there was a moment when I thought I might cry. I wanted so badly not to cry. I wanted to feel strong.

Nash had given me something I didn't know I needed.

Before Micah and Alexandria Hebert adopted me, I dreamed my mother or father or anyone who might love me would show up and whisk me away from the strangers who could never be my real family.

But I didn't want someone to save me. I wanted to save myself. If someone else was my hero, I would survive the situation, but if I was my own hero, I would survive the world.

"What's going on?" Chandra stood in the doorway of armory. I wondered if she still wanted to be in Nash's arms.

We dropped our embrace and put space between each other. Nash cleared his throat. "We talked to Lucifer."

Adrianna, Tom, and Kiran wandered in.

"What did she say?" Adrianna asked.

"Not much," Nash said. "We're on our own."

They all wore their training attire. Chandra wore a tank top, tight pants, and arm bracers. Kiran strapped his sword to his side. The hilts of Adrianna's daggers protruded from their sheaths. Tom wore an old t-shirt and jeans and carried his short sword. They assumed whatever Nash had to say meant they would have to fight.

"He's coming to Sheol?" Kiran's shoulder twitched as if a chill settled there.

Nash nodded. "He wants to get to her before Raphael does."

If he doesn't, Raphael would use me as a weapon to force Michael's hand into closing the gates of Heaven to humans. Michael's mission was noble. I cringed. *Had I called my murder noble?*

"But we won't let that happen," Nash said. Those were the words I wanted to hear from him. "We're going to fight him. We're going to up our training starting today." He motioned to the pile of silver weapons on the table.

Adrianna shook her head. Her eyes were distant as she spoke. I never saw a look of hopelessness in Adrianna's eyes, not even when Kiran, Nash, and Chandra had to pull her into the Circles to save her life. "Michael can't be hurt by Arcadian Steel."

"That's a rumor." Nash looked at me as he spoke. He tried to reassure me that I wouldn't die by Michael's hand. "All angels can be cut by Arcadian Steel. Michael can be hurt just like the rest of them."

My eyes darted back and forth. "But how can he come here?" I asked. "Bob warded Sheol, right?"

After the angels attacked, Bob warded Hell against intruders for three years. He explained that no angel, unless fallen, could get in, not even through a portal.

"He couldn't ward all of Sheol," Kiran said. "If Michael goes through the Circles, he could get in. The Circles are harder to ward because no one, not even Lucifer, wants to go down there."

Lucifer wouldn't go into the Circles? How could she control what went on down there if she never visited? That would be like a manager who never checked up on his employees.

"But someone should," I said. "What are the odds that Michael will try to get in through the Circles?"

"It depends on how much of a threat he thinks you are, Angel Killer," Chandra said.

ANGEL Killer.

Chandra was right. That's what I am.

My head leaned against the headboard of my bed. My guitar cradled in my arms, I strummed a few notes. The notes warmed me like the sun in winter.

I hadn't seen Adriel since the battle a few weeks ago. There was so much I wanted to say to him. But I knew that Nash wouldn't want me to see him. I wasn't sure why Nash didn't like Adriel. Maybe the two of them crossed paths before?

Whatever the reason, the last thing Nash had to know right now was that I wanted to find Adriel. But maybe he didn't have to know.

I knew someone who could help. And I knew right where to find him. I unhooked the amp and placed my guitar in its case.

Tom sat in the armchair in the library and read. He looked up from his book when I entered.

"You hear me every time," I said.

"I'm used to the quiet," he said. "I notice when it's disturbed."

"Sorry," I said.

"No problem." He closed the book. "I have an eternity. I'm afraid I'll run out of books."

I tried to imagine myself in Tom's shoes. He loved reading. What would he do if the world stopped making books?

"I have a favor to ask," I said.

"Ask away, but I can't promise I'll oblige." He smiled.

"I want to see Adriel. Where can I find him?"

My question hung in the air for a while, long enough that I felt awkward for asking. I wasn't ashamed of the question per se, but the silence was unsettling.

Tom leaned forward in his chair. "There's a special place in Hell for fallen angels."

"Will you bring me there?"

Tom smirked. "I don't think so."

"Why not?"

"Nash won't…"

"I'm not Nash's prisoner. He doesn't make decisions for me."

"Clearly," Tom said. "I guess I don't have much of a choice, do I? If I don't take you, you'll try to find it on your own, and that would be a disaster."

"So, you'll take me."

"If, and only if, you don't say anything to Nash," he said.

"I can't see why I would."

"Okay, but we have to be quick. You're hunting a demon tonight, a Balban. Tough suckers."

"Have you told Nash yet? I don't think he'll want to go. He wants to dedicate every spare minute to training to fight Michael."

"He knows Lucifer won't let him ignore demons while he hunts angels. Hope you don't mind walking. I hate to drive."

"That's fine." I didn't think my stomach could handle anymore race car driving.

The walk was therapeutic. Frustration, fear, and guilt flooded my mind, but the walk brought me some ease. I always walked home from school when I had a bad day. It calmed me.

It was a short moment of sanctuary among chaos. Tom let me have that moment. He didn't say anything as he walked with his hands in his pockets.

He probably had his own stuff to think about. I wasn't immune to the fact that what happened to me would affect others as well, including him. I hoped Lucifer wouldn't banish my friends to the Circles, or worse the Pit, if we failed.

Tom and I stood before a tall, iron gate. Beyond the gate was a city. The clouds above the city were darker than those surrounding it. Neon lights glowed from the buildings, which huddled close together.

Two men stood guard. Giants would be a better description than men. They each stood over seven and a half feet tall by my rough estimate. Their foreheads jutted out above their narrow eyes. They looked like twin brothers with the exact same bulbous nose, high cheek bones, and large lips except one had a swollen eye that made it look like he was eternally winking.

"What's your business?" Winks asked.

"Not business," Tom said. "Pleasure."

The way he said pleasure in a deep cadence made me uneasy. *Had Tom been here before?* Even from a distance the area looked seedy like the kind of place where murders happen in detective movies.

Each twin wrapped a massive hand around the bars of the heavy, iron gates and pulled them open.

I followed Tom past the gates and into the city.

"What is this place?" I asked.

"The Angel District."

Neon lights glowed in the gloom. Buildings stacked on top each other. Loud music assaulted my ears.

There was nothing *angelic* about this place. It was dark, grimy, and smelled like a mixture of vomit and alcohol.

The people, or the demons, wore a range of clothing from suits and dresses to leather jackets and crop tops. The only similarities were the smiles on their faces, the laughter, and the jeers.

But there were also people in chains, not people, angels. Their wings no longer had full white feathers, but were now bones, hanging useless from their backs. Large chains collared their necks, and more chains bound their hands and feet.

A few demons chose not to look like people. Some had red faces with pointed horns. Their eyes glowed yellow in the dark. Others had patchy skin that wrinkled in odd places like across the cheeks and scalp. They had muscled bodies and wielded whips and hammers.

One demon pulled a fallen angel around on his hands and knees like a dog. He barked orders, and the angel was obedient. The angel was once a beautiful winged warrior with white blond hair and soft feathered wings. *Was he one of the angels that I touched?* He ate food off the ground as a horned demon screamed in his ear.

Tears wet my cheeks, and I thought I might begin to sob.

Tom grasped my arms. "Lia," he said. "Stay close to me, and don't look at anybody. There are things down here you shouldn't see."

"I did this to them," I said.

Tom shook his head. "Lucifer did this to them. You think this is bad? Think of how bad the Circles must be, how bad the Pit must be. It's because of her that this is here. Not you. Don't look at anything, and don't meet eyes with anyone. Do you understand me?"

I swallowed and nodded.

I kept my head down and watched Tom's back as he moved through the crowd. The place was packed, and filled back in once Tom pushed through.

"Don't look away!" Someone grabbed my arm and turned me around.

"Don't look away!" the red-eyed demon bellowed as he pulled the chain connected to the angel's throat. Two demons, a man and woman from their figures, pawed each other over their clothes. His hands traveled to her tailbone. She twisted his shirt in her fists and crushed her lips against his. The angel tried again to divert his eyes, but the red-eyed demon grabbed his chin and forced his face forward.

The two demons undressed. I turned my eyes away.

"Look at this," a slurred voice said. "New blood."

A man in a leather jacket stood in front of me with a bottle of beer in his hand. He sounded like he had had a few beers before that one. He was tall and muscular and had the scent of alcohol on his breath.

He took a swig of beer as a woman put her hand on his chest.

"Who do we have here, Sam?" she asked. She wore a tight-fitting knee length dress, like she had come to the bar straight from an office job. Her dark, red lipstick was stark against her pale skin.

"New comer," Sam said. "Look, Delilah, I think she might be scared."

The woman turned her gaze to me. Her eyes widened. She looked up at Sam. "Sam, she's human."

Sam crooked his head back to take another swallow of beer, but when he heard that, he stopped. His bottle tilted away from his lips. "Is she now?" He smashed the bottle on the ground behind him. "What would a human be doing in Sheol?"

"Are you taking a spirit walk or something?" Delilah asked.

I couldn't tell if she was joking or not. She had a slight glint to her voice. She sounded too drunk to be sure.

"How did you know so soon, babe?" Sam asked.

"Look at her eyes. I could tell right off."

My eyes? Something in my eyes showed I was human. But what? Most demons looked like people. Often, I couldn't see any flaw in the disguise. Could demons lift the Veil on each other?

I turned around.

Oh, no, Tom!

I had no idea where he was.

"Hey, hey, wait a minute." Sam grabbed my arm as I tried to leave.

I pulled away from him. I doubt it would have been as easy if he hadn't been drunk.

My heart hammered in my chest as I pushed through the crowd. In the middle of the street people gathered shoulder to shoulder, elbow to elbow. It was difficult to push through.

Despite what Tom had told me and the disgusting things I had seen, my curiosity got the better of me. I could see between the bodies of a few people in front of me.

A tall, black demon with red eyes and curved black horns whipped an angel who stood with his arms spread.

Demons whipped the backs of angels. The people in the crowd threw golden coins at them.

The currency was unfamiliar. The coins looked ancient. I guessed on Earth the money had fallen out of use.

The demon swung the whip. Lashes bit into the angel's back, and black blood oozed onto the concrete. The whip must have been laced in Arcadian Steel. The demon forced the angel's head low to the ground. "Pick them up," he bellowed.

The angel scrambled to pick up the glittering coins from the ground while the others around her did as well.

I searched the crowd for Tom. I dared not yell out his name. I didn't want the attention of the demons on me.

"Lia!"

Far above me, in a window, a pair of darkened eyes gazed down at me.

Adriel.

Pushing through the crowd with more vigor than before, I hurried to the building and tore open the door. I found the steps. *Which room was it?*

A cockroach scurried down the hallway. The wallpaper peeled in curls down the walls. Graffiti marked either side of the hall. My feet pounded against the uneven laminate tiles that lifted from the floor.

Some of the doors were shut with numerous bolts and latches. Others had been torn off their hinges.

Cries echoed down the hall.

I opened a door. This had to be the one. The room was bare except for a twin-size bed in the corner. No sheets or blankets covered the dirty mattress. The walls were yellowed and brown in the corners where they met the ceiling and floor.

An iron collar hung around Adriel's neck. A chain went from the collar to a bolt in the floor.

He turned his head. His face was pale. His once-shiny, black hair had turned ashy and dull. His golden irises had darkened to black. Thick, black bones grew from his shoulder blades and thinner bones branched from thicker ones.

I destroyed something that was once so beautiful.

Tears welled up in my eyes, and I rushed into his arms. He enveloped me, but his embrace no longer held that intense feeling of warmth. That touch of bliss was gone. It felt no different than if I had been hugged by anyone.

"This place is so terrible," I whispered into his arm.

"I would have come to you, but I couldn't," he said. "I carried my headstone. Then, I had to come here."

"I'm so sorry for doing this to you."

He cradled my face in his hands. "Lia, you saved me."

My breath caught.

"There you are." Tom exhaled. He bent double with his hands on his knees. He looked up at me. "What the hell were you thinking?"

I turned away from Adriel and back to Tom. "I lost you in the crowd."

"You should have stayed where you were. Luckily, I heard him yell your name. Come on, we have to go back to Nash's place."

"I'm not leaving without Adriel," I said.

"What? We can't take him with us. The guards won't let him past the gate."

I wouldn't let Adriel stay another minute in this place, not after all he had done for me. He was my guardian angel for heaven's sake.

"Go," Adriel said. "I'm grateful you came, but don't come back. I can't bare for you to see me in this place."

I turned to him. "But Adriel."

"He's right," Adriel said. "Even if I could get pass the guards, they'll know I'm gone."

"What will they do to you?" I looked from Adriel back to Tom, challenging them with the question.

Tom grabbed my arm. "They'll hunt him down and throw him into the Pit."

four

HE air smelled of burnt leaves. We left the darkness that gathered around the Angel District behind us. Tom strolled silently beside me. The place burned me more than him.

I wanted to slap away Tom's stillness. He didn't care about Adriel the way I did, but no one could be bankrupt of pity after seeing Adriel in that place.

Nash's car sat in the driveway. The car had no license plate upon its sleek body.

Tom and I walked through the front door as Nash came down the stairs.

"Oh, great," Tom whispered in my ear. "Let me do the talking." He shut the door behind us.

I didn't care if Nash knew where I had gone. He knew where they had taken Adriel, and he didn't do anything about it. He hated him, but that place was sick.

"Where were you two?" Nash asked.

"We went to the Angel District," I said.

Tom, looking betrayed, glared at me and ducked into the living room.

"You what?"

"I saw Adriel," I said. "I don't want him there."

"Lia, what were you thinking?"

"He's living in squalor. Worse than squalor. I don't know what to call it. How could you not tell me? I want Lucifer to let him out."

"That's not going to happen."

"Make it happen."

"I don't understand why you have this sense of loyalty to him."

"He saved us. Have you forgotten? He fought with us, and you would let him live an eternity like that?" My voice trembled, and my fingernails bit into my palms.

"No one knows whose side Adriel is on," Nash said. "Before he fell, he might have wanted to hand you over to Raphael."

"He saved your life, Nash. He's protected me for more than half mine. He fought with us against the angels that came to Sheol. What more does he have to do to prove to you that he is on our side? Why would you think he would give me over to Raphael?"

"Perhaps he planned to hand you over to Michael. Michael would have killed you. He still might."

I pressed my lips together. "Adriel had plenty of opportunities to hand me over to anyone he wished, but instead he watched and protected me. Don't you think we might need him to defend ourselves against Michael? Angels can't be harmed by anything but Arcadian Steel."

Nash shook his head. "Fallen angels are different. They are more resistant to weapons than humans or demons, but they can still bleed."

I folded my arms. "We're talking about Michael. If he's really the badass you all say he is, we need as many weapon-*resistant* fallen angels on our side as we can get."

"It's not up to me. It's up to Lucifer."

I marched up the stairs and stopped on the step next to him. "You could help him if you wanted to. You hate him, and that's fine, but he saved us, and he suffered for it in the worse way imaginable."

I continued up the stairs, down the hall, and shut the door to my room.

If Nash wasn't going to help me, I had to find another way.

Adriel was chained to the center of that little room. He should have been able to break those chains. Maybe being fallen made him weaker.

Or maybe he thought it would be useless to run. Tom said they would find him. Could there be some way he could leave Sheol?

Only a few days ago, I made him fall. So, he hadn't been in the Angel District for long. Soon, they would take him down with the others to be tortured and ridiculed.

I rubbed my eyes.

Lucifer was a fallen angel. How could she do that to her own kind?

I needed time to think. I couldn't walk in unarmed and expect to walk out with an angel. I needed a plan, but that would take too much time. As soon as I came up with something, Adriel would have spent days, maybe weeks in that place.

My sheathed sword leaned in the corner of the wall. A dagger rested in my bedside drawer. I could awaken both weapons and tear down anyone who got in my way of taking Adriel out of the Angel District.

But what then?

They'll hunt him down and throw him into the Pit.

THE road twisted through the trees. Time faded the yellow lines that bisected the street. Naked branches reached over the highway on either side as if the trees tried to embrace.

Light glowed through the fog and caused shadows to stretch onto the road. Crows cawed, and leaves crunched in the distance.

"Tom said we're looking for a Balban." I stood in the middle of the street, which seemed like the safest place to be. Darkness draped the dense trees, but standing water reflected moonlight on the road. "What does one look like?"

"They don't often show their true form," Nash said. "Be careful. A Balban is a demon of delusion. It will try to trick you."

"But I'll be able to see through that," I said.

"Your sight isn't perfect," Nash said.

He was right. I could see demons. Sometimes I saw their full forms, other times I could only see the horns, the tail, or the eyes. I couldn't completely see through the guises Tom, Adrianna, Kiran, and Chandra wore. Maybe I didn't want to.

"The longer we spend with the Balban, the more time it will have to learn how to manipulate us." Chandra approached the tree line.

"Let's go." Nash waved us on.

Twigs snapped under our feet as we moved through the forest. Adrianna walked alongside me. We were a few feet behind Nash, Chandra, and Kiran.

"What do you think Nash plans to do about Michael?" I asked.

"I'm not sure." Adrianna watched the trees. She stayed vigilant as she spoke. "But I don't think he's going to let him near you."

"What if that's the only way to stop him?"

"Nash will find another way."

"He hasn't talked to me about it."

"Nash doesn't like to talk about his plans until he's worked them out completely. He doesn't like to be wrong. If he's going to solve something, he'll do it in private. He'll only talk about it once he's found the solution."

"I need to make Michael fall. That's the only—"

Adrianna grabbed my arm, and I stopped.

Nash, Chandra, and Kiran had their weapons drawn. Ahead of them stood hooded figures among the trees.

The cloaks the figures wore were dark and tattered at the hips. Their faces were shadowed. The legs looked strange like they were bent backward at the knees.

Ten figures stood at varying distances. The mist made the figures who stood further out look small and gray. They waited for something.

It wasn't one demon, but many. Tom was wrong again.

I drew my sword, and Adrianna drew her daggers.

Nash leaned in and spoke to Chandra and Kiran, but I couldn't hear what he said. Chandra and Kiran darted in opposite directions away from Nash.

Nash raced to me and Adrianna. "We have to go."

"What about Chandra and Kiran?" I asked.

"It can only follow one group at a time. It will choose the larger," Nash said.

"But," I said, "there's more than one of them."

"I don't have time to explain." Nash grabbed my arm and ran.

What was Nash up to? Did he want me to figure it out for myself? I ran with him and Adrianna. I couldn't hear footsteps behind me.

What if Nash was wrong and the demons chose to follow Chandra and Kiran instead? They were separated and would have to fight alone. If they were overwhelmed, they would die and go to the Pit like Chandra's brother, Alex.

But Nash knew what he was doing. He had sent thousands of demons back to Hell.

So, why did Adrianna set her teeth and tense her forehead? Was it possible that she was worried Nash's plan, whatever it was, wouldn't work?

"Put your weapons away," Nash said. "If it shows itself, we need to be ready to run as fast as we can. Having our weapons drawn will slow us down."

As I ran, I turned to look. I shouldn't have. The ground shuttered. A demon ran behind us. It stood twenty feet tall with muscled arms and legs. Four backward curved horns grew above its far-spread eyes. Its skin was gray and splotchy.

"What in the world is that?" I asked as I ran.

The thing made the ground quake as it knocked down trees in its wake.

"The hooded figures we saw in the forest," Adrianna said.

"But they were many," I said.

"No," Nash said, "they were one."

"It's gaining on us," Adrianna said. "Nash, what do we do?"

The ground rippled. Trees crashed in the forest. The crows were silent.

"Nash, say something," I said. "It's going to catch us."

"Keep running," Nash said. "Our ultimate duty is to keep you safe. We have to keep going."

But where? What would happen when that thing catches us?

"Lia, keep your eyes forward," Adrianna said. "You'll trip."

"I don't understand," I said. "We came to fight. Why are we avoiding it now? Is this not the demon we were looking for?"

"Just follow orders," Nash ground out.

No. I had a sword of the strongest metal that ever existed. I had the power to make angels fall. Why did I still depend on other people?

I drew my sword.

"What are you doing?" Adrianna asked. "Lia, you can't fight it."

I clenched my teeth. How was I supposed to avenge my parents if I wasn't brave enough to do what needed to be done?

No running, no hiding. I'd faced my demons. I'll face this one, and when Raphael comes, I'll be ready for him too.

"Think about what you're about to do," Nash said. "You should listen to someone with more experience."

"I can't run anymore," I shouted and turned with my sword drawn.

The Balban raised a massive fist, ready to bring it down on me, but it didn't get the chance. Kiran and Chandra jumped from the trees onto the creature's shoulders. It screamed as they stabbed it. Black blood oozed down its chest.

I stared wide-eyed as Kiran and Chandra cut the flesh between the demon's neck and shoulders.

Nash had a plan all along, and I almost ruined it. *Why couldn't he have just said something to me? Why doesn't he trust me?*

Nash and Adrianna rushed forward and cut at the beast as it swung its massive arms. The demon looked down at Nash, like it recognized him.

"Nash, look out," I screamed.

The massive hand gripped Nash around the chest and waist and brought him up into the air. It squeezed. It would kill him. It wanted to kill him.

I ran around to its back. Its legs were exposed. With my blade, I sliced the tendons behind one of its knees.

The creature howled and knelt on that knee.

I repeated the same to the back of the other knee and got the same result.

Adrianna jumped off the beast's chest and leapt onto its forearm. She hacked at the demon's fingers until it dropped Nash.

Nash scrambled on the ground, gasping for air, but it wasn't long before he was back on his feet. He leapt and plunged his sword into the Balban's chest. He dragged the blade down, using his weight as leverage.

He pulled his sword from the body and backed away as the demon fell face-first to the ground. The forest shook. The body of the Balban faded like a hologram, leaving only an impression of what had been.

I sighed and put a hand to my chest as it pounded.

Nash shook some of the inky blood from his sword. The ground absorbed the blood like water. He glared at me before he raised his hand and opened the portal.

The others put away their weapons and climbed through. I sheathed my own blade and approached the portal, but before I could enter, the portal closed.

Nash lowered his hand. "I told you to run."

"My legs were growing heavy," I said. A lie.

"If you can't follow my orders, you won't survive Michael."

How quickly the focus shifted from Raphael to Michael. I didn't care about Michael. He wasn't the one who killed my parents.

"If you're so concerned about Michael, you'd make sure Adriel gets out of that terrible place. He's my guardian angel. He'll do anything to protect me."

Nash laughed.

"What's so funny?"

"He wasn't tasked to be your guardian. He named himself that."

"How do you know anything about it?"

Nash's lips formed a hard line. "You need to start following orders."

"What if I don't?"

"You're stubborn."

"You're controlling."

"I'm the leader of this team."

"You're not a very good leader if you don't see things."

Nash narrowed his eyes. "What are you talking about?"

"Someone's trying to kill you, Nash. In Venice, those demons attacked you and now this. That monster looked at you. It wanted to kill *you*. It didn't go after the rest of us."

"That's because it spotted me first and hadn't finished killing me yet."

I pressed my lips together and folded my arms.

"I see what you're saying," Nash said. "But it could be a coincidence. Then again, a lot of demons want me dead. I've sent plenty of them back to Hell."

"You say that like you didn't want to."

"Why would I? Do you think I'm that cruel? I do it because if I don't, Lucifer would send me to the Pit."

"But demons are evil."

"Are Tom and Adrianna evil? Are Chandra and Kiran?"

I'd never thought of that before. All the demons I had encountered before I met Nash whispered horrible things they wanted to do to people. They crouched on people's backs and murmured to them. Sometimes the people they spoke to did bad things.

"Things aren't that black and white," Nash said.

How could someone with so much ink spilled into his soul see things clearer than I could?

"So why is there a Hell?" I asked.

"Because a mistake was made."

"What mistake?"

Nash looked away.

I grabbed his elbow. "What was it?"

"A mistake I made. That's all you need to know." His eyes locked on mine.

I squinted at him. "That's why you're in Sheol. That's why *you* sawed off your wings."

"I sawed them off before all the feathers burned away." His face was tense, pained.

I wanted to erase that pain, to burn it away. Something inside me vibrated like the string on a guitar. It was silent, yet I could *feel* the music. I touched the side of his face and brought my lips up to his.

As our lips touched, he backed away from me. His breath wavered, and his eyes trembled.

Had I made a mistake? I struggled to find words to fill the gulf between us. But I didn't need to.

Nash rushed towards me. His hands cradled the sides of my face, and his lips pressed urgently against mine as if he had been fighting himself the whole time, fighting not to kiss me. And now, he was.

My hands ran through his hair. His fingertips grazed my neck, and goose bumps erupted across my skin. I didn't want him to stop, but he did.

I pressed my lips together. They were still warm from his touch.

Nash backed away from me as if I was a rattlesnake.

"We should go." He opened the portal.

"Yeah, I guess so." I tried to meet his eyes before I stepped through, but Nash's eyes were to the ground. His hands were clenched. He acted like he graffitied a building rather than kissed a girl.

www.ingramcontent.com/pod-product-compliance
Lightning Source LLC
Chambersburg PA
CBHW020326180626
46812CB00001B/67